Four Months, Three Words

C.W. FARNSWORTH

FOUR MONTHS, THREE WORDS

Copyright © 2020 by C.W. Farnsworth

Editing & Proofreading:

Tiffany Persaud

Cover:

Sam Palencia

ALSO BY C.W. FARNSWORTH

Kiss Now, Lie Later

The Hard Way Home

First Flight, Final Fall

Come Break My Heart Again

The Easy Way Out (The Hard Way Home Book 2)

Famous Last Words

Winning Mr. Wrong

Back Where We Began

Like I Never Said

Fly Bye

Fake Empire

Heartbreak for Two

Serve

For Now, Not Forever

SYNOPSIS

He's the guy every girl wants...

Jace Dawson is less than a year away from accomplishing everything he's spent the past decade striving for. Not only has playing professional football been the dream since he was a kid, the financial incentive isn't one he could walk away from even if he wanted to. That is, until a chance collision has the unexpected outcome of making Jace realize he might want something more than the goal he's spent most of his life pursuing. Might want *someone* more.

...she's the girl he can never have.

For Vivienne Rhodes, the opportunity to attend Lincoln University represents what she's always craved more than anything: normalcy. One semester is all she has before returning to a future that's set in stone. Her mere presence on campus is only made possible by an elaborate arrangement. The essential component of it is that no one can know her real identity. Falling for the star quarterback is most definitely not part of the plan. But it will all be fine, just as long as she keeps those feelings to herself. Because that unchangeable future? Can't include Jace Dawson.

CONTENTS

For anyone who's wanted to swerve from what's expected. You only get one life.

PART 1

FOUR MONTHS, THREE WORDS

PROLOGUE

As soon as we emerge from the church, the cheers begin. I clutch my mother's hand tightly, overwhelmed by the flashing lights and loud sounds. Tugging at the hem of the satin dress I'm wearing with my free hand, I glance over at the two tall men in black suits standing next to us. I usually find their towering presence annoying, but the wall of noise makes me grateful, instead.

My father strides ahead of us to the metal barricade that lines the crowded street, shaking hands and passing off gifts to the agents that flank him. My mother begins to tug me along the stone path, but then halts to speak to someone. I don't bother looking up to see who it is.

A small, blond-haired boy who looks to be my age catches my attention as he walks over, carefully clutching a small bouquet of flowers. My mother stops speaking, and the woman she's been talking to leans down to speak to the boy.

"Give the flowers to the princess, Charles," she urges.

The boy thrusts out his tiny fist, offering the bouquet to me. I don't move, so my mother squeezes my hand in a silent command. I reluctantly grab one end of the ribbons streaming off the sides of the elaborate bow holding the stems together, letting the vibrant blossoms dangle against my bare leg. Their floral aroma engulfs me.

"Aren't they the sweetest?" the woman asks my mother.

I don't give her a chance to reply. "Can't we go home, Mother?" I ask, my tone a tad whiny. I'll be scolded for it later, but I'm eager to leave after having to sit quietly for the past couple of hours.

Predictably, my mother looks at me with vexation. "Vivienne, we're in public," she whispers.

I let frustration seep across my face in response.

Her expression softens. "Are you feeling all right?"

"I'm tired," I reply truthfully.

"Fine. Anders?" she calls, and one of the men trailing us appears at her side immediately. "Put the princess in the car," she instructs him.

I'm shuffled between the two, and then ushered away toward the long line of black cars parked to the side of the church. When we reach the middle one, Anders swiftly opens the door and lifts me into the backseat. The movement jostles my precarious hold on the bouquet. Rather than tighten my grip, I relax my fingers, and watch as the ribbon slips out of my grasp and the bouquet falls to the gravel ground.

I slide across the smooth seat and relax as soon as the door is shut behind me, hiding the abandoned flowers and crowds from view. I stretch out across the cool leather and enjoy the muffled silence after the din outside.

Tucking my hands underneath my chest, I listen to the uneven thuds of my heart as I wait for my parents.

CHAPTER ONE

W hen I was younger, I thought my life was ordinary. Boring, even. I thought everyone lived in palaces, had staff tend to their every need, wore elaborate, itchy dresses on a regular basis, and was greeted by cheers whenever they emerged from said palace, or anyplace else.

I can't pinpoint the exact moment that perception changed. It evolved in a gradual realization as I grew older and was exposed to more and more the outside world had to offer.

It began with a creeping awareness that most of the things I accepted as normal life were actually reserved for a select few, and was compounded at age ten when I finally recognized no one else in Marcedenia lived the same way that we did.

I was born with a congenital heart defect that required corrective surgery several times during my childhood. Thanks to my poor circulation, I spent most of my early years traipsing through the palace corridors draped in several woolen blankets to ward off the constant chill. My perpetually frigid skin earned me the moniker of "Ice Princess" from the palace staff when they thought

I couldn't hear them. My aloof demeanor probably contributed to the nickname as well.

My heart finally received a clean bill of health at age ten, which prompted my enrollment at the most exclusive and elite preparatory school in the country, Bridgemont Academy. Until that point, I was tutored privately at home. My interactions with anyone my age were limited to the children of dukes and lords at a few exclusive events.

While the main justification for the perpetual isolation was my poor health, I know my parents were also wary of the risks the outside world posed to me in particular, as their sole heir. As a result, they surrounded me with a constant rotation of nannies, tutors, and security that became a fixed presence in my everyday life.

An hour at Bridgemont Academy was all it took to permanently abate me of the notion that my life was ordinary in any way. Even amongst the offspring of the most privileged, wealthy, and powerful citizens in the country, my status was unchallenged.

Instructors didn't discipline me.

My peers looked at me with awe.

No one wanted to risk angering the future queen.

I took full advantage of the leniency, essentially doing as I pleased, especially once I realized my security detail would only intervene if they thought I was in physical danger. The deference I was treated with was flattering, but it was also boring.

Eight monotonous years later, my final days at Bridgemont Academy are rapidly approaching. This fall, I'm expected to start my university years at Edgewood College. A prospect I'm thoroughly dreading.

Although the shift to university means I will be living on my own for the first time—in a heavily guarded apartment with round-the-clock staff—my classmates will remain the same stuffy, serious, and spoiled group I've spent the past eight years with. The few peers I find remotely interesting were deterred years ago by my omnipresent security.

Adding to my already apathetic feelings about attending Edgewood College, three days ago, I learned of my father's Alzheimer's diagnosis. Since it was detected early, the doctors expect it will be at least five years before he begins experiencing any of the more serious symptoms. Hopefully longer, if he responds well to their treatment plan and medications.

The prospect of watching my jovial father slowly lose his mind is both devastating and terrifying. His diagnosis means the couple of decades of relative freedom I expected to have as the back-up are now gone.

My days as a princess now have a set expiration date.

The countdown to becoming a queen has begun.

My father's diagnosis prompted a rapid reshuffling of the future plans for the monarchy. Now, when I finish university in four years, as my fellow classmates decide on future careers and celebrate the end of academia, I will be preparing to rule the country they all reside in before my father's condition becomes public knowledge.

I resigned myself, from the very first day at Bridgemont Academy, to the fact that amongst the many privileges my charmed life as royalty offers, freedom is not one of them. My entire life was pre-determined for me before I even took my first breath.

Being the sole heir to the throne offers limited opportunities, but still slightly more agency than the ruling monarch. I hadn't realized how much that distinction mattered to me until I learned how soon it will become irrelevant.

Just hours ago, I was slammed with the second bombshell of my week, when I found out the antiquated law requiring a female heir to be married in order to become queen still applies to me. My father sought to abolish it as soon as he became king, and he finally convinced the misogynistic men comprising the Royal Council to change it. It was officially signed two days after my birth.

Turns out, I missed my chance at ruling solo by forty-eight hours.

My parents decided not to tell me until now, hoping they would be able to find a loophole, or that I would already be married and middle-aged before having to take the throne.

In light of recent events, the first is looking unlikely, and the second, impossible. I feel as though I'm clutching a bunch of balloons whose strings have just been snipped, now stuck watching the colorful circles float away with no chance of ever recovering them.

I was disinterested in attending Edgewood College before, but the past few days have been more than enough to change my feelings on the topic to strongly averse. Learning the next four years will be my last without the constraints and obligations of being monarch makes the prospect of having to spend them at Edgewood College sound all the more dreadful.

Since I have no alternatives, there's nothing I'd like to do more than consume a copious amount of whiskey. I've spent the remainder of the day, since the marriage bomb was dropped, contemplating a plan to sneak out tonight. My chances of actually leaving the palace grounds are low and my intentions for doing so are entirely selfish, but the allure of alcohol and complete solitude is too tempting to ignore.

Dinner with my parents is a mostly silent affair. The occasional clink of crystal or clatter of china are the only sounds that resonate in the massive dining hall meant to seat a hundred. My father sits at the head of the table, with my mother and me on either side of him. I know my parents are as worried and over-whelmed as I am, but I can't muster the words to comfort them as I grapple with my own feelings regarding recent events.

When the strained supper finally ends, I sneak into the kitchen corridor, where I snag a black hooded jacket from one of the lockers belonging to the staff. I slip outside without anyone spotting me. The cool night air is tinged with the scent of fresh rain, and I inhale deeply as I emerge from underneath the overhang into a heavy downpour.

I shove my hands inside the pockets of the borrowed jacket and discover the left one contains a keycard for the back gate, which will speed up my exit exponentially. The shiny new SUVs I spotted earlier are still parked in a row by the service entrance.

I snag the keys from the top of the rear right tire and climb inside the driver's seat. All of the palace's cars are typically stored in the main garage, but these were just delivered earlier today and haven't been moved yet. I let out a sigh of relief when the engine roars to life, then pull my phone out and power it off so my security team won't be able to track me.

The driving rain ensures the evening security guard remains in the booth adjacent to the massive wrought-iron gate. He simply waves me through after I scan the keycard. I've given no thought to my destination beyond it being an escape from both the physical confines of the palace and my own troubling thoughts.

I drive along the dark, wet streets, alone in a car for the first time, until I spot a grungy pub that suits my current mood perfectly. The obscure location has the added bonus of being one of the last places a citizen would expect to encounter a member of the royal family, significantly lowering the odds of anyone besides my annoyed security team ever knowing I even left the palace.

A long wooden counter spans the entire length of the pub,

9

where I order a glass of whiskey before taking a seat in the booth farthest from the front door. There are only two other patrons in the stodgy bar, and I use the rain as an excuse to keep my dripping hood up to cover my most distinctive feature: long strawberry-blonde hair.

I remain in the booth for a while after my jacket has dried, and long enough to down two more glasses of amber liquid. I stare across the dimly lit pub at the rain streaking down the outside of the dusty panes of glass, my mind blissfully blank. The dark wood that constructs almost every visible surface is soothing, and I feel stress leaching away as the whiskey warms me from the inside out.

I'm contemplating whether I should call my security team to come retrieve me now or if I should savor the rare moment of freedom longer when the front door swings open for the first time since I entered.

A boisterous group of five boys walk inside the previously silent pub and head over to the long counter. I watch them closely, intrigued by the chance to observe normal teenagers. They push and jostle each other in an attempt to order first, tossing around teasing remarks as they do. I don't realize how intently I'm staring until one of them turns away from the counter to survey the rest of the pub. He immediately meets my intrigued gaze. I look away, cursing internally for drawing attention to myself.

I pull my phone out of my pocket and power it back on. I learned the first time I snuck out of the palace to go for a run in the surrounding woods, it is a necessary step in order to have more than a few minutes to myself.

Instantly, the phone lights up with dozens of missed notifications. Sighing, I unlock the phone and tap on Michael's name, figuring he's the member of my security team least likely to yell at me.

He answers on the first ring. "Princess, where are you?"

"Just track me," I reply, then hang up.

I'm in no mood for pleasantries, and I'm slightly buzzed. Alcohol makes me more impertinent than usual. I also have no idea where I actually am. I didn't even take note of the name of the pub.

I set down the phone on the table just as two of the boys leave the group huddled around the barkeep to amble over to me.

One of them slides into the booth across from me with a friendly grin, while the other leans casually against the wooden divider separating my booth from the next.

"Looks like you've been here a while," the guy standing remarks, nodding to the three empty glasses on the varnished tabletop.

"I didn't have anything better to do tonight," I respond.

"Are you looking for a better offer?"

"What are you offering?" I reply, enjoying the flirty banter. Most guys are too nervous to hit on me.

"Come along with us and find out," he challenges.

I let out a short laugh. "How original. Unfortunately, I'll have to pass. I'm expecting some friends soon. They're pretty protective and highly unlikely to let me go off with a group of strangers." I smirk. "No offense."

"They can come along," the seated boy offers.

I grin broadly at the suggestion, trying to imagine convincing my burly security team to let me drag them along on a bar crawl. "Not really their scene."

I expect that to be the end of the conversation, but both boys linger.

"Feel free to stop bothering me at any time," I finally add, annoyed their persistence means I likely won't have any time to myself before my security team arrives.

The boy standing next to my table smirks.

"You've really lost your touch, Toby." A new voice joins the conversation.

I look to my right to see the remaining three boys are walking over toward my now crowded booth, each carrying a couple of beers. "Oh good, there's more of you," I state sarcastically, resting my head against the hard wood comprising the back of the booth and resigning myself to the fact that my precious solitude is over. The movement shifts my raised hood. I realize my mistake immediately.

The boy who just spoke stares at me intently. "You look really familiar. Have we met before?"

"I doubt it." I try to smother my unease with nonchalance. "But if we have, you weren't very memorable."

His friends guffaw at that, but their collective amusement shifts to surprise when the boy sitting across from me exclaims, "Holy shit, aren't you the princess?"

I let out a deep sigh of exasperation. "No need to bow. You can just leave me alone."

"Can we take a photo with you?" one of the latest arrivals asks excitedly.

"You can try," I reply, exhaling again. They glance at each other in confusion at my cryptic response.

I pull the black hood back fully, revealing my long hair. The group of boys take it as an invitation to crowd closer around the booth, and the one named Toby crouches down in front and holds his long arm out to snap a few photos of the six of us.

Just as he's standing back up, the front door to the pub is slammed open, revealing the eight men who comprise my security team. They're each dressed in full uniform and visibly armed. Looking at them, one would think they were here to rescue me from kidnappers in an underground bunker, rather than to pick me up from an empty, decrepit pub because I've had too many drinks to drive myself. Michael leads the squad, his expression thunderous.

"Aren't you glad I didn't invite them to your bar crawl?" I ask Toby.

He's too stunned to answer.

"Let's go, Princess," Michael barks, coming to a stop in front of the booth that was once blissfully empty.

All five boys are staring at the new arrivals in obvious shock. Michael and the other members of my security detail are far from subtle; their mere presence is intentionally meant to be intimidating. Each agent sports a stern expression, a head-to-toe black uniform, and is toting an array of deadly weapons.

"Wish I could say it's been a pleasure, boys," I say acerbically before pulling my hood back up and sliding out of the booth.

I'm surrounded as soon as I stand, and the boys trip over each other in their haste to move away from the booth as they're forced to back up from the protective wall my team forms around me.

"Did they take photos?" Michael asks as they escort me out of the pub.

"Yup," I reply cheerfully.

Michael makes a sound of distaste and turns to Kevin, the newest addition to my security team. Just like in any hierarchy, this means he is inevitably given any undesirable task. "Wipe the phones," Michael orders him.

Kevin complies, immediately turning around. The remaining seven agents continue marching along around me, and seconds later, we're back outside in the cool night air. The downpour has retreated to a light drizzle.

We head across the street toward the two black SUVs parked haphazardly on the opposite side of the road.

"I took that one." I point to the identical black car parked farther down the street.

Michael chuckles, his usual good humor restored now that I'm safely surrounded by security.

"Well, that explains it," he remarks.

"Explains what?"

"All our cars are outfitted with tracking devices. We just received a few new replacements, and they haven't been added to the system yet. But they *will* be added first thing tomorrow, so don't get more crazy ideas, okay?" He looks meaningfully at me.

I nod in agreement. It was a miracle I managed to sneak away earlier, and the teenagers in the pub reminded me of just how necessary my security can be. If the boys I encountered had more nefarious intentions than a group selfie, I could have put not only myself, but the future of the entire monarchy at risk. The sobering thought is enough to chase away the final remnants of the warm buzz I've been enjoying.

I pile inside one SUV along with Michael and two other agents. Kevin emerges from the pub seconds later and climbs into the car I took along with another agent. My remaining three agents bring up the rear of our entourage in the last car as we wind through the dark, quiet streets. I watch the car's headlights as they reflect and refract off the slick asphalt while we speed along silently.

Fifteen minutes later, we pull up to the front gates. The massive stone facade of the palace is just visible in the distance. Michael climbs out of the driver's seat and has a brief conversation with the security guard manning the gate. He climbs back into the car seconds later. The iron gates creak open, allowing the small parade of cars through.

Once back on palace grounds, we pull off to the right and into the cavernous garage. Automatically, the lights flicker on, illuminating the long array of gleaming cars considered property of the Crown.

We all pile out, and Michael walks me over to the door that connects to the residence. He types a few numbers into the keypad and the thick steel door opens with a loud click.

"Last nightcap off the grounds?" he asks sternly.

I nod. "I just needed…" My voice trails off. I don't know what exactly I needed. A way to make this all manageable. Or at least bearable. The joyride and whiskey helped in the moment, but back inside the familiar walls of the palace, the flash of ease feels very distant again.

"I can imagine," Michael says gently.

I shift awkwardly. The Royal Guard has been briefed about my father's condition, but having Michael acknowledge it makes it all the more real.

"But take someone with you next time you want to leave the grounds, okay? It won't help anything if something were to happen to you."

"I won't sneak off again," I promise, turning and beginning to walk down the tunnel. A thought occurs to me after a few steps, so I stop and turn back around. Michael is still standing there. "Any chance this outing could stay between us? Everyone else has enough to worry about."

Michael nods once. "I'll have to report this to Richard," he tells me. Richard is the head of my father's security detail, as well as the entire Royal Guard. "But I don't see why it should need to go any further than that."

I smile gratefully and turn to head back inside.

CHAPTER TWO

The next few weeks pass in a predictable pattern. First, my days at Bridgemont Academy come to an end. Over the past eight years, the completion of classes and the following week of exams have become a familiar ritual. The only difference this year is the afternoon of pomp and circumstance the entire Royal Guard spent weeks preparing for in order to map out every possible scenario and contingency.

The week following graduation is when the annual tradition of tutoring begins. Each summer since I started at Bridgemont Academy, I've been required to focus on one academic topic and one outdoor activity over the course of the summer break to supplement my already rigorous schooling.

This summer is art history and tennis. Last summer was filled with French poetry and archery. I usually articulate a convincing argument to my parents, outlining why the summer tutoring is wholly unnecessary. My protests were particularly vigorous last summer, partly from a bout of teenage rebellion, and mostly because I found the topic of French poetry to be incredibly boring.

I welcome the tradition of tutoring for the first time. It provides a distraction from the constant worries I'm otherwise plagued with. It's late at night, following dinner and a game of chess with my father, lying awake, listening to the owls and staring at the ornate chandelier in my bedroom, that I dread now.

Daily life continues within the palace with little indication anything at all has changed. I rarely see my father during the day, which was typical before, but surprises me now.

Through a mixture of snooping and eavesdropping, I discover his days are now spent mapping out the long-terms goals he's envisioned for the country to determine steps that can be taken now and projects I will have to take over. No sudden implementations can take place for fear of drawing unwanted scrutiny from the public.

I also come across a document in my father's desk that suggests he is still working to find a way around the marriage law. I try not to get my hopes up, now knowing he has unsuccessfully been trying to do so ever since he first learned my early arrival precluded me from its revision almost two decades ago.

My new reality sinks in more and more each day, and as it does, a sense of urgency grows that I'm squandering my days as princess before I become queen.

The feeling only increases when I wake up on Monday and realize the start of my studies at Edgewood College is now only six weeks away.

My mother brings the impending event up mid-way through dinner that night, which is uncharacteristic of her. She usually leaves logistical details for the staff to worry about. It's quickly revealed the source of her interest in the topic is the wildlife preservation meeting she attended earlier. It was mostly spent gossiping, if the volume of information my mother managed to compile regarding my classmates is any indication.

My father sends me a good-natured wink about ten minutes into the one-sided conversation. I grin back at him. We've always had a close relationship, partially stemming from a mutual weariness regarding the sacrifices royal life often requires. He's also an only child who was forced to take the throne long before he expected to, after the tragic deaths of both of his parents.

My mother has always had an easier time with royal life. This is a lifestyle she chose for herself. She also enjoys lighter responsibilities, knowing she'll never have to carry the burden of being the ruling monarch.

The kitchen staff is serving the final course by the time my mother finally runs out of moderately scandalous stories to share. I've completely tuned her out.

"You'll have to let me know if you see them together on campus, Vivienne." My mother ends her long soliloquy with the news of a rumored relationship between an earl's son and a duchess's daughter. Just your average coupling.

"What if I went somewhere else besides Edgewood this fall?" I ask, opting not to respond to my mother's request and instead finally voicing the thought that's been percolating in my mind for the past few weeks.

"Go somewhere besides Edgewood?" my mother echoes in surprise. "Like Varmish?" she questions, referencing the university considered to be the second best in the country after Edgewood College.

"No, I—" I start, then stop. I glance over at my father, who nods for me to continue. The encouraging gesture gives me the strength to finish my response. "I want to go someplace outside of Marcedenia."

"Leave the country for university?" my mother sounds shocked. She looks to my father, but his face remains blank.

"Not for all of university," I quickly add, trying to temper the extravagant request. Once my mother decides she's opposed to an idea, that's typically the end of it, and I doubt it'll take long for her to reach that conclusion in this instance. "It could just be for a year. One year in another country where I could meet new people, and experience new things, and—"

"It would be extremely difficult to guarantee your safety anywhere else," my mother interrupts. "And I don't understand why you'd want to leave Marcedenia for university. Edgewood College is considered one of the best schools in the world."

"It's not about the school itself, Mother," I reply. "Going to university is a chance to meet new people, to experience different things, to gain some independence. It won't be any of those things for me if I go to Edgewood College. It'll be another four years of being stared at and whispered about."

"That's just the reality of who you are, Vivienne," my mother lectures. "I know it is difficult at times, but being royal is not an accessory you can take off whenever it suits you. Either you are or you are not."

"I know that," I argue, growing increasingly desperate. I hadn't realized how badly I want this until I said it out loud. "But I could go someplace where no one knows I'm the Crown Princess of Marcedenia. We could tell everyone I'm going on some sort of humanitarian trip before university and withhold the location for security reasons. And you could send agents nearby just in case anything were to happen. Please. I know it's a lot to ask, but this is what I want, more than anything. You had the chance to experience a normal life, Mother. I never have."

She sighs, but doesn't immediately dismiss the idea, glancing over at my father instead. "Robert?"

My father looks over at me, his face serious. "I don't know if I can make this happen, Vivienne. But if this is what you really want, I'll call a few people and see if it's a possibility."

"It is, Papa," I assure him, trying to tamp down the hope that is rapidly blossoming. "Thank you."

My father nods, and the three of us resume eating dinner.

I don't dare to bring up the topic of attending university outside the country again. I'm both afraid of pushing my parents too far on the idea and reluctant to lose the small speck of hope I left our last conversation with.

My father is the one who raises the subject a couple days later during our nightly chess match in his study. Following his diagnosis, I quizzed the doctors on every possible way to help preserve his brain. Chess was suggested as a way to exercise his memory and mental acuity, and our matches have become my favorite part of the day.

"I made those calls," he states, and then moves a knight across the board.

I lean forward slightly in anticipation of what his next words might be.

"I think we can make it happen—"

That's as far as he gets before I leap out of my seat, almost upsetting the entire board, and dash around the table to throw my arms around him.

He laughs and pats my back gently. "I know you are having a tough time with things right now, Vivvi," he acknowledges. "You more than deserve a chance to enjoy yourself without having to worry about all this for a while. Just promise me no more evening outings without security. Deal?"

"Deal," I reply sheepishly. Apparently, Richard has a big mouth.

"And it can only be for one semester, not a full year," he

continues. "There are some events in the spring the Royal Council needs you to be home for."

I nod, my excitement not the least bit dimmed. I hardly expected this to happen at all. Four months sound like an eternity.

"What about security?" I ask anxiously.

"Richard agreed it's safe enough, as long as the school is located far enough away, the chances of any students being familiar with Marcedenia or its royal family are slim. He thinks the best option will be to follow your suggestion and not acknowledge your royal status. I gathered that is your preference."

I nod in vigorous agreement.

"We'll still need to take some security precautions, of course. There are a few ideas Richard has for obscuring your appearance, and you will have several agents there with you. Some under-cover, and then some additional agents nearby who could quickly intervene if necessary."

"So... I'll be able to act completely normal?" I'm shocked. This is more than I dared hope for.

"That was the idea, right?" my father replies, looking amused by my obvious surprise. "Just promise me you'll be careful. I couldn't stand it if anything happened to you."

"I promise, Papa," I answer, giving him one more hug before walking back over the fireplace hearth to return to my side of the table.

My father stands and walks over to his massive mahogany desk. He slides open one of the upper drawers and pulls out a sheet of paper. Returning to his chair opposite me, he slides over the sheet.

"This is the list of schools Richard and his team identified where they could pull this operation off from both a safety and a diplomatic standpoint. You only have a couple of days to decide;

they'll need to begin making the necessary arrangements immediately."

I glance over the paper quickly, which lists the names of each
school and their respective locations. Most of them are on the
outskirts of larger European cities, two are in remote locations,
and three are in the United States. Marcedenia's location in
southern Europe and relatively small size means it is often considered to be insignificant in comparison to its larger neighboring
counties, but I'm still surprised by some of the options. Once
again, it's more than I'd dared to imagine.

My thoughts must show on my face, because my father adds.
"Apparently nine in ten of the citizens of each of those countries
can't identify Marcedenia on a map, much less name any
members of the royal family. If it didn't allow you to have this
opportunity, I'd be deeply offended."

I can't help but laugh. We finish our game, and after thanking
my father again and wishing him good night, I leave his study and
rush back to my room, eager to begin researching the list of
universities.

The first school I search is one I've never heard of. I quickly
find the university's website, which displays a series of towering
stone buildings standing amidst a barren landscape blanketed with
a layer of untouched snow. I pull up the school's location on the
map and see that it is nearly a hundred miles from the nearest
town.

Pass.

I move on to the next school on the list. This one is closest to
Marcedenia geographically, and the landscape is familiar. The
campus is an eclectic mix of open-air villas and terra cotta
covered buildings surrounded with cypress trees.

Possibly.

The third school I look up is the first one located in the United

States. I find the university's site quickly, but the page doesn't load immediately. I drum my fingers against the glass surface of my desk as I wait.

Finally, the screen begins to load. The background of the website showcases a field of lush green grass interrupted by bright white lines. Seats filled with cheering students surround it. As soon as it finishes loading, the photo begins to disappear, small sections of it flipping around until the entire image has been replaced by a new one.

Now, I'm staring at another broad expanse of grass, this time divided into sections by winding paved paths dotted with small figures and surrounded by an array of stately brick buildings, which stand in stark contrast against the bright blue sky. I stare at the idyllic photo for a moment, trying to picture myself there. The background photos continue changing, showing a large lecture hall next, followed by a small, sterile room where two girls stand amidst a mountain of plastic bins and bags.

I go back to the search bar and type in the next name on the list. This school is located in one of the oldest countries in Europe, which the ostentatious architecture clearly indicates. The university's buildings are towering and imposing, carved with intricate details and framed by scrolling columns. I stare at the images displayed of smiling students riding bikes and sitting in the grass reading, once again trying to imagine myself among them.

An hour later, I've finished searching every school on the list. My eyes ache from staring at the screen for so long and my head pounds from the conflicting thoughts bouncing about my mind. This decision feels heavy. Important. It's no longer just an abstract dream; it's my one brief chance to experience a sense of normalcy.

I turn off the computer and walk over to my massive four-poster bed. I slide in between the crisp sheets, letting the warm comforter settle over me. As soon as I close my eyes, a slideshow of the photos I was just looking at flash behind them.

Eventually, exhaustion wins against my incessant thoughts, and I sink into oblivion.

CHAPTER THREE

The next morning, I open my eyes just as the first streaks of dawn are spreading across the darkened sky. I toss and turn for a few minutes, hoping to fall back asleep.

Finally admitting defeat, I roll out of bed and walk over to the bay window that takes up a large portion of the wall just past my bed, forming a cozy alcove that juts out from the rest of my enormous bedroom.

I stare through the panes of glass for a long time, studying the immaculately trimmed lawns and colorful gardens spread out before me. A quick turn of the small handle on the inside of the window frame allows a rush of fresh spring air in. The light breeze rustles the white gossamer curtains.

It doesn't take long to go through my usual morning routine before I'm outside, jogging through the woods at a leisurely pace. Right on cue, I hear footsteps that tell me an agent or two is not far behind. My early morning runs began as a way to appreciate the lack of restrictions my newly healed heart allowed after years of limited physical exertion, but now I employ them as a means of temporarily escaping the other constraints still in place in my life.

My runs started out solo. I would jog along the winding garden paths surrounding the palace since I was both easily exhausted and quickly bored. I grew more adventurous as my stamina gradually increased and began running farther and farther away from the perimeter of the palace as a small means of rebellion.

It didn't take long for my security team to catch on to the fact I was moving outside the gardens alone, and they started following me on each outing.

I've never protested.

I've heard the cautionary tales of reporters and stalkers climbing the massive wrought-iron fence that surrounds the entire royal estate in an attempt to sneak inside. That doesn't mean I make it easy for my agents to keep up with me. One of the maids let slip that my security team draws straws each night to decide who will be responsible for following me on my run the next morning.

I have no idea if that's true, but I let the rumor fuel me as soon as my legs protest the strenuous pace. The possibility that the formidable, fit agents that comprise the Royal Guard may struggle to keep up with me is a source of immense pride.

Once I've warmed up, I quicken my pace to a more arduous one, and smile to myself when I hear a couple of grunts behind me, suggesting this morning's agents would have preferred to stick with the slower speed.

I return to the palace almost an hour later as a sweaty, red-faced mess. My mind is blank and my muscles already ache. The hint of warmth I felt this morning has risen to a humid heat, despite the fact it's still early in the day.

I head inside and up the stairs. The chilly blast of air conditioning causes goosebumps to form on my damp skin. Back in my room, I swap out my sweaty shorts and tank top for a black bikini and then head back outside, clutching an oversized hat, sunglasses, and my laptop. I step out onto the terrace and follow the gravel path through the gardens and over to the patio that surrounds the pool.

Dropping everything onto one of the chaises, I immediately jump into the chilly, clear water, letting it wash away the coat of perspiration and cool my flushed skin. I emerge from the water a few minutes later, dripping and refreshed. One of the maids stands waiting by the edge of the patio, watching as I snag a folded towel and wrap it around my torso.

"Can I get you anything, Princess?" she inquires.

"I'll take my breakfast out here this morning."

She curtsies and leaves.

I flop down onto the cushioned chaise next to the one where I tossed my things and tilt my face back to soak up the sun. Rivulets of chlorinated water stream down my face as I bask under its warm glow.

I remain lying there until I hear footsteps approaching. Opening my eyes, I see a different maid approaching, carrying a tray that contains my usual breakfast of eggs, toast, fruit, and coffee. I sit up and put on my hat and sunglasses as she approaches. She sets the tray down on the table closest to me and then curtsies.

"Anything else I can get you, Your Highness?"

"I'm all set, thank you," I reply, already beginning to eat the delicious food.

She nods and curtsies before heading back inside the palace.

After I've finished eating breakfast, I open my laptop back up. The website for the last school I looked at is still displayed. It's one of the universities in the United States. A large white building with a red earthen roof is visible, surrounded by smaller structures designed similarly. Rather than the abundance of greenery show-cased on most of the other campuses I looked at, a cement court-yard sits in front of the main building with an elaborate fountain as its centerpiece.

I study the photo for a moment, then search the first school again. After I've gone through every university on the list twice more, I close the computer and lean back against the chaise. Now that I've fully dried off from my dip in the pool, the heat feels stifling rather than pleasant. I stand up and gather my things to head inside.

Back in my bedroom, I walk into the white tiled en suite. I yank off the bikini, drop it on the floor, and step inside the shower under the lukewarm spray. School logos and locations scroll through my head as I shampoo my long hair.

After I finish showering, I dress in jeans and a linen blouse and head downstairs to my father's study. I knock on the dark wooden door, and push it open when I hear him call "come in."

I step into the wooden paneled room. The soaring windows behind my father's desk flood the study with morning light and reveal an empty space.

"Papa?" I ask, taking a few steps forward.

"Up here, Vivvi."

I glance up to see my father standing along the edge of the iron railing above me, two books in hand. "I'll be right down."

I walk past the fireplace, where we typically play chess, and take a seat in one of the plush leather armchairs across from his imposing mahogany desk. I watch closely as he makes his way to the top of the spiral staircase tucked in the far corner of his study. Although there's a library in the opposite wing of the palace, my father prefers to have his favorites close by, so he had a second story constructed so that he could simply walk up the stairs once his collection outgrew the bookshelves already installed.

When I was younger, I would sneak up there and sit on the steel balcony that runs around the perimeter of the room, where I could lean against the packed shelves of leather-bound books and eavesdrop on my father's conversations with advisors and members of the Royal Council. I imagined them being about secret missions and confidential information. Most of the time, they were about ribbon cuttings and budgets.

"Had a hankering for some Tolstoy," my father explains, holding up the thicker of the two books when he reaches the bottom of the stairs. "You're a bit early for chess. We'll have to skip the bourbon and whiskey, or your mother won't be pleased." He winks.

I roll my eyes. "We can save the chess for later. I just wanted to let you know I've decided which school I'd like to attend this fall."

"Oh?" my father replies, taking a seat on the opposite side of the desk. "Which one did you pick?"

"Lincoln University. It's in the United States, in Michigan."

My father smiles. "I had a feeling about that one."

"What?" I laugh. "I had a hard time choosing!"

"I know you, Vivvi. You like to be challenged. Lincoln is the largest school on the list, and one of the only ones outside Europe. It almost wasn't included."

"Are you asking me not to pick it?"

"Hardly. I'm glad that you did. It's about as different from Edgewood College as a school can be. It seems like that is exactly what you're hoping for."

I nod, relieved I won't have to change my decision.

"I'll let Richard know, and they'll start making arrangements. We'll schedule a briefing for later this week."

I smile and stand. "Thank you, Papa," I tell him, walking around the desk to kiss his cheek. "This means a lot."

Three days later, I enter one of the ornate conference rooms where the Royal Council holds its regular meetings. A large oval table sits in the center of the room. It's surrounded by red velvet chairs, most of which are already occupied by men in suits. While they all look familiar, the only person I recognize at first glance is Richard. He's served as the head of the Royal Guard for as long as I can remember, and his brusque yet assuring manner makes it clear why he was chosen for the position to begin with.

My father stands off to the side of the table next to a large projector, filling a glass with water from a pitcher. There's a spread of food out, but I don't take anything since I just finished eating lunch.

The group of men all rise as I enter the room, each bowing respectfully in acknowledgment of my presence. I take a seat in one of the two available chairs, and my father takes the other.

"Ready to begin, Princess?" Richard asks once I've settled against the smooth velvet.

I nod in response.

"King Robert informed us of your wish to study at a university outside the country this fall. We came up with a list of schools that fit the basic requirements regarding international tensions and location. You chose Lincoln University in the United States, and plans are already in motion for that to take place. The purpose of this meeting is to provide you with an overview of the logistics and safety measures we plan to implement, and for you to ask any questions you may have."

I nod, and Richard shifts his gaze to my father. "Your Majesty,

I've made a few changes since our conversation yesterday to address the concerns you raised."

My father nods.

Richard stands and walks over to the screen that's been set up. The projector mounted to the ceiling hums to life, and several lines of black text appear on the screen.

"The essential component of this operation is complete and total discretion. Your safety depends on it. All the schools we selected are located in areas where press analysis and local demographics suggest no awareness of Marcedenia or its royal family, but that's far from a guarantee. We'll still take every precaution we can. You'll keep your first name, since it's a fairly common one in the States, but you'll go by the last name of Rhodes as a pseudonym. Your hair color was consistently cited as a memorable characteristic, so you'll need to dye and cut it. The university was told you're an American but have been at boarding school in England for the past eight years. Tell the same to any peers. That will excuse some cultural naiveté, but you'll still need to study some basic elements of American culture. Any questions so far?"

I shake my head, so he continues.

"The official story in Marcedenia will be this statement, set to be sent out next week."

Richard gestures to the words displayed on the screen.

"It says you're spending the next few months on an aid trip, and that the location is being withheld for security reasons. Not only will this provide a reason for your extended absence, it should also ensure no one is looking for you anywhere near where you'll actually be. We'll coordinate a meeting when you return to make certain you're able to accurately answer questions about the trip to the press, but your priority for the time being will be on preparing to pass as an American. Understood?"

I nod.

"Good. Now, for the logistics at the school itself. Lincoln is about an hour from Michigan's largest city. There's a small town that surrounds the campus, also named Lincoln. The location is obscure, but not desolate. You'll fly to London on a private plane, then take commercial flights from London to Michigan with two of the four agents who will be accompanying you. They will both have cover stories that allow them to spend time with you regularly and accompany you places without raising suspicion. One will be posing as your stepfather, who just received a position on campus as a professor. The other agent is one we pulled straight from the training academy here. He's only two years older than you. He will be posing as your stepbrother and a fellow student. The other two agents will be acting as campus security agents. They will be available for back-up at any time if it becomes necessary."

The faces of three men and a woman flash across the screen.

"We've arranged for you to live in Lincoln's only all-girls dorm, Kennedy Hall. Your roommate will be Katie Masterson. She's starting her second year, which means she can help you navigate campus. You'll be sharing a room and a bathroom with her. She did well at Lincoln last year despite her parents divorcing halfway through the year. She passed our background check and had glowing references from everyone we talked to."

A new image flashes on the screen, this time of a pale girl with short brown hair sporting a friendly smile.

"While your housing is all set, I'll need your class selections by the end of the day to ensure that's in order as well."

Richard returns to his seat and slides a thick booklet down the shiny table to me.

"The president of the university is handling all the arrangements at Lincoln personally. He's the only person on campus aside from the agents traveling with you who will know your true identity. Anyone else who has had to make arrangements has been told your father is an important government official and any leaks about your location could be a matter of national security. If that story comes out, it should give us enough lead time to remove you, and also create enough confusion when they can't verify any part of that narrative that your true identity will stay confidential. Questions?"

I shake my head, stunned by the effort and planning that's already taken place. I experience a twinge of guilt at the realization I've caused so much upheaval, but it's quickly engulfed by rising excitement at the prospect of spending the next four months almost entirely on my own.

"No questions at the moment," I answer.

"Good." Richard rises, his face as stoic as always. "You'll travel to Glendale Cottage the week before you depart. Your hair will be changed then. You'll also be quizzed on your cover story and American culture, so start studying." He slides a binder to me that I stack on top of the booklet already in front of me. "Make sure to get me those classes by the end of the day, Your Highness." He bows and then leaves the room.

The rest of the men follow his lead, leaving me alone with my father.

"Everything okay?" he asks.

"Yes, Papa," I reply. "Just a little overwhelmed. But also excited."

"Good." He smiles. "I've got another meeting now, but I'll see you for dinner. Your mother invited the Vanderbilts over, I believe."

"Okay," I reply. "I'm going to start working my way through this all." I lift the heavy stack of paper from the table and grin.

My father laughs. "Happy reading, Vivvi."

I spend the rest of the afternoon sprawled out on one of the overstuffed leather couches in the library, paging through the thick booklet listing all of Lincoln University's courses. Finally, I narrow the extensive options down to four selections: a medieval history course, a philosophy course, an English class, and an American government lecture. I write down all the course names on a piece of lined paper and leave the library to walk back toward the Royal Guard's quarters in the opposite wing of the house.

As I'm passing through the front foyer, I encounter my mother.

"Oh, Vivienne, good. I've had the staff running all over the place looking for you. Where have you been?"

I hold up the glossy booklet. "Picking my university courses. I have to bring them to Richard."

"Fine, but once you've done that, go put on something else." She eyes my shorts critically. "The Vanderbilts are coming for dinner tonight."

"I know, Papa told me."

"Be down here by six," are her parting words as she sweeps back out of the foyer.

I continue down the long hallway until I arrive at the door of Richard's office. I knock and push the heavy door open when he calls out for me to enter.

He's sitting behind his desk, sorting through the massive pile of papers that covers most of the wooden surface. Despite Richard's long tenure as the head of the Royal Guard, one would never know it looking at his office. Aside from one framed photograph, the small room is completely bereft of any personal details, merely containing the same dark wooden desk and chairs that fill the office of every member of the Royal Guard. The sparse space fits his no nonsense personality.

"I've made my course selections," I inform him as I step inside and hold out the booklet and sheet of paper listing my selections.

"Ah, very good. Just set them there, please." Richard nods toward one of the empty chairs across from his cluttered desk. I set them down where he's suggested, and head back toward the door.

"Have a good night, Richard."

"You as well, Your Highness."

I leave the security wing and head back into the residence. Entering my bedroom, I walk over to the massive walk-in closet and begin flipping through the long row of hangers as I decide what to wear for dinner.

Eventually, I come across a gray, raw silk cocktail dress I know my mother will approve of. I head into the bathroom and freshen up before slipping on the dress and a pair of gray heels that match it perfectly.

I descend the central staircase toward the front foyer just as the Vanderbilts enter the residence through the front doors, escorted by one of the butlers.

Lionel Vanderbilt is a duke, who also happens to be one of my father's oldest friends. They attended Bridgemont Academy together and were also classmates at Edgewood College for one year before my father was unexpectedly forced to take the throne. Lionel's wife, Margaret, is a petite blonde on the boards of all the same organizations my mother oversees. Their son, Charles, is the same age as me, although I haven't seen him in several years. Margaret is German, and Charles attends a prestigious boarding school her family founded there.

Lionel spots me first and bows, which catches Margaret's attention. She looks up and curtsies.

The butler leads the Vanderbilts into one of the many sitting rooms that line the main entryway, and I enter the room behind them. My parents are already seated inside.

My mother has changed into a flowing pink organza dress, and she nods approvingly when she sees my choice of attire. The Vanderbilts bow and curtsy to my parents, and then take seats on one of the antique couches. I drop into the armchair next to my father's, and he gives me a warm smile.

"Productive afternoon?" he asks with a wink.

"Very."

He nods, then turns to talk with Lionel. One of the butlers brings me a glass of whiskey immediately, making me glad that my drink preference is well known by the staff. The Vanderbilts request their beverages, and I listen absentmindedly as they socialize with my parents while I take small sips of the aromatic liquid.

"Vivienne, are you excited about starting at Edgewood College?" Lionel asks, shifting the conversation to me. "Your father and I had quite the time there back in the day." He chuckles.

I take my time swallowing the whiskey, unsure how to reply. Thankfully, my father jumps in. "Actually, Vivienne won't be at Edgewood this fall. She's decided to go on an aid trip before starting there. We're very proud of her decision."

I shoot him a grateful look.

"An aid trip?" Lionel echoes in surprise. "Where?"

"Somewhere in South America, likely," my father replies vaguely. "We have a team still sorting out the final details."

"That's wonderful, Vivienne," Margaret tells me, smiling. "You truly are your mother's daughter. Charles will be disappointed, however. We told him you'd be classmates this fall."

"How is Charles?" my mother asks, clearly eager to steer the conversation away from my plans.

Margaret and Lionel accept the subject change readily, and begin boasting about all their son has accomplished while in Germany. I take the opportunity to tune the conversation out once again.

One of the maids enters to announce dinner is ready just as I'm taking the last sip of my drink. As we're all exiting the sitting room to make the short trek to the formal dining room, Lionel Vanderbilt falls into step beside me.

"I doubt the place you'll be staying in this fall will look anything like this." He chuckles, gesturing to our luxurious surroundings. "If you get a chance between teaching children or any other tasks they have you helping out with, you should really make a trip to our beach house in South Carolina. You've never been across the Atlantic, have you?"

I shake my head.

"Beautiful scenery over there, especially along the coast. South Carolina is our favorite. We spend March through May and parts of the summer there every year. If you get a chance, you should feel free to visit."

"I appreciate it, Lionel," I reply politely. "But I doubt I'll be anywhere near an airport. And I'm not planning to be jetting off on any beach vacations while I'm there."

"Of course, of course. But should you change your mind..." Lionel slips a card out of a pocket inside his suit jacket and jots something down on it before handing it to me. "Here is the number for the personal pilot we have over there. He can pick you up from anywhere and fly you to South Carolina to see it in person."

I take the card. "Thank you."

I'm quiet during dinner. Although Lionel doesn't know it, his gushing over the scenery the United States offers has only increased my excitement for my upcoming time there. Aside from the campus photos I looked at, I have no idea what to expect of the country I'll be temporarily living in.

After dinner, my father and Lionel retire to his study for a nightcap. My mother and Margaret invite me to the drawing room with them, but I decline, faking a headache.

I return to my room eagerly, pulling off the fancy dress and dropping it carelessly on the gleaming wooden floor. I put on a matching set of silk pajamas and climb onto my bed to begin reading through the binder Richard gave me earlier.

I'm quickly inundated by page after page of information about music, movies, television shows, and celebrities an American teenager would be expected to know. I reach a section titled *Football* that lists out the rules for an American sport where players throw a ball and tackle each other on a grass field divided into segments by white lines. The description pulls at a memory.

I grab my computer and pull up Lincoln's website. Sure enough, the first image displayed in the background is of a field exactly like the one described in the binder.

A search of *American football* causes millions of results to come up, discussing professional teams, games, statistics, and players. The sheer volume is overwhelming. I click through a few of the first sites, but they are all articles that use nonsensical words.

I close my computer and move on to the next section in the binder.

CHAPTER FOUR

The next few weeks pass rapidly. The day I'm set to depart for Glendale Cottage, a royal residence located closer to the coast, arrives before I know it.

Neither of my parents are traveling with me, so I stand and wait for them in the foyer as my security team loads bag after bag into the trunk of a black SUV. My mother and her team found a Marcedenian stylist who attended fashion school in New York to consult with on my wardrobe. Their lengthy conversations mean an array of new sweaters, jackets, and boots unnecessary in Marcedenia's temperate climate have been added to bags already filled with my substantial wardrobe.

The last of my suitcases are being loaded into the back of the car when my mother appears. She looks as poised and elegant as always, but I notice her hand is shaking as she straightens the lapels of the linen blazer she's wearing over a slim sheath dress.

"You're sure you have everything, Vivienne?" she asks, glancing around the now empty entryway.

"I'm certain," I reply. "If anything, I overpacked."

A ghost of a smile appears. "Well, this is it, I suppose." She steps forward and wraps her arms around me. I rest my chin on the tailored shoulder of her blazer. We stand like that for a long moment.

After eighteen years of keeping me contained within the fortress of the palace under heavy guard, the prospect of sending me to another country and hoping no one recognizes me must seem like a terrifying prospect.

"I'll be fine, Mother," I tell her. "I'll be careful, I promise."

She drops her arms. I raise my head and step away, giving her what I hope is a reassuring smile.

"Your bags are all loaded?" my father asks, appearing in the soaring entryway to the foyer and glancing around. "I thought it would take them all day to figure out how to fit that massive pile in the car."

I scoff at his dramatics. "They got them all."

My father walks over to where my mother and I are standing. My mother is wearing a forlorn expression, but it disappears when he reaches us and gives her a quick kiss on the cheek.

"Evelyn, we had to kick her out of the nest sometime."

My mother smiles slightly in response, and my father steps forward to give me a tight hug.

"Be safe, be smart, and have fun," are his parting words to me. His tone is light, but I see my mother's worry reflected in the blue eyes I inherited.

I nod.

My father steps back and rests his arm around my mother's shoulders. She leans against him, and I turn to walk toward the tall ornate doors that mark the main entrance to the palace. One is still propped open from when the car was being loaded. I pause when I reach it, and glance back at my parents. They're still standing in the same spot, watching me leave. I smile at them, then step outside the palace and into the warm summer sunshine.

The shiny black SUV is parked just outside the main doors. Richard and Michael are both standing next to the car.

"Ready, Princess?" Richard asks.

"Yes, I am," I reply confidently.

Richard climbs into the front passenger seat next to the driver, and Michael climbs in next to me in the back. We pull up to the massive iron gate. The doors creak open slowly, revealing the expanse of open road ahead of us. Crowds of tourists mill about just outside the gates. I look out at them from behind tinted glass as they point and exclaim at the car.

Progress is slow as we drive away from the palace and wind through the city, but we eventually reach the highway. I relax against the seat in preparation for the two-hour drive to the coast as tree-lined roads fly by.

I doze off during the drive and am jolted awake by the bumpy country road that signals our arrival at Glendale Cottage. To call the royal residence a cottage is an understatement. At one point, it was a fairly modest dwelling, but years of restorations and renovations have made mansion a more appropriate noun.

We pause at the gated entrance so the driver can flash his identification. Once he does, the gate slides open, allowing us to roll up the clamshell drive to the front of the house. I head inside as soon as we park, while Richard and Michael begin unloading the car.

Over the course of the next four days, I'm quizzed relentlessly by Richard on every single aspect of my cover story. Once he's satisfied I remember each detail, he passes me over to Michael to test me on my knowledge of American culture.

Our sessions of preparation are much more enjoyable, mostly

thanks to Michael's easy-going nature, which I appreciate even more after enduring days of Richard's taciturn manner. The subject matter is also more interesting, although the one topic I remain unable to master is American football. I make the mistake of mentioning my confusion regarding the sport to Richard at dinner one night.

He decides it is absolutely necessary for me to have some understanding of football to pass as an American student, thanks to its widespread popularity throughout the country. I'm immediately tasked with reading a book on the sport, which makes me more confused. Michael tries to help, but seems equally baffled by it.

The day before I'm scheduled to depart, Richard enters the suite as my hair is being cut and dyed from strawberry blonde to light blonde to inform me he has set up a call with a retired professional football player to teach me about the sport.

As soon as my new hair is finished, I'm ushered into the office down the hall, where a video chat has already been pulled up. I take a seat behind the wooden desk to see a middle-aged man displayed on the computer screen.

"Hello there," he says, giving me a friendly smile. "I'm Jerry Lewis. Nice to meet you."

"It's nice to meet you too," I reply. "I'm Vivienne…Rhodes."

Richard gives me an approving nod from the opposite side of the desk and then exits the room, leaving just Michael with me.

"You've been at school in London but are going to college in the States?" Jerry asks.

"That's right," I confirm.

"Well, I can understand why you'd want to brush up on your football, then. Hard to escape it in this country, although to be honest, I can't say I've ever really tried to." He winks, and I smile in response.

Jerry proceeds to recite the same terminology and rules I've already read about repeatedly, but he takes the time to draw diagrams and come up with comparisons that make me feel as though I finally have a solid grasp of the basic concepts.

"Any questions?" he asks me at the end.

"Why do you think football is so popular in the States, but no place else?" I wonder, marveling at the complexity of a sport played in only one country rather than around the world like most.

"That's a good question," Jerry replies, shrugging. "Wish I knew the answer to it. It seems to just be getting more and more popular here, though."

"Do you think it's changed since you played? Why has it become more popular now?"

"More good questions." Jerry laughs. "You should consider taking some journalism classes in college. But to answer your question, no. I think it's become less innovative, and I think it's become more commercialized. Teams look for the quarterback who can throw the farthest, not who's most inventive. There's no way I would make it to the professional level these days. I wouldn't have back in the day if not for the Kamanski technique. It was creativity that mattered then, not just yardage."

There's a shout on his end of the call, and he glances to the side before looking back at me apologetically.

"I'm afraid I've got to go, Vivienne. Kids are looking for food. I hope this helped, and good luck in school. Think about what I said about journalism. I could make some calls!" He winks, then the screen goes black.

I look at Michael, who's still sitting across the table. "Did you follow any of that?"

"Parts," he replies, glancing up from his phone. "I did some research, and I'm pretty certain he was downplaying his talent at the end there. This says he won three football championships with a team called the Ducks. 1998, 2001, and 2002."

"Well, hopefully this appeases Richard. I think I can pass for an American who doesn't follow football now, at least," I joke.

We leave the office and head downstairs to discover that the four agents who comprise my new security team have arrived. Richard looks over from speaking to one of them as Michael and I enter the living room.

"Princess, perfect timing. How was the call?"

"Useful," I reply. "Thank you for setting it up."

"Thank Lionel Vanderbilt. He was the one who had some connection in the American football world. Someone he knows from his time in South Carolina."

I nod, then glance over at the four agents curiously. As soon as the group realizes they've caught my attention, they all bow, with the exception of the solitary woman, who drops into a deep curtesy. Members of the Royal Guard aren't typically required to display the formal greeting in the presence of royalty, except when approaching a member in public or meeting them for the first time. I look the four agents over with interest as they all straighten.

"Your Highness, let me introduce you to your assigned team," Richard states. "First, we have Agent Thomas Lee." A tall man who looks to be in his mid-forties gives me a kind smile. "He'll be posing as your stepfather and also as an engineering professor at Lincoln."

A younger guy just a couple inches taller than me stands next in line, a serious expression on his face. His blond hair is closely cropped; his stance is rigid. He gives me a brief smile before returning to the same stoicism.

"Next, we have Agent Philip Matthews. He'll be known as your stepbrother and a fellow Lincoln student."

A short woman with a long braid of blonde hair gives me a warm smile.

"Agent Julie Williams will be undercover as a member of campus security," Richard continues. "Along with her partner, Agent Steve Jackson."

A bulky man with dark brown hair nods to me respectfully.

"Agents, this is Her Royal Highness, Princess Vivienne of Marcedenia. As we discussed in your individual briefings, I cannot overstate the importance of this mission and your responsibilities enough. She is the sole heir to the throne, a role that just became of even greater importance in light of recent events. Anything happens to her, and I guarantee you will wish it had happened to you instead. Understood?"

"Yes, sir," the line of agents chant in perfect unison.

Studying their cowed expressions, I realize Richard's brisk attitude over the past few days was actually a glimpse of his most patient and friendly self.

"Good. Now settle in for the night. We've got a big day tomorrow. The plane leaves at eight sharp."

I don't sleep well that night, anxiously tossing and turning as I contemplate the complete and utter upheaval that's about to take place in my life.

I wake from a fitful sleep to find the cottage already bustling with activity as everyone prepares to depart. The car is reloaded with all my luggage while I say goodbye to Richard and Michael before they head back to the palace.

My number of companions whittles down further when we arrive at the airport. Julie and Steve are traveling separately on a commercial flight later in the day. I board a private plane with

Thomas and Philip to London, and from there we embark on a commercial flight to New York, and finally one from New York to Michigan.

Philip stays quiet throughout most of the long trip, but Thomas and I make small talk during the multiple flights. I learn both his father and grandfather were members of the Royal Guard and that his wife is expecting a baby at the end of the year. That last revelation is a reminder of the upheaval I've caused over the last few weeks. People are uprooting their lives and making major sacrifices so that I can have this opportunity. The monarchy is a massive force, and it requires total dedication. This is a temporary arrangement, a stop on the way to stepping up and fulfilling my duty. A selfish act before dedicating the rest of my life to service. A pursuit of new experiences I hope will make me better prepared to take on big responsibilities. Make me a better ruler.

Once we land in Michigan, there is a car waiting to transport the three of us to Lincoln. Most of the drive is along a tree-lined interstate. We eventually exit the highway and drive through a small downtown area before we arrive at the periphery of the campus.

A massive stone sign carved with *LINCOLN UNIVERSITY* marks the entrance. We enter the campus and drive past a few buildings before we stop. I step out of the car in front of a brick, ivy-covered building with a large sign reading *Kennedy Hall* displayed above the front doors.

Thomas and Philip unload all of my luggage from the trunk, as I stand and take in my new surroundings. It's almost nine in the evening now, and my body sags with exhaustion as we walk toward the entrance to the dorm.

I check in and receive my student identification card, along with a folder of welcome materials. One of the student volunteers leads me down a long hallway, with Thomas and Philip close behind. She departs after bringing us to the last of the nondescript wooden doors, and I swipe my new keycard.

The door swings open to reveal a room that's roughly the same size as my walk-in closet back home.

The two sides of the room are mirror images of each other, separated by a paned window that sits in the very center of the wall we're facing. A long shelf just below it butts against the edges of each of the twin beds pushed against the walls. A desk and dresser on each side of the room complete the reflection.

One half of the room is already partially decorated. A couple of posters hang on the wall, and the bed is neatly made with a navy comforter. Two zipped suitcases lean against the wooden frame of the bed, atop a plush white rug.

I walk a few steps into the room and spot a door off to the right. I push it open, revealing a small but clean bathroom containing a toilet, sink, and shower stall.

Thomas and Philip are already in motion when I turn back toward the room. Philip is making the bed with clean linens we brought while Thomas stacks notebooks, binders, and pens on my desk. They move efficiently, and are finished with unpacking everything I brought except my wardrobe within minutes.

"Would you like us to unpack your clothes, Princess?" Thomas asks.

"No, it's all right," I'm quick to reply. "Go get some rest. You must both be exhausted."

Thomas slides a sleek phone out of his pocket. He hands it over. "This is your new phone.".

I left my old one at the palace, since it wouldn't receive any service outside the country.

"It has an American number, and is already programmed with the numbers for the palace as well as the numbers to reach Philip, Steve, Julie, and me. There's a secure app installed that requires facial identification to open. That's how you should contact us for regular check-ins. Only call the numbers listed for us if it's an emergency or it's a conversation that can be had on an open line. Understand?"

I nod.

"All right. Good night, Princess."

"Good night."

Thomas and Philip leave the tiny dorm room. I stand still, suddenly too overcome to move. I'm more alone in this moment than I have ever been in my entire life. Not only am I thousands of miles away from my family, but also from the palace and the country I've called home for the past eighteen years. The feeling is so foreign, I can hardly begin to process it.

Bit by bit, exhaustion begins to seep back in. The long day of travel and sleepless night overwhelm the paralyzing novelty of unfamiliar isolation.

I take a quick shower, dress in my usual silk pajamas, and finish unpacking. It takes some creative maneuvering, but I finally fit all the shoes and clothes I brought into the small dresser and closet.

I'm storing my empty suitcases under the bed when the door swings open. A girl with shoulder length hair and brown eyes enters the room. She spots me crouching down by the edge of my bed and smiles tentatively.

"You must be Vivienne. I'm Katie—Katie Masterson."

I shove the last bag under the bed and stand. "Yes, I'm Vivienne Rhodes," I reply formally. "Pleasure to meet you."

"You're unpacked already?" Katie asks, looking at my stuffed closet. "I'm impressed. I just dumped everything earlier. Did you bring any decorations?" She eyes my bare walls and empty shelves.

"No, there was limited space on the plane, and I prioritized my clothes," I tell her.

She smiles at that. "We can stop by the campus store tomorrow, if you'd like," Katie offers. "They have a bunch of stuff for decorating."

"I'd like that," I reply, just before a large yawn escapes me. "Sorry, it's been a long day of travel."

"You're from London?" Katie questions. "How come you don't have an accent?"

I'm suddenly grateful for Richard's relentless preparation. "I've been at boarding school in London for the past eight years," I answer. "But I was born and raised here in the States, so I never picked up an accent."

Katie nods as though that makes perfect sense, and I let out a subtle sigh of relief.

"Did you like London?" she asks.

"Yes," I respond. "I was planning to stay there for university, but then my stepfather, Thomas, got a position here as a professor, so it seemed like the right time to come home. My stepbrother, Philip, is also starting here this semester. He's a junior, but he transferred because he wasn't happy at his last school."

I study Katie's reaction closely, hoping my background didn't sound like the carefully rehearsed story it is.

"Lincoln's the best," she tells me, accepting my explanation. "You both definitely made the right choice. What does your step-father teach?"

"Engineering," I reply, glad the answer comes to me imme-diately.

"I definitely won't have him, then." Katie laughs. "I'm a drama major."

"That sounds cool."

"Any idea what you want to major in?"

This time I don't have to lie. "No idea."

"That's how I was, too. You're only a freshman, right?"

I nod.

"You've got plenty of time."

Another yawn overtakes me. "Sorry. I'm exhausted. Do you mind if I head to bed?"

"Of course not," Katie replies, giving me a friendly smile. "I totally understand. We've got the whole year to get to know each other."

I smile back, although her final words form a twist of unease in my stomach. I've been here for less than an hour, but I already have a sinking sensation that four months won't feel like long enough.

CHAPTER FIVE

The next morning, I wake up just before seven. It takes me a few minutes to process the unfamiliar surroundings before I climb out of bed.

I brush my teeth and wash my face in the small bathroom, then pull on a pair of athletic shorts and a tank top. I grab my new phone and keycard before heading outside. It's a beautiful morning. Bright sunlight illuminates the deserted campus. I jog away from my new dorm along a paved path, keeping a close eye on the landmarks I pass to make certain I'll remember how to get back to Kennedy Hall.

One of the few times Philip spoke on the trip here was to ask me whether I would be continuing my early morning runs at Lincoln, indicating he did some research and spoke to members of my usual security team. I'm pretty certain I deterred him by replying I only ran at home as a means of getting out of the palace.

Having to call him because I'm lost on campus in the midst of a morning run would undoubtedly alert him to that lie.

I successfully return to my new room a half hour later. Katie is still asleep. I quickly shower and dress in a blue cotton dress. My phone dings just as I finish putting on a pair of sandals. I look at the screen to see a notification from the messaging app Thomas mentioned last night. I tap it, and it scans my face before opening a group chat. I quickly reply to the message asking if I'm doing all right and confirm I'm not planning to leave campus today.

"You're up already?" Katie's sleepy voice distracts me from my phone.

I glance across the room to see her sitting up in bed, yawning widely. Her brown hair looks like a bird nested in it.

"Yup. I'm an early riser," I reply.

"Ugh, my mom is too. Wish I could say the same. I'm sure I could get a lot accomplished if I dragged myself out of bed before nine."

"It's a blessing and a curse," I reply, thinking of the many mornings I toss and turn, trying to sleep in just a little longer.

"Do you want me to show you around campus this morning?" Katie asks hesitantly. "We could stop by the school store so you can see what they have for decorations."

"Yes, that sounds great."

Katie smiles. "Okay, let me just get ready."

I browse through my phone while she swaps her pajamas for a pair of shorts and a t-shirt and then heads into the bathroom, emerging just a few minutes later.

"Ready?"

I nod, and we each grab our phones and keycards. I take my credit card out of my wallet and copy Katie when I see her slide her cards into the back of her phone case.

When we emerge outside, the air temperature is much warmer than during my run earlier. Katie and I chat easily as we walk along, and I'm grateful Richard chose her as my roommate. She asks me a few more questions about my background, all of which

I have prepared answers to. She also shares some details about her own, describing her hometown, and even mentioning her parents' recent divorce. I school my expression carefully when she shares that detail, recalling how Richard mentioned it during the briefing.

Katie leads me to a coffee shop on the fringe of campus. We each order an iced coffee and a pastry before taking a couple of seats at one of the small metal tables to consume our breakfast. After we finish eating, Katie guides me back toward the center of campus for the promised tour.

My eyes are wide as I follow her across the campus, which is now bustling with activity. Massive brick buildings surround us as we walk along the gray stone pavers that comprise the wide central path.

Katie points out each building we pass, telling me which academic departments it houses. Just as she's beginning to talk about the political science building, a skateboarder suddenly zips past us on the right. He calls out an apology to the pedestrians he's displaced over his shoulder before continuing to career down the smooth path.

"You've got to watch out for the skater guys along here," Katie tells me. "They never pay attention to where they're going."

She's barely finished speaking when another male voice calls out, "Coming through!"

His voice sounds as though it's coming from directly behind me, so I reflexively jump to the other side of the path.

A gust of warm air blows by me as the skateboarder passes, sending strands of my hair flying about. I'm more distracted by the firm male body I've just collided with.

Breath leaves my lungs in a harsh *whoosh* from a mixture of surprise and impact.

"Girls normally at least buy me a drink before feeling me up."

I steady myself and glance up into the most startling pair of gray eyes I've ever seen, peeking out at me from underneath the rim of a black baseball cap. Their stormy color match the annoyed expression of the stranger I'm currently pressed against.

I inhale sharply. "Well, I'm fresh out of cocktails at the moment," I reply, dropping my hands from his muscular chest and taking a step back so we're no longer touching.

The guy looks momentarily startled, as though he didn't expect me to respond to him. He quickly regains the same arrogant, vexed expression he was wearing before I spoke.

"Then at least look where you're going," he lectures me haughtily.

I scoff. "Advice better suited for the guy who almost just ran me over, don't you think?"

"He wasn't the one who just collided with me." The guy flashes me a condescending smirk, and my temper flares.

"Next time I'll take my chances with the skateboard," I retort. "Couldn't possibly be worse than talking with you."

I don't wait to see if he'll respond, brushing past him to stalk over toward Katie. She's stopped a few feet away on the opposite side of the path and is staring at me in shock.

"Do you know who that was?" she asks when I reach her side.

"An arrogant jerk?" I fume.

"Jace Dawson!" Katie exclaims. I can practically see the stars in her eyes.

"That name means nothing to me."

"He's our quarterback. The hottest guy at Lincoln," she informs me. "Everyone on campus knows who he is. He's like royalty here."

I laugh at the irony of her statement. "I don't see the appeal." That's a lie. Until he opened his conceited mouth, I was struck speechless by the sight of his chiseled features and the feel of his muscular body.

Katie gives me a look that clearly indicates she doesn't believe me, but she doesn't comment further as we continue on the tour of campus. As promised, she brings me to the school store at the end of the tour, and I pick up a couple of posters along with a Lincoln pennant to hang on my currently empty wall.

The following morning marks the first day of classes. Although I didn't choose Lincoln for its academics, I discover I love the courses I selected, particularly the philosophy one. Part of the novelty is the knowledge they're subjects I chose myself, but I'm equally buoyed by the fact I walk to the classes alone, or with Katie, rather than with a group of armed agents.

My parents call at the end of the first week, and we have a long conversation. As soon as I've finished answering their questions about Lincoln, my mother launches into a rendition of all the gossip she heard at her latest board meeting. My father remains on the line, despite the fact I suspect he's already heard it all once before. While I'm usually annoyed by her speculating, I'm surprised by the amount of nostalgia I experience listening to her. It feels like we're all sitting together at dinner rather than thousands of miles apart.

After my mother finishes with her stories, my father contributes to the conversation by informing me he's finished *War and Peace* again, and that he beat Lionel in a chess match in a matter of minutes.

I quickly settle into a new routine consisting of classes, morning runs, calls home, and check-ins with my agents. The days begin to fly by rapidly, and before I know it, I've already been at Lincoln for over a month.

The sprawling campus is as gorgeous in person as it was on the university's website. The woods that encircle the campus quickly become my favorite place to be. Each morning, I start my day jogging through the cool morning air to the welcome sound of complete silence.

Now that I've learned my way around campus, I'm no longer concerned about getting lost and having to call Philip, so I take every obscure path I can find.

I've also discovered how to set the location tracker on my phone to a specific spot, a trick Katie taught me one night while she was celebrating having successfully done so herself to escape her mother's constant monitoring. I no longer have to worry about one of my agents waking up early and seeing I'm not in my room. As guilty as I feel editing my location, I figure it's better to do that than go running without it.

The Monday marking the start of my fifth week at Lincoln, I wake up later than usual. One of the girls on the floor above us spent the better part of the night blasting rock music, and my eyes feel gritty from lack of sleep when I finally pry them open. I roll out of bed, groggily dressing in my usual running clothes before heading into the bathroom to finish getting ready.

There's a chill in the air when I step outside; the first traces of fall evident in the slight breeze rippling through my hair. I veer left, opting to follow a deserted path that heads toward the opposite end of campus. The gravel makes a satisfying crunching sound beneath my sneakers as I run toward a massive elm tree that's just off the path up ahead.

A flash of movement catches my attention, and I turn my head to see a lone figure to my right.

I experience a flash of irritation as I recognize the same football player I bumped into my first day. He's jogging across the grass toward the same tree I'm about to pass.

Jace Dawson, I suddenly recall, thinking of Katie's strange reaction to our infuriating encounter and of the many times I've heard the name repeated since. I quicken my pace, hoping to avoid another interaction. Based on our last conversation, he would likely accuse me of stalking him.

I think I've made it past without him noticing, when suddenly I hear footfalls behind me. I'm about to increase my speed even more when I hear a "Hey!" shouted behind me. I speed up anyway, but when I hear another yell, I finally slow my pace and then turn around reluctantly.

Jace Dawson stands in front of me. To my annoyance, he's barely winded and even better looking than I remember.

"I'm not stalking you," I state.

Jace looks surprised, but quickly recovers. "That sounds like something a stalker would say," he notes.

"Well, since you were conceited enough to think I staged a near-death experience just to touch your chest, I figured I would save you the hassle of accusing me of stalking you because I'm out running on a public path."

"I would hardly call someone skateboarding past you a near-death experience," Jace says easily.

Beneath my annoyance, I'm both surprised and strangely pleased that he remembers our brief encounter over a month ago.

"He was skateboarding toward me, not past me," I correct.

"Matter of opinion."

I roll my eyes at that, but he's given me the perfect opening to end the conversation. "I'm not interested in yours, so goodbye."

I turn and start jogging again. Jace falls into step beside me, and I bite back a groan.

"I'd accuse *you* of being the one stalking *me*, but I'm not a self-absorbed narcissist," I inform him.

"You're awfully focused on stalking for an innocent bystander," Jace replies. "Guilty conscience, perhaps?"

"Hardly," I scoff. "But it's nice to know I was right you would accuse me of it."

"I do run here every morning," Jace responds.

"I'll make sure to avoid it in the future."

"And girls have done much crazier things for my attention," Jace adds.

"They must not have ever talked to you, then, or they'd know to just ply your ego with a few compliments."

"Compliments get old when they're always the same ones."

"You get sick of people telling you what an amazing football player you are? I'm shocked."

Jace sends me a pleased grin. "You asked around about me?"

I curse internally. I hadn't meant to let slip that I know he is considered Lincoln's star athlete.

"Nope. I have no control over the fact that most of this campus seems to have an unhealthy obsession with your ability to throw a ball." I have yet to make it through a single day on campus without overhearing at least twenty people mention Jace Dawson. No other person seems to dominate Lincoln gossip more. "Not sure why," I add.

"Doesn't seem fair that you know who I am, but I don't know who you are," Jace replies, ignoring my dig.

"Life is full of disappointments," I tell him loftily.

"True, but like you already said, I have some clout on this campus. If you don't tell me who you are, I'll just find out some other way, and then you'll have to explain how you stalked me and I needed your name for the restraining order."

"Funny." My voice conveys I found his comment the opposite.

We run in silence for a few hundred yards.

"Well?" Jace finally prompts.

I sigh. "Vivienne."

"Vivienne."

The sound of my name rolling off his tongue does strange things to my stomach.

"So, where are you from, Vivienne?" he asks.

"I don't think that's information they'll need for the restraining order."

"Has anyone ever told you that you're difficult to get to know?"

"Has anyone ever told you that you're annoying?" I retort.

Jace lets out a dry laugh. "Handsome, talented, athletic, yes. Annoying is a first."

I snort. "Shocking."

We continue running in silence. I'm pushing myself faster than usual, but Jace keeps up easily. The same massive tree where I first encountered him is visible in the distance, and I'm surprised to realize we've run the entire trail together.

I slow my pace as we return to the gravel path, eventually stopping in the shade of the broad branches so I can pull my quarter zip over my head and tie it around my waist.

"I have to get to an early class," I tell Jace, who's watching me closely. I shift uncomfortably under the scrutiny. I contemplate tossing out another barb, but decide to just tack on a lame "See you."

He smiles. "See you, Vivienne."

I jog back toward Kennedy Hall, resisting the temptation to look back at him the whole time.

CHAPTER SIX

I spend the rest of the day thinking about Jace Dawson, and it irks me.

The next morning, I leave my dorm room and stand outside of Kennedy Hall for longer than usual, conflicted. A large part of me wants to turn left and see if Jace is at the tree again, but I squash down the troublesome inclination and turn to the right before I begin jogging.

The rest of the week, I purposefully wake up especially early and choose long, winding routes that take me as far away from the elm tree where I encountered Jace as possible.

With each passing day, the decision to do so becomes easier and easier, like I'm slowly being cleansed from an addictive substance.

The following Tuesday, I push through Kennedy Hall's front door to embark on my usual morning run, stretching my arms as I do. I round the large bush that stands just outside the entrance and unexpectedly slam into a hard body.

I glance up, about to apologize, when I'm struck silent by familiar gray eyes.

"Morning," Jace greets me, grinning.

"Are you lost?" I ask. "This is the all-girls' dorm."

"I know. It also seems to be a safety hazard. Do you ever watch where you're going?"

I ignore him and start jogging. It only takes a few seconds for the telltale sound of footsteps to start behind me. I look over at Jace, annoyed.

"What part of our last run together gave you the impression I wanted to repeat the experience?" I ask. Despite my harsh words, I'm disgruntled to find that I'm actually excited to see him.

Jace returns my gaze and grins again. "I'm training. Your endless insults make me run faster."

"I like my runs to be peaceful, not to be a verbal sparring match."

Jace chuckles. "I can be quiet. The disdain radiating off of you is motivation enough."

I can't help but crack a small smile at that.

To my surprise, Jace keeps his word and doesn't say anything else as we continue running along the outskirts of campus side by side.

Unfortunately, his silence allows me to focus on other, inconvenient details, like the way he smells like pine and clean laundry. His bare hand brushes mine at one point, and I experience a startling rush of heat.

We pass the student center, and I notice the stone steps leading up to the entrance have been lined with carved pumpkins.

"Are those for Halloween?" I ask, finally breaking the silence.

Jace glances over at the steps. "No, they must be for Valentine's Day," he tells me seriously.

I ignore his sarcasm. "I thought only little kids celebrate Halloween."

Jace looks at me with surprise. "Seriously? A chance to wear a ridiculous outfit and get drunk? It's one of the craziest nights of the year here."

"Are you speaking from experience?"

"Don't they celebrate Halloween in London?" Jace asks, ignoring my question.

I have no idea, but I try to sound confident in my response. "They do, but the school I went to was pretty strict." Unless you were set to rule the country one day, I add silently. Another thought occurs to me. "Wait, how do you know I went to school in London?" My voice is accusing.

Jace's is unfazed. "I asked someone to find out. Wasn't hard to do." He sounds disgruntled about that for some reason.

"That's not an invasion of privacy or anything," I grumble. I'm surprised he actually followed through on his earlier threat to ask around about my background. "Did this unnamed informant also dig up the incident with the headmaster's son?"

That question catches his attention, and I laugh when his startled eyes meet mine. His expression relaxes when he realizes I'm kidding.

"So, are you a big fan of Halloween?" I ask curiously.

"When I was younger, yeah," Jace replies. "It was mostly the dressing up part I liked. I've never had much of a sweet tooth."

"What did you dress up as?"

"A race car driver. I was obsessed with them when I was six. My grandfather had a stock car he spent years trying to restore, and I used to sit out in our barn for hours pretending to drive it."

I smile at the mental picture. "Did you ever actually get to drive it?"

"Nope. I had a grand plan of restoring it and beating Chris Morgan one day, but that never happened."

"Who is Chris Morgan?"

"Jerk I went to high school with. His family is crazy rich, and he made certain no one ever forgot it. His parents got him a Porsche when he turned sixteen. He looked ridiculous driving it around town, but man did I want that car. No one could beat him in our street races."

"You should buy a Porsche when you sign your first professional football contract," I suggest, smiling. I lost track of the number of people who mentioned that Jace Dawson will be drafted to play professional football after my first week here.

I expect some sort of cocky response, but Jace replies, "Not likely." His tone has shifted from nostalgic to solemn.

He doesn't elaborate further.

"So...are you dressing up as a race car driver this year?" I ask, trying to return to the easy conversation we were having before. "Revitalize an old classic?"

"I haven't dressed up as a race car driver since high school," Jace replies. "We always have a game Halloween weekend."

"You dressed up as a race car driver starting when you were six all the way through high school?"

"It was a crowd pleaser." Jace winks.

"You mean girls liked it?" I roll my eyes, and Jace's smirk answers for him. Something tells me Jace could have dressed up as just about anything and still have been wearing the most coveted costume, but I keep that thought to myself.

We near the main entrance to the campus. The large stone sign that marks it also has a line of pumpkins displayed across it, this time uncarved.

"Pretty sure those are the ones they use to make the pumpkin bars in the dining hall," Jace tells me.

"Pumpkin bars?" I scrunch up my nose in distaste.

"You don't like pumpkin?"

"I've never seen the appeal of squash," I reply. "Your informant didn't find that tidbit out about me, either?"

"You could have just told me where you were from last time."

He's right, and I'm not sure why I was so reluctant to answer his questions. I've had no trouble sharing my fake background with Katie or anyone else here. I don't respond to his statement, and we run in silence for a while.

"How come you're so anti-football?" Jace suddenly asks.

"Who said I'm anti-football?"

"You've made some sort of disdainful comment about it every time I've talked to you," he replies.

"I didn't even know you played football the first time we spoke," I argue. "And if I've made a 'disdainful comment' it's been about how conceited and arrogant you are because you're a big football star," I add. "That has nothing to do *with* football. I'd be just as judgmental if you acted the way you do because you won a pool tournament."

Jace rolls his eyes. The end of the trail appears, indicating we're almost back to Kennedy Hall.

"This is me." I nod to the assortment of dorm buildings just visible down the path. "I'll see you around, maybe."

I turn to start running back onto the central campus, but I'm stopped by the feel of Jace's warm skin against my own. Butterflies swarm my stomach, and I fight to keep my expression neutral as I turn back to him and raise an eyebrow expectantly.

"I want to show you something," is all he says.

I stare at him for a moment, confused. This is the first mostly cordial encounter we've managed, and he wants to extend our time together?

"Okay." To my surprise, I find myself agreeing.

Jace nods, then lets go of my arm and continues jogging, this time heading straight toward the heart of campus. It's entirely abandoned at this hour. The only signs of life are the squirrels rummaging through the metal trash cans.

We run along the same main path where I first encountered him, passing one of the libraries and a long assortment of academic buildings. My curiosity is piqued as we pass through most of campus without stopping.

Finally, Jace turns off on a side path. A massive structure looms ahead, and I realize where he's taking me.

"Is this some sort of test to prove I don't hate football?" I ask as we stop in front of the entrance to the enormous stadium.

"Yup," Jace replies, pulling a key out of his pocket and unlocking the metal gate. He jerks it open and gestures for me to enter first.

I roll my eyes, but walk past him through the gate and into a cement hallway. Glancing up, I see the undersides of the thousands of seats that must surround the stadium.

We keep walking for about a hundred feet, until green turf is suddenly visible in front of us. I quicken my pace, until suddenly I'm no longer under the stadium, but rather inside of it.

I continue walking forward slowly. My sneakers press on the soft ground as I advance. I'm amazed as I take in the pristine field covered with stark white lines.

Row after row after row of dark green seats surround the field, glimmering in the early morning sun.

"Wow." I breathe, spinning around to take in the spectacular view from all angles.

"Pretty impressive, huh?" Jace asks, coming to stand next to me.

I nod in agreement.

Jace jogs over to the sideline, where a white mesh bag sits, filled with an assortment of weathered footballs. He fishes one out and then returns to my side.

"Ready?" he asks, spinning the ball on his index finger casually.

"I'm sorry. What gave you the impression I wanted to play football with you?" I ask incredulously. "The repeated discussions about your cockiness when it comes to, well, everything, but especially this sport? Or your comments about how uncoordinated I am?"

Jace just laughs and strolls about ten feet away from me.

"C'mon Viv," he coaxes. "You said you don't hate football, so humor me. If you manage to catch it a few times, I'll even stop mentioning the fact that you're a one-woman wrecking ball."

The only person I've ever allowed to call me by a nickname is my father, but for some reason, I don't feel the urge to correct Jace. I simply scowl as I tighten my ponytail and hold my hands out in a silent acquiescence.

Well-worn leather brushes one of my outstretched fingers and then goes spinning off to the right for a couple feet before dropping onto the grass.

"Solid start." Jace grins widely.

I groan. "Aren't you good enough to throw it to me with minimal effort on my part?"

"I could make a trained monkey look like a first-round draft pick," Jace retorts.

"Great, why don't we find one of those for you to practice with instead?"

"Notice how I didn't make fun of you for missing the perfect pass I just threw you?" Jace counters.

"This is *not* filling me with an undying love for the sport of football," I inform him.

Jace simply tosses the ball to me again. I miss, again.

The same pattern continues until I've lost count of the number of throws and missed catches.

"You can't honestly expect me to think you're not uncoordinated after this," Jace remarks, returning to my side.

"Okay, well, this has been fun," I say sarcastically, turning to leave.

"Wait." Jace grabs my arm for the second time this morning, and my traitorous body refuses to move away from his touch. "Just try one more thing." He leads me out further onto the empty field, then suddenly bends over.

I come to an abrupt stop, bewildered. "What are you doing?"

"I'm going to snap the ball to you," Jace replies.

"What does that even mean?" I question, trying to recall any mention of snapping from my football lessons. I come up blank.

Jace straightens and glances over his shoulder at me. "It's when the center passes the ball to the quarterback."

"That clarifies nothing."

"Haven't you seen players do this during the game?" Jace asks, squatting down in the same position before standing again.

"Ah, yeah, so...I've never actually watched a football game," I admit.

Jace makes a face that seems like a more appropriate response to telling him I murdered someone.

"You've *never* watched a football game?"

"Nope. Have you ever been sailing?" I counter.

"I'm from Nebraska," Jace informs me.

"So? What does that have to do with it?" I ask.

"Nebraska is the only triply landlocked state. Not a lot of sailing done there."

"Pretty sure we're in Michigan at the moment," I point out.

"No, I've never been sailing." Jace lets out an exasperated sigh.

I attempt to mimic the same look of shocked outrage he just gave me. Jace shakes his head, but I catch the ghost of a smile before he turns back around and crouches on the grass again, holding the football between his outstretched legs.

"Ready?" he calls. I don't have much time to respond before he spouts a few words of gibberish and sends the ball sailing between his legs and directly at me. Unsurprisingly, I miss catching it.

In addition to the lack of coordination I was already struggling with, I am now also having to contend with the very distracting view of Jace's defined calves and tight shorts directly in front of me.

He's surprisingly patient, offering me suggestions between each of my fumbled catches. Finally, my growling stomach forces me to focus, as I grow increasingly concerned Jace plans to keep us out here until I complete some sort of football play.

At long last, the odds I catch the ball finally seem to outweigh the odds I won't. The weathered football lands neatly in my outstretched hands.

I stand there in shock for a split second, then do the only logical thing.

I run.

Despite the exhausting workout I've already put my legs through today, they cooperate without complaint as my long strides eat up the green grass. White lines fly past me in a blur. Dimly, I imagine how this sensation must feel coupled with a packed stadium of screaming fans and the thrill of an opponent close behind.

I'm imagining the encouraging roar of a sold-out crowd when I feel an arm wrap around my abdomen. Suddenly, I'm weightless, flying through the air until I hit the ground with a soft thud. I'm breathing heavily, but Jace looks barely winded as he lands beside me. He rolls over so that he's hovering on top of me.

"Nice catch," he compliments, smiling broadly at me.

"You seriously tackled me?" I groan. "I'm going to be covered in bruises tomorrow, thanks to your attack."

"Attack is pretty harsh," Jace replies, still looking amused. "I know you've never actually seen a game, but this is how it's played. You try to keep your opponent from scoring. It wouldn't be very entertaining if we stood around cheering each other on."

"Well, it's not very fun having your arm dislocated either," I retort, rolling the shoulder that took the brunt of the impact gingerly.

The movement shifts my torso closer to his, and I momentarily forget about the dull throb as I become keenly aware of every inch of my body that is currently pressed against Jace's. Nervous flutters fill my stomach.

"As someone who's actually had their arm dislocated, I would agree with that."

"DAWSON!" suddenly echoes across the empty stadium.

"Shit," Jace mutters under his breath.

He quickly clambers to his feet and offers me a hand. I take it, and am lifted from the damp grass, only to be greeted by the furious face of a tall, broad-shouldered man with a hefty mustache I assume must be the Lincoln football coach. Standing behind him is what looks to be the entirety of the football team, minus the player standing next to me.

"What in the hell are you doing, Dawson?" the coach shouts. "Is my morning practice interfering with your date? I don't care how many touchdown passes you throw, if—"

I step forward, interrupting his tirade.

"I'm Vivienne," I tell him. "And you are?"

The coach shifts his angry gaze from Jace to me in utter astonishment.

It's obvious he's a man accustomed to speaking uninterrupted, but unfortunately for him, I was raised to never show deference to anyone outside my immediate family. I let the innate sense of superiority bleed across my face as I watch him expectantly.

He opens and closes his mouth twice before he speaks again. "I'm Coach Alberts.". His tone is still saturated with authority, but absent of the rage that was coloring his words before.

"I assumed that based on where we are, but what's your first name?" I probe. "I'm guessing it's not coach. Unless your parents were really set on that career path for you from the start."

A few snickers sound from the players assembled behind Coach Alberts, but I don't look away from our silent stare-off.

"Andrew Alberts," the coach responds evenly.

"Nice to meet you, Andrew," I reply. "There's no reason to blame Jace for this. We had a bet going, and thanks to the competitive spirit you seem to foster in your players, Jace refused to stop until the winner was clear. I told him that based on his playing style, he should try implementing the Kamanski throwing technique. He insisted you know best. I suggested we meet before your morning practice so I could ask for your thoughts as well."

I feel dozens of curious eyes on me, but I don't let my own waver from Coach Alberts as I infuse as much confidence as I can muster into my hastily concocted explanation.

Andrew Alberts eyes me skeptically. "What do you know about the Kamanski throwing technique?"

"I know it won Jerry Lewis and the Ducks three championships."

Andrew gives me a grudging look of respect. "You know your football."

Jace makes a low sound of incredulity beside me, but otherwise remains silent.

"How come you're so invested in Dawson's throwing technique?" Andrew asks. "Are you a groupie?"

I have to work to hold back the laugh that threatens to escape in response to that accusation. Based on my understanding of the term, I'm the furthest thing from one.

"No one wants to go see their football team lose," I reply instead. Andrew looks unconvinced, so I improvise further and quickly add, "I'm also writing an article comparing this year's starters to the 1998 Ducks team. Jace is the obvious choice for Jerry Lewis."

Andrew harrumphs, but seems appeased. "Dawson, go get changed," he barks. "Cotes and Anderson, go ask Coach Jestings to warm you up using the Kamanski method, so when Dawson gets back, we can try running it."

I allow myself a quick glance over at Jace, who's staring at me in blatant shock. I wink at him, then begin walking back over to the entrance we'd come in.

CHAPTER SEVEN

"Care to explain how you've never seen a football game but knew about some obscure throwing technique I've never even *heard* of?" That's how Jace greets me the following morning for what has apparently become our daily run.

"You're welcome," I retort, continuing to jog past the tree he's leaning against as he waits for me. "Pretty sure you were about to get kicked off the team before I intervened," I call over my shoulder.

Jace pushes off from the bark and begins running after me, his footfalls pounding the ground.

"Was the whole I'm-so-clueless-about-football act just some ploy to get my attention?" he presses, drawing even with me.

I scoff loudly, incensed by the accusation. "You were the one who showed up at my dorm and dragged me to the stadium when I was planning to go on a run by myself and then eat breakfast. Not sure what sort of master plan that would have been."

Jace doesn't reply, acknowledging I have a valid point.

After a moment of silence, he persists. "Did one of the guys on the team put you up to it?"

"Of course not. I only talk to you because you refuse to leave me alone. You seriously think I'm coming up with elaborate plots with other football players?"

"I didn't ask if you've been plotting with them, I asked if they told you to do it," Jace replies evenly.

"You're unbelievable. But in this hypothetical situation, I obviously would have been the brains behind any supposed plan."

"Sounds like a confession to me."

"You are the most infuriating and conceited person I've ever met," I inform him. "But if you *must* know, I was telling the truth about never having watched a football game. I knew football is big here, so I read a couple books about it before classes started to see what all the fuss is about."

"Here?" Jace asks in confusion.

"At Lincoln," I add quickly.

"So you read about the Kamanski throwing technique, and that's how you knew what to say to Coach?"

I waver on what should be an easy "yes." For some reason, I don't want to lie to him. "No, Jerry Lewis told me about it."

He scoffs at the truth. "Fine, I'll drop it."

He's giving me another out, but I still don't take it.

"I'm serious," I insist. "He mentioned it when I asked him how he thought football has changed since he played. He told me it was less innovative and mentioned the Kamanski technique as an example."

Jace looks over at me, all traces of annoyance gone. Surprise is written all over his handsome face.

"You've *met* Jerry Lewis?" he asks incredulously.

"Well, over video conference," I clarify.

"Why?" Jace questions.

"The books I was reading barely made any sense, so a family friend asked him to help explain things."

"Jerry Lewis personally answered your questions about football because a family friend asked him to?" Jace sounds stunned.

"Yup."

"Is this family friend a sports agent or something?"

I focus my gaze on the entrance to the wooded trail we're rapidly approaching. "No, he's not. He just knows some important people." Including me.

I feel Jace's eyes on me, clearly expecting an elaboration on my vague response. He doesn't press the topic further when I don't say anything, and the remainder of our run is silent.

The rest of the week passes by quickly. Jace and I run together each morning. I tell myself his persistent presence is annoying, but it's disappointment and not relief that I feel when he never shows up on Saturday morning.

I run harder and farther than I have in a while in an attempt to erase that realization from my mind.

When I arrive back at my room, I'm surprised to find Katie is already awake. A rare occurrence. She's dressed in jeans and a sweatshirt with *LINCOLN* written across the front.

"Do you want to come to the game?" Katie asks as I pull off the light fleece jacket I'm wearing. "I'm going with a few friends."

"Game?"

"Yeah, the football team has a home game today."

This is not the first time Katie has invited me to a football game, but it's the first time I've felt any compulsion to go. I tell myself it stems from a desire to experience a normal American college activity and has nothing to do with Jace Dawson.

To Katie's surprise, I accept her invitation. After I've showered and dressed, we head to one of the numerous cafes on campus to grab coffee and breakfast.

As we walk, she regales me with stories about some of the more entertaining events at past games she's attended. I nod along in all the appropriate places, but only half listen to the anecdotes, distracted.

I blurt out "How early do the players have to arrive before the game?" as soon as she finishes telling me how a head cheerleader choreographed the squad's halftime routine to "Before He Cheats" after she caught her wide receiver boyfriend with another girl last season.

Katie laughs as we leave the coffee shop and head in the direction of the football stadium. "That's your response to that story?"

"I'm just curious to know more about the team than who can't stay monogamous."

She gives me a strange look. "They have to be at the field a few hours before the game starts, I think."

The rush of relief startles me.

"You think?" I tease, my mood suddenly lightened. "I thought you were the football team expert."

"Hardly," Katie replies. "I'm practically oblivious compared to most of the girls here. I just pay attention to gossip about the guys I think are hot. I'm not memorizing all their stats, hoping I'll run into one of the players and be able to compliment him on his number of interceptions this season."

The football stadium appears up ahead, and I'm taken aback by the hundreds of students milling about, most of them clad in Lincoln's signature shade of dark green.

We meet up with Katie's group of friends underneath one of the trees that surround the stadium. I recognize a couple of them from fleeting interactions in our shared room.

They all introduce themselves to me, but I'm so preoccupied, I forget most of their names almost immediately. My attention is being drawn to the massive banner displayed at the stadium's entrance. It displays a photo of Jace mid-throw that reaches from the very top of the stadium to the edge of the front gate, about thirty feet high. The rippling muscles of his extended forearm span several feet alone.

One of Katie's friends follows my gaze. "Stupid hot, isn't he?" She grins conspiratorially as we move to join the long line of students waiting to enter the stadium.

I smile back at her, but internally I'm trying to reconcile the jolt of possessiveness her words incited. Jace is the most attractive guy I've ever seen, so it's completely irrational for me to be bothered another girl finds him good looking as well. I shake off the strange reaction as we move closer to the entrance and inside the cement tunnel that leads into the stadium.

After a long wait in line, we finally enter the stadium. It's a beautiful fall day. Bright sunlight illuminates the green field spread before us. I feel as though I've stepped into the photo I saw on Lincoln's website in my bedroom weeks ago. The smell of popcorn and freshly mowed grass permeates the crisp air, while the sound of thousands of chattering spectators surrounds us.

As we walk along the pathway, looking for seats, I'm surprised by the number of students who smile at me or greet me by name. Katie gives me a series of curious looks between the brief interactions. I rarely take her up on any social invitations, and I can tell she's wondering if I've been doing so in order to take advantage of other ones. I give her a quick shrug to indicate I'm just as mystified by the attention as she is.

It takes a while for our group to find a section of open seats, but we finally claim a spot. I end up sitting between Katie and a dark-haired girl with a heart-shaped face who looks vaguely familiar.

She gives me a warm smile as we all sit down.

"I'm Claudia," she reminds me. "We have medieval history together."

"Right. I thought you look familiar," I reply. "Sorry, I'm terrible with names."

Claudia smiles again. "No worries. How do you like Lincoln so far?"

We talk for a while about the university in general, and eventually the topic shifts to our mutual class. I learn Claudia is part of a study group that's formed for the upcoming exam, and she invites me to their next meeting.

"I'll definitely come," I promise. "I can hardly pay attention to anything that happens in that class, it's so warm in the room."

Claudia laughs. "I noticed that too. I've started wearing a t-shirt under my jacket on Mondays and Thursdays just because of that class."

"There's a vent that sometimes blows cooler air on the right side by the whiteboard," I tell her. "You should come sit by me next class."

"I'll try," Claudia replies. I feel a crease of confusion form between my eyes. "You haven't noticed the seats around you always fill up first?"

I shake my head and laugh at her unexpected observation. "What? No they don't!"

Claudia grins. "Yeah, they do. You're the hot commodity in that lecture. The two guys sitting behind me last class were trying to decide how to ask for your number." She pauses and laughs. "Based on the look on your face, I'm guessing neither of them ever did."

The stadium loudspeaker suddenly crackles to life, echoing

feedback around the stadium for a brief second before the booming sound of the announcer's voice replaces it. He welcomes everyone to the game, and then reads through the list of starting players, pausing for each of them to run out onto the field. The announcer continues rattling off a long series of unfamiliar names, aside from a few I think I've heard Katie mention. Just not the one I'm waiting to hear. I start to lose interest as the announcer drones on.

There's a dramatic pause that recaptures my attention.

"And now, number twelve, your quarterback and captain... Jace Dawssooonnnnn!"

Jace's gorgeous face flashes across the giant screens displayed around the stadium.

I thought the stadium was loud before, but it was nothing compared to the defeating roar greeting Jace now. His solitary figure jogs out of the tunnel and onto the field.

Jace turns toward Lincoln's bench, revealing the number twelve and *DAWSON* printed across the back of his jersey. I would have known it was him just based on the familiar, confident stride.

It's a strange sensation: sitting in a crowd of strangers, watching him. I've never been an anonymous face in a large audience before. Equally foreign is the chance to see the hero worship of Jace firsthand. Although I'm fully aware of his status on campus—even joked about it—it's a wholly other thing to experience it. It's a struggle to reconcile the star football player with the guy who made me stop running yesterday so he could tie my shoelace in the midst of the loud cheers now.

I watch him while he talks animatedly with the other green-clad players, clearly in his element, and realize it's not just Jace's looks or athletic ability that make him so magnetic. He's pulled off his helmet and is now talking with one of the referees intently.

There's something intrinsic in Jace's confidence; it permeates the air around him no matter what he's doing.

"He's the guy you collided with on the first day of the semester," Katie whispers to me. "Remember?"

As if I could forget.

"Oh yeah, that's right," I acknowledge instead, keeping my voice casual and detached.

"You ran into Jace Dawson? Literally?" Claudia asks.

I brace myself for disbelief or incredulity, but instead she chuckles. "Me, too."

"What?" Katie and I ask in unison.

"Yeah, I literally bumped into him last spring when I was leaving the library. Highlight of my freshman year. He was walking in with a bunch of his teammates."

"How am I just hearing this now?" Katie exclaims. She sounds offended, although it's difficult to tell whether it's genuine or not.

"Please, you were in your peak football player obsession period then. You would have grilled me for twenty minutes about the ten second interaction."

Katie grins, unabashed. "That doesn't sound like something I would do."

"What did he say when you bumped into him?" I ask, unable to help myself. "Was he rude?"

"Rude?" Claudia looks surprised by my question. "No, I don't think he said anything at all. I apologized and then he just kept walking."

"Huh," I reply.

"Was he rude to you?" she asks.

"He was arrogant," I reply.

"Keep watching the game, and you'll see why." She winks.

My gaze returns to the field. Names of positions and rules run through my head as I try to remember the intricacies of the game, but eventually I give up. I just sit there and absorb the electric atmosphere. Being incognito in a crowd is a novelty I'll only get to enjoy for a couple more months, and I try to appreciate it while I sip on my now lukewarm coffee.

I attempt to take in the entire game, but my eyes refuse to leave number twelve for very long.

CHAPTER EIGHT

"Hey! Hey! Blondie!" someone shouts behind me as I walk to the library the following Saturday afternoon. I turn to see a tall, lanky guy with shaggy hair jogging toward me on the deserted sidewalk.

"Blondie?" I ask, raising an eyebrow.

The guy has the good sense to look sheepish. "Sorry, I wasn't sure what your name is. One of the guys pointed you out on the quad yesterday, but they won't actually defy Dawson and tell me. The one day I miss practice…" He rolls his eyes.

"You're friends with Jace?" I ask. The mere sound of his name sends a ripple of annoyance through me.

The guy grins. "We were freshman year roommates. I was planning to play soccer, but he talked me into trying out as kicker instead. Dawson is pretty persistent."

"I hadn't noticed."

He laughs at my dry sarcasm. "I'm Joe, by the way, but everyone calls me Anderson."

"I'm Vivienne—Vivienne Rhodes."

Anderson smirks. "I knew they were full of it."

The confusion must be clear on my face.

"One of the guys told me your name was Violet, but I was pretty certain he was messing with me."

"The guys?"

"The team," Anderson clarifies. "I told them I was going to invite you anyway, and they tried to get creative to stop me from asking you and pissing Dawson off. No one wants to deal with his moods or risk our undefeated season. Well, except for me, cause I think this is funny as hell."

"You completely lost me," I admit.

Anderson laughs again. "Just come to the blue house on Fourth Street tonight. Number thirty-four. Any time after eleven."

"Why are inviting me to a football event the football team doesn't want me to attend?" I ask, perplexed.

"Oh, they want you to attend," Anderson replies confidently. "They're just listening to Dawson."

"You're inviting me to an event Jace asked the whole team not to invite me to?" I'm still confused and also miffed.

"Event," Anderson scoffs. "It's a party. But aside from that detail, yes, you've pretty much got all the main points."

I open my mouth to question him further, but just then, his phone rings. He pulls it out and glances at the screen.

"I've got to get this." He starts to back away. "Remember, blue house on Fourth Street!" he calls out before turning and walking back the way he came.

"Do you know anything about a football party tonight?" I ask Katie when I return to our shared room from the library.

"Yeah, it's the first one of the season," she replies. "The girls behind me in Psych spent class yesterday planning their outfits. They're arriving at nine so they can at least make it onto the lawn."

"What?" I ask, totally confused.

"I forget that you're still new to all of Lincoln's traditions," Katie tells me. She stands up from her desk chair and moves over to her unmade bed, flopping down onto it. "Okay, so the football team is treated like they're the shit, right?"

"Right," I reply.

"So, during the season, their schedule is super intense, but they throw a few parties during it when there's a bye, or a major win. Everyone wants to go, but the house can only hold a couple hundred people, so you have to be invited by a player to actually get inside. Everybody else just hangs around outside, hoping to get a last-minute invite or at least be able to say that they went. Last year, I went to one and two girls got into a fight on the front lawn over which of them would sneak in through the window to Jace Dawson's room. You know who he is now, right?"

"Yeah, I know who he is." I should finally tell Katie about our runs, but I'm too annoyed and hurt by his unexplained absence this past week. There's no real justification for my feelings, though, so the resulting embarrassment keeps me silent.

"Well, he's famous for never inviting anyone to their parties, so people—mostly girls—take extreme measures to get inside to talk to him. I heard he moved to a second-floor bedroom after what happened last year. It was all people talked about on campus for weeks."

I want to ask Katie if Jace's lack of invitations has ever extended to ensuring someone *doesn't* receive an invite, but there's no way I can do that without explaining all of our interactions since that day I literally collided with him.

"Well, I got invited, if you want to go." I hadn't decided yet if

I would take Anderson up on his strange invitation or not until now, but after hearing Katie's depiction of the parties, I'm curious enough to attend. And if I'm being honest with myself, I know the opportunity to see Jace is also a factor.

"You *what*?" Katie looks completely dumbfounded by my revelation.

"I just ran into a guy who's on the football team, and he invited me. Said to come to the blue house on Fourth Street after eleven."

"What guy?" Katie asks skeptically.

"He said his name is Anderson," I relay.

Katie's eyes widen. "He's one of the starters," she informs me. "Are you interested in him?"

"Interested in him?" I echo.

"Yeah, Anderson must like you if he invited you."

"Uh—I've never really talked to him before, so I'm not sure whether he likes me or not," I reply honestly.

"You've never talked to him before, but he invited you to the party tonight?" Katie's voice is thick with disbelief.

"Yes, and now I'm inviting you. Let's go shopping for outfits to wear tonight," I urge her, eager to stop discussing the finer points of my invitation.

"Don't you already have enough clothes?" Katie asks, laughing as she gestures toward my overstuffed closet.

"No such thing," I tell her, winking. "And you need something special to wear, too. My treat. C'mon, if this party is as big a deal as you say it is, we'd better plan to make an entrance."

"I still have a lot of reading to do," Katie says as she glances back toward her desk, but the words are half-hearted at best.

"It's Saturday," I remind her. "You have all day tomorrow to get your work done."

"Okay, let's go." Katie climbs off her bed and begins gathering her things.

"Let me call Philip. He can give us a ride. He's been wanting to go to that bookstore in town." He hasn't, but I'm not supposed to leave campus without him and it's the most believable excuse I can think of.

Philip picks up on the first ring. "Everything okay?"

"Hello to you too," I reply. "Katie and I want to go shopping in town. Can you drive us? I know you've been wanting to go to that bookstore," I tack on for Katie's benefit.

"Sure. I'll let Thomas and Julie know you're leaving campus and pick you up in five minutes."

"See you then," I reply. I turn back to Katie. "He'll be here in five minutes."

We head outside to wait for Philip in the sunshine. We've just sat on one of the benches outside the dorm when Philip pulls up in his black sedan. I smile at him as I climb into the front seat.

"Thanks for the ride."

"Of course," Philip responds before turning to greet Katie.

It's only a ten-minute drive to Lincoln's small downtown area from campus. The town is busier than either of the other two times I've been before. The narrow sidewalk is crowded with a mix of both Lincoln students and local residents.

"Text when you guys are ready to leave," Philip tells me after he parks alongside the curb outside of the bookstore.

I nod in acknowledgement, although I know he'll likely be keeping tabs on us the entire time and won't actually need the update.

Katie and I integrate into the crowd and begin strolling along in front of the cute storefronts that line the block.

"Let's go in here." I nod to a clothing store with a colorful display of patterned woolen scarves in the window. We head inside to discover the interior of the shop is filled with a wide assortment of cute sweaters and warm jackets. Not at all what we're shopping for, but I stop to browse through the scarf collection anyway. I spot a black and white herringbone patterned one that I grab for myself, along with a navy plaid scarf I see Katie eyeing.

"Vivienne, you don't have to do that," she protests as I bring them both up to the register to purchase.

"I told you this trip was my treat." I hand her the bag containing her new scarf after I've paid. "Now come on, let's find some outfits that are less weather appropriate."

We strike out at two more stores before Katie points to one with a light blue awning.

We walk inside to find several other college-aged girls browsing inside as well. I spot a red velvet dress with a plunging neckline on a mannequin in the corner and immediately head toward it. Katie follows me.

"This would look amazing on you," I tell her.

She fingers the soft fabric gently. I glance around and spot several more of the same red dress hanging on one of the many racks lining the walls. I grab her size and hand it to her, nodding to the changing rooms in the back of the small store.

"Just try it on," I encourage her.

She complies, stepping out a few minutes later in the curve-hugging dress.

"You're getting it," I inform her. "You look amazing, Katie."

She smiles at her reflection bashfully. "Okay, I'll wear it."

I smile victoriously.

"What about you? Did you find anything?" Katie asks.

I hold up the gray suede miniskirt and silky navy top I grabbed while she was changing. "What do you think of these?"

Katie comes over to stand beside me and strokes the soft materials. "Wow, I love them both," she tells me. "Try them on."

I duck into the changing room to pull off the black sweater dress and leather riding boots I'm wearing before replacing them with the skirt and top. I step out in front of the wide, full-length mirror that spans the back wall of the store, and Katie looks at me with awe.

"What do you think?" I ask, turning to stare at my reflection.

"You look incredible."

The buttery material of the skirt hugs my hips and upper thighs, emphasizing the remnants of my summer tan and my toned legs. The silk top gathers around my neck and dips low in front, showcasing my cleavage. I smile, pleased with the outfit, although my face morphs into an annoyed frown when my first thought while looking at my appearance is to wonder what Jace will think when he sees me in it.

"You okay?" Katie asks.

"Of course," I exclaim, pushing thoughts of Jace away. "Let's get these and get out of here!"

We both change back into our previous clothes. Katie tries to buy her dress, but I refuse to let her. She finally acquiesces and thanks me profusely as we head back outside.

The sidewalk is emptier than it was earlier. The sun is setting in the distance, casting a muted orange glow over the street. We start to walk down the block, and I see Philip leaning against the car a block ahead.

We reach him a couple minutes later. He eyes our multiple bags with amusement before placing them in the sedan's trunk.

"Looks like the trip was a success?" he asks as we all climb inside the car.

"Yup, we'll be the two best-dressed girls there tonight!" Katie replies from the backseat.

I groan internally as I realize I forgot to ask her not to mention the reason for our impromptu outing to Philip.

"What's tonight?" Philip questions, shooting me a confused look.

"You didn't hear about the football party, either?" Katie asks, laughing. She proceeds to fill Philip in on the same details she provided me with earlier.

"You're planning to go to this party, Vivienne?" Philip asks me.

"Yes." I sigh. "But it will be fine. Katie's coming with me."

"I'm coming too." Philip states.

"That's really not necessary," I tell him. "I can just call you if I need anything." I guess the party is *technically* off campus, but I was viewing it as a gathering of students, not unlike the lectures I attend. If no one's figured out who I am by now, there's no reason to think tonight will be any different.

"There's not a chance I'm letting you go to a football party without me." Philip's tone leaves no room for argument. "I've heard the stories about the guys on that team around campus."

"The parties *can* get kind of wild…it might be nice to have another person there with us," Katie adds. "I only know one other girl who'll be there, and she's been friends with one of the wide receivers for years. If Philip comes, we'll have another person to hang out with."

"Okay, fine. He can come." I act as though I have a say in the matter, although I'm certain I would have needed to ask Richard to call Philip personally to keep him from attending this party.

We stop to pick up a couple of pizzas on the way back to campus, and then Philip drops us off outside Kennedy Hall with the steaming boxes and a promise he'll be back for us at 11:30.

Katie and I head back into our room and put on comfy sweatpants before hunkering down in her bed to eat the hot pizza and start an episode of the reality television show she's obsessed with. The series is terrible but extremely entertaining, and before we know it, it's already almost eleven. We both leap out of Katie's bed, cleaning our greasy hands and mouths on the napkins from the pizzeria.

Katie heads into the bathroom first, and I busy myself by plugging in my curling iron and twisting portions of my blonde hair around the barrel. I went to the salon to get my roots touched up earlier this week, and the newly lightened strands shine under the light from my desk lamp.

Katie re-emerges from the bathroom just as I'm brushing through the curls I've created.

"All yours," she tells me, heading over to her own dresser.

I clip back my freshly styled hair and walk into the bathroom to finish getting ready. I head back into the room just in time to see my phone light up with a text from Philip. It's already 11:35.

"Philip's here," I inform Katie as I pull the clip out of my hair. She's changing into the red dress.

"I'm almost ready," she replies.

I grab the bag that contains my new outfit and quickly change as well.

"Ready!" Katie caps the small cylinder of lipstick she just applied.

I grab my phone and slide it underneath my top into the waistband of my skirt. Katie slings a small crossbody bag across her chest, and we're out the door.

The cold air hits us as soon as we step outside. Neither of us bothered with a jacket, and I'm grateful it's a short trip to the black sedan already pulled up alongside the curb.

Philip turns in the driver's seat as we climb in, studying first

Katie's outfit, then mine. "That's what you're both wearing?" He sounds horrified.

"You look nice too, Philip," I reply caustically.

"Are you sure you don't want to change and put on something...warmer?" he suggests.

"We're sure."

"It'll be hot inside," Katie adds.

Philip lets out a long sigh, but pulls away from the curb and follows Katie's directions to the edge of campus.

A few minutes later, he turns the car onto Fourth Street. It's immediately evident which house is our destination. Philip parks as close as he can to it, and the three of us clamber out of the car.

Philip casts another disapproving glance at my outfit, but doesn't say another word about my attire as we approach the big blue house. Smart choice. It's not even midnight yet, but the front yard is crammed to capacity and littered with empty plastic cups, bottles, and cans. As we approach, I see a short girl with red hair stumble off the porch.

There's a brick pathway that leads to the front door. It's the only part of the yard that's still visible through the throng of people. I take the lead and stride confidently up the bricks toward the front door, sensing Katie's uncertainty and Philip's disapproval lingering behind me.

Dozens of stares weigh on me as I climb the porch steps and reach the front door. I knock loudly.

"You're wasting your time!" the red-haired girl calls to me from the side of the porch. "They're not letting anyone else in."

Just then, the front door swings open. To my relief, Anderson is the one standing there, and there's no sign of Jace. His face lights up when he sees me standing on the other side of the door.

"Vivienne! You made it!"

I'm surprised by his greeting. His enthusiasm makes it seem

90

as though we've known each other for years, rather than a matter of hours. I decide to play along, smiling widely, and am grateful I do when I see his exclamation has drawn the attention of several people inside the house. Two guys amble over to the doorway, both of them sporting apparel that identifies them as members of the Lincoln football team.

"I thought you said this would be a quiet night in, just the two of us?" I ask Anderson in mock confusion.

He grins. "I'm saving that for the second date."

"You actually invited her?" one of the guys asks. His tone is a mixture of disbelief and annoyance. "I owe Jones fifty bucks now."

"I know you think Dawson won't make *your* life miserable," the other adds, "but the rest of us aren't as confident."

"Lighten up, boys. It's a party," Anderson tells them. He doesn't seem the least bit perturbed by their reaction, but I experience a spasm of unease. "Come on in."

He steps aside and opens the door wider. I walk into the front hall, grateful for the change in temperature once I'm inside the warm house. I turn to see both Philip and Katie are hovering on the doorstep, listening to the exchange. Katie wears a look of awed confusion, and Philip just looks annoyed.

"We can leave in an hour," I promise them both.

That's enough to propel Katie through the door, and Philip has no choice but to follow. I introduce Anderson, who greets them both warmly before turning his attention back to me.

"You clean up pretty well, Vivienne." He examines my outfit appreciatively. "That all for me?" He winks.

"This old thing?" I shrug, falling into the banter easily. Apparently, Jace Dawson has decent taste in friends. "Just wait until you see my outfit for our second date."

Anderson laughs. "I hope I live that long."

I glance around the house curiously. It's sparsely furnished and quite crowded, although nowhere near as packed as the lawn outside. Anderson beckons us farther into the front room and past a solitary couch pushed against the wall. A catchy pop song blasts through invisible speakers as we pass a group flipping cups on a round coffee table and a few couples making out.

Anderson leads us through the living room area into a second room that contains a round wooden table. Ordinarily it must serve as the dining room, but at the moment, the large table is entirely surrounded by at least a dozen guys, each holding a hand of cards. Only one chair sits empty.

A small pile containing watches, cash, cigarettes, and other miscellaneous items sits in the center of the table, so I quickly surmise they must be playing poker. One of the guys glances up as Anderson enters the room, and he grins. His eyes flicker to me, and it widens further.

"Thanks, Anderson," he calls out loudly. "You just made me two hundred bucks."

A few groans sound from around the table as more of the guys look up. "Didn't the rest of you fools know better than to bet against me?" Anderson asks. I can't tell if the outrage in his voice is fake or real.

The entire group of guys is looking at us now, wearing expressions that range from amusement to worry.

"Seen Dawson yet?" one of them asks.

"Obviously not, or Anderson wouldn't be walking," another responds. That draws several laughs from the table. I feel a second flicker of uncertainty.

"What the hell are they talking about?" Katie whispers in my ear.

"No idea," I reply, mostly truthfully.

Anderson meets my gaze and nods to the right. Philip, Katie, and I follow him into the next room, which turns out to be a large kitchen. This is the least crowded room yet, with only ten people milling about as they grab drinks from the broad assortment of alcohol spread across the kitchen counter. There's a pool table sitting in the far corner of the room, which a small group of girls are gathered around. Several of them glance over when we enter the kitchen.

Anderson leads us to the fridge. "What do you guys want to drink?" he asks.

"Do you have whiskey?" I question.

"Sure," Anderson replies, grabbing a familiar glass bottle. He pours a generous amount into a plastic cup and adds a few cubes of ice. "What do you want added? Ginger ale?"

"No, just the whiskey," I reply.

Anderson looks surprised, but hands me the cup without further comment. I take a long sip of the amber liquid, enjoying the slow burn as the alcohol slides down my throat. Katie stutters out that she'd like a beer, while Philip unsurprisingly opts for water.

We stand next to the kitchen counter as I continue taking sips of my drink, keeping a close eye on my surroundings. There's no sign of Jace yet, and the anticipation of his arrival is putting me on edge.

I'm distracted by the sound of glass breaking, and look over to see a bowl has been knocked off a side table. Anderson goes over to investigate the mess. Philip walks over as well, dutifully helping him clean up the shards and move the table out of harm's way.

I take advantage of the temporary distraction as an opportunity to pour more whiskey into my cup. I know Philip will be keeping a close eye on my alcohol consumption, and I want some liquid courage for whenever Jace appears.

Katie's eyes are wide as she takes in our surroundings. She glances over at each person who enters or leaves the kitchen.

"Everything you thought it'd be?" I tease her.

She laughs. "I can check it off my bucket list."

Anderson and Philip return to our spot by the fridge. "Happens every time," Anderson says, shaking his head.

"Breakables don't fare well at college parties," I remark. "Shocking."

Anderson grins at my sarcasm and opens his mouth to say something in response. He's interrupted by the sound of his own name being called from the poker room.

"Shit, it must be my turn again already," he tells us. "Any of you want to come watch the game?"

Philip and Katie both remain silent, but I jump at the opportunity. I've played plenty of poker with the children of diplomats following my parents' dinner parties, but I'm mostly curious about what other comments Jace's teammates may make.

"Do you guys mind?" I ask Philip and Katie innocently.

Philip sends me a sharp look that makes it clear that he does mind, but he stays silent.

"I'm good as long as Philip's keeping me company," Katie replies, eyeing Anderson bashfully.

"Okay, I'll be back soon," I say before following Anderson back into the dining room.

He takes the one empty chair at the table, but stands right back to grab a small rectangular bookshelf that he moves beside his chair for me to sit on.

"How chivalrous, Anderson," the guy sitting next to him remarks.

"Can it, Owens," Anderson responds. I take a seat on the sturdy wood next to him.

Owens leans forward and gives me a smirk. "Nice to see you again, Vivienne."

"Have we met before?" I ask, confused.

"Not officially. But you became my new favorite person after you lectured Coach on his throwing technique history." He winks, then leans back.

By the time the poker game ends, my cup is empty and my cheeks hurt from all the smiling I've done in response to the lively banter flying around the table. At the moment, the guys are all complaining about Anderson's victory, thanks to his wise decision to follow my strategic suggestions.

"Unbelievable," one groans.

Owens grins at me. "Time to show us whether you were just lucky."

He and Anderson scoot further apart so that I have room to move closer to the table as new hands are being dealt. I spot a few liquor bottles sitting in the corner of the room, so I stand and refill my cup with more whiskey, eager to prolong the pleasant buzz I'm experiencing.

When I return to the table, I'm dealt in, and the second game begins. My dry sarcasm proves to meld well with the rest of the playful digs being tossed around the table, and I'm surprised by how much I'm enjoying myself. The game progresses quickly, and I'm just about to lay down my winning hand when chatter around the table ceases.

I glance up in confusion, and am met with a pair of stormy gray eyes.

This is the first time I've seen Jace in anything other than athletic clothes, and I'm struck by how ridiculously attractive he looks in a simple pair of faded jeans and a cotton t-shirt, standing in the wide opening in the wall between the dining room and the packed living room.

He shifts his piercing gaze from me to appraise the rest of the room, keeping his expression cool and detached. Despite his calm demeanor, the guys surrounding me shift nervously as he looks around the crowded table. Two girls hover behind him. One is a petite blonde, and the other is slim with long black hair.

"Nice of you to finally grace us with your presence, Dawson." Anderson bravely breaks the awkward silence that's descended over the room since Jace entered.

"Looks like he had his hands full," Owens comments next to me, causing a few snickers around the table. My stomach twists uncomfortably.

Jace doesn't respond to their teasing, but shifts his intense gaze back to me. I meet his stare defiantly, recalling Anderson's blunt declaration that Jace didn't want me here. He certainly isn't acting happy to see me, and I feel an extra surge of irritation as I recall all the solo runs I've taken lately. Since he made me accustomed to his presence, the very least he could do was continue to show up.

"Come on, Jace. You said we were getting some drinks," the dark-haired girl finally says after another stretch of glaring silence. Jace is still watching me, so I hide the burst of annoyance I experience at the sound of her sultry voice.

"Go get them without me." Jace's tone is short.

"Don't you want anything?" the girl persists. "I can just grab—"

"I'm fine." Jace doesn't bother to hide his irritation.

Both girls linger for a moment longer, clearly hoping Jace will change his mind. However, he just continues standing there stoically, so they both slink off into the kitchen. The darker-haired girl lets out an annoyed little huff as they exit the room. Jace doesn't seem to notice.

Everyone around the table remains silent, seemingly waiting to see what Jace will do. I decide to take matters into my own hands. First, I take another fortifying sip of my drink, and then I lay down my royal flush. The move elicits several groans from the group.

"Oh, did you boys think I was bluffing?" I ask with a cheeky grin.

That finally breaks the thick tension in the room, and banter resumes around the table. I keep my gaze firmly fixed on the table. I don't see Jace move, but I suddenly hear his voice.

"Owens, can you go check on the beer supply? See if someone needs to make a run."

"I'm actually quite happy with my spot right here. How about you go check it, Dawson? I hear you're wanted in the kitchen anyway."

Talking ceases as there's a collective intake of breath around the table.

"Owens," Jace growls.

Owens laughs. "Not interested, huh?" He scoots his chair back and stands. "Sure thing, Dawson." He remains standing for a moment, but I don't look up to see why. Eventually, I hear him walk away.

The chair next to me makes a scraping noise against the scarred hardwood floor as Jace pulls it out to accommodate his taller frame. As he settles into the seat, his bare arm brushes against mine, sending a jolt of electricity through my system. The other guys are still revealing their hands, so I have nothing to do but fiddle with my own cards as I sit there and pretend I'm oblivious to Jace's presence mere inches from me.

"What are you doing here?" he asks me in a low voice.

"Playing poker."

Jace sighs. "Why are you at this party?" I'm startled and hurt by the frank question, but I fight to keep it off my face.

"I heard it was the place to be tonight." I keep my eyes straight ahead, still refusing to let myself look over at him.

"Who let you in?"

"Way to make me feel welcome, Dawson." I emphasize his last name. "I'm surprised anyone bothers showing up to these parties at all, if this is the way they're greeted."

"Vivienne, how did you get in here?" Jace persists with his interrogation, and my temper flares in response.

"I knocked on the front door, and the person who opened it has much better manners than you do. Is there any particular reason why I'm the only person here you're cross-examining? Next time, I'll climb in through a window to make for a more interesting story and give you an actual reason to throw me out."

"No one else here hates football the way you do. It's a little ironic that you, of all people, are at a team party."

"Are you seriously telling me I have to be a football expert to attend your stupid party?"

Jace opens his mouth to reply, but I don't give him a chance to.

"And didn't we already cover this? I thought I made it clear it's your condescending attitude I have a problem with, not the sport you play."

Anderson chuckles from my other side, and Jace leans forward to glare at him. I look up from my cards to see that several of the other guys are grinning, evidently listening to our tense conversation.

"Did you do this, Anderson?" Jace asks, nodding to me.

"Dawson, I have no idea what you're talking about," Anderson lies. "But I would suggest you shut up about her not being welcome here, or Vivienne's not going to want to come to any of our other parties. We'll all be richer but much less entertained."

I smile at that, and then stand to refill my empty cup again. Jace tracks my movements closely as I walk back and sit down next to him.

"How many of those have you had?" he asks me quietly.

I don't answer him. Instead, I tip my cup back defiantly and drain half of it in one gulp. Jace doesn't say anything else, but I see his jaw clench out of the corner of my eye. The alcohol I've just imbibed sears my throat as it travels down my esophagus and settles in my stomach. My muscles feel languid and loose, and I realize I'm rapidly on my way from feeling tipsy to being drunk.

Another game begins, and I remain sitting. I've entirely lost interest in playing poker, but am unwilling to move. Jace opts not to play, although he remains sitting at the table by my side. Owens doesn't return from his errand, but the two girls Jace entered with earlier come back to the room mid-way through the game. They loiter in the corner for a moment before the dark-haired girl approaches Jace.

"Jace, you said you would teach me how to play pool." Her voice is low and seductive in a way that suggests she's interested in a lot more than just playing pool.

"I'm busy," Jace replies. Since he's not even participating in the game, I'm tempted to ask him what he's busy with, but I refrain.

The blonde comes over to join her dark-haired friend.

"Come on, Jace, everyone's waiting for you," she cajoles. "What are you doing in here? You never play poker with the team."

Her gaze flickers to me briefly, the insinuation obvious.

"I said I'm busy," Jace states. The aggravation is clear in his tone. "Go find someone else to play with, Maria."

The blonde's eyes flash. "It's Megan."

I can't contain the small snort that escapes me, and I hear Anderson chuckle as well.

Jace's eyes flash to mine as the two girls leave in a huff, and I finally meet his intense gaze.

"Looks like Jace Dawson Fan Club membership might be dwindling," I comment.

"In my experience, it's a lot more difficult than that to lose members," Jace predicts confidently.

I roll my eyes and look away. "I met another girl who bumped into you once."

Jace's eyes focus on me. "What the hell are you talking about?"

"Well, in case you've forgotten, I ran into you while trying to escape a near-death experience—"

"That skateboarder was at least a foot away from you," Jace asserts.

"—And you weren't very pleasant about it," I finish, ignoring the interruption. "I met a girl who bumped into you outside the library, and you didn't say a word to her or—"

"How did you meet this girl?" Jace asks, looking completely bemused.

"At your game. But that's not the point—" I start, although I'm losing track of what the point is myself, likely thanks to the whiskey muddling my thoughts.

"You were at our game?"

I didn't mean to tell him that. "Yes."

"What did you think?"

I don't have to look over to know he's sporting a cocky smirk.

"It was fine," I reply simply.

"Fine?" Jace questions. "You know I broke two school records?"

"I vaguely remember something about that being announced."

"If you weren't going to pay attention, why did you even bother going?" Jace asks, his voice angry now.

"Maybe I wanted to make sure you hadn't gotten hit by a car," I retort, and immediately regret the words. Another thing I wasn't going to mention.

"What are you talking about?" Jace looks confused. "Why—" Understanding dawns on his face.

There's suddenly a new influx of people into the dining room, and the commotion they cause interrupts the progress of the third game entirely. Each new arrival looks over to Jace as they enter the room, and I quickly realize it's his presence drawing everyone into here.

One of the guys who's just entered comes over and asks Jace something. I quickly seize the opportunity to escape, standing and grabbing my empty cup. I'm relieved to find I can stand without the room spinning, although I can still feel the alcohol coursing through my veins, making my movements feel sluggish.

Anderson looks over to me as I stand.

"I'm going to find Katie and Philip," I tell him.

He nods, and I walk toward the kitchen. I have no idea how much time has passed since I started playing poker, but it's certainly been a lot longer than I expected Philip to have allowed me out of his sight.

As soon as I enter the kitchen, I realize why. Philip is leaning against the wall that runs along the edge of the doorway, providing him with a clear vantage point of the entire dining room. Katie stands beside him, talking to a smiling girl with light brown hair I've never seen before. Katie smiles when she spots me approaching and waves me over to where they're standing.

I see her eyes widen in surprise, which is the only warning I receive before a calloused hand grabs my bare forearm.

I'm spun around, and almost collide with Jace's tall frame. We're only a few inches apart, standing close enough that I can feel the heat radiating from his body and spot a small freckle just beneath his bottom lip. I thought his proximity was potent before, but it was nothing compared to now.

"Are you leaving?" he asks me quietly.

"Isn't that what you want?" I counter.

"No, I—shit." Jace rakes a hand through his short, dark hair. "I didn't think you cared, okay? We've had extra practices this week, and—"

Our conversation is suddenly interrupted.

"Let's go, Vivienne," Philip states, appearing next to me and standing there protectively. I don't reply, continuing to hold Jace's probing gaze. I start to feel light-headed from the intensity.

"Vivienne." Philip says again, his voice more insistent. We're standing within clear view of everyone in the dining room, and I tear my eyes away from Jace's to see most of them are watching our silent stand-off.

I start to turn away from Jace, and as I do, my foot catches on the edge of the throw rug I've been standing on. I tip forward. My stomach experiences a sickening jolt as the wooden floor draws closer.

My momentum is broken by a muscular forearm. I look up, expecting to see Philip's face. Instead, I'm met with Jace's concerned one. My entire body heats as he pulls me upright. My legs don't cooperate, still shaky from surprise and further addled by the alcohol swimming in my system. I end up pressed against Jace's chest as he supports my weight, keeping me vertical.

Dimly, I hear Philip saying something. Jace's arms automatically tighten around my body in response to whatever it was. I turn my heavy head to see Philip standing close by, his face a mask of concern and anger.

"Let's go, Vivienne," he tells me in a hard voice. "You're drunk, I'll take you home."

"You can't," Jace replies.

"Are you going to try and stop me?" Philip draws himself up to his full height, clearly preparing for an altercation if necessary. Although his stance is intimidating, he's still several inches shorter and a couple dozen pounds lighter than Jace, leaving little doubt as to who the alpha in the situation is.

"Kennedy is an all-girls dorm," Jace tells him. "Whoever's at the front desk won't let you take a drunk girl up to her room. They'll call Campus Health, which will end up on her permanent record. It's better that she sleeps it off here. I'll keep an eye on her."

The front desk attendants were told I'm the daughter of an important American government official, so all Philip would have to do at the front desk is flash his official badge and they'd let him take me to my room. However, he can't say that to Jace without blowing my cover. I watch the indecision war on his face as he tries to decide what to do.

"I'm not leaving her alone with you," he finally states.

Jace lets out a humorless laugh. "I don't think that's your call. Vivienne can make her own decisions."

"Not when she's drunk, she can't," Philip retorts.

Despite my role in the center of their argument, my entire body feels calm and relaxed. I would like to think it's just another effect of the whiskey I've consumed tonight, but if I'm being honest with myself, I know it has more to do with the person I'm pressed against.

I can't make out the blinking green numbers on the stove to tell what time it is, but my body is steeped in exhaustion and my heavy eyelids start to close without my permission. My head fits perfectly in the nook between Jace's shoulder and neck.

"Vivienne, we're leaving." Philip tries to reason with me again. Frustration is evident in his tone.

If I were less exhausted and sober, I'd feel bad for the difficult position I'm putting him in. He has no way of removing me from the house and guaranteeing my safety without either attracting a horde of unwanted attention or revealing who I really am, neither of which he wants to do. However, my tired, tipsy self wants nothing more than to remain in Jace's arms, which is exactly what I choose to do.

Philip tries tugging at my arm, and I clench Jace's t-shirt tightly in response, mumbling "No" into the soft material.

Jace intervenes again.

"Look, man, I get that you're protective of Vivienne, but I promise nothing will happen to her. I'll put her upstairs in one of the empty bedrooms and make sure the door is locked. She'll be perfectly safe and can leave whenever she's slept it off, okay?"

Philip doesn't reply. I pry my eyelids open and shift my head to meet his concerned eyes.

"I'm fine, Philip," I tell him earnestly. "I have my phone. I'll let you know if I need you, I promise. Go home."

Philip studies my face for a moment, and I hold his gaze, trying to convey as much authority and assurance as I can.

"Fine." His tone is curt, but resigned. I wouldn't be surprised if he spends the night sitting outside the house in his car, but I can't muster the energy to care about anything besides remaining right where I am at the moment.

Philip finally turns to leave. Another thought suddenly occurs to me.

"Make sure Katie gets home safely," I call out after him. He looks back and nods.

I turn my head back against Jace, effectively tuning out the rest of the world. We remain standing in the same spot where he'd caught me. I can feel eyes on us, an ability I've honed over years of attending public events as the center of attention.

I didn't realize how quiet the kitchen became until it gradually begins to return to a normal volume, interspersed with muttered whispers.

Jace suddenly sweeps my feet off the floor, keeping my head closely cradled against his chest. My eyes fly open as he walks back through the house toward the front door, passing an array of surprised faces. He carries me through crowded rooms effortlessly, and I turn my face back against his chest and close my eyes. The swirl of curious faces is not helping my uneasy stomach.

Jace adjusts my weight as we begin to climb up a staircase. The rocking motion stops for a moment, and he then proceeds to walk straight for a while before stopping again. He shifts me and I hear the creak of a door before he continues moving.

I'm gently placed on a soft surface, and I snuggle against the cozy fabric. Just as I've curled up on the comfortable bedding, Jace holds a bottle of water in front of me. Condensation drips down the outside of the plastic container.

"Drink this."

I force myself to sit up and twist open the plastic lid. I take several hearty sips of the cool liquid, which seems to appease Jace.

He sets the half-empty bottle on the small table next to the bed and doesn't protest when I lay back down. "I'll be back in a little while to check on you," Jace tells me. "I have a key to the door, so don't let anyone else in, okay?"

I grunt in acknowledgement, already half asleep. The door creaks open, then quietly shuts.

It seems like only moments later when I hear the door squeak open again. I still feel tired, but my stomach has settled and the buzz of alcohol is absent.

I open my eyes and watch Jace as he enters the room, turns to shut his door, and walks over to his dresser. He flicks on the small lamp sitting on top of the dresser, and I cringe as my eyes adjust to the harsh appearance of light. The glow cast allows me a glimpse of what must be Jace's bedroom. I glance around, but can only make out shadowed shapes in the feeble light.

My attention is diverted from studying Jace's room when I look back over and see he's started undressing. He pulls off his t-shirt and jeans before turning toward me in just his boxer briefs. He stills when he sees I'm awake, looking like a perfectly carved Adonis in the shadows that emphasize the angles and ridges of his body. He takes a few cautious steps toward me and takes a seat on the end of his bed.

"How are you feeling?" he asks, looking at me with concern.

I don't answer at first, distracted. "Better," I finally tell him, my voice scratchy with sleep.

The presence of Jace's muscular, mostly naked body so close to me is all-consuming, and I'm struggling to focus on anything besides the overwhelming lust slowly spreading through me.

Jace and I stare at each other for a long moment. I wonder what he sees on my face.

He moves to stand just as my hand reaches toward the bottom of my top. Jace freezes as I slowly drag the silk material higher and higher, until my entire chest is exposed. I pull the shirt over my head, revealing the lacy bra that's all I'm wearing underneath. I toss my shirt on the floor and pull my phone out from my skirt, setting it on the table next to me. Then, I begin to shimmy out of the suede material, eventually sitting up so I can pull the stretchy fabric down my long legs.

Jace doesn't move or say a word as I undress. I toss my skirt down next to my shirt. We sit side by side in our underwear, studying each other in the light from the lamp that barely reaches the edge of Jace's bed.

I shift forward. Jace's athletic reflexes anticipate my movement. We collide at the same moment, and I fall back against the soft comforter. Only our arms are touching. The rest of Jace's weight is suspended above me, although he's just as close as he was in the kitchen. I study the shades of gray in his eyes as we resume our silent stare-off. The color is darkest close to the pupil.

"What are you doing, Vivienne?" Jace whispers.

"Can't you tell?"

Although he's grasping my arms, I still have enough range of movement to raise my head and close the small gap between our lips. The heat that flares within me when our mouths touch is staggering; it dazzles my mind and invigorates my senses. Jace freezes for a moment, but then begins to kiss me back. We become a tangled mess of heated touches. Nothing exists beyond the sensation of his tongue in my mouth and his hands running along my body.

He pulls away abruptly with a muttered "Fuck." I'm thrust back to reality, feeling as though I've had a bucket of cold water thrown over me.

The outside world rushes back into the room, and I once again become aware of the muffled bass beat playing downstairs and the cool rush of air coming in through Jace's open window.

"Why did you stop?" I ask, hoping he can't see the hurt and confusion on my face in the meager light.

"You're drunk."

"No, I'm not," I insist. "Well, not anymore," I amend.

"You drank half a bottle of whiskey earlier. Trust me, you're still drunk."

"You're turning me down? Seriously?" I ask. "Is it because you already fucked Maria or Megan or whoever?"

I try to mask the sting of his snub with anger, but it bleeds into my voice anyway.

"Jealous?" Jace smirks.

I don't reply, because we both know I am, although there's no way I'll admit it to him or myself. He doesn't answer my question, which prompts a bothersome ache I fight to ignore.

Something shifts in his expression as he studies my own, but I can't identify what it is before his face returns to an indifferent mask.

"I thought you go through girls like Kleenex," I accuse, my tone tinged with judgement as I recall the rumors I've heard circulating around campus. "You'll sleep with any girl who compliments you, but the one night I want you to be the arrogant football star, you're not interested?"

Jace shoots me a hard glare, then climbs off the bed. For one wild moment, I think he's going to kick me out of his room. Instead, he opens the top dresser drawer and pulls out a gray t-shirt. He tosses it to me and turns out the lamp on the dresser, plunging us into near darkness. There's just the barest hint of light from the hazy moon beaming in through the open window.

I feel the bed shift as his shadowy figure climbs under the covers beside me. I don't move, disoriented by the rapid shift of events that have taken place over the last few minutes. Embarrassment, anger, hurt, and confusion swirl and mix with the remnants of lust.

Finally, I settle on annoyance as I sit on top of the bed, holding the t-shirt. I contemplate leaving, but have no idea what the state of things is downstairs or how to even get back to my dorm at this hour. My best option would be to call Philip, but I have no desire to deal with the inevitable lecture about how irresponsible my actions tonight were right now.

I glance over at Jace's still body, resolving I'll sleep for a little while and sneak out early before I have to talk to him. Having decided, I slip on the cozy t-shirt and slide under the covers.

Jace's bed is much more comfortable than my dorm's. Despite my lingering annoyance and shifting kaleidoscope of emotions about the boy lying beside me, I find myself falling asleep in minutes.

CHAPTER NINE

I wake up to a dark room. I sit up quickly, trying to assess my barely visible surroundings. My navy top and gray skirt lay on the floor, illuminated by a sliver of moonlight.

Details from the night before slowly filter back into my consciousness. As my brain begins to awaken, I'm seized by a desperate thirst. I turn to see the barely visible outline of a small table next to the bed. Carefully, I reach out and trace my fingers along the surface, hoping to encounter a light.

I freeze when I hear the sound of rustling sheets behind me, followed by a quiet click that bathes the room in warm light.

I whip my head around. The motion exacerbates the pounding headache I'm suddenly keenly aware of. Jace's disgruntled, sleepy face stares back at me as he sits up on the other side of the bed. White sheets pool around his waist. I look at him, simultaneously marveling over the uninterrupted view of the carved ridges of his abdomen and wincing as more of my memories from the night before begin to return.

"What," Jace asks, "are you doing?"

"Looking for water," I croak out. My throat feels rough and dry.

Jace nods to the table I'd been fumbling with, and I look back to see a half-empty water bottle in the center of the table. I grab it and gulp the remaining liquid gratefully.

"How much of last night do you remember?"

"Parts," I reply, my voice still hoarse.

"Your stepbrother hates me," Jace says, his voice pleased.

"What?" my still-sleepy brain tries to catch up. "You mean Philip? Why?"

"He tried to get you to leave with him, but you wouldn't let go of me," Jace explains, sounding amused.

I cringe at the revelation, and the memories it unearths. "He's protective," I respond, attempting to sound nonchalant. "My step-father trusts him to look out for me, and would be really mad if he found out he didn't." I half-grin at the understatement. Thomas would likely kill Philip if he found out he'd been negligent in his duties regarding me.

"Protective is right," Jace agrees. "But he's also jealous. He looked ready to punch me out when you started snuggling me."

I flush at his characterization of my behavior. "He's not jeal-ous, he just thinks all the 'football gods' at this school are breaking hearts and beds left and right. I'll make sure to let him know he has nothing to worry about, since I offered you sex and you turned me down cold."

Jace stares at me, obviously surprised I've brought my disas-trous attempt at seducing him up. "I don't think I'm the one who should be worried about breaking hearts," is all he says in response.

I roll my eyes. The motion draws my attention back to my pounding head. "Can you turn the light out?" I request. "I've had too much alcohol and too little sleep to have a conversation with you."

Jace looks at me for a moment, but then nods and turns out the light, returning us to darkness once again. I try to return to blissful oblivion, but the renewed awareness of his close proximity alights each of my senses and keeps sleep evasive.

I must fall asleep eventually, because when I open my eyes again I'm greeted by a broad expanse of golden tan skin. Hesitantly, I lift my head off Jace's chest and slip out of his loose embrace. We fell asleep on opposite sides of the bed, so I have no idea how we ended up entangled in its center.

The first hints of morning sun filter through the transom window, softly illuminating my surroundings. I slide out of the warm bed, wincing when my toe jabs against a textbook lying on the hardwood floor.

The gray t-shirt I'm wearing has *Fulton Football* written on the front in white block letters. Snagging my wrinkled top and skirt off the floor, I pull the t-shirt off and drape it on Jace's desk chair before re-dressing in last night's outfit.

I start to make my way toward the door, but then catch a glimpse of myself in the full-length mirror on the inside of Jace's ajar closet door. My blonde hair is completely disheveled, so I quickly pull it up in a messy bun and brush a few stray flakes of mascara off my face.

Glancing down at the deep creases in my revealing top, I pivot and tiptoe back over to Jace's desk. I retrieve his t-shirt and yank it back on over my head. It covers most of my outfit, with only a small strip of my short skirt still visible. I twist the soft material into a tight knot on my right hip so it's clear I'm wearing some sort of bottoms. Spotting a pad of post-it notes on the desk, I grab a pen and scribble *thanks for the water (and nothing else)*. I sign it -*V* with a flourish, and place the neon paper on the creased pillow.

The quiet house is in a state of disarray and littered with trash. I'm thankful I don't encounter a single person as I sneak through the house and out the front door.

As I walk down the brick path, I pull out my phone. A flash of movement catches my attention, and I look up to see Philip pulling the black sedan up in front of the house. I sigh before walking over to the car and climbing into the front passenger seat. The hard set of Philip's jaw makes it clear that all is far from forgiven regarding the previous evening's events.

"Did you stay here all night?" I ask.

"Yes."

"I'm sorry," I tell him earnestly. "I know I made things difficult for you last night, and that you're just trying to keep me safe. It's just—" I look out the window, trying to come up with a way to describe the reckless emotions driving my actions last night. "I just got a taste of what it's like to be a normal college student, and I didn't want it to end. It won't happen again."

Philip's expression softens somewhat.

"Did you tell Thomas?" I question. "Or Julie and Steve?"

"No," Philip replies. "I didn't see any reason to worry them too."

"I'm sorry."

He nods in acknowledgment. "So, what's the deal with the football player?"

"There's no deal," I reply. "It was just a stupid drunk thing."

"How does he know you live in Kennedy Hall?"

"I don't know," I lie.

Philip's jaw tightens again. "He didn't try anything…" he starts.

"I'm *fine*, Philip." I cut him off, eager to stop discussing Jace. "Can we please just act like last night never happened? I have a bad headache and I just want to take a hot shower and eat some breakfast."

Philip complies with my request and remains silent for the rest of the short drive back to my dorm. I thank him for the ride, apologize for last night again, and head inside. I smile at the tired woman sitting at the front desk. She eyes my disheveled appearance critically, although she doesn't comment as I head down the empty hallway.

I enter my room and am relieved to see Katie fast asleep in her bed, her brown hair barely visible under the navy comforter. I quickly grab my toiletries and a fresh set of clothes before heading to the bathroom.

Twenty minutes later, I emerge feeling somewhat refreshed. My headache is mostly gone thanks to the steam from the shower and the two painkillers I swallowed before it, and I'm dressed in my favorite pair of leggings and a cozy fleece pullover.

I toss the suede skirt and wrinkled top into my laundry hamper and stand there, staring at the gray t-shirt I'm holding for a long moment. My pride is screaming at me to throw it in the trash can, but something stops me from actually doing so. I finally toss it on top of my dresser before leaving the room to go get some breakfast.

The dining hall is practically empty at this hour. The only other students are either athletes dressed in Lincoln sports gear or overeager academics in neatly pressed clothes. I load a plate high with eggs, bacon, and an array of fresh fruit, grab a mug of fresh coffee, and make my way to one of the many empty tables.

I've just sat down and taken my first bite of fruit when a tall, muscular black guy saunters up to my table and takes a seat across from me. I don't recognize him, but he's wearing a long-sleeved shirt with the outline of a football and the words *Lincoln*, suggesting he's a member of the football team. I eye him curiously as I hastily swallow.

"So, what's your deal?" he asks, as though it's entirely normal to interrupt a stranger's breakfast early on a Sunday morning.

"Excuse me?" I question, affronted.

"What's so special about you?"

I'm completely taken aback. "What are you talking about? I'm flattered you think I'm 'so special,' but it would mean a lot more if I knew who you are, what you're talking about, and why you're interrupting my breakfast."

The stranger simply raises his eyebrows, so I take a sip of my coffee, wondering if I'm still asleep and this is a bizarre dream where my subconscious is trying to tell me something.

"I've known Dawson a long time, and I've seen him with a lot of girls," he finally elaborates. "Never seen him act like he did last night."

"He spent most of the night trying to convince me to leave," I tell him. "So I wouldn't read too much into it. We can hardly stand each other."

"That's exactly why I *am* reading into it. Dawson ignores people he doesn't like. He doesn't care enough to ask a girl to leave once, much less spend all night at her side and then carry her upstairs."

"Look, I still don't know who you are or why you care about what Jace does at a party, but I can assure you Jace does not care about me at all, and the feeling is mutual. Now, could I please eat my breakfast in peace?"

The guy studies me for a long moment. "He has a lot riding on this season," he states, then finally stands to leave, departing as suddenly as he appeared.

I let out a deep breath and dig back into my breakfast, musing over the bizarre interaction.

The return to my peaceful meal is short-lived. Minutes later, I see Katie walk into the dining hall. Her hair is tied up in a messy ponytail, and the creases from her pillow are still evident on her face. She heads over to the drinks station and fills a mug with coffee. Then, she turns toward the seating area and spots me. Her eyes light up, and she makes a beeline over to my table.

I take a long sip of my steaming coffee, bracing for what I have no doubt will be my third inquisition of the day. Katie plops down in the seat Mr. What's-So-Special-About-You just vacated and leans back in it with a groan.

"How on earth do you look so alert and put together?"

"Trust me, I'm neither," I reply.

Katie lets out a small laugh and snags a piece of strawberry off my plate.

"Okay, so spill," she prompts, resting her chin on one hand with an expectant expression.

I raise an eyebrow and play dumb. "Spill what?"

"Vivienne! I told you Jace Dawson is treated like a god on this campus, partly because he acts like one. He hardly ever bothers to interact with us mere mortals who are not on the football team unless he has to. I've never seen him say more than a couple words to a girl, much less carry her up to his room in front of the entire football team. What the hell was that about? I didn't even know you two know each other!"

"We don't know each other, we've just…" I pause, unsure how to characterize our interactions. "We've just talked a few times. Actually, argued would be a more accurate description."

"Argued about what?" Katie inquires.

I think back on the wide range of topics we've covered on our early morning runs. "Pretty much everything," I reply honestly. "We can barely have a civil discussion about anything."

"That's not what it looked like last night."

My cheeks burn. "He just felt bad for me and took pity on my drunk self."

"Took pity on you?" Katie shakes her head. "Vivienne, have you been listening to anything I've been telling you? Jace Dawson does not take pity on anyone or take the time to acknowledge a situation that doesn't directly involve him. Or even some that do. He looked ready to punch Philip when he was trying to get you to leave with him last night. That is not pity."

I don't answer. I take a bite of my eggs and hope she'll drop the topic. Unfortunately, she persists.

"Did you guys hook up?"

"No!" I exclaim, feeling my cheeks warm as I recall our heated kiss. "He let me sleep it off in his bed, and when I woke up this morning he was still asleep, so I left."

Katie raises her eyebrows and sends me a disbelieving look.

"That's what happened." I insist, unwilling to dredge up the details of the exhilarating and humiliating encounter that took place between those two events.

"What was his room like?" Katie asks, not missing a beat.

I laugh. "You don't know this already? I thought you're some sort of Jace Dawson fangirl expert," I tease.

"Vivienne, if you still haven't figured it out yet, every single girl at Lincoln, and most of the guys, are obsessed with Jace Dawson. Every girl wants him, and every guy wants to be him. He's one of the best college football players in the country, he's hot as hell, and completely unattainable. If you took anything from his room, you could hold a bidding war."

I laugh, but think of the gray t-shirt wadded up on my dresser.

"Well, no wonder he has such a massive ego," I remark, eating my final piece of bacon. "Are you going to eat anything?"

"No, I convinced Philip to stop and get doughnuts on the drive home last night, and I ate the leftovers when I woke up."

"I'm glad he took you home. Sorry I was such a mess last night."

Katie shrugs. "Getting drunk at a party is a freshman rite of passage. The rest of us just didn't get to have Jace Dawson sweep in like our own personal knight in shining armor."

I roll my eyes. "Can you manage to go more than a minute without mentioning his name, please? The rest of the day, maybe?"

Katie lets out a dramatic sigh, but nods in agreement.

"You ready to go?" I ask, draining the last remnants of my coffee. "I'm planning to head straight to the library. I've got a lot of work to do today."

Katie nods in agreement, and we both rise from the table, heading toward the exit. I deposit my dirty dishes in the bin along the way. The aroma of various breakfast foods and freshly brewed coffee fades away as we step outside into the crisp fall air.

We head back to Kennedy Hall first to gather books and grab our backpacks. It's a brief stop, and then we walk through the center of campus toward the massive, imposing library, chatting easily about classes and assignments. Laughing at the other hungover students just beginning to emerge out into the light of day.

We snag a coveted table on the second floor that overlooks the heart of campus. A broad expanse of green grass spreads out before us, only interrupted by the tidy walkways that cut across to connect the surrounding sidewalks.

Katie keeps her word and doesn't mention Jace again as we each unpack our books and papers on the polished wooden table. I put in a pair of headphones and try to focus on creating the outline of the paper due Tuesday. I flip through the thin pages of the novel I'm writing the essay on, attempting to ignore the students passing by our table and the slowly awakening campus visible outside.

I eventually tune out the distracting activity, but thoughts of Jace continue to invade my mind.

I thought getting Katie to drop the topic of Jace Dawson would allow me to forget about him.

Unfortunately, it's my own thoughts I can't seem to shake.

CHAPTER TEN

When I wake up on Monday morning, it's earlier than usual. I went to bed before ten, still tired from Saturday night and drained from a long Sunday mostly spent in the library. However, I know my inordinately early wake-up has more to do with the decision I have to make this morning rather than an early bedtime.

I reach out and pull the curtain away from the lone window situated between my bed and Katie's, revealing an overcast, dreary sky. I let the fabric drop back into place and flop back down on my bed to stare up at the white plaster ceiling, warring internally with myself. I left Jace's house on Sunday morning determined I wouldn't venture anywhere near the elm tree where we used to meet, but my resolve has gradually chipped away over the past day to the point where it hardly exists anymore.

I'm still annoyed with Jace.

I'm still embarrassed by both my actions and his rebuff.

I also still want to see him.

Remaining under the warm covers for a while longer is my only option to put the decision off longer. Finally, I climb out of bed and go through my usual morning routine before dressing in a pair of leggings and a lightweight polyester jacket. I pull my hair up in a high ponytail and zip my phone in my jacket pocket before heading outside. The morning air is brisk, saturated by the light drizzle that's just started to fall.

I hadn't made a conscious decision about my route, but my feet turn automatically as I start to jog.

Several minutes later, the towering elm tree appears. Its vast form is silhouetted against the dark storm clouds spreading languidly across the sky.

I battle a mixture of relief and disappointment when I see the damp grass surrounding the broad trunk is as deserted as the rest of campus has been. I stop jogging when I reach the base of the tree and use its trunk for support as I double knot my laces and stretch my hamstrings. The rain has picked up. Heavy drops of water patter against the colorful leaves overhead.

The sound of a familiar voice startles me. "I've got to say Sunday morning was a first for me. I'm usually the one sneaking out."

I turn around. The surge of happiness I experience when I see his features startles me, so I quickly cover it with snark. "I hope your ego has had time to recover," I reply. "Do the girls you sneak out on usually show up on your run the following day?"

"You're the one waiting at the tree you know is on my normal running route."

"I'm not waiting. I was stretching."

Jace raises his eyebrows in a silent challenge, but doesn't reply. I look away from him and resume the stretch he interrupted.

"You stole my favorite t-shirt." Jace breaks the silence.

My cheeks warm, and I hope they were already flushed from the chilly fall air. "I don't know what you're talking about."

121

"I guess you must have forgotten you were wearing it in your rush to sneak out without waking me up."

I don't answer, choosing to keep my gaze on the fallen leaves dotting the emerald grass. I startle when Jace's warm hand tilts my chin up. His discerning eyes probe mine as a few stray droplets of rain roll down his face.

"Why did you sneak out, Vivienne?" he asks softly.

"I woke up, and you were still sleeping, so I left," I summarize succinctly. Jace opens his mouth to say something in response, but unbidden words continue to pour out before he has the chance to. "I've never done that before, but it seemed like it would simplify things."

Jace's brow furrows, and he drops his warm hand from my flushed face.

"Never done what before? Snuck out?"

"Slept with someone," I blurt. Fresh heat floods my cheeks, which I doubt Jace will miss.

"Slept with someone or had sex with someone?" he clarifies.

"Either," I whisper.

Jace looks startled. "Oh."

"I told you my family is overprotective, and they're pretty strict about who I'm allowed to socialize with and when. But—" I look up, and the tenderness in Jace's gaze prompts me to keep speaking. "—even with all that, I probably could have managed to, if I'd known someone that I wanted to be with that way."

I shut my mouth quickly, realizing what I've inadvertently implied. Not that Jace isn't aware of my attraction to him, especially after Saturday night. I drop Jace's stare, feeling exposed and vulnerable in front of someone I never expected to feel that way with once, let alone twice. I don't even have alcohol as an excuse this time.

Jace Dawson is the last person who I should be entrusting

with my secrets, and yet I can't seem to lie to those slate-colored eyes. I risk a glance up, and there's no sign of the god-like persona Katie described yesterday in the soft look he gives me. The tree branches shelter us from the precipitation plummeting from the sky around us, and it feels as though we're the only two people who exist under their green canopy.

Self-conscious, I tighten my ponytail and nod toward the path.

"Ready?" I ask, trying to dispel the intense moment. Jace nods, and we set off at an easy jog, side by side.

We run in silence for a while, until I finally ask, "What's Fulton?"

Jace gives me a sideways glance. "As in the Fulton Football t-shirt you've never seen?"

I try to contain the grin his words elicit, but don't do so very successfully. "Maybe."

"It's from my high school team. The town in Nebraska I'm from is named Fulton."

"Oh," I reply. "Is it a big town?"

"No, it's tiny. Only a few thousand people live there."

"Were you a big deal there, too?"

Jace sends me a smirk that suggests the answer should be obvious. I roll my eyes.

"Do you miss it?" I ask, curious to hear more about his upbringing.

"Yeah, it was hard to leave and come here," Jace replies. "My family is pretty tight-knit."

"Do you have siblings?"

"Yeah, I'm one of five."

I look at him in surprise. "Seriously?" I pictured him as a fellow only child.

"Yup. I'm the oldest, and then Mike is next. He's a junior in high school and thinks he's the shit."

I laugh, and Jace glances over at me. "Wonder where he might have learned that," I speculate.

Jace scoffs. "Then there's Max and Alden," he continues. "They're identical twins and are starting high school next year. Claire is the youngest. She's only eight." A fond smile forms on his handsome face as he talks about his younger siblings.

"What are your parents like?" I wonder, eager to learn more about his family.

"They both grew up in Fulton and were high school sweethearts. They planned to go to college together, but my grandfather died right after graduation, so they got married and stayed in Fulton to help my grandmother run the family farm. She passed away right after the twins were born, so they decided to stay for good. My mom runs the farm stand and my dad oversees most of the farm operations."

"I'm sorry about your grandparents," I tell him.

"Thanks."

"Your parents sound pretty amazing," I remark.

"Yeah, they're great. We didn't have a lot of money growing up, but they still made sure I had all the football equipment I needed and that I could go to all the best camps, even with all the other stuff my siblings needed. There's no way I would be here otherwise." A brief flash of uncertainty crosses his face, but it quickly disappears as he turns to look at me. "What about you?" he asks.

I think back to Richard's relentless drilling in preparation for exactly these sorts of questions, but once again, I find myself unwilling to lie to Jace.

"I'm an only child," I tell him. "I think my parents wanted more kids, but I had some heart problems when I was younger, and that dissuaded them for a while. If they started trying again, my mom never got pregnant. I don't know for certain though, they tend to avoid talking about anything difficult. Especially my mom."

"Are you close with them?" Jace asks.

"Yeah, I am. Especially my dad. We would play chess together every night."

"What is it with you and games?" he asks. "First poker, and now chess?"

I laugh. "Some of us can be good at more than one game."

"My family plays board games every Friday night," Jace replies. "I play a mean game of Monopoly."

I grin widely, trying to reconcile the image of Jace playing board games alongside his large family with the cocky football player everyone worships. "I seriously cannot picture that," I tell him honestly.

"I'll send you a picture next time I'm home," he promises.

We run in silence for a bit, and then Jace asks, "What about your step-brother?"

I wince. I was hoping he wouldn't notice the exclusion of my supposed step-family from my answer.

"Are you guys close?" Jace prompts when I don't immediately answer.

"He's nice."

I keep my response vague, and I feel Jace's eyes on my face. Thankfully, whatever he sees there causes him to drop the subject. The rain falls faster. My damp clothes are soon completely soaked.

The remainder of our run passes quickly. We emerge from the wooded trail next to the elm tree, both breathing heavily from the exertion. We stop underneath the extended branches and I peel off my wet jacket to let the cool water roll down my bare arms.

"I've got to get to practice," Jace states after we've stood there for a moment, catching our breath and enjoying a respite from the rain.

I nod. "I can probably find that t-shirt if you want it back," I admit, recalling our earlier conversation in this same spot.

"You can keep it," Jace tells me, smiling.

I smile back and turn to head back toward Kennedy Hall.

"Viv?" Jace calls from behind me, and I spin back around.

"It wasn't because I didn't want to." He turns and starts jogging toward the direction of the athletic center.

I stand there for a moment longer, letting his words wash over me.

CHAPTER ELEVEN

"What are you doing for Thanksgiving?" Katie asks me as we're leaving our philosophy class.

"Thanksgiving?" I ask.

"Yeah, you know, that one day a year where we stuff ourselves with too much food and argue with family members?" she jokes.

That sounds like most every day prior to my arrival here, but I don't share that with Katie as we continue walking across campus.

"Oh, right. Thanksgiving." I try to play off my unfamiliarity with the holiday as simple forgetfulness.

Katie gives me a strange look, but then understanding washes over her face. "I guess they don't celebrate it in London, huh? Did you not get to come home while you were at boarding school?"

"Not usually."

"Then what are you doing this year?" she asks.

"I'm not sure yet," I reply. "How about you?"

We walk into the student center. I pull my mailbox key out of my bag as we approach the post office.

"Well, since this is the first one since the divorce was finalized, my mom just told me she's planned a trip to New York City as a surprise."

"That sounds fun."

"We'll see," Katie remarks. "She's been pretty depressed every time I've talked to her lately."

"Sounds like this trip is a good idea then."

"Yeah, it probably is." After a brief pause, she adds, "It will be strange not watching the Lincoln game with my dad, though."

I unlock my mailbox. Katie moves farther down the row to unlock hers. There's nothing inside my box except for a folded piece of notebook paper. I slide it out of the metal box and into the back pocket of my jeans as I hear Katie's footsteps approaching.

"What Lincoln game?" I ask as she appears beside me, clutching two envelopes and a magazine.

"Lincoln plays our main rival on Thanksgiving each year."

"Oh," I reply. "Does that mean the football team will be staying on campus all break?"

"I think so, aside from traveling to Boston for the game," Katie replies, then looks over at me. "Why? Because of Jace?"

"No, I was just wondering," I reply quickly.

"I'd invite you to come with me and my mom, but I'm sure my mom will get all emotional at some point, and I don't want to subject you to that. I figured you already had plans with Thomas, Philip, and your mom."

I have to hide the smile that forms when I imagine what that would look like.

"It's fine," I assure her. "We're not very big on holidays, but we'll probably do something."

"You'd better figure out your plans soon," Katie advises. "You have to let Student Services know if you're planning to remain on campus by the end of the week."

"That soon?" I ask in surprise.

"Thanksgiving is next Thursday," Katie informs me.

"Wow," I reply. "I didn't realize it was already that close."

My phone buzzes in my jacket pocket, and I pull it out to see a message from Thomas asking if I can meet him in his office. I reply, telling him I'll be there in a few minutes.

"I'm going to go see Thomas."

She nods. "Ask him about Thanksgiving!"

As soon as I'm outside the student center, I pull the creased paper from my mailbox out of my pocket. I unfold it to see a series of numbers scrawled across the top. Underneath it is a message. *So you don't have to subject yourself to another football game.* A reluctant grin tugs at my mouth before I shove the paper back in my pocket.

I make my way across campus and arrive outside Thomas's office in the engineering building minutes later. I knock, and he calls for me to come in.

"Hello, Princess," he greets me, since we're alone. The title sounds foreign after weeks of being just Vivienne.

"Thomas," I acknowledge. "What did you want to discuss?"

"I have some extended family in Texas," he begins. "My wife mentioned to them that I'm in the country at the moment, so they've invited me for Thanksgiving. Your father has already approved the trip, but I wanted to make certain that you're comfortable with it as well."

"Of course," I assure him. "You're free to spend the break wherever you'd like. Does Philip have plans?"

"I haven't asked him yet, but I was planning to invite him to travel with me. You're more than welcome as well, but if you choose to remain here, you'll remain protected. With most of the campus empty, Julie and Steve will be able to remain close by."

"You and Philip should both go," I state firmly. "And thank you for the invitation, but I'll plan to remain here."

"Thank you, Princess," Thomas replies. "Are you sure you don't want any arrangements made for your own travel, though? Home or anywhere else?"

"I'm certain," I reply. "I'm actually looking forward to having some time to enjoy a quieter campus."

"All right," Thomas says. "I'll speak to Philip and update Julie and Steve as well."

"Very well." I turn to leave.

"Everything else all right, Princess?" Thomas interrupts my exit.

"It's fine, Thomas, thanks," I reply, then head back out into the empty hallway.

The next week passes quickly, and before I know it, the first day of Thanksgiving break has arrived. I wake as early as usual, but rather than the usual silence, I hear shouts and thuds in the hallway as residents of Kennedy Hall prepare to depart. Katie's alarm goes off right as I'm getting dressed in my running clothes.

She looks at the time and groans, but climbs out of bed.

"Crap, my taxi will be here in twenty minutes." She yawns widely as she grabs her toothbrush.

"Can I help with anything?" I ask, tying the laces on my sneakers.

"Actually, yes," Katie replies. "Pack whatever you think people in New York City wear. I've never been before."

"You haven't packed yet?" I exclaim.

"I was going to last night, but then I fell asleep." Katie heads into the bathroom to get ready.

I roll my eyes as I survey the mess of clothes draped around her side of the room, then start sorting them into neat piles. By the time Katie emerges from the bathroom, I've laid out several outfits.

She looks them over and smiles. "I knew you were the right roommate for the job!"

"Was 'I fell asleep' code for 'I want you to pack for me?'" I tease.

"Maybe." Katie winks before quickly getting dressed in one of the outfits I selected. Her phone rings right as we finish shoving the clothes into her oversized suitcase.

"That's my taxi. Thanks, Vivienne. You're the best!" She gives me a quick hug and grabs her bag. "Happy Thanksgiving!" she calls out as she rushes from our room.

I finish getting ready, then leave the room as well. Instead of the deserted campus that usually greets me at this hour, there's a flurry of activity as students rush around carrying suitcases.

I ignore the commotion and set off on my usual route along the outskirts of campus, passing idling taxis and excited families. There's a pang of homesickness as I think of my own parents.

It's the middle of the afternoon in Marcedenia, so I imagine my father meeting with his advisors in the study, while my mother plans some type of charity event out in the gardens. Nostalgia hits me, but as I look around the campus I've become so attached to, it's overcome by despair at the thought of my rapidly approaching departure. I reach the elm tree and go through my usual routine of stretching before I begin the more strenuous part of my workout.

Once I complete my stretches, I start to run. It's been a week since Jace has been waiting for me at the tree. Instead of reveling in the tranquility that's been restored, every morning he's absent results in a fresh twinge of disappointment.

After the first three days of solo runs, I caved and texted him, asking where he was. I expected a sarcastic response stating he must have put his number in the wrong mailbox, but instead he said his practice schedule has shifted in preparation for the all-important Thanksgiving game. He sent a final message saying *don't miss me too much*. I laughed at the time, but the despondency each morning I approach the elm tree to see no other figure in sight has become more annoying than amusing.

I push my pace faster than usual, and by the time I return to the tree, I'm panting heavily and soaked with sweat. I stop underneath the increasingly barren branches and lift my hands overhead to open up my lungs. Hazy sunlight warms my damp face as I suck in greedy gulps of the cool air.

"Was someone chasing you?"

My eyes snap open and my arms fall back to my sides. I turn to see Jace walking toward me, his hands shoved in the pockets of his sweatpants. He gives me an easy smile that I don't return. I'm preoccupied by the dizzying rush of emotions his appearance has sparked.

"Because if that's just your normal running pace, then I know you've been taking it easy on me," he adds when I don't say anything.

"What are you doing here?" I ask. "I thought you have practice every waking moment until the Thanksgiving game."

"I did. Until we found out there isn't going to be a Thanksgiving game."

"What?" I reply, confused. "Why?"

"Most of the opposing team has the flu. Apparently, they kept it quiet for a few days, hoping they would still have enough people to play, but Coach found out this morning it's being officially postponed."

"Wow. I'm sorry."

Jace shrugs. "We'll get to annihilate them next week instead."

"So do you still have practice all break?"

"Nope, Coach is giving us a few days off. Said we earned it after the crazy schedule this past week, but that if any of us get sick at home and can't play next week, he'll kill us himself. He's sentimental like that."

I laugh. "So, are you staying on campus?"

"Nope, I'm headed home. Just got off the phone with my mom. Pretty sure she'll have cooked a week's worth of food by the time I get there. I was at football camp most of the summer, so it's been a while since I was home."

I smile, smothering the rush of disappointment. "I'm glad."

"When are you leaving?"

"I'm not."

Jace looks at me with confusion. "Your family is staying here?"

"Uh, no. Philip and my stepfather left last night to visit extended family in Texas, but I decided to stay here."

Jace studies my face, and I shift under his scrutiny.

"Make sure to send me that board game photo. Pics or I won't believe you even know how to play Monopoly, much less win," I tease. "Happy Thanksgiving, Jace."

I turn and start to jog back toward Kennedy Hall.

"Vivienne!" Jace shouts from behind me. I look back over my shoulder to see him still standing in the same spot.

"Be ready in thirty minutes," he tells me, then walks away.

I open my mouth, but no sound comes out. I simply stand there, frozen. Excitement fills me, followed closely by indecision. With the end of my time here creeping closer and closer, I truly have been looking forward to enjoying the extra time on campus. After seeing the hordes of students eagerly departing for home, I'm more melancholy than exhilarated at the thought of remaining on the mostly empty campus.

Then I think of Jace. Do I want to be with him for the entirety of break?

The answer comes to me without hesitation, so I turn and begin running back to Kennedy Hall to pack.

CHAPTER TWELVE

Twenty minutes later, there's a knock on my door.

"Coming!" I call, zipping up my second overstuffed suitcase and flinging open the door to reveal Jace leaning against the metal doorframe. He's now wearing a pair of jeans and a dark green hoodie.

"Ready?" he asks with a broad grin.

"How did you even get in here?" I wonder. Kennedy Hall takes its status as an all-girls dorm very seriously.

"Turns out Cheryl at the front desk is a football fan," Jace replies, strolling into my room as though he owns the place. The small room feels even tinier in his domineering presence.

"Of course she is." I roll my eyes.

Jace looks around. "Nice room." He glances at the large pile of rejected clothes strewn across my bed.

I ignore his comment. "Jace, are you sure about this?" I ask tentatively. "I wanted to stay here. It's not like I didn't have anywhere to go, and I don't want you to feel obligated to—"

Jace stops appraising the room and gives me his full attention. "Do you want to come?" he asks me seriously.

"Well, yes—" I start.

"Then you're coming," Jace declares. "I wouldn't have invited you if I didn't want you to, okay?"

I nod.

"Now, where's your stuff?"

I gesture to the two suitcases sitting in a pile on the rug.

"You know break is only five days, right?" Jace eyes the stack dubiously.

"You didn't give me enough time to decide, so I just packed anything I thought I might want."

Jace chuckles. "Why do I feel like there would still be this many bags even if I'd given you days to pack?"

I don't deign that with a response, because he's right.

Jace grabs the suitcases while I toss a few more odds and ends into my tote bag.

Droplets of water fall from my hair occasionally, the strands still damp from my hasty shower. I twist them back in a messy bun. Taking a final glance around the room, I decide that I have everything I might need. "Let's go."

We leave my room and begin walking down the long, carpeted hallway. We pass a few girls, and each one looks at Jace in shock.

I'm pretty certain one of them actually takes a photo on her phone.

We enter the lobby, then emerge outside. One girl is just approaching the entrance with her parents, and her mouth gapes when Jace holds the door for the trio with his foot. She stammers out a thank you, and her parents eye Jace curiously.

"You could have just waited in the car," I grumble as we head for the parking lot.

"Embarrassed to be seen with me, Viv?" Jace teases.

"Yes," I retort.

He smiles at that. "You would have had to carry these by yourself if I had." He lifts the two heavy bags he's carrying.

"Beats having my entire dorm gossiping about you."

We approach a faded red truck with rusted fenders, and Jace tosses my luggage in the back before climbing into the cab.

"Now I believe you live on a farm," I tell him as I open the passenger door and hoist myself up. "This truck looks like it's been to the county fair one too many times."

Jace bursts out laughing. "The county fair? Did you see that in a movie about the Midwest, or something?"

"Maybe," I admit. "Does that mean you've never been to a county fair?"

"No comment."

"I'm going to take that as a yes."

Jace starts his truck with a deafening roar that quiets to a dull thrum after a few seconds. I eye the vibrating dashboard dubiously.

"How reliable is this thing?"

"It gets me where I need to go about eighty percent of the time."

"Great. And the other twenty?" I ask skeptically.

"Don't worry, things are completely under control."

We pull out of the near-empty parking lot. The radio plays softly in the background as I take off my leather boots and down jacket. I pull my long legs underneath me to sit cross-legged on the worn leather seat. We pass through downtown Lincoln. The small storefronts all boast window displays decorated with an assortment of vibrant fall leaves and cut-out turkeys.

Jace turns onto the highway a couple of blocks later, forcing the truck's growling engine to a faster speed. Bare trees line the asphalt road, turning the scenery to a blur of brown as we motor along.

About an hour later, I look over at Jace. "Are we almost there?" I ask expectantly.

"Yes," he replies seriously. "Only seven hours to go."

"Seven hours?" I exclaim.

"What, did you think Nebraska was just down the road?" Jace asks, grinning.

I don't reply, which Jace correctly interprets as a yes. The length of the trip was probably something I should have clarified before agreeing to this journey, but despite my initial surprise, I don't actually mind being stuck in this tiny cab with Jace for that length of time. There's a sense of ease when I'm around him, even when we're bickering, that I've never experienced with anyone else.

A couple hours later, I'm staring out the window when I notice Jace trying to shrug out of his dark green hoodie. The truck's vents are weak at best, but the dry heat has finally permeated every recess, raising the temperature inside the truck to near tropical levels. I laugh as he attempts to shake one sleeve down his arm while holding the steering wheel tightly with his other hand. I've already pulled the sleeves of my cashmere sweater up as far as they'll go, regretting having thrown it on with nothing underneath but my bra in my haste to get ready.

"Little help here?" Jace asks.

I take off my seatbelt so I can scoot across the bench seat to help him tug off the sweatshirt. I've just jerked the hoodie down his other arm when I suddenly lurch forward. The truck's suspension bounces wildly in the immediate aftermath of the pothole we've just driven over. I end up half-sprawled across Jace's lap, with his arm tucked around me like I'm an oversized football.

"Sorry. I couldn't swerve to avoid that one," he tells me. "Are you okay?"

"Yeah, I'm fine," I reply, pushing myself back to an upright position. Ease has been replaced by a swarm of butterflies. My skin tingles where Jace's hands have just been.

Jace glances over at me as I continue sitting here, trying to reconcile the extremes his presence and touch elicit from me. How I can feel comfort and familiarity in his company one moment and shockwaves running across my skin a moment later baffles me.

"You sure?"

"I'm sure," I confirm, sliding back to my original spot and clicking my seatbelt in order to avoid any more acrobatics. "It's just guys usually buy me a drink before asking for a lap dance."

Jace smirks at my thinly veiled reference. "Too bad I don't have a cocktail," he replies.

I bite back a grin and resume staring out the window.

Halfway across Iowa, Jace flicks on his blinker and guides the truck off the busy highway down one of the exit ramps. "We need gas." He turns into the first station we come across, pulls up to the pump, and opens his door to climb outside.

A cold gust of wind invades the warm cab. The icy air nips at my bare arms. I pull down the soft sleeves of my sweater and climb out of the now-chilly cab, taking advantage of the stop as an opportunity to stretch my cramped muscles. Jace finishes fueling the truck and returns the nozzle to its holder.

"I'll be right back," he tells me, and heads inside the small convenience store.

I finish stretching and pull my hair out of its bun, letting the wind whip the dry strands around my face before climbing back into the truck. Jace emerges back outside a couple minutes later, clutching a couple of waters and a bag of pretzels.

"Slim pickings." He climbs into the cab, tossing the snacks on the seat between us. "We can stop for something else soon."

He turns the key in the ignition, but instead of the deafening roar of the engine, the only sound is a soft click. Jace curses.

"Bad sign?" I ask.

Jace leans his head back and lets out a deep sigh. "Looks like we hit the twenty percent." He opens his door again and climbs back out of the cab. "Stay here. I'll go see if there's a mechanic nearby who can take a look at it."

I busy myself by checking the settings on my phone. Before we left, I set my location to stay at Lincoln. To my relief, that's still where I'm showing up.

Jace returns about ten minutes later.

"There's a garage down the road that's sending someone to take a look. They're going to call me when they know more. Apparently, there's a diner down the street we can wait at."

I nod and climb out of the cab, pulling on my coat and grabbing my bag. We start to walk along the bereft road, passing a run-down motel and a drive thru fast food restaurant before we reach the recommended diner.

The long, narrow building looks deserted. Red marquee letters atop it spell out *Josie's Diner*. Jace and I walk inside, and are greeted by warm air saturated with the potent scent of fried food. A couple of older men sit on two of the stools that line the Formica countertop, while the three booths across from them sit empty.

A gray-haired woman walks out from the kitchen over toward us. "You kids want a booth?" she asks, giving us a tired smile.

"Yes, please," I reply. She motions for us to follow her, and we walk across the checkered tile floor over to the row of booths.

"Take your pick. Menus are on the tables. Just holler when you're ready to order."

Jace and I each slide into our own side of red synthetic

leather. He hands me one of the plastic menus stashed behind the napkin dispenser.

"Sorry about this, Viv." He smiles sheepishly. "Didn't mean for you to have to spend the first day of break in a diner in the middle of Iowa."

"What's a good road trip without a few problems along the way?" I joke.

Jace smiles. "I'm pretty sure it's the lack of problems that make it a good road trip," he informs me.

"Maybe if you're a pessimist."

"Seriously, I'm sorry about this. I can't wait to replace that hunk of junk."

"I like the hunk of junk," I assure him. "It got us this far."

He leans back against the booth. "Guess I should have taken it on fewer trips to the county fair."

I laugh, appreciating his attempt to lighten the mood, although he's still looking at me with a touch of trepidation, as though he's afraid I might bolt from the booth at any moment.

"It's really fine," I tell him. "There's no place I'd rather be." I meant the words as a joke, but they come out more seriously than I intended, and ring with sincerity.

Jace's smile turns relieved.

"Are you two ready to order?" The same woman who greeted us reappears, a pad of paper at the ready.

I haven't even glanced at the menu yet, but I already know what I want. "Burger and fries, please."

"I'll have the same," Jace adds.

The woman jots down our order. "Coming right up."

Jace's phone rings, and he pulls it out of his pocket. "Hello," he answers. Whoever is on the other end of the line talks for about a minute, and then Jace thanks them and hangs up. "They think they know what's wrong with the truck. It should be ready in an hour."

Our food arrives quickly. I dig in eagerly to the greasy fries and juicy burger. Jace watches me with amusement as I inhale my food. When we've both finished eating, we continue sitting in the booth, talking until the hour has passed.

We arrive back at the gas station to find Jace's truck has been moved to the side of the convenience store. I get back into the truck while Jace talks briefly with the mechanic. A few minutes later, he climbs into the cab as well.

He grins over at me. "Let's hope this guy knew what he was doing."

Thankfully, as soon as Jace turns the key, the truck starts with its distinctive rumble. Jace guides it out of the gas station and onto the road that leads back to the highway.

As Jace merges onto the interstate, a familiar melody begins playing. I bounce in my seat and turn up the volume on the old radio.

Jace glances over, raising an eyebrow as I belt out the lyrics to my favorite song.

"What are you, sixty?" he teases.

"The classics are timeless," I inform him between verses.

He scoffs, but doesn't comment further as I continue singing.

"You're a terrible singer," he informs me a minute later, grinning widely. I ignore him, just singing louder.

Night approaches rapidly, and the open plains that line the highway become less and less visible in the fading light until they disappear from view entirely. My eyelids grow heavy as I lean my head back against the seat. I've shifted farther toward the center of the cab, taking advantage of all the additional space I can in the close confines of the truck.

I'm roused by Jace's voice. "We're here, Viv." He shakes my shoulder gently.

I groan in protest as consciousness slowly begins trickling back in. I'm still in the truck. Somehow, I traveled across the rest of the bench seat. I'm now pressed against Jace's side, using his bicep as a pillow. My seatbelt is stretched to capacity, the stiff material digging into my shoulder.

I sit up fully, disoriented. Darkness surrounds us, but I glance to the right and see a large, faded white farmhouse. Its blazing lights illuminate the silhouettes of several figures standing on the wooden porch that wraps around the front of the house.

Jace opens his door. The rush of cold air and the bright light that flickers on in the cab of the truck chase away the final remnants of sleep.

I put on my jacket and grab my bag before sliding out onto the dirt driveway. Jace has already grabbed our bags from the bed of the truck and is walking toward the front porch. I trail after him hesitantly, feeling like an intruder as I watch him hug a middle-aged woman with short brown hair who must be his mother and a tall, dark-haired man who I assume is his father. Several shorter figures in pajamas surround them, bouncing around in excitement. I hover on the lowest step, watching as Jace steps out of his father's embrace and glances back at me. I climb the next two steps to stand on the very edge of the porch.

"This is Vivienne, everyone." Jace beckons me forward. "Vivienne, this is my mom, dad, Alden, Max, and Claire."

They all eye me curiously, but none of them look surprised to see me, so Jace must have already told them he was bringing me.

Jace glances around the porch. "Where's Mike?"

"He's spending the night at Jason's," Jace's mom replies. "He promised he'd be back first thing to help get everything ready, or else he's just asking for a grounding." She steps forward and smiles warmly at me. "It's so nice to meet you, Vivienne." She gives me a quick hug.

"You too, Mrs. Dawson," I reply. "Thank you for having me."

"Call me Ellen, please," she responds. "Now come inside. You must be exhausted."

I follow her into the warm house. A row of cubbies line the right side of the front hallway. The floor is littered with an assortment of muddy rubber boots and the hooks in each cubby boast an assortment of jackets in different sizes and colors. A wide, wooden staircase is located just beyond the tiled entryway that leads upstairs.

Ellen veers to the left, and I trail after her into a cozy living room containing a long couch and two overstuffed armchairs. The walls are covered with bookshelves. A wood stove sits in the corner. It fills the room with the sound of crackling wood, and casts enough heat to erase the remaining chill from outside.

The living room transitions into a massive kitchen. The wide wooden floorboards creak beneath my feet as I walk toward the long tabletop decorated with smudges of paint and faded scratches. A handmade ceramic bowl sits in the center, filled with a mix of green and red apples.

"Your home is beautiful," I compliment Ellen as we stop in the kitchen.

"Thank you, dear," she replies. "We'll make sure to give you the full tour tomorrow morning when it's light out." Shifting her gaze away from me, she adds, "Time for bed, you three. I let you stay up until your brother arrived, but there's lots to be done tomorrow to get ready for Thursday, so get some sleep."

I turn to see a young girl with blonde hair in braids and two boys with identical mops of curly brown hair studying me closely. I smile, and they all look away shyly.

"Come on. Vivienne and Jace will still be here tomorrow," Jace's mom tells them. "Patrick, can you herd them upstairs?"

I turn to see Jace's dad adding a log to the wood stove. He shuts the grate and comes into the kitchen to follow Ellen's request. "Let's go, kiddos." His voice is low, but the three kids listen to him immediately, scurrying out of the kitchen back toward the staircase. Mr. Dawson gives me a kind smile. "Lovely to meet you, Vivienne," he says before heading toward the stairs himself.

"Let me show you where you'll be staying," Ellen tells me once the kitchen has cleared out. "Jace, bring her bags." I bite back a smile at her bossy tone and follow her out a side door from the kitchen.

We walk down a short hallway decorated with framed photos and crayon drawings until we come to an open door. Ellen steps inside and switches on the light, revealing a small, tidy room. The wall to the right is taken up by a twin bed with a colorful quilt spread across it. The left side of the room holds a washer and dryer with a couple of woven baskets sitting atop them. The entire wall we're facing is lined with floor-to-ceiling shelves, containing a random assortment of items that includes books, board games, and a sewing machine.

"I'm sorry it's not larger," Jace's mom says apologetically. "We usually use Jace's old room for guests these days, but with him home, this is the only other option. Good news is it's the closest bed to the kitchen and the wood stove, so you'll be warm and have first dibs on food."

I smile. "It's great, Ellen. Thank you."

She smiles back. "I'll go grab you some clean towels. The bathroom is just across the hall."

Ellen bustles out of the room, leaving me and Jace standing in the tiny room. He sets my two suitcases down in the corner next to the washing machine.

"So this is where the great Jace Dawson grew up, huh?"

"It is," Jace replies. "What do you think?" His voice is teasing, but there's an undercurrent of uncertainty I'm surprised I detect.

"I love it," I tell him honestly. "Definitely an improvement from my double in Kennedy Hall." And much homier than the palace I grew up in.

He grins. "I'm beat, so I'm going to head to bed. My room is the one at the top of the stairs, first door on the left. Get me if you need anything, okay?"

I nod.

He steps forward and gives me a quick kiss on the forehead. "Night, Viv." He smirks at my startled expression before ducking out of the room and closing the door.

I change out of the jeans and sweater I've been wearing most of the day into a t-shirt and sleep shorts. A soft knock sounds on the door. I open it to reveal Mrs. Dawson. She hands me a stack of white fluffy towels.

"Let me know if you need anything else. See you in the morning."

I thank her, then walk down the hallway into the white tiled bathroom to finish getting ready for bed. Once I'm done in the bathroom, I make my way back into the hallway. The house is completely silent. The only light comes from the thin beam cast through my half-open door. I hurry inside and shut the door behind me, turning out the light and slipping between the soft flannel sheets. Despite the unfamiliar surroundings, I immediately feel myself drift toward unconsciousness as I burrow under the warm blankets.

CHAPTER THIRTEEN

I wake up to the delicious aroma of freshly brewed coffee and baked goods. I climb out of bed, wincing when my feet hit cold hardwood, and head down the hallway to use the bathroom.

Once I've freshened up, I return to my room and face the dilemma of what to wear. I study the many options I brought. I have no idea what one wears on a working farm or what I'll spend the day doing. The safest option is jeans and a sweater.

I head back out into the hallway, this time walking in the opposite direction toward the kitchen. I enter it to find Mrs. Dawson standing at the farm sink washing dishes.

She turns when she hears me enter. "Morning, Vivienne," she greets me with a wide smile.

"Good morning, Mrs. Daw—I mean, Ellen." I correct myself mid-sentence.

"Grab some coffee, if you'd like. I just brewed a fresh pot and I have some muffins in the oven for breakfast."

I grab one of the mugs sitting out on the table and fill it with hot liquid.

Ellen finishes rinsing the dish she's holding and sets it in the drain rack before taking a sip from her own mug. "You ready for that tour?" she asks, turning to face me. "I've got about twenty minutes before these muffins will be ready."

"Sure," I reply, following her out of the kitchen.

We walk back through the living room and pause by the front door. Jace's mom grabs a fleece jacket and pulls on a pair of rubber boots.

"You should be warm enough in that." She nods to my heavy sweater. "But you might want to wear a pair of these." She hands me a pair of boots, and I pull them on over my jeans. We head outside.

The air is chilly, but tempered by the bright sunshine as we descend from the porch steps and cross the front yard, passing Jace's truck.

Aside from the dirt driveway, the yard is comprised entirely of green grass. Fields filled with neat rows of corn, wheat, and other crops I can't identify surround us in every direction, as far as the eye can see.

"Are you always this early of a riser?" Ellen asks as we walk along.

"I am," I reply. "I used to fight it when I was younger, but now I've learned to appreciate having some time to myself before most of the world wakes up. I usually go running first thing."

Ellen lets out a low laugh. "Jace mentioned he's been running every morning. Extra runs make a lot more sense now." She gives me a conspiratorial wink.

"Extra runs?" I ask.

"Even on the mornings he already has team ones."

"Oh," I reply, feeling silly. When Jace tells me he's heading to practice, I always imagine him standing around doing something similar to the simple drills he coached me through, not running. I think of the many mornings I pushed my stamina to its limits in hopes of avoiding or impressing him, and resolve to set an easier pace on our next run.

We walk across packed dirt, passing another truck and a silver SUV. A massive red barn sits before us, with two silver silos towering directly behind it.

One half of the barn is painted a darker shade of red, as though someone added a new coat more recently and then left the other half. I don't ask if that's the case, because I feel some strange compulsion to ensure the woman beside me has a positive impression of me.

Ellen pulls open the massive barn door. It groans as it slides along the track, revealing a couple of tractors parked in the center aisle. The first one has wheels roughly the same height as me.

A low whinny sounds to my left, and I look over to see a chestnut horse peering over a stall door. It nickers softly as Ellen walks over, nudging her pockets in a quest for food. She laughs and pats its large head before opening a plastic bin and scooping out a generous serving of grain that she pours into a bucket and feeds to the hungry horse. She fills two more buckets, then walks farther into the barn. I follow her around the corner, where two more horses are eagerly awaiting their breakfast. One is a paint, the other entirely black.

Ellen offers me one of the buckets.

"Want to feed Patches?" she asks, nodding to the paint.

I take the bucket from her. "Creative name," I joke.

Ellen laughs. "We let Claire pick out their names. This is Black Beauty"—she nods to the black horse—"and the first one you met was Firewood."

"What do you use them for?"

"They do some of the plowing in the smaller fields that are tough to navigate in the tractor. But aside from that, they're mostly just pets. We got Firewood first, and then a neighbor was moving and gave us these two as a package deal."

"Do you ride them?" I ask.

"Not regularly, but they can be. Do you ride?"

"No, but I've always wanted to try," I confess.

"Well, now's your chance," Ellen tells me with a smile.

I stroke the soft lock of hair resting between Patches' brown eyes, watching as he inhales the grain eagerly.

Once the horses are fed, Ellen moves across the aisle and opens a door made of wooden slats. With a loud series of squawks, about a dozen chickens fly out from another stall.

Ellen tosses a handful of cracked corn on the ground, and they immediately begin pecking around and scratching on the cement floor. She grabs a basket that's hanging on a hook and walks inside the stall, emerging a couple minutes later to reveal the basket's been filled with brown and blue eggs.

"Farm fresh eggs with your muffin?" she asks, winking.

I laugh. "Sounds great."

We walk back outside the barn just as a white truck is beginning to move down the driveway. It pauses next to us. The passenger side window rolls down, revealing a smiling blonde boy who looks a bit younger than me.

"Hi, Jason," Ellen greets.

"Morning, Mrs. D.," Jason replies, smiling. "Happy early Thanksgiving."

"You, too. Did Mike remember to give your mom the jam I sent?"

"He sure did," Jason replies. "She said to tell you thanks, and that she'll be dropping off some fresh pumpkins at the farm stand later today."

"That sounds great," Ellen responds. "Do you want to stay for breakfast?"

"Nah, I can't today," Jason says. "But thanks. I'll see you tomorrow." He gives me a curious glance, then continues driving down the dirt road.

"Jason is one of Mike's best friends. His mother Caroline is one of my oldest friends," Ellen explains. "We grew up here together, just like our boys."

We walk back into the house and enter the kitchen to find a dark-haired boy slumped in one of the chairs.

"Morning, Mike," Ellen says as she walks over to the oven and pulls out two trays of lightly browned muffins. Their mouthwatering aroma fills the kitchen.

"Hey, Mom," Mike replies. "Jace get back okay?"

"Yes, and he brought a guest. Vivienne, this is Mike."

Mike's gaze slides over to me. He has the same dark hair and striking features as his older brother, but it's the lazy, confident grin he gives me that makes the resemblance seem uncanny.

"Oh, really," he drawls out. His eyes scrutinize my appearance closely. "Are you one of the Lincoln football groupies?" he asks with a smirk.

"Michael Neil! You do not speak to *anyone* that way, much less a guest of ours," Ellen scolds, turning away from the stovetop where she's scrambling eggs to give Mike a disapproving frown.

"Relax, Mom, I just want to make sure she knows she chose the wrong Dawson brother if she's after an actual football star."

Jace chooses this moment to walk into the kitchen. He's simply wearing a pair of worn sweatpants and a cotton t-shirt, but still manages to render me speechless for a minute.

"Knock it off, Mike," he warns, hitting his younger brother on the back of the head as he passes his chair.

"Nice to see you too, Jace," Mike replies. "You bringing random girls home to meet Mom now?"

"Mich—" Mrs. Dawson starts, but Jace interrupts her.

"I brought one special girl home to meet all of you," he tells Mike evenly. "Now, drop it."

Mike scoffs, but doesn't say another word. He does watch closely as Jace walks over to where I'm awkwardly lingering in the doorway.

"Sleep okay?" he asks

"Like a rock," I inform him. "Lot less bumpy than the truck."

Jace smiles. "Did you go running?" he asks, looking at my outfit.

I shake my head. "Your mom gave me a tour of the barn."

Jace's father appears in the kitchen, and the younger Dawsons follow closely behind, making me think they were waiting in the hallway for any conflict between Jace and Mike to blow over.

The kitchen becomes a hub of activity as everyone helps themselves to the steaming pan of scrambled eggs and the warm blueberry muffins.

As we're all finishing up breakfast, I ask Mrs. Dawson what I can do to help around the farm today.

"That can wait until later. Jace, Vivienne wants to go for a ride. You two should take out a couple of the horses."

Jace looks over at me. "I'm not sure it's the best idea to subject a helpless horse to someone with your lack of coordination," he says solemnly.

I let out an indignant scoff. "I can't believe you're still bringing this up. I collided with you once—"

"Twice," Jace interjects.

"—And I don't care what other people on campus say," I add. "Your throws are not that great, especially the snaps or whatever they were called. I had no idea when it would come flying at my face or what the gibberish mea—"

I'm interrupted for a second time by the sound of giggles. I look over to see that Alden, Max, and Claire are all laughing, while Mike sports a wide grin. Jace's parents also wear amused expressions.

I blush. "I can handle it," I conclude lamely, embarrassed by my outburst.

"Jace taught you to play football?" one of the twins asks.

"Jace tried to teach me football," I reply. I can't tell if I'm talking to Max or Alden. "Tried being the operative word."

"It would have gone a lot better if you'd been a more engaged student," Jace remarks, finishing his eggs.

"Or if you hadn't tackled me when I finally caught the ball. Talk about negative reinforcement."

"I was trying to teach you how the game works and—" Jace begins, but is cut off by Mike.

"You *tackled* her?" he asks. "Smooth moves, big bro. Thought you could flirt better than that."

"Mike, shut it," Jace grits out. I notice his ears are red.

"He was smoother when the whole football team showed up," I tell Mike unhelpfully. "Just stood there while I got him out of trouble."

Jace groans.

"Are you two always like this?" the other twin asks, looking between Jace and me.

"It's usually worse," I reply.

"Much worse," Jace adds, grinning.

A half hour later, I stand in the barn aisle watching Jace saddle Firewood and Black Beauty. I watch in surprise as his fingers nimbly buckle all the leather straps.

"I had no idea you were some sort of expert horseman," I tell him, impressed.

Jace laughs. "Hardly. I've just had a lot of practice with the tack."

Noticing my puzzled expression, he elaborates. "Claire loves riding, but she can't get the horses ready by herself yet. I'm usually the one who gets them saddled for her."

"That's nice of you."

"I'm a nice guy."

I laugh. "I know you are. Sorry I got a little carried away at breakfast. I want your family to like me, not think I'm overly sensitive and argumentative."

"Are you kidding? They loved you already, and after breakfast, you're probably their new favorite person. Ordinarily, they're the only ones who give me shit. They all found it extremely entertaining, if you didn't notice."

Jace leads the two horses out of the barn. I follow, coming to a standstill next to the massive animals.

"Okay, put your foot in the stirrup here when I give you a boost," Jace instructs.

I nod, then am suddenly propelled off the ground into the saddle atop Black Beauty. I shift around in the firm leather as I try to get more comfortable. Jace hands me a pair of smooth reins to guide the horse's movement and then climbs onto Firewood.

"Squeeze your boots along her side."

I do as he instructs and lurch forward when the horse begins walking. Jace pulls up Firewood next to me. My horse seems content to keep pace with his, requiring little input from me.

"What do you think?" Jace asks, glancing over at me.

Now that I'm becoming accustomed to the rocking motion, I relax in the saddle and allow Black Beauty to amble along. "I like it," I answer, smiling.

We ride along in silence for a few minutes, and then Jace

speaks. "I'm sorry about how Mike acted earlier. He's a real brat when he wants to be."

"It's fine," I assure him. "I did crash your family's time together. I wouldn't be happy if a stranger showed up at my house."

"We've always butted heads. We're pretty similar, like you already pointed out. And Mike would never admit it, but I think it's also his way of protecting me. He visited campus last spring and saw some of the craziness first-hand. Now that I'm about to enter the draft, he knows it's about to get even worse."

"What do you mean, you're about to enter the draft?" I ask.

Jace looks over at me, his eyebrows raised. "College players are eligible for the draft after their junior year. This is my last year at Lincoln."

"But don't you want to finish college?"

Jace lets out a humorless laugh. "College *is* football for me. I'm at Lincoln on a full athletic scholarship. They're making millions off of the team that I'm leading. I miss half my classes for practices or meetings, and professors give me A's on assignments I never even knew about. College has always just been a way to get to the pros for me."

"But you won't be able to play football forever. Wouldn't it be worth it to stay just one more year and get your diploma? Take full advantage of what you can from the scholarship?"

Jace lets out a deep sigh and looks around the sprawling fields we're riding through. "I need the money," he confesses. "My parents are close to losing the farm. If Mike doesn't get a scholarship too, there's no way they'll be able to afford to send him to college."

I'm silent for a moment. "Jace, I'm so sorry," I tell him. "I had no idea."

"I know."

"Do your siblings know?" I ask tentatively.

"No," Jace replies. "Money's always been tight, and they know that, but my parents wouldn't even tell me how bad it was. I had to call the bank to finally find out how much they owe."

I glance over at his profile. His broad shoulders and strong jaw show no glimpse of the heavy burden he's carrying that includes his entire family's futures.

"I'm glad you told me. If there's anything I can do..." I let my voice trail off, feeling guilty about the millions sitting in my own bank accounts.

"No, it's nothing you should be concerned about," Jace replies. "Things will work out."

I nod, sensing he doesn't want to discuss the topic further. We reach the end of the cornstalks, and an unplanted field stretches before us.

"Ready for the fun part?" Jace asks. "Hold on!"

His horse surges forward, and mine follows. Clouds of dirt trail after us in the wind as the horses canter along across the smooth soil. We leave the heavy conversation behind us and fly across the packed earth.

Despite my initial apprehension, I relax into the leather saddle as I allow my body to move in time with the horse's rhythmic movements. I laugh in sheer bliss, feeling freer than I ever have before.

Jace eventually pulls Firewood back to a walk, but I continue to urge Black Beauty forward, guiding her around the open area in several wide circles before tugging on the reins to slow her back to a walk.

I push my windswept hair back and grin at Jace. "That was amazing!"

I spend the rest of the day trying to help out around the farm, with varying degrees of success. I burn the mushrooms Mrs. Dawson asks me to sauté and accidentally uproot several tomato seedlings while weeding in the greenhouse alongside Mr. Dawson. I apologize profusely for both mistakes, but Jace's parents take them in stride.

Mrs. Dawson simply smiles and hands me a new bag of mushrooms, while Mr. Dawson shows me the distinctive shape of the tomato leaf and tosses the ones I uprooted in the plastic bucket along with the weeds. After we finish the weeding, Mr. Dawson informs me he's headed out to one of the back fields to plow and asks if I'd like to come along. I agree and soon find myself perched on the side of the massive tractor as Mr. Dawson guides it along the dirt path.

"Jace said this farm has been in your family for a while?" I ask as we roll along.

"Sixty years," Mr. Dawson replies. "Fulton has a long history of family farms. Most everyone I grew up with has had land here for generations. Of course, half of them have had to sell parts or all of it to developers by now just to make ends meet. Farming's a tough business."

I nod, understanding the statement more than he knows after my conversation with Jace.

I've never given any thought to the intricacies of farming before. I gain a new appreciation for the back-breaking work over the next couple hours spent creating meticulous rows out of the freshly churned dirt.

Mr. Dawson and I chat as he drives the tractor back and forth. He explains more about the planting process and entertains me with stories about various harvesting mishaps they've had over the years.

Once the field is finished, we drive back toward the barn. Mr.

Dawson comes to a stop underneath an overhang that juts off the side of the looming red barn.

The front yard is bustling with activity. Mike is raking leaves, while one of the twins sits on the front steps removing green husks from a pile of corn cobs. I think it's Max, but I'm not certain. Claire stands in the center of the yard, scattering handfuls of grain from a bucket. The flock of chickens are clustered around her, scurrying from pile to pile as each new handful hits the ground.

Mr. Dawson climbs down from the tractor and offers me a hand to get down as well.

"Thanks for the trip."

"Anytime," he tells me, eyes twinkling.

I head toward the house and am greeted by the distracting sight of Jace chopping a log of firewood. Despite the chilly November air, he's stripped down to just a t-shirt. The muscles and tendons in his arms bulge and shift as he carefully splits each block of wood.

For the second time today, I'm dumbstruck by the mere sight of him. I hoped I was finally desensitized to messy dark hair and muscles. At the same time, I never want the moment when he glances up and catches me staring to end. A flash of heat over-whelms me as I meet his knowing gaze.

Jace winks.

I flush and turn away. I beeline toward the front porch, but slow when I reach the twin shucking corn. "Need any help?" I ask, studying him closely to try and determine which twin he is.

"Sure." He hands me a couple ears of corn that still have their husks. "I'm Max," he adds, grinning.

Clearly, I wasn't very subtle in my inspection. "That was going to be my guess," I tell him, smiling sheepishly.

"Of course it was." He sends me a cheeky grin that looks exactly like Jace's.

I take a seat on the step next to him and start shucking. "Jace said you're starting high school next year?" I haven't spoken to a thirteen-year-old boy since I was that age myself, so school seems like the safest topic.

"Yup," Max replies. I wait, but he doesn't elaborate further.

"Are you excited about starting high school?" I prompt.

"Yeah, I guess. I know other guys who are nervous about combining with Arlington." He glances over. "That's the next town. Kids there are richer, but we're the bigger town, so they come to us."

"Are you nervous?"

"Nah. Mike will still be there, and we're Dawsons. No one gives us a hard time once they know we're related to Jace." He gives me a side glance. "Is he a big deal at Lincoln, too? Mike said it was nuts when he visited."

"Yes," I reply honestly, setting the freshly shucked corn in the basket. "He's a big deal. Everyone on campus idolizes him."

"Do you?"

I cringe, realizing I set myself up for that question and unsure how to answer. I've avoided labeling and examining my feelings for Jace, knowing they'll eventually hit the barrier of my inevitable departure. "I admire him," I start slowly, realizing with surprise I genuinely mean the words. "But I wouldn't say I idolize him. To me, he's not a big football star, he's just Jace."

And I like that to him, I'm just Vivienne. By nature, I'm not deferential. Part of it is personality. Another piece is taught. Rulers and leaders aren't supposed to need guidance or reassurance. They're the people we look to for guidance and reassurance. But I've relied on—trusted—Jace more than I have anyone else, outside of my parents. He makes me feel stronger, not weaker.

"Are you his girlfriend?" Max asks.

Goodbye unsure, hello uncomfortable. I shift on the hard step, certain I'm blushing. "Uh…" I stall for time, not certain how to respond.

A slam sounds behind us, and I turn to see Alden rushing through the front door.

"Caroline dropped off the pumpkins at the farm stand," he informs us. "Mom told me I could take the cart." Alden turns to me. "Do you want to come, Vivienne?" His voice holds a hint of nervousness.

I'm tempted to leap up immediately, but instead I make a point to glance down at the basket piled high with freshly shucked corn as though I'm contemplating my answer. I don't want Max to think I'm avoiding answering his question, even though I absolutely am.

"Sure, it looks like the corn is all set," I reply cheerfully. "Thanks for letting me help, Max."

I follow Alden over to one of the small outbuildings scattered around the yard. He lifts the long wooden board that's holding the front doors in place, and they swing open, revealing what looks to be a green golf cart without the canopy overhead and with less seating. There are two seats in the front, but the back is just a cavernous opening similar to the bed of a truck.

"Climb in," Alden tells me, as he settles in the driver's seat.

I eye the small vehicle apprehensively, but walk inside the shed and climb onto the other seat. Alden turns the key and the engine sputters to life. He taps on the gas pedal, sending us lurching forward down the slight ramp and onto the grass.

We make rapid progress along the packed dirt driveway, but Alden slows as we turn off it and drive down a thin strip of grass situated between two fields that's just wide enough for the vehicle we're in.

A building slightly larger than the one we retrieved the cart from appears ahead. It's set about twenty feet back from an asphalt road, which I don't notice until a car breezes by. A small white sign hangs on the side of the building that reads *Dawson Farm*.

Alden turns off the cart and jumps out.

"Where are we?" I ask.

"Mom runs this farm stand during the summer when we've got fresh vegetables. People in Arlington will pay a ton for them, unlike the grain and corn we sell to the cattle farms. In the off months, we use it for storage, and people will drop stuff off here rather than driving all the way up to the house."

Alden disappears around the front of the stand and re-emerges a moment later, clutching a massive pumpkin. He sets it in the back of the cart and disappears again, returning with another, slightly smaller one seconds later.

"Wait until you try Mom's pumpkin pie," he adds as he loads the second pumpkin.

I try not to grimace.

"Do you want to drive back?" Alden asks, coming back around to the front of the vehicle.

"I've never driven anything like this before," I reply.

"Well, you've driven before, right?"

One joyride and some time on a closely supervised course is the extent of my driving experience, but I nod.

"Then you'll be fine. Here." Alden holds the keys out. I take them, and we switch seats.

The cart starts immediately when I turn the key in the ignition, and we sit there idling for a moment before I lightly tap on the gas pedal. We move a few inches.

"Come on, give it some gas!" Alden encourages.

I comply, pressing the pedal down with more force. The cart

surges ahead, and soon we're rapidly barreling down the grass path.

Suddenly, I see brown dirt ahead. I start to turn the wheel, then realize I'm driving too fast. I stomp on the brake, and we careen around the corner back onto the dirt driveway. The front wheel promptly slides off the side of the road into a shallow ditch.

"It's fine, I've done this before," Alden comforts me. "Just put it in reverse and get back on the driveway."

I don't move, so he leans down and fiddles with the gear stick.

"Okay, hit the gas now," he instructs.

That I know how to do, so I tap on the gas pedal once again. The engine snarls, and a spray of dirt appears on my left.

Rather than return to the road, we both feel the cart sink lower in place.

"It's fine," Alden says again. "I'll get my dad. He'll know what to do."

With that, he's off, running back up the driveway toward the house. I let out a resigned sigh and lean back against the seat, staring out at the sea of waving golden stalks in front of me.

"How did you even manage to do this?"

I turn to see Jace walking toward me, shaking his head in disbelief. I sigh. "No idea."

"It's a smooth, even, dry patch of dirt. You found some way to get stuck?"

I scoff in response. "I'm not exactly used to driving in these conditions."

"Open road, no other drivers, no rules of the road? Yeah, I can see how that could be a challenge."

"Are you going to help me or not?"

Jace grins. "My dad's bringing the tractor."

Sure enough, the massive tractor I spent a couple hours riding on earlier appears around the corner. Mr. Dawson is sitting in the seat, and Alden is perched next to him. The tractor stops a few feet away from us.

"Someone call for a tow?" Mr. Dawson asks, grinning.

"I'm so sorry," I tell him. "I honestly have no idea how this happened."

Mr. Dawson laughs. "Don't worry about it. Jace, you ready?"

Jace attaches a couple of chains from the back of the cart to the tractor. "All set."

The tractor begins to move again, this time taking the small cart with it. Once the cart's wheels are all back on the road, Mr. Dawson backs the tractor up slightly so Jace can undo the chains.

"See you two back at the house," he calls before he and Alden disappear from sight.

I slide over to the passenger side of the cart, and Jace gets in beside me. We sit there for a moment, and then he starts laughing. Loudly.

"What?" I ask, looking over at him. "Is this still about the cart?"

"It's about you. You always manage to do what I least expect."

"Is that a bad thing?"

"Not to me. For all the vehicles on this farm, maybe."

I can't help the small smile that forms in response before Jace drives us back to the house.

We all sit down to dinner a few hours later. Mrs. Dawson serves a large platter of roast chicken and vegetables along with a fresh green salad, and we dig in eagerly.

"Do you remember the Williams' oldest son?" she asks Jace as she joins the rest of us at the table.

"Yeah, Charlie, right?" Jace replies. "He was one year ahead of me."

"Yup," Mrs. Dawson confirms. "He's getting married this Saturday."

"Married?" Jace echoes in surprise. "Seriously?"

"Your mother and I were two years younger than that when we got married," Mr. Dawson says. "It worked out pretty well for us." He gives his wife a loving look, and I smile.

"I guess," Jace allows.

He and his siblings all make identical faces of disgust when Mrs. Dawson gives Mr. Dawson a kiss on the cheek.

"Mom, Dad, I'm eating here," Max complains.

"Anyway," Mrs. Dawson continues, ignoring her son. "We were invited to the wedding. I replied yes, but that was before I knew you would be home. I'm sure Susie will understand if I tell her we can't make it now."

Claire pouts in her seat next to me. "Then I won't be able to wear the new dress I got from Caroline!"

"We'll find another time for you to wear it," Mrs. Dawson replies.

Jace looks at me from his seat across the table. "Do you want to go?"

All of the Dawsons turn to look at me as well.

"Uh, well, unlike Claire, I don't have anything that I could wear to a wedding—"

"How is that even possible?" Jace interrupts. "You brought *two* suitcases of clothes!"

I roll my eyes at him. "You all should go, though." I smile at Claire. "I want to see your new dress."

"You don't have to worry about that, dear," Mrs. Dawson tells me. "We can certainly get you something to wear. The wedding will be casual. They're holding both the ceremony and reception at their farm."

Claire looks at me hopefully.

"Okay, then." I watch her face light up with glee. "I'm in."

"All right, then," Jace confirms, looking over at his mother.

Mrs. Dawson looks surprised, but doesn't comment further.

Dinner turns to a discussion of the Fulton High football game tomorrow, which Mike will be playing in. I had no idea the Thanksgiving football tradition extended past college, but I keep that to myself, knowing it'll likely set me up for ridicule from Jace about my lack of football knowledge.

I eat the delicious meal and listen to Jace and Mr. Dawson give Mike suggestions for plays to run and techniques to implement. He acts annoyed by their suggestions, but I notice he listens closely in a way that suggests he actually values their input.

After dinner, Jace, Mike, and I start a movie in the living room. I only make it through an hour before I say good night to them and head back to my cozy bedroom.

As soon as I've changed and gotten ready for bed, I pull out my phone to see Julie sent a message earlier, checking in. I quickly reply, saying I'm fine. I make certain my location settings are still showing me in Michigan, then promptly pass out on the soft mattress.

CHAPTER FOURTEEN

I emerge from my room on Thanksgiving morning, freshly showered and dressed, to find the Dawsons all standing in the front hallway next to the row of cubbies.

The only one missing is Mike, who left a couple hours ago to get ready for the game. The Dawsons are each sporting some variation of *Fulton Football* apparel. Mrs. Dawson is wearing a baseball cap, the twins are wearing faded jerseys, and Mr. Dawson, Claire, and Jace are all wearing sweatshirts.

"Guess I missed the Fulton pride memo," I joke, joining the group in what has become my daily uniform of jeans and a sweater. I should go put on Jace's t-shirt, although I'm not sure I want his family speculating over why I have it.

"Come on." Jace grabs my hand and pulls me up the stairs. "We'll meet you in the car," he says to his family over his shoulder.

I don't look back to see their reactions as we reach the top of the stairs and turn to the left. Jace opens a wooden door and we enter his childhood bedroom.

The room is not very large, and a four-poster bed takes up

most of the limited space. A wooden desk and dresser are pushed up against the wall opposite from the bed. A white shelf hanging above the furniture boasts a row of shiny trophies.

Jace walks over to his dresser and opens a drawer, while I study the two framed photos hanging on the wall next to the door-frame. One depicts a high school aged Jace standing with three other guys wearing football gear. The second is Jace, when he looks to be Claire's age. He's standing atop the same tractor I rode on yesterday. A younger Mr. Dawson stands next to him, laughing.

I smile at the sweet photo. "You were so cute," I tell Jace as he walks over to stand next to me. "What happened?" I ask, grinning.

Jace shakes his head. He's now holding a navy sweatshirt. He tugs the soft fabric down over my head and his scent surrounds me as I guide my arms through the sleeves and tug the oversized material down around my waist. It fits easily over my bulky sweater.

I glance down to see *Fulton Football* is printed across the front in white block letters.

"Now you look like a local."

I tug my hair out from underneath the hood and push the blonde locks to one side so I can adjust the bunched fabric. One stray piece falls back in my face, and Jace takes a step closer to brush it behind my ear.

His proximity inundates my senses, and I feel my heart race in response. I forget all about the sweatshirt as I glance up at him. His gray eyes probe mine as we stand inches apart.

Jace fingers one of the strings hanging from the hood of my new sweatshirt. Suddenly, he tugs it. Unprepared, I stumble forward and collide against his hard body.

"I thought you hate it when I run into you," I whisper.

"It's grown on me," Jace admits.

Then he kisses me; a heady, deep kiss that overwhelms every cell of my body. I melt against him and he wraps his arms around me, crushing the layers of soft material between us.

I convinced myself the explosive chemistry of our first kiss was simply an effect of the whiskey coursing through my veins at the time, but I experience the same dizzying rush as his mouth moves against mine.

Jace pulls away first. "Come on, we'll be late for the game."

He tugs my hand and I stumble, this time thanks to the stupor his touch seems to elicit. Jace grins at the dazed expression on my face as I follow him out of his room and back downstairs.

The rest of Jace's family has already piled inside the silver SUV. Jace and I slide into the middle row of the car next to Claire. The twins are seated behind us in the very back.

Mrs. Dawson looks back from her spot in the front passenger seat and winks when she takes in my new top. Mr. Dawson drives down the long dirt driveway and out onto the asphalt road. I look out the window, seeing Jace's hometown for the first time. We pass a series of dirt driveways identical to the one we've just left, interspersed between fields full of corn and waving stalks of grain.

Gradually, the farmlands give way to development, with new subdivisions lining either side of the road. We pass a general store, post office, and library before Mr. Dawson pulls into an expansive parking lot just past a sign that reads *Fulton High School*.

Unlike everywhere else we've just driven past, the parking lot is full of cars and people. Mr. Dawson has to take several laps around the bustling lot before finally finding a space to park in.

If I hadn't actually experienced it firsthand, I would think walking with the Dawsons through the crowded high school parking lot was what it was like to be seen with royalty.

As soon as we all exit the car, we're swarmed by everyone in the immediate vicinity.

Once we emerge through that group, we continue to be stopped every few feet by another person. The Dawsons know everyone who approaches them by name, chatting about kids, pets, and Thanksgiving plans with an easy feeling of familiarity.

Jace fields the most questions, continuously being asked about his current season and future plans. He's still holding my hand and continues to grip it tightly as we slowly make our way across the parking lot. Each person we encounter is clearly invested in his future, and beams with pride as he answers their football questions.

We finally manage to finish crossing the parking lot, and the football field stands before us. It's the same size as Lincoln's but seems smaller without a massive stadium surrounding it. Instead of soaring rows of seats, metal bleachers line the field. To my surprise, they're already mostly filled with spectators, despite the large crowd still in the parking lot.

"I'm surprised they haven't named the town after your family yet," I whisper to Jace once we're clear of the last well-wisher.

"They tried. There's already a Dawson, Nebraska," he replies. I glance at him in surprise, and he laughs. "I'm kidding."

Progress is slow up the steps of the metal bleachers as the Dawsons encounter more friends and neighbors. By the time we've taken our seats, the players are already out on the field, signaling the game is about to begin.

Before it does, a tall guy with shaggy hair jogs up the metal steps toward the row where we're sitting. I recognize him from the photo I saw in Jace's room. As soon as he spots the guy, Jace stands, and they clap each other on the back in greeting.

"Dawson!" the guy exclaims. His friendly, easy-going manner reminds me of Anderson. "Had no idea you're in town."

"It was a last-minute trip," Jace explains. "Other team got the flu, so our coach gave us a few days off."

"I'm so glad you're back. Man, you should hear Morgan griping about you," the guy tells Jace. "Carrie and Melissa were talking about you, and that really set him off."

"Ask him if he's been moved up to second string yet," Jace suggests, and both guys laugh loudly.

"Did you hear about the Williams wedding? Should be like a mini-reunion with you in town."

"Yeah, I'll be there," Jace replies.

"Awesome. Mike better kick some ass with the whole family here to watch."

The guy's eyes leave Jace for the first time to skim over the Dawson family, finally coming to rest on me. They widen in surprise, and he glances at Jace. "Long-lost cousin?" he asks.

"You've met all my cousins," Jace responds. "Vivienne, this is one of my best friends, Sam Evans. Sam, this is Vivienne."

Sam holds out a calloused hand. "It's really nice to meet you, Vivienne." He smiles warmly as we shake hands. His face shifts to a mischievous smirk. "You should know, many a girl has tried and failed to be sitting where you are. You must have an endless source of patience to be willing to put up with this guy's bullshit." He winks at me.

"Now I remember why I didn't tell you I was back in town," Jace tells Sam, punching his shoulder lightly.

"Yeah, yeah," Sam replies. "I guess I'll leave without sharing the story of how you got nominated for Homecoming King freshman year in just a towel for the sake of our friendship."

"Great idea," Jace affirms.

"I'd love to hear that one at the wedding though, Sam," I

chime in with.

Sam sends me another smile before he bounds back down the stairs after greeting the rest of the Dawsons.

The game begins right after Sam's departure. Jace murmurs explanations of everything that's happening throughout the game, correctly assuming I won't know what's going on otherwise.

However, his attempt to help me follow the action actually has the opposite effect. I'm so distracted by his proximity that I have absolutely no idea what is happening in the game. The frequent celebrations around me suggest Fulton is winning, which is confirmed each time I glance at the scoreboard. The higher the number, the better is a concept I understand.

The game ends as a blowout. We flock back into the parking lot amidst a crowd of celebration. Everyone seems eager to get home to eat with their families, so there's much less socializing as we walk back toward the car.

When we arrive back at the Dawsons' house, it's filled with the mouth-watering aroma of roasting turkey. Everyone returns to their rooms to change. I put on a black sweater dress before heading back out into the kitchen.

Mike's friend Jason arrives shortly thereafter, along with his parents. His father is a quiet, soft-spoken man, but his mother bustles into the kitchen and introduces herself as Caroline.

As we sit in the kitchen making the final food preparations, Caroline and Ellen regale me with stories from their teenage years growing up in Fulton. Their tales of field parties and school dances sound like a different world than the isolated one I grew up in.

"So, Vivienne, you were at school in London before starting at Lincoln?" Caroline asks. No one in Jace's family has questioned me about my background, so I assumed he already told them, but Caroline's question confirms it.

I feel bad lying to her, but also recognize my cover story is the only reason I'm currently sitting in the Dawson's kitchen. I experience an extra stab of guilt thinking of how I'm lying to my security team. The least I can do is ensure there's no reason they will need to fly to Nebraska, so I quickly summarize my concocted background for Caroline. Thankfully, she doesn't press for details about my family, instead informing me she studied abroad in London during college and then peppering me with questions about the city. The questions are all ones I have prepared answers to.

Caroline and Mrs. Dawson finish getting dinner ready with my limited input, and then Caroline heads outside to grab a cranberry sauce she brought. Mrs. Dawson finishes transferring the potatoes from the pan to a dish and comes over to stand next to me at the kitchen island.

"I'm sorry about Caroline," she tells me. "Jace mentioned you don't like talking about your background or family very much. I should have thought to say something to her, so she didn't inundate you with so many questions."

"Jace is perceptive," I reply with a wry smile. "But don't worry about it. I know Caroline didn't mean any harm. My parents and I just have a...complicated relationship."

"Families can be tricky. My parents didn't speak to me for two years after I told them I wasn't going to college and was staying here in Fulton with Patrick. They gave up a lot to provide me with the opportunity and didn't understand how I could throw it away. But eventually they accepted my decision, and one day your parents will understand your view of things, too. Don't tell my kids, but we parents don't always know what we're doing. We're just doing our best."

I nod, giving her a grateful smile.

"And know I'm always here to talk if you want to," Ellen adds.

To my surprise and embarrassment, I feel tears prickling beneath my eyelids. I pull Mrs. Dawson into a hug. I'm not normally overly emotional or affectionate, but something about her maternal words elicits the urge in me.

She hugs me back tightly, and we don't break apart until the sound of footsteps indicate someone has come into the kitchen. I look up, expecting to see Caroline, but instead meet Jace's puzzled gaze.

"Everything okay in here?" he asks, glancing back and forth between his mother and me.

"Everything's fine," Ellen replies. "Tell you father the turkey's done, so he should come in here to carve it."

Jace looks to me again. I give him a quick smile to let him know I'm okay.

Caroline returns to the kitchen at the same time Patrick enters to carve the turkey. Suddenly, the kitchen is bustling with activity as the final dinner preparations are made and we all sit down at the long table to eat.

The room is filled with the chatter of lively conversations and a delicious blend of aromas as we all dig into the feast spread before us. I end up sitting between Jace and Caroline.

Jace is pulled into a recap of the football game with Mike and Jason, and I continue chatting with Caroline about London and my classes at Lincoln.

Dinner passes quickly, and then Mrs. Dawson carries over a few browned pies fresh from the oven.

"We aren't having pumpkin pie this year?" Alden asks in confusion as pecan pies appear in front of us.

"Not for Thanksgiving. I have something else in mind for those two big ones these guys brought us."

"They were obscenely large this year," Caroline admits, laughing.

I lean toward Jace. "Did something happen to the pumpkins?" I whisper.

"You mean after their traumatic trip here?"

"Yes!"

Jace smiles at my distressed tone. "No, they're fine."

"Vivienne, do you want some?" Alden asks. I look over to see he's holding out a small white plate with a generous slice of perfectly browned pie.

"Sure, thanks," I reply, taking the plate of offered dessert.

Despite my full stomach, I sink my fork through the layer of hardened nuts and into the flaky crust. The nutty, sweet flavor explodes on my tongue as I sample the first bite.

As we eat dessert, the group conversation shifts to Jace's draft prospects. Caroline's husband joins the discussion for the first time.

"I talked to a couple of old college buddies last week," he shares. "They both think Jace'll go first round for sure. Of course, I've been saying that ever since he started playing. His group would always play before Jason's, and even then I would tell Caroline he had something special."

"Hear that, Jace?" Jason asks. "Better make my dad your publicist!"

Everyone laughs good-naturedly.

Later that night, Jace and I stand in the kitchen, putting dishes away after everyone's dispersed.

"Thank you for bringing me here," I tell Jace as we stack the clean plates back in the cupboard.

He looks over at me. "Thanks for coming."

We work in silence for a few more minutes.

"Does it ever bother you? How people here are always talking about you making it to the pros?" I wonder, thinking of the many times the topic has come up just over the course of the day.

"I've gotten used to it. But hearing it over and over again does get old."

"I thought you hadn't been home in a while?"

"I hadn't, but it's no different at school. My teammates, coaches, random people on campus? They all bring it up in some form. But next spring I'll either get drafted or I won't. The number of people who bring it up to me won't change that."

We're both silent again.

"Max asked if we're dating." I blurt. I don't look over at Jace, instead focusing on sliding the plates into place. "Actually, first he asked if I idolized you, and *then* he asked if I'm your girlfriend."

Jace lets out a wry chuckle. "He didn't bother with any small talk, huh?"

"We were pulling the green stuff off the corn," I inform him. "So it was actually the perfect time for a serious discussion."

"Sure it was." Jace smiles. "So, what did you tell him?"

"That I have a shrine to you in my dorm room."

He smirks. "I know that's not true."

"I told him the truth. That I don't idolize you, but I admire you."

Jace looks at me with surprise. "You do?"

"Yeah, I do. That surprises you?"

"I haven't exactly gotten the sense it's admiration you're experiencing when we've discussed football."

"Who said I'm talking about football?" I counter. "But since you brought it up, I may know barely anything about the sport, but even I can tell you're good. Really good. But you don't just take it for granted, you work hard at it, too. You go for extra runs. You help out your teammates. That's admirable."

"My extra runs don't have much to do with football these days," Jace admits. He takes a step closer, effectively caging me against the countertop. "So…what do you admire about me, aside from football?" His voice is husky and his stare is intense.

I consider making a joke about his looks, but something in his earnest expression keeps me from doing so. I open my mouth to speak, still uncertain of what I should say. The list of things I admire about Jace Dawson is long—longer than I realized until he asked.

The prospect of admitting that to him is both exciting and terrifying.

"Okay, Claire finally—" Mrs. Dawson walks into the kitchen, and abruptly stops speaking when she sees Jace and I standing inches apart in the corner of the kitchen.

I startle at the unexpected interruption, not having heard her come downstairs.

"—Oh, sorry," she finishes. "I'll give you two a minute."

"No, it's fine," I reply, suddenly grateful for the intrusion. "I was just telling Jace I'm headed to bed. Thank you for dinner tonight, Ellen. Everything was delicious."

Mrs. Dawson smiles warmly. "I'm glad you liked it. Don't forget we're going shopping tomorrow morning for the wedding."

"I won't. I'm looking forward to it," I promise her.

I risk a glance at Jace to find he's studying me closely.

"Good night, Jace." My words are heavy, bogged down by all the others I decided not to say.

"Night, Viv," he replies.

I leave the kitchen quickly and am in bed within minutes, but it's hours before I'm able to actually fall asleep.

CHAPTER FIFTEEN

We spend Friday afternoon wandering along the two blocks that comprise the downtown section of Fulton, Nebraska. I thought shopping options in Lincoln were limited, but they were copious in comparison to here.

Despite the lackluster choices, I'm enjoying myself more than I expected to. As we browse through the small selection, I realize I've never been on a shopping trip with my own mother. The thought sends a pang of sadness through me. I push the unpleasant realization to the back of my mind, determined to enjoy this outing.

Claire insists on trying on every piece of clothing she takes a fancy to, which makes for slow progress through the first store. The second shop is even smaller than the first and also has a limited amount of apparel more conducive for farming than a wedding. In the last store we enter, I immediately spot a long rack of velvet dresses.

I walk over to the display and start flipping through the options. Halfway through, I come across a deep scarlet dress. It has full length bell sleeves gathered at the wrists and a long row of velvet buttons up the front of the bodice. I grab my size and hold it up against myself. It flows to just above my knees.

I turn and hold out the dress. "Ellen? Claire? What do you think?"

They both come over from a display of hats to where I'm standing. Claire strokes the soft material gently.

"That dress will look beautiful on you," Jace's mother compliments. "And it'll be perfect for the wedding."

"Mrs. Dawson?" a voice says behind us.

The three of us turn to see a girl with wavy blonde hair.

"Gretchen!" Mrs. Dawson exclaims. "How are you, dear?" She steps forward and gives the girl a brief hug.

"I'm good, just picking up a few extra hours while I'm home for break."

Gretchen smiles at Claire and then glances at me. Her eyes widen.

"An unfamiliar face in Fulton?" she asks. "Don't think that's happened to me since middle school." Her voice is friendly, but somewhere underneath lurks a slight edge.

Mrs. Dawson laughs lightly. "Vivienne, this is Gretchen Williams. We've known her family for years. I went to school with her mother, and she and Jace were the same year as well."

I smile. "It's nice to meet you, Gretchen." I don't miss the way her eyes look over me appraisingly.

She's clearly curious why I'm here, but too polite to ask. "You, too," Gretchen returns the smile. "Speaking of Jace, how's he doing?" she asks, looking at Ellen. Her voice has a new, eager tone to it. "I saw Lincoln's Thanksgiving game was postponed. Too bad he wasn't able to get home."

"Oh, he's home," Mrs. Dawson replies. "He and Vivienne arrived late Tuesday night."

Gretchen's eyes flash to me following this revelation. "You're friends with Jace?"

A surge of possessiveness shoots through me, but I quickly tamp it down. "Yes, I am."

Gretchen looks as though she wants to press the subject further, but doesn't. "Can I help you all find anything?" she asks instead.

"Nope, we've found all we need." Mrs. Dawson snags the dress out of my grasp and begins walking over to the cash register. "We'll take this, please."

"Ellen!" I exclaim, rushing after her. "I can't let you do that. Let me pay for the dress, please."

"Nonsense," she replies. "You're our guest, and we're the ones who invited you to the wedding."

"You really don't need to do that." I feel terrible as I watch Ellen hand over her card, reflecting on what Jace confided in me about his family's financial situation.

"I want to." Ellen smiles and hands me the bag with the dress after Gretchen rings it up.

"You're all going to Charlie's wedding tomorrow?" Gretchen asks.

"We'll be there," Ellen confirms. Turning to me, she adds, "Gretchen's cousin Charlie is the groom." She looks back to Gretchen. "Is the family all excited?"

"They're all over the moon," Gretchen replies. "We haven't had a family wedding in a decade."

"We're looking forward to it, too," Ellen replies. "See you tomorrow!" After exchanging goodbyes, the three of us head out of the store.

Our shopping trip is the main topic of discussion at dinner.

"Wait until you guys see Vivienne's dress," Claire informs everyone as we're eating the pasta Ellen made. "It's *so* pretty!"

She beams over at me and I smile back, touched by her excitement. Jace grins at me, and I wink.

"Gretchen was working at Larson's," Mrs. Dawson adds. "She said they're all looking forward to tomorrow, and she was excited to hear you're back for break, Jace."

I don't know if Ellen is bringing Gretchen up intentionally or not, but I'm grateful for the chance to scrutinize Jace's expression when she does. He doesn't react to the name. His response is a noncommittal "Great" that doesn't provide me with any insight.

As we're finishing up dinner, Claire disappears and then reappears clutching a stack of board game boxes so high she can barely see over the top.

"It's game night!" she exclaims.

"No Scrabble this Friday," Mike tells her. "You just made up words last week."

"It's called being smart, Mike," Claire retorts, and I smile at her sassy response along with the rest of the Dawsons.

"Let's play Monopoly," Jace suggests.

"No way, you always win," Alden complains.

Jace sends me a triumphant look. I roll my eyes in response.

Eventually, everyone agrees on charades.

"Girls versus boys," Claire declares. "I want Mom and Viv on my team."

It's the first time any of Jace's family members have used his nickname for me, and the sound of it in Claire's innocent voice fills me with a cozy warmth.

We each huddle in our respective groups to scribble the most challenging books, movies, television shows, and songs we can think of. I'm grateful for Richard's relentless preparation as names I studied in the binder on American culture get tossed around. My first trip to the front of the room goes smoothly, but the second slip of paper I draw contains the word cow.

It takes five minutes of silent imitation for Claire to finally guess it. The Dawson boys spend every second of them laughing uproariously. Soon after that, the game entirely dissolves into banter and jokes. Mrs. Dawson intercedes, instructing everyone to get to bed when she realizes how late it has gotten.

"I think you missed your calling in the theater, Viv," Jace teases as he heads for the stairs.

"Take notes. Your swimming impression looked like a spastic octopus," I retort.

"Funny. I thought the same when you were dancing in the car."

I stick out my tongue at him, and Jace winks in response.

Mike walks past me over to the stairs. "I am seriously going to miss this entertainment," he says, chuckling as he gestures between me and Jace.

Saturday morning, I wake up feeling melancholy. This is my last full day in Nebraska, something I never expected to feel so sad about. I employ my usual strategy to escape emotions I don't feel like facing; I roll out of bed and pull on my running clothes.

I can hear Ellen in the kitchen when I pass it, but I bypass the room and head straight outside, transitioning into a brisk pace as soon as my sneakers touch the grass.

The air is cool, but the sun is warm on my face as I pass the parked cars. I survey the farm fondly as I run past the barn and head down the long dirt driveway. I reach the end of the packed dirt and stand there for a moment, surveying the swaying stalks filling the fields that surround me. Finally, I turn around.

I enter the warm house just as Claire comes down the stairs dressed in a fluffy robe and slippers.

"Hi, Vivienne," she greets me happily.

"Morning, Claire," I respond, smiling as I watch her skip into the kitchen. I follow her to find everyone else gathered in the room, helping themselves to eggs and coffee.

After breakfast, Jace and I go for another horseback ride. When we return to the house, everyone is running around getting ready for the wedding. I take a quick shower and slip into my new red dress. I pad barefoot to the bathroom to dry and style my hair, and also add a light layer of makeup before returning to my room to put on a pair of black tights. I look through the bag of shoes I brought, grateful for the variety I packed despite Jace's teasing. Finally, I decide on a pair of black suede heels.

"Viv, are you almost ready?" Claire asks from outside the door.

"I'm ready," I reply. "I'll be right out."

"Okay, Mike is still getting dressed, but the rest of us are ready."

I glance in the full-length mirror on the back of the door, pleased with the results. I grab my long black wool jacket and step out into the hallway. My heels rap against the wooden floorboards as I emerge in the front hallway.

Like a magnet, my gaze is drawn to Jace. He's leaning casually against one of the beams that marks the opening between the entryway and living room with his hands tucked into the pockets of his black dress pants. The matching blazer is unbuttoned, revealing the blue dress shirt he's wearing underneath. His eyes meet mine, and I'm seared by the heat in his gray gaze.

"Oh, that dress is perfect on you, Vivienne!" Ellen exclaims, looking me over. "I'm so glad we found it."

"Me, too," I reply, dropping Jace's gaze to look over at her. "Thank you again, Ellen."

"Of course, dear." She smiles warmly.

I glance over at Claire, who's standing on the last stair bouncing eagerly. "I love your dress, Claire."

She beams in response to my compliment, tugging on her own velvet dress. It's a brilliant shade of dark blue that hangs just past her knees, revealing a few inches of the white tights she's wearing underneath. A thundering sound draws my attention to the top of the stairs, where Mike has appeared. He's dressed identically to Jace, except his dress shirt is white rather than blue.

"Okay, I'm ready." Mike comes to a stop next to Claire at the bottom of the stairs.

Everyone else grabs their jackets as I button mine up.

"You look beautiful." Jace appears at my side as he shrugs into his coat. I glance up to see him smiling softly down at me.

"Thanks," I reply quietly, feeling uncharacteristically shy.

His smile turns sly. "I was kind of hoping you'd break out that outfit from the football party again."

I raise my eyebrows. "I didn't realize you even noticed what I was wearing that night, let alone had any particular feelings about it."

"Every guy at that party noticed what you were wearing, Vivienne."

"Well, I didn't wear it for every guy at the party," I admit, holding his gaze. He opens his mouth, but I answer his question before he has a chance to ask it. "I took your efforts to keep me from attending to mean you would be there."

"Vivienne! Jace! You guys coming?" Mike's voice interrupts our conversation.

I turn to see everyone else is already headed toward the car. Jace and I follow. The air has warmed since my run earlier, the temperature hovering in the high forties now that the sun is at full blast.

Mike, Jace, and I squeeze across the middle seat. Once

everyone is situated, Mr. Dawson begins to drive down the driveway. He turns the opposite way from how we drove to the high school.

About ten minutes later, he turns up a long driveway marked by a black sign that has *Williams Farm* written on it in white letters. Three gold balloons are tied to the wooden signpost. We drive up a dirt driveway that is identical to the Dawsons', aside from the fact it is much more uneven.

As we bounce along, Jace tells me, "Imagine the damage you could do to the cart on a road like this."

"Shut up, Jace," I groan, although I'm grinning along with everyone else.

Mr. Dawson pulls the SUV off into a large dirt field already filled with parked cars. I open my door and eye the soft earth below skeptically.

"What's wrong?" Jace asks as I hesitate.

"Nothing. I just didn't think the heels through." I admit, laughing to try and cover my embarrassment.

Jace doesn't say anything in response, he just climbs out past me. Rather than turning around, he stands there with his back to me.

"What are you doing?" I ask. "I was already going to have trouble getting out. There was no need to complicate things further."

Jace snorts. "Get on, Viv."

I scoot forward and place a hand on one of his broad shoulders. I move to wrap my leg around his waist, but the fabric of my skirt stops me. Groaning, I shimmy it up until the material nearly reaches my upper thigh.

"Any day now," Jace tells me, his voice amused.

"I had to make some outfit adjustments," I inform him, finally climbing onto his back.

"What kind of outfit…" Jace stops speaking when his hands encounter my tight-clad thighs rather than velvet material.

Sizzles of electricity skitter through me as the heat from his hands burns through the thin material. Jace starts walking across the field. I'm grateful for the length of my coat, which conceals both his intimate touch and my mostly exposed legs.

We attract a fair amount of attention from other wedding guests as Jace's long strides eat up the spongy ground, and I'm unsure if they're staring because it's Jace or because they're surprised to see one wedding guest carrying another.

We reach the brick path that leads to the large barn, where the rest of the Dawsons are standing, watching Jace and me with expressions of amusement. Jace slides me down his back gently, and I quickly tug my dress down under my coat.

"Had no idea you were such a gentleman, big bro," Mike teases as we all start walking up the path. Jace opens his mouth to reply, but Mrs. Dawson beats him to it.

"You could learn a thing or two from your older brother, Michael."

Jace grins while Mike rolls his eyes. We reach the small side door of the massive barn. It's propped open, and I look around in awe when we step inside.

Rather than the assorted farm equipment and tools that fill the Dawsons' barn, the interior of this building doesn't offer any glimpse that we're on a working farm.

The walls have been cleared of any dust or cobwebs and the wide wooden planks that comprise the floor gleam as though they've been freshly scrubbed. Twinkling lights are wrapped around the beams. Dozens of round tables pepper the central space, each displaying a carefully arranged assortment of bitter-sweet. Long tables line the walls of the room, holding empty serving dishes, glasses, plates, utensils, and bottles of champagne.

A raised stage is set up with instruments and microphones for a band and an empty stretch of floor in front of it is clearly meant to be a dance floor.

The massive doors at the opposite end of the barn are pushed open, revealing an expanse of grass spotted with neat rows of straw bales that have brightly colored woolen blankets spread across them.

Before the rows, a minister stands under an elaborately carved wooden trellis talking to a man in a suit who I surmise must be the groom. A woman stands to their right, holding a violin.

"Need another lift?" Jace whispers to me as we emerge from the barn out onto the grass.

"I think I can make it," I reply, smiling.

Jace takes my hand. "Just in case."

Most of the bales are already full, but there are several sitting empty, about halfway back on the right side. Jace's parents head in that direction, and the rest of us follow.

The violinist begins playing, and most of the chatter ceases as guests fall silent to listen. It seems as though everyone we pass waves at the Dawsons.

I'm seated at the end of an aisle between Jace and Mike. The blankets make the bales surprisingly comfortable. I slip off my heels as soon as we're seated to give my pinched toes a break, something I'd never be able to do at an official engagement back home.

As soon as we've settled in our seats, the violin music changes to traditional refrain. Everyone stands and turns to watch a smiling girl wearing a lace dress walk down the central aisle on the arm of a beaming middle-aged man. He escorts her to the trellis, where she takes the hand of the man already standing there.

Everyone takes their seats as the minister begins speaking. As he talks, Jace begins tracing small circles on the palm of my hand, eliciting the exhilarating mix of ease and excitement I only feel around him.

Goosebumps cover my skin, although I'm plenty warm under my wool coat in the late afternoon sun. I lose track of what the minister is saying as I bask in the exquisite sensation.

The applause that erupts from the crowd of wedding guests alerts me to the end of the ceremony, as the bride and groom kiss under the trellis. Jace pulls his hand away as we stand and clap with the rest of the attendees while the newly married couple walks down the central aisle toward the barn.

Once they disappear inside, all the guests begin to gather up their belongings and gravitate back inside the large barn after the newlyweds. The sound of cheery voices fills the air once again.

It takes a while for us to navigate through the crowd back into the barn. The building is now filled with throngs of people milling about. I shrug off my long coat as soon as we're inside. I'm not sure if there are heaters installed or it's simply the proximity of so many other people, but the temperature inside the barn is much warmer than I expected it to be.

I hear "Jace!" called to my left and turn to see Jace's friend from the football game, Sam Evans, walking toward us. The girl from the dress store, Gretchen, follows him over to where Jace and I are standing.

"Hey, Sam," Jace replies, grinning.

"Hi, Vivienne," Sam greets as he reaches us.

"Hey, Sam," I respond. "How's it going?"

"Not too shabby."

Gretchen comes up behind Sam, her gaze fixed on Jace. The same surge of possessiveness I experienced in the store suddenly resurfaces.

"Hey, Jace," she greets quietly. Her voice is breathy. She moves to give him a hug, and Jace reciprocates.

"Hi, Gretchen, how are you?" Jace's tone is casual.

"Great! Everything turned out well, didn't it?" She gestures around at the decorated barn.

"It all looks beautiful," I compliment, jumping into the conversation. "Nice to see you again, Gretchen."

She looks over at me for the first time. "You too," she replies, giving me what looks to be a forced smile. She eyes my outfit. "That dress looks really nice on you," she offers, begrudgingly.

"Thank you."

"Gretchen and I were just heading to get some drinks." Sam breaks the brief silence that's descended over our foursome. "Can we get you guys anything?"

I open my mouth to reply, but Gretchen jumps in first. "Jace, you can help me, right? We can give Sam and Vivienne a chance to get to know each other better."

I eye her innocent expression cynically, fairly certain she has a different motivation for changing her escort to the bar. I don't make any objection, though. Jace looks to me, and we have a silent conversation where he raises his brows questioningly, and I nod in assent. I'm surprised to realize we can communicate wordlessly.

"Whiskey?" he asks me.

I nod, and he and Gretchen walk off toward the bar set up alongside the makeshift stage. She's beaming.

"That was nice of you," Sam comments, drawing my attention away from their retreating figures.

"Huh?"

"Gretchen's had a thing for Jace since we were kids. She's spent years waiting for him to wake up and decide they're soul mates. It made more sense when we were younger. We all grew up together, our parents are all friends. I was hoping she'd get over it at college, but…" He lets his voice trail off, and glances over at me. "It's good for her to see you two together. I think part of it was that Jace never looked twice at any girl. But finding out he brought you home, brought you to his brother's game, was bringing you to this wedding, it's been a much-needed wake-up call for her. It's obvious Jace is crazy about you."

I shift uncomfortably in response to his last sentence. "Does Jace know? How she feels about him?"

"I think he had an idea in high school. I'm guessing he thinks —or hopes—that she's over it now."

"So she's never said anything to him?"

"Not that he's told me. I only know because I found her crying at Homecoming our junior year after Jace went off with— uh…" He glances awkwardly at me.

I laugh. "Don't worry, I'm well aware of Jace's effect on girls. And that he's taken advantage of it."

"Does it bother you?"

"It'd be a bit hypocritical of me. It's not like I don't see the appeal." I wink at Sam, and he laughs.

"Was that the same Homecoming Jace was nominated in a towel?" I ask, recalling our previous conversation at the football game.

Sam grins. "Ah, no that was—"

"It seems like we've returned just in time."

I turn away from Sam to see Jace and Gretchen have returned, each clutching two drinks. Jace hands me a glass of whiskey, and I take a sip of the smoky alcohol.

"If you don't let him tell me what happened, I'm just going to imagine it's worse than it really is," I inform Jace.

"Oh, that's not possible," Sam interjects.

We both laugh, and Jace shakes his head.

"Gretchen's got the inside scoop on everything, and apparently dinner's about to be served. We'd better get to our seats," he tells me.

"Are you trying to tempt me with food to stop me from finding out embarrassing stories about you?" I inquire.

"Is it working?" Jace counters, smirking.

"Yes." I sigh. "Let's go. Sam, find me later!"

I grin at him and give Gretchen a small smile, unsure of how to act around her now that I know the truth about her feelings toward Jace. She smiles back, but it's clearly forced.

I follow Jace over to the table where the rest of his family is already seated. Each round table is surrounded with eight chairs, so there are two seats open for us.

We take our spots just as the servers move through the room, setting plates of mushroom ravioli and green salad in front of everyone.

While everyone is eating, various family members and close friends get up to offer well wishes to the newlywed couple.

After the speeches end, the violinist from the ceremony climbs up onto the raised stage with two men, one who is clutching a guitar, and the other a cello. They all begin playing in perfect synchrony as the bride and groom wander out onto the dance floor. They waltz in circles under the shimmering lights in time with the sweeping, slow music. As the final notes of the first song fade away, everyone applauds.

"Let us know if you have any requests!" the violinist offers, the microphone echoing her voice around the large building. "If we know it, we'll play it!"

She steps back, and the band starts playing again, an upbeat number that causes a couple dozen guests to stand and head to the dance floor.

"Vivienne, what do you say?" Mr. Dawson asks from across the table. His eyes twinkle as he nods toward the dance floor.

"Sure, I'd love to," I reply, standing. We head toward the dance floor. Mr. Dawson takes my hands, showing me the proper steps as he twirls me around. I'm quickly breathless from laughter as I try and fail to follow the intricate moves.

"Jace is going to have a field day with this," I tell Mr. Dawson as I fudge another spin.

He laughs. "I've never seen Jace so happy. I'm so glad he brought you home to meet us."

"Thank you, that means a lot," I reply sincerely, although his words prompt an uncomfortable twinge. "I've loved spending time with you all."

The song comes to an end. We stop and applaud with everyone else.

"I'm going to head to the restroom," I tell Mr. Dawson. "I'll see you back at the table."

There's no line for the bathroom, so I quickly slip in and lean my forehead against the door once I've locked it. Jace's father's words have caused the gloom I woke up with to resurface. I know that I will never see any of his family again after Jace and I leave tomorrow, and that bothers me a lot more than I expected it to. A lot more than I can afford it to.

Someone knocks on the door, breaking me out of my depressing thoughts. I quickly use the restroom and force the worries out of my mind. I head back into the main area of the barn and immediately run into Gretchen. She's standing with two other girls next to the buffet.

"Hi, Vivienne." Gretchen greets me reluctantly. It's clear she's no more eager to interact with me than I am with her.

"Hey, Gretchen," I respond.

"I'm Carrie," one of the girls interjects.

"And I'm Melissa," the other adds.

Neither of them mention Jace, instead asking about how I like

Lincoln and where I went to high school. I give them my prepared answers and then finally make up an excuse to leave after a few minutes. I glance back behind me on my way back to the table to see Melissa and Carrie have gathered around Gretchen. The three of them are speaking intently, leaving me with the uncomfortable inclination she asked them to find out more about me.

I reach the table to find Jace is the only one still sitting at it. He's typing something on his phone, and looks up when I approach.

"I saw you socializing," he tells me when I reach the table.

"It felt more like an interrogation." I laugh lightly as I sit down. Jace's eyebrows rise. "It's fine," I quickly add.

"You sure?"

I nod.

"Do you want some champagne?" Jace asks, nodding to the glasses sitting on the table. "They just brought these."

"No thanks, I'm not a fan of anything carbonated," I reply.

"Really?"

"It tickles my throat."

Jace laughs.

A familiar melody begins to play. I glance over at the band in surprise, then at Jace's grinning face.

"Did you do this?" I ask, shocked.

Other emotions threaten to overwhelm me, but I beat them back as I focus on the beginning strains of my favorite song reverberating throughout the barn.

"Maybe," Jace replies. "Dance with me?" He stands and holds out a hand. I take it, and we wind our way among the assortment of tables and out onto the dance floor.

Jace pulls me tightly against his body, and I collapse against him, resting my head in my favorite crevice just above his shoulder.

We sway slowly as I observe the other laughing couples on the dance floor, framed by the weathered wooden beams and twinkling lights above us. I can't help but smile contentedly at the serene image.

I've never given much thought to what my own wedding will be like, even since learning of its impending date due to my father's diagnosis and the antiquated marriage law.

It still feels like a distant event; not to mention one that will no doubt be micro-managed by my mother and her team of event planners to the point where I'll hardly have any input in the day at all. The only aspect of the day I know I'll have some say in will be the groom. My mother has strong feelings on the topic, her favorite option being the Vanderbilts' son Charles, but I know the ultimate decision will be my own.

On the rare occasion the thought of my wedding crossed my mind, I envisioned details such as a freesia bouquet and a long lace train, but it was always an average, nondescript face I was walking toward.

Swaying back and forth in Jace's arms in the midst of decorations and a venue I would have never chosen for myself, those details suddenly seem irrelevant. As I try to picture my own wedding, the image that forms is absent any details regarding the flowers or dress. The only thing I can picture with absolute clarity is the face I want waiting for me at the end of the aisle. The brief flash of joy the image fills me with is quickly replaced by a cold trickle of panic.

I stiffen, and Jace notices.

"You okay?" he whispers in my ear. The sound of his voice is enough to pull me out of the state of anxiety and back to the present.

"Yeah," I reply, relaxing back against him. I force troubling thoughts from my mind for the third time today, determined to enjoy this moment while it lasts.

A couple of hours later, the festivities gradually begin to die down. Claire is falling asleep at the table when Ellen announces it's time to go.

We all gather our coats, thank the Williams family, and head outside into the cold night air. I wrap my jacket tightly around me to ward off the chill.

I entirely forgot about the dirt field we crossed until we reach the end of the path and Jace scoops me up against his chest without a word. I'm transported back to the night he carried me up to his room at Lincoln, grateful I get to experience the comforting rocking of his arms without the unpleasant nausea I was contending with the last time. The ride back to the Dawsons' farm is quiet. Everyone is tired after the excitement of a long day.

Mr. Dawson parks the SUV in front of the farmhouse, and we all hustle from the car to get inside the warm house. Mr. Dawson heads directly to the wood stove to put another log on the fire burning inside, and Mrs. Dawson hangs up everyone's dress coats in the closet. Claire ambles sleepily to the stairs, and the twins follow closely behind.

"Good night, everyone," I state, shooting Jace a quick smile before bypassing the staircase and heading down the hallway to the bathroom.

After washing my face and brushing my teeth, I enter my room. I take the velvet dress off carefully and lay it down atop the washing machine before pulling Jace's gray t-shirt out of one of my suitcases. The soft material slides down my body, and then I pull off my tights. I take a seat on the bed, checking my phone for messages.

Katie sent me two photos from New York City, and there is one message from Julie asking if everything is okay. I reply to

Julie first and assure her that I'm fine. I'm pulling up Katie's text to respond to her when there's a soft tap on my door.

"Come in," I call out.

The door creaks open, and Jace walks into the small room. My heartbeat stutters, then races as he closes the door behind him. He's shirtless, wearing nothing but a pair of athletic shorts. Butterflies swarm my stomach as I stare at the defined ridges of his torso.

"I just wanted to say good night," he tells me, taking a couple more steps forward so he's standing at the edge of the bed. I turn my phone off and let it fall onto the bedspread.

I lean my head back against the wall and smirk up at him. "Good night."

He remains standing in the same spot. "Nice shirt."

"I'm starting to like it a lot," I reply, well aware I'm talking about more than just the shirt.

"It looks really good on you." His voice is low and suggestive; his eyes smoldering.

"You look better without one." The words slip out unbidden, a product of the lust I've held in all day in front of his family and the strangers at the wedding.

Jace crouches in front of me, so we're at eye level. The flirtatious gleam in his eyes captivates me.

I move first this time, sliding off the bed onto my knees. Now we're both on the woven rug that covers most of the floor. Jace relaxes his posture so that he's sitting with his long legs outstretched. I crawl into his lap, so I'm sitting between his open thighs.

The distance between us slowly shrinks, until our lips are only millimeters apart. We're so close I can feel the pull of oxygen entering and carbon dioxide leaving his lips as I hover there for a moment.

Jace rests his large hands on my calves, then slowly begins to slide them up my legs. I shiver at the enticing sensation. My response shifts me even closer to Jace, and the slight movement is enough to close the minuscule gap between our mouths.

The touch breaks the tantalizing anticipation that's been steadily building. Jace's tongue invades my mouth hungrily. I straddle his waist and rock against him, feeling him harden under me. His hands creep higher and higher under the oversized shirt as I moan against his mouth, spurring him on.

A soft knock sounds on the door and we break apart, gasping for air.

"Jace?" Claire's soft voice comes through the door. "You said you'd be right back to read me the story. Mom says I have to go to bed soon."

Jace curses quietly under his breath. I slide off his lap, pulling my shirt back down.

"Okay, Claire," he calls back. "I'll be right up." He gives me an apologetic look and stands. "Better than being one of my brothers," he says, helping me up off the floor. "They would have just barged in."

I laugh. "Not the impression I want to leave your family with."

"Get some sleep," Jace tells me. "I'll see you in the morning."

He gives me a quick kiss, but I step closer to him, deepening it. Electricity pulses between us again.

Jace pulls back with a groan. "Viv, that's not helping."

I smirk at him. "You're the one who came to say good night."

"Best and worst decision I ever made," Jace says before he opens my door and disappears into the hallway.

CHAPTER SIXTEEN

The entire Dawson family stands out in the front yard early the following morning. Everyone except for me, Jace, and his parents are wearing pajamas. I took advantage of the long drive as an excuse to put on a comfy pair of yoga pants and the oversized *Fulton Football* sweatshirt Jace gave me before the game on Thanksgiving as a farewell gesture to a place I'll never forget.

"I double-checked the whole engine," Mr. Dawson tells Jace as he loads up the truck's bed with our bags. "You shouldn't have any trouble this trip."

"Thanks, Dad," Jace replies, giving him a quick hug.

Ellen hands me a heavy paper grocery bag. "Here are some snacks for the road."

"Thank you," I reply, feeling a lump form in my throat at the love behind the gesture. The emotion must show on my face, because she immediately pulls me into a hug.

"I'm so glad Jace brought you home, Vivienne," she whispers to me. "I've never seen him happier, and I've loved getting to know you. You'll always be welcome here."

I'm too choked up to form a response, but I give her an appreciative look I hope conveys my gratitude.

Mr. Dawson hugs me as well, and then I'm passed along through the younger Dawsons. I hug Claire first.

"Will you come back and visit again?" she asks me.

"I would love to," I reply truthfully, although I know I never will.

Her face lights up. "Even if you don't marry Jace?"

"Claire, no one else is getting married," Alden chimes in, giving me a hug next.

"But Mom said boys and girls only stay in the same room at night if they're getting married, and Jace was in Viv's room last night."

Silence follows this announcement. I'm certain my face has never been redder.

"He must have been in her room to read her a bedtime story," Mike suggests, grinning widely.

"Well, on that note," Jace announces, glaring at his younger brother. "We should get on the road." He heads for the truck.

Mike gives me a hug. "Sorry I called you a groupie," he mutters.

I smile at him affectionately.

I hug Max last, then climb into the truck next to Jace. He backs up and starts driving down the dirt road. I wave out the window until the white farmhouse fades from view behind us.

Eight hours later, I enter my room in Kennedy Hall, lugging my two heavy suitcases. Jace offered to bring them in, but I could tell he was tired after the long drive and know he has a team meeting soon, so I promised him I could manage them myself.

Katie is already back in our room. She's lying on her bed, talking on the phone. She looks up when I enter and flashes me a wide smile of greeting. I set my bag on the desk and pull off my heavy jacket.

Katie ends the call and bounds over to give me a big hug. "Hi! I was just about to call and see where you were. Where did you go? Home?" she asks, looking at my suitcases. "I thought you were staying here for break."

"That was the plan," I reply. "Things changed last minute."

"What do you mean? Where did you go?"

"Nebraska."

"I thought Philip and your stepfather were going to Texas, not Nebraska."

"They did."

"So…why did you go to *Nebraska*?"

"Okay, promise me you won't freak out," I implore.

Katie raises her eyebrows.

"Or tell anyone else," I add.

"Okay, I promise," Katie says impatiently, her face alight with curiosity. "Now tell me."

"Jace is from Nebraska."

"You saw Jace Dawson while you were in Nebraska?"

"Yeah, a fair amount actually…considering I was staying with him."

Katie's jaw literally drops in the wake of this information. "You spent Thanksgiving with Jace Dawson?"

"Yes."

"You and Jace Dawson spent Thanksgiving together?" she repeats.

"Yes." I confirm again.

"Was his family there?"

"Yes."

"Jace Dawson took you home to spend Thanksgiving with his family?" Katie still sounds stunned.

"Yeah, I—" I'm interrupted by the chime of my phone. I pull it out of my bag to see a message from Claudia asking if I'm coming to the study session.

"Crap, I've got to go," I tell Katie, quickly grabbing my medieval history notebook and cramming it into my bag.

"Are you kidding me?" Katie exclaims. "You can't just drop something like this on me and then disappear."

"I'll fill you in on everything later," I promise. "I'm late for a study group meeting, and we have an exam on Tuesday."

A couple of hours later, I walk out of the library with Claudia. She's telling me about a yoga class she's taking, trying to convince me to come to it tomorrow morning, when I feel my phone buzzing in my pocket. I pull it out and smile when I see the name on the screen.

"Hey," I answer. "Give me one sec."

I pull the phone away from my ear and turn back to Claudia. "I'll come tomorrow."

She grins. "Yay! Okay, I'll see you then. I'll text Katie about it, too."

"Okay, sounds good," I reply. We say goodbye, and I raise the phone back up to my ear. "Okay, I'm back."

"You hungry?" Jace's voice resonates through the speaker.

"Yeah, I am," I reply. "I haven't eaten since the sandwiches your mom packed. I'm just leaving the library."

"The main one?"

"Yes."

"Okay, I'm leaving the gym now. I'll meet you at Casey."

I walk across campus. The path is crowded with students rushing to catch up with each other along with the work they ignored over break. I stop outside the dining hall, taking a seat on one of the benches. I'm still wearing the same yoga pants and *Fulton Football* sweatshirt I wore in the car.

My hair keeps blowing in my face, so I pull back the wayward strands and weave them together in a loose French braid. I look up to see Jace walking toward me seconds later, his hands shoved deep in his pockets.

He's changed from earlier, now wearing a matching set of athletic apparel embroidered with *Lincoln Football* and the school's insignia. He gives me a tired smile as he reaches the metal bench and holds out a hand.

"C'mon, let's get some food. I can't sit down, or I won't get up again for a few hours."

"Long day?" I tease, taking his outstretched hand and letting him pull me vertical.

"Just an eight-hour drive followed by three hours of watching film," Jace replies. "All in a typical day's work."

"At least it was only a couple traffic delays this time and not another engine issue."

We walk into the large dining hall. To my surprise, Jace keeps his grip on my hand.

"And I did offer to drive," I remind him, trying to focus on our conversation and not the attention Jace's entrance has drawn.

"You did," Jace replies. "But I wanted to make it back to campus alive, so…"

"You can't judge my driving skills based on what happened to that little cart!" I reply indignantly. "I'd never driven one of those before, and they're different from a car."

"You're right," Jace responds dryly. "They're a lot easier to drive than a car."

I look over at him, and he's grinning widely. He must have showered just before leaving the gym, because his dark brown hair is still damp. The water droplets glimmer under the bright lights of the glorified cafeteria.

"Alden said he has trouble with it sometimes," I inform him defensively.

"Alden's been driving the cart since he was ten. He only said that because he has a crush on you and was trying to make you feel better."

"Looks like you've got some competition, then." I wink.

"Alden will be thrilled. Maybe he can take you out for a ride in the cart for your first date," Jace suggests.

"At least it'd be a first date." I bite my bottom lip, wishing I could shove the words back into my mouth.

"Is that what you want? To go on a date?" Jace asks. His voice has shifted from joking to serious.

We've reached the beginning of the buffet, which displays an assortment of leftovers from dinner, along with a random array of eggs, pizza, and doughnuts for late night study fuel. I grab a plate and begin filling it with food. Jace does the same.

"Viv?" he asks as I silently grab a piece of chicken.

"The idea never occurred to you?" I ask, moving farther down the line.

Jace follows. "Of course it occurred to me," he replies. "I just have a lot going on right now, and you—you complicate things."

"I complicate things?" I ask. "You brought me home to meet your entire family! I didn't ask you to do that."

"I know," Jace replies. "And I'm glad I did, it's just I still—"

The sound of my name being called distracts us both. I turn away from my overloaded tray to see Katie standing a few feet away with a couple of her friends.

"Hey, Katie." I smile despite my annoyance as I notice her

awestruck expression when she realizes who is standing next to me.

"This is my roommate, Katie," I inform Jace, keeping my voice neutral despite my churning emotions. "Katie, this is Jace." I try to remember the names of her friends but come up blank for both.

"Hey." Jace flashes Katie an easy grin, then glances over at me. I don't return his gaze.

"These are my friends Liza and Alex," Katie finally says, nodding to her two companions. They're both staring at Jace with wide eyes.

"It's nice to see you guys," I tell them.

Out of the corner of my eye, I notice a long line has started to form behind the point in the buffet where Jace and I stopped moving. The girl closest to us is waiting patiently, her eyes glued to Jace. He seems to notice the bottleneck at the same moment I do, and he lifts both of our trays off the rack to let the other students in line pass us.

Without another word, he strides over to an empty table while carrying both trays. Katie and her friends watch his wordless departure closely, along with what seems like most of the other students in the dining hall.

"I'd better go eat," I tell them. "You guys are welcome to join us."

"No, it's fine. We're just grabbing a quick snack before rehearsal," Katie answers. "I'll see you back in the room, okay?"

"Sounds good," I reply.

I walk over to the table Jace chose, only stopping to fill one cup with still water and the other with sparkling at the drink dispenser.

I set the glass of fizzy water down in front of Jace when I reach the table and take the seat across from him.

"Peace offering?" he asks.

"It's just a glass of water, Jace."

"Water is rarely just water with you," he replies. I can't help but smile at that, and he returns it. "I'm sorry," he surprises me by saying.

"You don't have to apologize. You didn't do anything wrong."

"I don't want you to think I regret anything that's happened between us," Jace says, his gaze imploring. "Well, maybe some of the early stuff," he amends, and I smile. "But this is my last chance to win a college championship, and it could have a major impact on my draft chances. I'll have slightly more time next semester," he promises.

I smile sadly. There won't be a next semester for me. "I get it, Jace, I really do. I'm not asking you to choose between me and football. I would never do that. I know how hard you've worked, and how important it is that you succeed." There's more emotion behind the words than I intended, so I quickly change the subject, asking Jace about his practice.

He fills me in on stories from some of his teammates' Thanks-givings as we eat our late dinner. By the time we've finished eating, the dining hall is even more crowded than when we arrived. With each new arrival, I feel the number of eyes on us multiplying.

"Are you ready to go?" I ask Jace.

He nods, and we gather up our dirty dishes to deposit on our way out.

"Does it ever bother you?" I wonder as we head toward the main door.

"The attention?"

I nod.

"I found it flattering at first, then it got annoying. Eventually, I just came to accept it. I just do what I want to do, and if people want to talk about it, they can."

"You're a publicist's nightmare."

Jace laughs. "I'm not stumbling out of strip clubs in the middle of the night. I'm just saying people noticing what you do doesn't mean you shouldn't do certain things. Life's too short to conform to what others want or expect, you know?"

"What if it's bigger than you, though?" I press. "What if other people will be hurt if you don't conform?"

Jace opens his mouth to respond, but before he can reply, we're interrupted by another familiar voice.

"Jace Dawson gracing us with his presence in the common dining hall?" Anderson asks.

I turn to see him approaching from our right. He's followed by three other guys I recognize as being on the football team but who I've never spoken to.

"Fuck off, Anderson," Jace says, but he's grinning.

"I was wondering where you were rushing off to after practice," Anderson continues. "Never seen you move so fast before. You better bring that hustle on Thursday."

Jace flips off his friend, but doesn't comment, so Anderson shifts his attention to me.

"Good to see you, Vivienne."

"You too, Anderson," I reply, giving him a grin. "How was your Thanksgiving?"

"Loud. My mother was so thrilled to finally have me home this year, she invited our entire extended family over. It's quieter in the team locker room after we win a game."

I laugh.

"And I didn't get any of Mrs. Dawson's pumpkin pie. She usually sends a couple dozen to the team for our Thanksgiving game. Did she not make any this year?" His eyes glint with mischief, and I send a quick glance Jace's way.

He sighs, looking resigned. "She made pecan this year. Vivienne doesn't like pumpkin."

I look at Jace in surprise. "Wait, that's why we didn't have pumpkin pie?" I don't bother waiting for a response. "How did you even know I don't like pumpkin?"

"You told me," Jace replies simply. I think back, surprised to realize he's right, and even more surprised he remembered the offhand comment.

Anderson looks amused by our exchange. "Well, we'll leave you two to start covering each other's favorite movies," he quips before heading toward the food line. The other players follow him after giving Jace fist bumps and me curious glances.

We emerge back outside. The peaceful night air is a relief after the crowded and noisy dining hall.

"Do you want to spend the night?" Jace asks abruptly as we walk along the paved path. I can't see his face very well in the shadowy light.

I experience an exhilarating mix of excitement and nervousness at his question, but my response is immediate. "Sure."

Philip and Thomas are arriving back on campus early tomorrow morning. I'm eager to take full advantage of my time removed from their watchful presence to pretend I'm an ordinary girl for just a little while longer.

Jace takes my hand again as we walk side by side through to the parking lot to his truck. I shift uncomfortably as I settle on the leather seat, my body protesting the position after the many hours I've already spent sitting here today.

It only takes a few minutes before we pull up outside the blue house. The front porch light is on, but the rest of the house is dark. I follow Jace up the brick path, thinking of how much has changed since the last time I spent the night here.

Jace unlocks the front door and pushes it open, gesturing for me to enter first. He flicks on the lights, revealing the scuffed floors and furniture that were hidden by the couple hundred people crammed inside before. I walk toward the staircase, looking around with interest.

"Want me to carry you again?" Jace asks, coming to stand next to me after he closes the door.

"I think I can manage," I reply, ascending the wooden staircase.

The stairs creak with each step until I reach the top and walk down the hall to Jace's room. The door is slightly ajar. I push it open fully and flick on the light switch.

Familiar surroundings appear as I lower my backpack to the ground next to Jace's desk. Jace tosses his practice bag down next to it and turns the light on his dresser on as well. He opens the top drawer, pulls out a black t-shirt, and holds out to me.

I look at the offered fabric. "What's this for?"

"I'm assuming you didn't pack pajamas in there," Jace replies, nodding to my backpack. "And if you did, that was awfully presumptuous."

"You're giving me clothes to put *on*?" Confusion colors my voice.

"What, did you think I was inviting you over for a booty call?" Jace asks.

I don't reply, because that's exactly what I was thinking, and it's clear to me now that's not what Jace has in mind. I battle a combination of disappointment and relief.

"I'm smoother than that, Viv." Jace smirks at me.

"How would I know?" I challenge.

"Oh, you'll know." He sends me a sexy grin.

"'Spend the night' is usually code for sex, Jace," I state the obvious.

"I'm well aware. But when I asked you to spend the night, I was not using code."

"Well, how was I supposed to know that?" I ask in frustration, ripping off Jace's sweatshirt. "Most guys—"

"I'm not most guys," Jace interrupts.

"That's for sure," I mutter.

Jace grins.

"That wasn't a compliment," I snap.

Jace takes off his own jacket and pulls off the tight sweat-wicking t-shirt he has on underneath, exposing his impressive physique. I trace the stacked muscles of his torso with my eyes. Jace glances up, and I don't even attempt to hide my blatant ogling.

"So exactly how set are you on this no sex thing?" I ask.

Jace smirks, then tosses me the same t-shirt he offered me before. I manage to snag it out of midair.

"Get changed, Viv," is all he says.

"You're going to give me a complex," I tell him as I pull down my yoga pants and put on his t-shirt. "The campus player who won't sleep with me. You're bad for my ego."

Jace lets out a dry chuckle. "You're bad for mine."

He takes off his pants. We stand facing each other in his room, me in his t-shirt and him in his black boxer briefs. I feel a flash of déjà vu.

"Seriously, Jace," I implore. "Why not? I'm sober and your sister is a couple states away."

Jace smiles slightly, but then turns serious again. "Because you deserve for it to be perfect. It's never meant anything to me before, but it'll mean something to me just because it's you. But you deserve better than this." He gestures to his messy room.

"Jace…" I start, my throat thick with emotion.

"Plus, my housemates will be home soon, and I doubt you'd be able to stay quiet," he adds, lightening the heavy moment.

He walks over to his bed and climbs in. "Get in."

I turn off the light and feel my way through the dark over to his bed. The warmth from Jace's body is already radiating throughout the entire bed. He pulls me close to his side and plants a soft kiss on my forehead before promptly falling asleep.

I try to stay awake longer to contemplate some of the questions swirling through my head, but I quickly succumb to my own exhaustion and fall asleep.

CHAPTER SEVENTEEN

The second time I wake up in Jace Dawson's arms, I'm less hungover, but more confused.

Jace is still asleep, so I lie in bed and study his strong jaw and sharp cheekbones, trying to figure out how I got here. If someone had asked me on my first day at Lincoln University who I would most be dreading saying goodbye to, I never would have even considered the arrogant guy with dark hair and gray eyes I collided with.

Somehow, our bickering morphed into a deep-rooted fascination, followed by a magnetic attraction. I can't pinpoint the exact moment where it became more than that, but as I recall watching Jace play board games with his family and carefully carrying me across a dirt field, I realize I'm just as enchanted by the vulnerable side of him few get to see.

I study his peaceful expression and recall his words from the night before. I thought Jace Dawson would be the perfect candidate for a college fling. Experienced, unattached, uncaring. Someone I could barely stand but was insanely attracted to.

I've refused to listen to anyone who's suggested it, but I

suddenly realize what I've hardly let myself hope for. That Jace really does see me differently from the many other girls he's been with in the past. I did everything I could to distract myself from the possibility while I was with his family, but now that it's just the two of us again, I have no way to hide from the truth. More so, I realize I *want* it to be true.

Jace deserves someone who will be there on the day he gets drafted and bake pies with his mom for Thanksgiving without lying to her friends.

That's someone I can never be.

I feel a surge of panic in response to the pain I experience imagining some other girl, like Gretchen, being the one Jace spends those moments with. It forces me to confront the other truth I've been in denial about.

It's not just Jace's feelings I've underestimated.

It's my own as well.

As I trace the lines of Jace's sleeping face, the first word that comes to my mind isn't like, or lust. It's love. That realization sends a fresh bolt of horror through me that's enough to propel me out of bed to get dressed and gather my backpack.

I slip out of Jace's house and start to walk back to campus in a daze. I finally manage to tamp my thoughts down to a manageable level of alarm as I arrive back at Kennedy Hall.

When I enter my dorm room, I'm surprised to see Katie is sitting on her bed, already dressed in workout clothes. She lets out a loud sigh of relief when I enter our room.

"Where the hell have you been?" she asks. "I was worried sick."

"Sorry, I meant to text you last night," I reply. "How come you're already awake?"

"Claudia texted me yesterday, inviting me to a yoga class this morning with you guys. She said you already said you would go."

I completely forgot about my conversation with Claudia outside the library last night.

"Oh, right," I reply, grateful for the reminder. "Let me just change."

I'm still wearing the same clothes from yesterday, so I quickly pull on a pair of leggings and a spandex tank top before putting on my down jacket. "Okay, I'm ready."

Katie and I head out into the cold morning.

"You were with him, right?" she asks as we walk along the path toward the athletic center.

"Right." I let out a deep sigh as her question recalls my previous consternation.

Katie takes in my troubled expression. "Are you okay?"

"Yes. No. I don't know," I waver. "I like him. I like him a lot," I finally admit.

"And that's a bad thing because…" Katie wonders. "He seems to really like you, too."

"It isn't part of my plan," I tell her, coming as close to the truth as I'm able to. "It could never work between us."

"How do you know?"

"I just do," I reply firmly.

Katie casts me a concerned look as we head inside the athletic center. "Maybe…" she starts.

I shake my head, and she stops speaking. "I don't want to talk about it anymore right now."

We're already a couple minutes late for the start of the class, so we both hurry through the main entrance into the massive central gym that's filled with neat lines of various exercise equipment and machines. I spot a sign that reads *Intermediate Yoga.*

I open the door and we enter the room quietly, each grabbing a yoga mat and laying them down next to Claudia, who smiles over at us in greeting.

An hour later, the class ends. My body feels relaxed, and I've successfully shoved my worries away again for the time being.

I head back out into the main gym with Claudia and Katie. The sun shines brilliantly through the paned windows that take up most of the opposite wall, allowing students a sprawling view of campus as they exercise.

Glancing around, I see the gym has become much more crowded than it was when we arrived. I quickly discover why. Jace is standing in the far corner with the rest of the football team huddled around him, writing workout instructions on the whiteboard. Katie and Claudia both spot him as well.

"Should we go over and see if he remembers either of us?" Claudia jokes.

Katie sends me another look of concern.

I force a laugh in response to Claudia's comment. "Let's get breakfast instead."

We turn to head toward the exit, passing a long rack of weights. Three guys stand around the equipment, their muscular builds indicating they spend a lot of time in this building.

One of them whistles as we walk by. "Hey, blondie," he calls.

I turn my head, since I'm the only blonde in the group. The guy in the middle of the trio is looking directly at me, smirking confidently. He's handsome in a manufactured way. His light blond, almost white, hair is carefully styled and his tight, sleeveless shirt is clearly meant to emphasize his bulging biceps.

"What's your name, sweetheart?" he asks. I can feel the arrogance coming off of him in thick waves.

For some reason, I immediately think of my first interaction with Jace, and how taken aback I was by his arrogance. Standing a few feet away from this stranger, I suddenly realize the pull I felt toward Jace was not simply the thrill of challenging his cocky attitude. My body doesn't react to this guy's confident tone the same way it always responds to Jace's, even when I'm genuinely annoyed with him. I'm simply indifferent to this guy's abrasive charm.

"I'm not interested," I tell him bluntly, not missing the way his eyes are running over the tight clothes I'm wearing. One chuckles at my rude rebuff. "Let's go, guys," I tell Claudia and Katie before I start walking again.

"Blondie!" the guy calls more loudly. Everyone in the immediate vicinity glances our way.

I turn back around, my temper flaring. Claudia and Katie look between us, wide-eyed.

"What?" I retort. "I told you I'm not interested."

"Are you sure you're not just playing hard to get?" The guy persists. "Just tell me what your name is." My skin crawls in response to his leer. A large part of me wants to hurry away. But pride keeps me in place, meeting his entitled expression and not wavering.

"What the fuck are you doing, Stevens?" Jace is suddenly standing next to me, his face furious.

Anderson, Owens, and the black guy who talked to me in the cafeteria all hover a few feet behind him. I glance past them to see we've captured the attention of the entire gym, including the rest of the football team still standing in the same corner as before.

Stevens' face hardens at the malice in Jace's voice. His two buddies straighten behind him, but don't move any closer. Normally, I would be annoyed by someone intervening on my behalf, but I feel nothing besides overwhelming relief in Jace's protective presence.

"Just being friendly," Stevens replies. "Nothing you need to be concerned with, Dawson. Just keep throwing those touchdowns." His voice is mocking, but I detect a hint of nervousness in his expression.

"I'm plenty concerned," Jace replies. His voice is like steel. I can feel the anger radiating off him. "I better not see or hear about you harassing anyone else, or you'll have me to answer to."

"Harassing?" Stevens scoffs. "Please. I don't need to harass anyone. I've got a line of girls just hoping I'll look twice at them. You know how that is." He gives Jace a grin, clearly hoping to diffuse the stifling tension with some playboy camaraderie.

"Keep telling yourself that. In the meantime, stay away from mine." A jolt of surprise hits me when I register Jace's words, but I quickly school my features to remain neutral.

Stevens' eyes shoot to mine. He doesn't hide his own surprise. "That's what this is really about? You're marking your territory, Dawson?" Stevens smirks. "I didn't think you were a one-woman kind of guy."

Jace takes a step forward, and Stevens' two friends both shift uncomfortably before moving back slightly. Stevens holds his ground, but his jaw twitches.

"You're fucking right I am," Jace warns. "We clear?"

Stevens' bravado has entirely disappeared. "We're clear," he mutters, turning back to the rack of weights.

Jace looks to me, and the hard expression melts off his face. "I'll be right over," he calls out to his three friends. They all return to the corner where the rest of the football team is standing.

I glance over at Claudia and Katie. They both look stunned.

My hand is suddenly surrounded by a larger, calloused one as Jace tugs me away from the weight rack and against the wall about ten feet away.

"Are you okay?" he asks, looking down at me with a worried expression.

"You didn't have to come over. I was handling it."

"I know, but I've wanted a reason to intimidate Stevens since freshman year. The guy is an asshole."

I decide not to press the issue further. "You called me your girl." I state instead.

"Yeah, I did."

"Did you mean it?"

"Yes."

"Were you going to ask for my opinion on the topic?" I ask.

"In the midst of defending you?"

"At any point," I reply.

"I was waiting for the hot-air balloon ride I scheduled later."

I roll my eyes. "Fine, forget it."

"Do you want to be mine?" Jace asks, his teasing tone gone. His eyes bore into mine.

If I hadn't already realized the depth of my feelings toward Jace, this would have been the moment. The weight in the back of my mind disappears as I realize I wouldn't change a single thing that's led me to this point in time. I know it's not fair to Jace. I know it will only make my inevitable departure harder, but I simply stare at him and let myself fall.

"Yes." I've done my best to avoid lying to him about anything important—least of all this.

Jace's answering smile is breathtaking. "We're going to need to talk about the sneaking out in the morning," is how he breaks the poignant moment.

"We're going to need to talk about the no sex thing, too," I reply.

Jace laughs. "I could probably be persuaded pretty easily on that one."

"Me too."

"I've got to get back to the team," Jace tells me, his voice tinged with regret. "I'll talk to you later, okay?"

I nod. To my surprise, he tugs me closer and gives me a quick kiss.

"What was that for?" I ask when he pulls back.

"Just saying goodbye to my girlfriend." He grins and leaves me standing there as reality slowly trickles back in.

I manage to walk over to where Claudia and Katie are still standing. Katie is wearing the same stunned expression and Claudia looks completely floored.

"Let's go," I instruct, careful to not make eye contact with any of the many stares I can feel on me.

Katie and Claudia follow after me silently, but the short walk back outside the athletic center is all the time it takes for them to find their voices.

"Holy shit!" Katie exclaims as we start walking down the path. "I don't even know where to begin. Holy shit!"

Claudia's comments are completely unintelligible. "He—you —what?"

"Forget what I said earlier," Katie insists. "Jace Dawson does not just like you. He's in deep, maybe even deeper than you."

"What happened earlier?" Claudia asks, finally stringing a coherent thought together. "Why didn't you tell me you know Jace Dawson?"

"She more than knows him," Katie states. "He took her home for Thanksgiving to meet his family, for Christ's sake." She glances at me, likely realizing she promised not to tell anyone that detail. "Sorry."

"It's fine," I tell her. "Thanks to Jace, everyone in that gym knows something's going on between us now, anyway."

"Everyone in that gym?" Katie repeats. "Vivienne, everyone on *campus* is going to know about this by the end of the morning. Jace Dawson does not interrupt football training to tell the hockey team captain to fuck off and then kiss a girl in the sports center. This is all anyone will be talking about for weeks."

Claudia nods in agreement. "Those poor guys in our history class. I think one was going to finally talk to you this week."

I smile. "I'll let him down easy."

Claudia laughs. "Are you kidding? I doubt a single guy on this campus is going to dare to talk to you after the way Jace Dawson just acted."

My phone rings. "Hello?" I answer.

"Princess, it's Philip," Philip's voice comes through the line. "I'm calling on one of our encrypted phones. Thomas and I are in the car about fifteen minutes out from campus. Phone and internet were spotty in Texas, so I'm just receiving the reports from here. Julie said everything was fine there."

"Yes, it was," I reply.

"I'd like to catch up in person. I'll meet you in the library in half an hour?"

"Fine," I reply, and hang up.

"Who was that?" Katie asks.

"Philip," I reply. "He wants to catch up from break. See, some guys on this campus are still talking to me."

Katie rolls her eyes. "It doesn't count if they're related to you."

After grabbing a quick breakfast, I head to the library to meet with Philip. I spot him sitting at one of the secluded back tables. He looks up and sees me.

I'm surprised to see a look of anger on his face. I experience a flash of panic, worried he's somehow found out about my spontaneous trip to Nebraska.

"How was Texas?" I ask when I reach the table.

Philip ignores my question. "Why is everyone on campus talking about you kissing that football player in the gym this morning?"

Apparently, Claudia and Katie *weren't* exaggerating earlier.

Me kissing a guy in public would be front page news back home. I'm disgruntled to realize that's now the case here.

"It's not a big deal, Philip." I take a seat across the table.

"Yes, it is. Jace Dawson is bad news."

"I'm not allowed to have a college fling?" I ask petulantly.

Philip looks even angrier. "Not with Dawson. You know the level of scrutiny around him. If someone starts looking into you because you're associating with him, your cover could be blown. Is this fling worth all the blowback that would create?"

"It's none of your business," I retort, standing. I'm abruptly furious, partly because I'm annoyed by Philip's interference, but mostly because I'm worried he might be right. "And I suggest you remember what your place is in all this, Agent Matthews." I emphasize Philip's formal title. "You work for the Crown, not the other way around. Don't forget that."

"I'm trying to *protect* the Crown," Philip hisses. "And you."

"Your job is to look after my physical safety, not to cast judgements about my personal life."

"I'm trying to keep you from getting hurt. You must have heard the rumors about him. You're just another conquest. Imagine what it'll be like if he finds out who you really are and leaks it to the press. He'll be considered a legend, while you'll be labeled a slut."

I flinch at his harsh words. "You don't know anything about Jace, or our relationship."

"I know it won't end any other way besides badly."

"I'm done having this conversation. Don't mention anything about this to me again, or you'll be gone." I storm out of the library, leaving a fuming Philip in my wake.

CHAPTER EIGHTEEN

The remainder of the week passes quickly. I only see brief glimpses of Jace, since he travels with the team to Boston on Wednesday to make up their game that was meant to be Thanksgiving.

He texts me on Friday morning as I'm leaving my English class, letting me know he won't be back on campus by noon, as originally planned, since their flight has been delayed. I'm typing a response when my phone lights up with an incoming call.

I answer.

"Vivienne? Are you there?" my mother's voice comes through the line.

"Yes, I'm here, Mother," I reply.

There's a pause on the other end of the line. My calls home have become less frequent and more stilted as the months in Michigan have passed. As Marcedenia has begun to feel further and further away.

"How's Papa?" I finally ask.

"He's still at the cottage," my mother replies. "He says he

thinks better out there. I speak to his nurse every day, and he's doing fine. No changes."

"His nurse?" I question, my voice rising in alarm.

"She's more of a secretary at the moment," my mother assures me. "The doctors suggested it would be best to already have someone familiar in place whenever things do start to progress."

"That makes sense, I guess," I respond. I spot an open bench along the side of the path and take a seat so I can set down my heavy backpack.

"We had the Vanderbilts over for dinner the other night." My mother is clearly eager to change the subject. "Charles came too. He is such a lovely young man. He's very happy at Edgewood, so you two will be classmates next semester."

I nod absentmindedly, already beginning to tune her out. Belatedly, I realize she can't see me. "That's nice, Mother."

"He told the most charming story about being nervous to hand you a bouquet of flowers when you two were little. He's a very nice young man. I invited them over again the week after you return. They're all eager to hear about your aid trip. Which reminds me, I had Richard set up a meeting with Helga's daughter. She actually did one of those trips a couple years ago and said she'd be willing to tell you about it so you have some stories."

"Mm-hmm, okay," I reply.

"I really do think he'd be an excellent choice," she continues. "So keep that in mind when they come over."

"Excellent choice for what?"

"Your husband." That word certainly catches my attention. Not because it's surprising my mother would mention it—she's made her feelings toward Charles quite clear—but because a heavy ball of dread settles in my stomach at the prospect of marrying him. I know my epiphany in the Williams' barn is the source.

"Mother, I still have another few years before I'll have to get married." I fight to keep the trepidation out of my voice.

"I know, but these things do require a lot of planning, you know. And Charles is such a catch. You don't want some duchess to snap him up."

I roll my eyes, relieved my mother can't see me and amused by the thought of placing a hold on my future husband like he's a library book.

"Sure, mother. I'll keep that in mind. Now, I've got to get to class. I'll talk to you next week." Thankfully, she's never asked for a copy of my schedule, so she has no idea I've just left my last class of the day.

"All right, dear," she responds. "Make sure you're being careful over there."

I shift uncomfortably as I think of the idea that's been forming in my mind all week, which my mom would undoubtedly strongly disapprove of. Once again, I'm grateful she's not here in person to see the guilt written all over my face. I've let my guard down here more than ever before, meaning I'll have to practice my poker face before returning to the palace.

"I will. Say hello to Papa."

Thanks to his extended stay at the cottage, I haven't talked to him in several weeks. I miss his gravelly voice, but I'm also grateful. My father has always been more perceptive of my true feelings than my mother, which is the last thing I need right now.

I end the call but remain sitting. The same anxiety that overtakes me every time I receive some reminder of the life I'll be returning to in a matter of weeks lingers.

A crushing wave of sadness engulfs me as I think about how little time I have left here and how soon I'll have to leave this life, this campus, and Jace.

I'm distracted by a text from Katie. *Leaving campus now*, it reads. *Have fun this weekend!*

I quickly reply, telling her to do the same. She's going to visit her dad for the weekend. I pull up Jace's name in my texts and stare at my half-composed message for a moment.

Finally, I delete what I started writing previously and send *Are you free this weekend?* He usually has practice on Saturdays, but I hope his game yesterday might mean he has both days off.

He responds immediately. *Nope playoffs start next weekend so extra practices.*

I turn off my phone, embarrassed by how disappointed I feel.

The screen lights up again.

Why? I could be convinced to skip…

I type back, *it's a surprise.*

I'm in appears on the screen.

Crippling disappointment is replaced by giddy excitement.

Be ready at 7 tomorrow morning, I reply. Then, after a moment of thought, I add, *pack a swimsuit.*

I was considering renting a cabin for a weekend getaway, but my mother's mention of the Vanderbilts has given me another idea. I pull a folded scrap of paper out of my wallet and dial the number I saved.

"Hello?" a deep voice answers.

"Hello. Duke Vanderbilt gave me this number to use if I required your services," I say. "Are you available for a flight tomorrow morning?"

"Yes, ma'am," the voice replies. "What time?"

"Eight, at whatever private airport is closest to Lincoln, Michigan."

"I'll look and send an address to this number."

"Okay, thank you," I reply, giddy now that my plan is actually in motion. I dial the next number I need to call before speaking with Thomas and Philip.

~

"Thomas, isn't your wife due to give birth soon?" I ask, trying to appear casual as I stroll around his office twenty minutes later.

"Yes, in just another month or so," he replies. "Two weeks after we return home."

Eagerness overwhelms the pang in my stomach at yet another reminder that the end of my time here is rapidly approaching. "You should travel home this weekend to see her. I've already made all the travel arrangements for you."

Thomas starts to protest. "Princess—"

I hold up my hand, silencing him.

"Please, let me do this for you. I have plans with Katie to have a girls' weekend, and Philip is perfectly capable of looking after me on campus. I feel badly that you've been away from home on my account for so long, and it would make me feel better if you allow me to do this."

The last sentence is true, but the grateful look Thomas gives me makes me feel guilty for the selfish motivations I have for arranging this trip.

"The car's outside now," I state. "Your flight leaves in two hours. And I've already gotten Richard and my father's approval for this," I add, knowing that's likely to be his next objection.

Sure enough, that sentence is all it takes for the conflict to leave his expression. He quickly gathers his things into his brief-case and starts walking toward his office door.

"Thank you for this," Thomas tells me fervently. "You're going to make a wonderful queen, Princess."

I smile at his kind words, although they cause a flare of panic inside me. Thomas turns to leave.

"Wait." I stride over to the doorway. "Give me your phone," I order.

Thomas opens his mouth to argue, but I don't give him the chance. "I know if you take it you'll be badgering Philip every hour, making sure everything is okay. You deserve a weekend completely off. I'll be fine."

Thomas thinks it over for a moment, then finally pulls his phone out of his pocket and hands it to me. I try not to let the elation show on my face.

"Be careful, Princess," are his parting words.

One down, one to go.

"Thomas already agreed to go with me," I lie, taking a seat on Philip's dorm bed. "You deserve a chance to be a real college student for the weekend, without constantly having to look out for me."

"It's my job," Philip argues. "I'd feel much better if both of us are there."

"I already told Katie that Thomas is going to Radcliffe for a meeting and that's why he's driving us," I argue. "It will seem strange if you come along on our girls' trip and our supposed father's work meeting. We're going to a small city, not a war zone."

"I still don't feel comfortable about letting you leave campus with only one agent," Philip states.

"I'm not. Steve and Julie are coming too."

Philip opens his mouth to argue further, so I play my last card desperately. "Please, I just need a chance to get away from this campus. Away from him." We both know who I'm referring to.

"You were right, okay? I got too caught up, and I just want a chance to enjoy myself away from him before I have to go home."

The argument fades from Philip's face, replaced by understanding and relief. "Okay, fine. But I'll be checking up on you guys."

"That's not necessary," I reply. "Don't tell him I mentioned this, but Thomas finds it offensive when you check up on him while he's guarding me. Since he's the senior agent, it's considered an insult." I feel a wave of guilt as I utter the untrue words, but I have no choice if I want to get away with this.

Philip looks shocked. "I—I had no idea," he stutters. "I thought he'd appreciate I was checking in even when I was off duty…"

"I know you meant well," I interject, feeling increasingly nauseous with each lie I spew. "That's why I decided to tell you, to make sure you know for the future."

Philip nods, looking crushed.

"I've got to go get my things together," I state, standing. "I'll let you know when we're back on Sunday night. Enjoy the weekend."

I walk out into the hallway of Philip's dorm, shocked that all the moving parts actually seem to be falling into place. I do a quick search on my phone and pull up the number for the nearest car rental company. It ends up being a local car dealership.

After a brief conversation, they assure me they'll have a car here by quarter of seven tomorrow morning. I thank them and hang up, hurriedly swiping into my dorm and then entering my room.

I grab an overnight bag and begin stuffing it with an assortment of pants, shorts, dresses, shoes, and tops. Satisfied I have at least a week's worth of options, I move on to my underwear drawer. I take out my favorite blue bikini, along with several sets of lacy lingerie. I add them to the overflowing bag before moving to my dresser to collect my various toiletries.

Tossing them all into a zippered bag, I add it to my tote. It takes me four tries to zip up my overnight bag, but I finally get it closed. I flop on top of my comforter, exhausted and exhilarated.

I wake up the following morning at six. Excitement propels me out of bed immediately. I use the bathroom, then get dressed in a pair of faded, ripped jeans and a cotton sweater.

Once I finish getting ready, I do a final scan around my room to make certain I haven't forgotten anything vital. I switch off the light and make sure I've locked the door behind me before shouldering my tote bag and carrying my overnight bag down the empty hallway.

When I emerge outside, I'm relieved to see a black SUV idling by the curb. A middle-aged man with a kind smile steps out of the driver's side door.

"Ms. Rhodes?" he asks.

"Yes, that's me."

"I just need your signature here, and then we'll be all set," he tells me, handing me a clipboard.

I sign my fake name with a flourish and pass it back to him.

"Here's my card, in case you have any trouble. Otherwise, it's all yours until Tuesday."

"Thank you." I open the trunk and toss my bags inside. I start toward the driver's side door, when a sudden thought occurs to me. I turn back to the man.

"You sell cars too, don't you?" I ask, recalling the listings on their website.

"Yes, we do," the man replies.

"Do you sell Porsches?" I ask.

His eyes widen slightly, but his face otherwise remains

neutral. "I've had a few in the past, but I don't have any on the lot at the moment."

"Any chance you'd be able to get one by Monday?" I ask. "Whichever model you think is best?"

He studies me, clearly trying to discern if I'm serious. "I could, but it will cost extra to have it shipped so quickly," he replies.

"That's fine," I reply. "I'll send the payment. You have my contact information. I'll let you know the address it should be delivered to once it's here."

He nods and smiles widely, likely thinking about the commission he'll be making off this sale. I climb into the car and pull away from the curb. The sensation of driving myself feels foreign at first, but I quickly readjust and enjoy the quiet morning as I drive toward Fourth Street.

I pull up in front of the blue house, and Jace appears in the doorway. He walks down the brick walkway with a duffle bag slung over his shoulder. He tosses it into the trunk and climbs into the passenger seat before kissing me hello.

"Sweet ride," he tells me, looking over the brand-new interior.

"Buckle up," I reply, shifting the car into drive.

"Any chance you're going to tell me where we're going?"

"None," I reply, grinning over at him.

"Any chance you'll let me drive so we make it there in one piece?"

"None."

We arrive safely at the small airport about an hour later. Julie and Steve are already waiting on the runway as I carefully park the car in the private lot.

Jace looks around in confusion. "Where are we going, Vivienne?"

"Have a little faith," I tell him. "Come on."

I climb out of the car and grab my bag. Jace does the same before I lock the SUV.

We walk over to the small plane parked on the runway. A tall older man who must be the Vanderbilts' pilot stands next to Julie and Steve. He bows slightly as Jace and I reach the runway, suggesting he's either been told or simply figured out who I really am.

Jace looks understandably bewildered.

"Princess," the pilot greets me. I say a bad word in my head. "It's my pleasure to fly you and your friend today."

"Thank you for accommodating this in your schedule so last minute."

"I do whatever Duke Vanderbilt or his guests ask, especially when it's for our future queen." The man smiles. I nod to Julie and Steve and grab Jace's hand, pulling him up the short set of stairs.

"What the hell is going on?" Jace whispers to me as we settle into the luxurious leather seats on the plane. "Who are those people? Why was he talking to you like that?"

"I'll explain everything when we get there, I promise," I implore. "Just trust me, please."

Jace looks far from appeased, but he nods and stops asking questions.

The pilot gives me a respectful nod as he climbs the stairs and heads into the small cockpit. Julie and Steve take two of the seats several rows behind us. The door automatically raises and closes. A couple of minutes later, we're whizzing down the runway and are airborne. Jace looks out the window, his handsome face impassive.

It takes us just over three hours to arrive in South Carolina. Jace dozes off about twenty minutes into the flight, while I stare out the window, trying to decide what I'm going to tell him when it's just the two of us again. I could still concoct some sort of story to explain it all away, but there's a large part of me that just wants to reveal the truth. Explaining my departure by telling him the same packaged story as I'm supposed to share with everyone else, that I've decided to leave Lincoln and transfer to a university in London because I miss the city, seems ludicrous now.

Beyond that, I also want him to know the truth. To understand why I have to go.

I glance back at Julie and Steve and think of all the work that has gone into allowing me to have this opportunity in the first place. The key component has always been that no one can know who I really am. Entrusting Jace with my true identity is the largest leap of faith I can take.

By the time we land, I'm still undecided.

We disembark into warm sunshine, and I thank the Vanderbilts' pilot again. He promises he'll be back to return us to Michigan tomorrow afternoon.

I pile into a waiting taxi alongside Jace, Julie, and Steve. Jace and my security team exchange curious looks, but none of them speak as we wind through streets lined with luxurious houses to the address the pilot gave us. The taxi driver leaves the car windows down, and I'm quickly sweating in my jeans and sweater.

"Y'all picked a good weekend to visit," the driver informs us. "Unseasonably warm at the moment."

We pull up to a gated entrance. Julie climbs out to speak to the security guard. After a brief discussion, she gets back into the car and the gate slides open.

A short stretch of tree-lined driveway lies ahead, leading up to a wide curve. We reach the bend, and the Vanderbilt's beach house appears before us. It's every bit as ostentatious as I expected it to be.

The base of the three-story house is made of stone, contrasted against wood shingles that have turned a weathered gray in the salty air. We all step out of the taxi and stand in front of the mansion, taking in the luxurious sight. We're surrounded by lush greenery on all sides, which makes the house seem as though it's in the midst of a tropical oasis.

Jace grabs our bags from the trunk, and I take the opportunity to pull Julie and Steve aside on the cobbled driveway.

"We're all set here," I promise. "I won't leave this property, and I'll call if anything comes up."

They nod, although I can tell they're both hesitant to leave. I'm guessing it's because Jace wasn't who they envisioned when I told them I was taking this trip with a good friend.

Finally, Julie and Steve climb back into the taxi after promising they'll be back tomorrow afternoon to pick us up and return to the airport.

I walk up to Jace's side.

He glances over at me. The sea breeze ruffles his dark hair. "You've got a lot of explaining to do."

"I know," I tell him, grabbing his hand and pulling him forward.

We step into the front foyer. The walls of the entryway are lined with white shiplap, and a bench made of weathered wood is pushed against the wall. We keep walking deeper inside the house until we reach a short stretch of stairs, climbing them to emerge into a massive gourmet kitchen equipped with sparkling marble countertops and brand-new appliances.

To the right is the dining room, which boasts a long, gleaming table set for twenty people. A large living room sits off to the left, containing three long couches covered in woven material. An elaborate coffee table artfully composed of driftwood sits in the middle of the room atop a braided jute rug.

Four sets of glass doors comprise the far wall. I walk toward one and slide it open. An expansive wooden deck stretches before me. To one side sits an outdoor kitchen, complete with a grill and a bar counter that seats eight. Another corner of the deck contains a stone firepit with several plush armchairs gathered around it. Just past it is a wrought-iron spiral staircase that leads to an upper deck. A long dining table sits close to the railing that encircles the edge of the deck, made of slatted wood. This one is set for ten.

I walk over to the railing, which overlooks an oval shaped pool with a hot tub sectioned off to one side. The smooth tile that encircles it leads to a boardwalk that gradually is swallowed by the grains that comprise the private stretch of white sandy beach.

Jace comes to stand next to me, letting out a low whistle of appreciation. "Promise me we're not trespassing."

"I promise. This place belongs to friends of my parents. We have an open invitation to visit whenever. Did you pack a swimsuit?"

Jace nods.

"I'll meet you at the pool in five minutes." I take my overnight bag from Jace and carry it into the master bedroom, which boasts a sweeping view of the turquoise water and has a bathroom that's about the same size as my dorm room. I quickly change into a navy blue bikini and put Jace's gray t-shirt on over it.

I head back downstairs, passing four of the other eight bedrooms. Jace is already waiting for me by the pool. He's wearing swim trunks, a t-shirt, and a baseball cap, and grins when he sees my choice of attire.

We walk down the boardwalk, side by side. The coarse grains of sand rub against my bare feet. I smile triumphantly when I see the small white sailboat lying just past the dunes.

232

"Help me get it into the water." I turn, and Jace is standing in the sand, looking at me in confusion.

"Please tell me we're not about to steal someone's boat."

"It comes with the house," I reply. "Just help me get the boat in the water, and I swear I'll explain everything."

Jace studies me for a long moment.

"I watched a football game," I finally say.

That's enough to make him step forward and help me haul the boat toward the waves lapping against the shore. I pull off the t-shirt and toss it onto the sand. I feel Jace's eyes on me as I start to adjust the lines on the boat. Out of the corner of my eye, I watch him pull off his own shirt and hat, so he's standing next to me in nothing but his swim trunks.

We start to push the boat into the salty water. The waves lap against my feet, calves, and soon I'm submerged up to my waist. The air may be warm, but the water feels freezing. The sailboat bobs, and I raise the sail. The boat tilts precariously on the surface of the water.

"Climb on," I call to Jace, raising my voice to make myself heard over the sound of the waves and the wind.

To my surprise, he does as I instruct without comment. Once he's on board, I hoist myself up as well. The boat sways under our combined weight but remains vertical. We're past the break point now, starting to drift away from shore rather than toward it.

I crawl around the small hull, adjusting lines and lowering the tiller. The sail whips taut in a strong gust of wind, and we're rapidly propelled farther away from the shoreline.

I look over at Jace. "Now you've been sailing."

He grins in response as the wind tousles his dark hair into a casual disarray. The stretch of beach we departed from is now just a thin white strip beyond the tranquil waters that surround us.

A carpet of shimmering blue stretches endlessly around us,

marred only by the occasional whitecap. We're pushed along for another couple hundred feet, until the wind dies down and our speed lessens to nothing more than a slight rocking motion.

Jace looks over at me, eyebrows raised. "You have a plan to get back to shore, right?" he asks. The Vanderbilts' enormous house has become little more than a speck on the horizon.

I shrug. "Wait for some more wind?"

Jace stares at me in amazement for a moment, then bursts out laughing. "So, we're stranded?" he asks.

"Looking that way."

"I thought you've been sailing before?" Jace asks, shaking his head.

"I have. I just haven't been the one doing the sailing," I reply.

"Who was?"

I haven't made a conscious decision yet, but the words come out anyway. "Some of my father's men. Technically, the Royal Yachtsmen."

"The Royal Yachtsmen?" Jace asks, grinning. It dies when he sees my serious expression. "You're not joking?"

I shake my head.

"So...when the pilot called you Princess..."

"I didn't go to school in London," I admit. It's a relief to say the words out loud. "I'm from a small European country by the Mediterranean Sea. It's called Marcedenia. It's a monarchy still, and..." I let my voice trail off, unable to say the words.

Jace stares at me for an elongated moment. "This isn't happening," he mutters to himself. "This isn't happening," he says again, louder this time. "This is some sort of joke, right? What are you talking about?"

"Jace, it's the truth," I reply, my voice pleading. "I'm sorry I didn't tell you sooner. I had to make certain my cover story was protected, and I didn't think—well, I didn't expect—"

Jace cuts me off, his voice shifting from disbelief to anger. "What the hell are you talking about? You've been lying to me this entire time?"

"No, Jace, you're the only person I haven't lied to," I reply. "I swear."

"Maybe not directly, but you let me believe a lie. You let me tell my family lies."

"Jace, believe me, if I could have told them the truth—"

"And now, what? You've dragged me out to the middle of nowhere and dropped this bomb on me while we're stranded at sea? Why would you do that? What was the point of any of this?"

"There was no point!" I exclaim, frustrated. "I've been stuck in a palace my entire life. I saw the same people every day and did the same thing every day. The only people my own age back home are afraid to even look at me wrong. Anything I said to anyone could end up leaked to the press. My father was diagnosed with Alzheimer's, and I found out I only have a few years until I became the monarch, not a few decades. I begged my parents to let me start college someplace new, where I could experience some normal, and they agreed to let me come to Lincoln for one semester. These past few months have been my only chance at experiencing anything close to a normal life. I couldn't tell anyone the truth. Especially you."

Some of the anger has ebbed from Jace's expression. "What do you mean, especially me?"

I smile at him ruefully. "I expected to like the campus. I expected to meet new friends. I expected to like choosing my own classes. I expected to feel free after years of having my every move scrutinized. I didn't expect you. Going to class, eating in the dining hall, watching TV with Katie in my dorm room, that all made me feel normal. You make me feel happy. I knew telling you the truth would ruin it. Would ruin us."

Jace opens his mouth to speak, but I continue talking.

"And you only took me home last week. Before that we were just flirting, at most. You seriously think I should have been spilling my deepest secrets to you?"

"You seriously think we were just flirting?" Jace replies. Some anger has seeped back into his tone.

I turn my gaze out to the open water. "I didn't know what to think," I whisper.

"So what does this mean?" Jace asks. "You said your parents agreed to one semester? So in two weeks, you leave to be royalty and we'll never see each other again?"

I keep looking at the shimmering waves, unable to meet his eyes. "That's exactly what it means."

Jace is silent, and I'm afraid to look over at him. I don't know which would be worse: pain or indifference.

"I'm sorry," I break the silence first. "I know it's not enough —not fair—but I'm truly sorry. I didn't see this—you—coming. I thought it was just the challenge, at first. I liked arguing with you, and then I wanted you to just be a meaningless fling. By the time I realized you weren't, I couldn't change things. I didn't want to change things."

"You didn't want to change things? God, Vivienne, do you have any idea how selfish that sounds?"

"I know it was selfish."

"So you were just stringing me along, making the most of your time here until you just up and disappear?"

"Stringing you along? Jace, no—you have to know that I— that the only reason—" I stutter and trip over my words as I attempt to answer him.

"You let me think we could work, while knowing full well it never could, right?"

"Well, yes, but—"

"Sounds like stringing along to me."

"Fine, maybe you're right," I tell him. "But you have to know I never did it to hurt you. I tried to avoid you as soon as I realized —when I started to…" I give up on trying to explain the draw I fought from our first encounter. The way he captivated me, even when he annoyed me. How I literally ran in the opposite direction to fight the pull. "I wasn't strong enough to stop it. I didn't want to stop it. And you—I mean you're Jace Dawson. You're a legend. You're the one who's royalty here. I didn't think I would mean anything to you. I thought this would just run its course."

"Run its course?" Jace repeats, anger filling his tone again. "It sounds like I'm the one who didn't mean anything. Was any of it even real to you?"

"Of course it was real." My voice is rough with emotion. "It was all real. Jace, you know I have feelings for you. I feel things with you I've never felt with anyone. I lo—" I pause, unable to finish the sentence.

Jace scoffs. "You can't even say it."

"Not because I wouldn't mean it. I won't be able to leave in two weeks if I say it."

"Would that be such a bad thing?"

I smile sadly. "I won't be able to live with myself if I don't. Could you? Could you walk away from playing football profes-sionally? Could you let down your family, your coaches, your teammates, all those years of work? Because that's what I would be doing. I'm an only child. There's no other direct heir. I would be walking away from my parents, from my country, from the millions of people depending on me to lead them the way my ancestors have for hundreds of years."

"That's what you meant. When you asked about conforming being bigger than just you."

It's not a question, but I answer it anyway. "Yes."

This time, Jace is the one who looks away to the water. "Fuck," he curses. There's a new note of resignation underneath the residual annoyance and anger in his voice.

There's not much else to say after that.

We sit in silence on the tiny sailboat until the wind picks up again and I'm able to navigate us back toward the sandy shore. When we get close enough to the beach, I slip off the boat, guiding it in through the shallower water. Jace follows my lead and helps me pull it to shore. We drag the boat back to its original spot. Jace turns wordlessly toward the house.

I grab his forearm, and he stops.

"Do you want to leave?" I ask quietly. "I can make the arrangements. We can be back at the airport within an hour."

Jace turns and studies my face for a long moment. "No," he finally says. "I don't want to leave."

Relief fills me.

"I must be a masochist." Jace turns and grabs his hat and shirt from their spots on the sand before heading inside, leaving me standing there in the sunlight.

I sit alone on the beach for a while. By the time I follow him inside, it's nearing dusk. I walk into the large house, and there's no sign of Jace anywhere.

Strolling around the empty kitchen, I peer in cabinets and the fridge. We were stranded at sea during lunchtime, and I realize I haven't eaten all day. The kitchen is stocked with ingredients, but nothing that's ready to eat.

I open the freezer to find a full bottle of vodka and pour some in a glass tumbler before I head over to the living room, then flop down onto one of the couches. I spot a remote on the coffee table and hit the power button.

The flat screen television hums to life, displaying some sort of soap opera that fills the wide screen. I don't pay any attention to it, instead sipping the vodka and letting the dialogue fade to background noise as I stare out of the sliding doors at the water barely visible in the receding light. The alcohol burns my empty stomach as I lose myself in my thoughts.

I'm pulled back to the present when I hear footsteps on the stairs.

Jace appears in the doorway of the kitchen, still dressed in the same clothes he wore sailing earlier. We stare at each other for a minute, and then he walks over to the fridge and begins pulling random items out.

I stand and walk over to the kitchen island, abandoning the show and my empty glass. "What are you doing?"

"Cooking." Jace's voice is absent of anger, or any other emotion.

"Can I help?"

He slides a red pepper to me. "Chop this."

I look around the kitchen, finally spotting a cutting board and knife.

Jace starts cutting up a large chunk of broccoli. The only sounds in the kitchen are the sharp thud of our knives and the muted exclamations coming from the television.

Finally, I can't take the charged silence anymore. "I really am sorry, Jace," I whisper.

He sighs. "I know you are. I'm mad at the situation, more than you."

"But you are mad at me." My voice is soft, and I don't bother to hide the hurt.

"Wouldn't you be?"

I try to put myself in Jace's position and imagine finding out something like this about him.

"Yeah, I would be," I reply truthfully.

We resume chopping.

"How much of it was a lie?" Jace suddenly asks.

"What do you mean?"

"Like Philip. Is he actually your stepbrother?"

"No," I reply. "He's part of my security detail. They had him pose as a student so that he would be able to stay close to me on campus without arousing suspicion."

"Security detail?"

"It's normally eight agents. But since no one knows who I am here, they decided four would be enough."

"Who were the other three?"

"Thomas joined the faculty as a professor and my supposed stepfather. The two others were the people who came with us on the plane earlier. They've been undercover as campus security to provide back-up to Philip and Thomas if they need it."

"And your father is a king?"

"Yes."

"Do you really play chess together?"

I smile, pleased he remembered that detail. "Yes, the doctors suggested it to help with the Alzheimer's."

"Did you really learn about the Kamanski method from Jerry Lewis?"

Jace continues to pelt me with questions as we finish making dinner and eat it, verifying things I've told him, and then moving on to questions about my upbringing and Marcedenia.

Eventually we move to the couch, where the interrogation continues. It's a relief to respond without thinking, to reveal the final pieces of myself I hid from Jace before.

Finally, he falls silent. "I'm going to bed," he says, standing and walking out of the living room.

I let out a disappointed sigh and lie down on the couch. The cushions are still warm from where Jace was just sitting. I remain there for a while longer before I stand and start to walk upstairs myself.

The hallway is dark, aside from a thin beam of light coming from one of the guest bedrooms. I hesitate, but pass it and walk into the master bedroom. I brush my teeth and wash my face before unzipping my overnight bag.

Brightly colored lingerie spills out of the top. I stare at the bag for a moment, disappointment overwhelming me. I grab the lacy pink slip that's almost entirely see through and put it on before I slide in between the crisp sheets. I toss and turn, until finally I manage to fall asleep.

I'm awoken by a creak in the hallway. My heart pounds as I sit up in bed.

"Jace?" I whisper. There's no response.

I slide out of the warm bed and tiptoe over to the door. The hallway is dimly illumined by the same strip of light I passed earlier. I walk down the hallway and pause outside the slightly ajar door. I push it open a couple more inches to reveal Jace leaning against a stack of pillows on the left side of the bed, shirtless, and scrolling through his phone.

A nightlight is plugged into one of the electrical sockets in the wall, providing a small glimmer of light. The door hinges squeak as the door opens farther, which catches Jace's attention.

His gaze turns heated as he takes in my appearance, and he rubs a hand across his face. "What the hell are you wearing?" he asks in greeting.

"I thought the campus playboy would know what lingerie looks like," I reply. In the darkened room it's easy to pretend the past day never happened.

Jace sends me a look that makes it clear he's not amused by my flippant comment.

I take slow, deliberate steps over to his side of the bed before climbing up on the mattress next to him. Jace takes an unsteady breath and turns off his phone.

"What are you doing, Viv?" he asks. The sound of the familiar nickname makes my heart clench. "This is hard enough already, don't make it worse."

"I know," I whisper into the darkness. "And I know it's not fair to ask you this, but I want it to be you, Jace."

"Vivienne." My name comes out as a tortured whisper.

"Please, Jace," I plead.

I don't see his hands move in the darkness, but suddenly their warm weight settles on my bare thighs. They rest there for a moment. I remain completely still, hardly daring to breathe for fear of ruining the moment.

I'm suddenly flipped around onto my back by the practiced dexterity of Jace's hands. He hovers over me for a moment, and I'm reminded of the night of our first kiss. The same heady suspense floods my system.

This time, Jace kisses me first. Hesitantly, and then hungrily. I run my nails across his back as his tongue explores my mouth, and he groans, pushing himself closer to me so there's no space between our bodies at all. He moves his mouth to my neck and then to my chest, kissing every expanse of exposed skin he encounters. There's no shortage, thanks to my choice of sleep-wear. I moan loudly, the pleasure overwhelming.

Jace's hands slide up and under the lacy nightgown, and he discovers I'm not wearing anything underneath. He tugs the material higher and higher until it's over my head. I lie completely naked beneath him. He traces his hands up and down my body slowly, reverently, leaving goosebumps in his wake.

I tug at the waistband of his boxer briefs, and he laughs.

"Hang on," he tells me, climbing off the bed and walking over to where his duffle bag sits in the corner. He pulls something out of it, and then returns to the bed, lying back down beside me.

"Awfully presumptuous, weren't you?" I ask, nodding to the foil packet he's holding.

Jace grins. "Says the girl who came into my bedroom in the middle of the night wearing *that*." He nods to the scraps of pink lace resting next to my head.

I wiggle closer to him. Bolts of lust shoot through me as his bare skin makes contact with mine, mingling with the tingles of nervousness I'm also experiencing. Jace gazes down at me, his expression unreadable and his body motionless. I panic, thinking he's changed his mind.

"I thought you would be a little more efficient about getting naked," I tell him impatiently. "Maybe sometime in the next minute?"

Jace smiles as he finally pulls off his boxer briefs. A new wave of trepidation courses through me as he sheaths himself with the condom, and I hope it's not clear on my face.

"Was that an order?" Jace asks, brushing a hand against my stomach. I clench my abdominal muscles in response to the sensuous touch.

I raise my eyebrows, confused by his question.

"This may come as a surprise to you, but I've never fucked a future queen before," Jace adds, giving me a sexy smirk. "I'm not sure how it works."

Love, pure and unadulterated, courses through me as I realize what Jace is trying to do. It's exactly what I need right now. I roll on top of him and begin kissing him again, fueled by the feel of his entire body naked beneath mine. He returns my passion and then some. His hands roam over every inch of my exposed skin as he rolls us again, so he's back above me.

I'm a needy, writhing mass of limbs by the time Jace finally begins to ease inside of me. My slick walls part easily for him at first, but I feel a sharp twinge of pain as he pushes farther inside.

Jace immediately stills. "Are you okay?" he asks, hesitating.

I raise my hand and trace the side of his stubbled cheek. "Keep going," I urge.

He slides forward another inch, and then another, and keeps going until he's fully seated inside me. I shift slightly as my body adjusts to the foreign sensation.

Jace's eyes never leave mine. The connection between us feels tangible. The outside world has ceased to exist as I lie beneath him, vulnerable and exposed. The house around us could collapse and I don't think I would even notice.

Jace moves, and the motion creates a delicious friction inside me. I moan loudly, and he moves again. He quickens his movements, and I wrap my legs around his waist to pull him even closer. He shifts deeper within me, and I cry out in pleasure. Jace begins whispering in my ear, and the sound of his deep, rough voice is all it takes to send me over the edge.

Every cell of my body lights up as I experience wave after wave of pleasure, while my inner muscles convulse around him. Jace thrusts into me a few more times before he lets out a low groan and stills. He remains hovering above me for a moment longer, resting his weight on his forearms on either side of my face.

He slowly slides out of me and reaches over to the bedside table to grab a couple of tissues. He pulls off the condom and wraps it in one, then uses the other to wipe gently between my legs. He drops the tissues in the trash and then lies back down in bed next to me. Only our arms are touching now, and my body immediately grieves the loss of contact.

"Is it always like that?" I ask as the transcendent sensation begins to fade.

"Not for me."

I roll onto my side and snuggle up against the firm planes of his body, resting my head in its favorite spot between his chin and his shoulder. Jace wraps his arms around me to pull me closer, and I sigh in contentment.

"Thank you," I whisper against his warm skin. Jace doesn't reply, but his grip around me tightens.

Neither of us acknowledge the late night events that occurred the following morning.

The day passes by quickly. I cook eggs for breakfast, and we eat them out on the porch. I sunbathe on one of the lounge chairs that surrounds the pool, while Jace swims laps in the heated water. We make sandwiches and walk along the beach before eating them amongst the dunes.

It's as though nothing ever happened. I never told him the truth, and we never had sex. The only reminder of our night together is the ache I woke up with between my legs.

Four o'clock arrives before I know it. I reluctantly zip the bag filled with the many outfits I never actually wore. I walk down the hallway to find Jace closing up his own bag. I pause to look inside his bedroom for a moment. Flashes of last night play back in my mind, and my cheeks flush. Jace glances up and catches me blushing. He grins in a way that suggests he knows exactly what I'm thinking about, but doesn't say a word.

We head out onto the cobbled driveway and the front gate opens immediately, announcing Julie and Steve's arrival in another taxi. Jace and I climb inside silently after depositing our bags in the trunk.

"Good trip?" Julie asks, looking between our somber faces in confusion.

I nod, my stomach sinking as we pull away from the lavish beach house where the best and one of the worst moments of my life took place.

The drive to the airport, the flight back to Michigan, and the drive back to campus are all mostly silent.

I pull up in front of the blue house just before nine. The lights in every window seem to be on, blazing in the darkness.

We sit in the silent car for a long moment. I don't know what to say, and he doesn't seem to either.

"I should go," Jace finally says, but he doesn't move.

"Okay," I whisper.

Jace sits in the passenger seat for a while longer, then finally opens his door and climbs out. He reaches into the back seat to retrieve his duffle bag and stands there, gazing at it in his hands. Cold air rushes past him into the interior of the car and I shiver, still dressed for South Carolina's temperate climate. Jace notices the movement, and it seems to jerk him out of his reverie.

"I wouldn't change it," he tells me. "Even knowing it all now. How it will end. I still wouldn't change it, Viv."

I simply nod, unable to speak as I desperately try to hold the prickling in my eyes at bay. Jace gives me a sad smile, then shuts the car door. He turns and walks up the brick path. I drive back toward Lincoln's campus.

I find a spot near Kennedy Hall and grab my own bag from the backseat. The campus is quiet. I only pass a couple of people as I walk inside the dorm and enter my dark bedroom. Katie isn't supposed to get back to campus until tomorrow morning, and I'm grateful to have the room to myself.

I drop my bags and flip on the light. Then, I lie face down on my bed and start to sob.

CHAPTER NINETEEN

When I wake up, my face feels stiff, coated with a long night's worth of dried tears. I don't get out of bed and dress in my running clothes like usual. Instead, I just lie under the covers, allowing myself to drown in heartbreak for a little while longer.

After forty-five minutes, I talk myself into becoming a functioning person again. I still have two weeks left at Lincoln, and spending them being miserable won't make leaving any easier. With that thought in mind, I climb out of bed, determined not to wallow further.

I head to the bathroom first to wash the salty streaks off my face. I slather on a heavy coat of moisturizer, which has become an essential ritual thanks to the increasingly chilly Michigan weather. This morning I put on even more than usual, hoping it will alleviate some of the puffiness around my eyes.

I dress in black jeans and a soft gray cashmere sweater before pulling my black wool jacket on. My phone buzzes on the bedside table, and I pick it up, scanning the list of notifications. The only name I want to see isn't there.

Instead, I see several messages from Philip asking if I'm back on campus yet. The final one says he spoke to Julie and is glad we're back safely, so I don't bother replying.

The latest message is from an unfamiliar number. I tap on it to see it's from the car dealership. The message reads *Car is ready, what's the drop-off address?*

I reply with Jace's address, and seconds later, a response appears. *Will be there in fifteen minutes. Keys on back right tire as requested.*

I respond, thanking them and confirming the payment has been received.

Realizing it's already later than I thought, I quickly sort through the large stack of binders and books on my desk, pulling out the ones I'll need for today and shoving them all in my bag before I head out the door.

I walk toward the crowded parking lot, grateful I still have a car for the time being. I locate the black SUV quickly, climbing in and tossing my bag on the passenger seat.

When I arrive at a coffee shop on the periphery of campus, I order a coffee and muffin, keeping a watchful eye on the large clock that hangs behind the register.

After paying, I walk over to the end of the counter to wait for my coffee.

"Excuse me, aren't you Vivienne?" a girl's voice says to my left.

I glance over to see a slim girl with long, jet-black hair. She looks vaguely familiar, but I can't place her.

"Yes, I am..." I let my voice trail off. "Have we met before?"

Irritation flashes across her pretty face. "We were both at the football party a few weeks ago. Although I guess it's not too surprising that you don't remember. You were pretty wasted."

I look down at her disdainfully, grateful my tall frame allows me a few extra inches of height over her. "Or I don't remember you because I was a bit preoccupied," I retort.

Her face twists in a cruel smile. "You know, I came over here to warn you about Jace Dawson, but now I'm not going to bother."

A sharp stab of pain pierces me at the sound of his name.

"You're just his flavor of the week, and I can't wait to watch when he drops you for the next one."

Despite Jace's reputation, I don't experience even the slightest twinge of doubt that she might be right. I know in two weeks she'll think that she was, but for the moment, I savor the opportunity to defend our relationship.

"So thoughtful of you to warn me," I reply sweetly. "But are you sure you're not just jealous?"

If looks could kill, I would no longer be standing.

The barista chooses this moment to call my name. I give the girl from the party a regal wave before grabbing the hot cup and heading back out the front door.

I'm both annoyed and amused as I climb back into the car and start driving toward Jace's house, alternating between taking sips of the hot coffee and bites of the warm blueberry muffin. It was an unfortunate choice—it reminds me of eating breakfast in the Dawsons' cozy kitchen.

When I reach the blue house, there's a gray Honda sitting in the driveway and a gleaming silver Porsche parked in front of it. I smile, imagining the look on Jace's face when he sees it. I pull into the end of the driveway and park, pulling a pen out of my bag and putting it in my jacket pocket before stepping outside.

I walk over to the Porsche, feeling along on top of the back right tire. As promised, my fingers graze the cold metal of a pair of keys. I grab them and walk back around to the driver's side, clicking the button to unlock the door. Sitting on the front seat is a white envelope. I open it to see a wad of papers which list Jace Dawson as the car's owner. I stuff them back inside the envelope and pull the pen back out of my pocket. I stare at the blank envelope, debating about what to write.

Everything I think of seems either too sappy or not meaningful enough.

Beginning to feel foolish, I finally scribble *Every moment meant everything*. I don't bother signing my name the way I did on the last note I left him. I don't think Jace will have any doubts about who is gifting him a car worth a hundred thousand dollars. I place the envelope back on the supple leather seat, then shut and lock the car door.

I walk up the brick pathway and ring the doorbell.

The same guy who talked to me in the dining hall after the party opens the door. I groan internally. I was hoping Anderson would be the one to answer.

Jace's housemate simply stares at me.

"I'm Vivienne," I state.

"I know." His tone is flat.

"And you are…" I prompt.

"Kenny," he answers. "That car your doing?"

"It's a gift for Jace."

Kenny scoffs. "The weekend getaway wasn't enough?"

I look at him in surprise, well aware Jace told his teammates he had a family obligation this past weekend.

Kenny notices my confusion. "Please, no one on the team bought that story for a second."

"Can you just give these to Jace when he gets back, please? I have to get going or I'll be late for my first class."

I hold the keys out, but Kenny doesn't take them.

"I've known Jace since middle school. We grew up two towns

apart and went to all the same football camps. He's never missed practice for a girl. Never."

"Jace can make his own decisions. I didn't force him to do anything he didn't decide to do," I contend.

Kenny studies me. "It seems like you actually care about Jace, so let me give you some advice. Despite what might have happened this weekend, football is the most important thing to Jace. Money is tight for Jace's family. He's got a real chance to play professionally, and if he does, it'll make a huge difference for not only his future. People don't make it to the pros by missing practice the week before playoffs for a vacation. Jace may have decided to go, but the only reason he went is because you asked him to."

His words play on a loop over and over again through my head. *He went because you asked him to. He went because you asked him to. He went because you asked him to.*

I was so focused on the possible repercussions our getaway could cause me that I never even considered the consequences they could have for Jace.

I wonder what Kenny will think when I permanently disappear from Jace's life in just a couple of weeks. Based on the scowl he's wearing, my absence will be welcome. Despite the uncomfortable sensation of being glared at, I'm glad Jace has friends who are protective. Who care about his success and his future.

"I have to go. Just give him these, please." I hold the keys out again. This time, Kenny takes them.

I rush back down the brick path, cursing when I climb in the car and see the time on the dashboard. Quickly, I shift the car into reverse and zoom down the empty street, grateful Jace lives so close to campus. I follow the signs to Bryant Hall, pulling into one of the last available spots in the lot. Grabbing my bag off the seat, I take off toward the building's entrance, pressing the lock button on the car key over my shoulder as I do.

I enter my philosophy class just as the professor is starting to speak and give her an apologetic smile as I slide into the seat Katie has saved for me.

The lecture drags by slowly as the professor reviews the long list of topics that will be covered on the final exam.

"So, how was your weekend?" Katie asks eagerly as soon as class ends.

I pause, unsure how to respond. Every possible adjective could apply to some part of it.

We emerge out of the massive lecture hall into the crowded hallway. The surrounding noise and activity doesn't distract Katie, who continues looking at me intently.

"It was bittersweet," I finally reply.

"Bittersweet? What does that mean?" Katie looks puzzled.

"It means it contained some perfect moments I'll never forget and some horrible moments I'll never forget. Jace and I are over."

"What?" Katie gasps, looking over at me in concerned confusion. "You guys broke up? Why?"

We've reached the tall wooden doors that mark the entrance to the building. I open my mouth to spew the lie about transferring, already knowing it will justifiably spawn a whole new series of questions I don't want to answer. Before I can say a single word, we walk outside into a sea of bright flashes.

"Princess! Princess!"

"Princess Vivienne!"

"Over here, Princess!"

"It's her! Princess!"

The cacophony of shouts assaults me as I stand there frozen, completely stunned. The sudden collision of my royal status and time as Vivienne Rhodes is too overwhelming to process.

Paparazzi continue to clamor, unfazed by my impersonation of a statue as noise swirls around me.

"When will you become queen now that your father is ill?" a reporter yells.

That snaps me out of my daze. It's one thing to be confronted with my true identity, but another entirely to hear a stranger casually question information that's been carefully guarded. Dimly, I'm aware of Katie calling my name next to me, but I'm too overcome to think straight, much less respond.

I turn and fight back against the tide of students streaming out from the building behind us. My progress is slow thanks to the uproar the paparazzi are creating, but I eventually manage to get back inside the building. I duck into an empty lecture hall and pull my phone out of my pocket.

The absolute silence of the massive auditorium is eerie in comparison to the echoes of the shouts I can still feel reverberating in my mind.

I pull out my phone to see the screen is covered with notifications. I chastise myself for not having checked it right after class. Fingers shaking, I unlock the phone and tap on Thomas's name. He answers before it even has a chance to ring.

"Where are you?" he asks urgently.

"One of the classrooms in Bryant Hall. Second floor," I answer.

"We'll be right there."

I hang up and sit down in one of the empty seats in the front row. Resting my head in my hands, I try to quell the panic rapidly building inside of me. That many reporters, here at Lincoln, suggests the situation is well beyond the point of any containment.

Philip and Thomas burst through the door a couple minutes

later. They both scan the large lecture hall I'm sitting in and relax slightly when they see it's empty.

"Are you okay?" Thomas asks me.

I nod mutely.

"Where were you this weekend?" Philip asks. "Julie won't tell me, but Steve let slip you flew someplace. Did someone recognize you there? Were you with that football player? Did you tell him the truth?" He fires the questions rapidly at me.

"Philip," Thomas chastises. "Now is not the time. We need to get her out of here safely."

I'm silent. The panic continues to build as Philip's questions set in. I told him everything two days ago. Everything about me, about my family. He's the *only* person I told. My heart struggles against rational thought. Did I misjudge everything?

"He wouldn't have told," I whisper, not sure who I'm trying to assure. Myself, maybe.

"Wait a minute. You actually told him?" Philip looks stunned. "Why would you—"

"Philip," Thomas interrupts. "Go out to the hallway and see if you can find a back entrance."

Philip looks incensed, but follows Thomas's instructions, walking back out into the hallway and leaving the two of us alone.

"Thomas, I'm so sorry for lying to you about this weekend," I tell him, my voice breaking. "For once I just wanted... I just wanted to be normal. To truly feel like I escaped it all. As incredible as the last few months have been, it's still hard to feel free when you're both around reminding me that I'm not."

Thomas nods sagely. "I know your life is not easy, Princess. And believe it or not, I remember what it was like to be young and in love once myself. Things become clearer and more complicated."

"I'm not in love with him," I dispute. The false words hang heavily in the massive hall.

"Aren't you?" Thomas asks with a sad smile. I drop my eyes from his knowing gaze. "I'm just glad that nothing happened and you're safe."

"Thanks." I tell the scuffed floor.

Thomas pulls out his phone and types something quickly.

"I found the back door." Philip re-enters the room.

"We've got a car service waiting outside. Julie and Steve are here. We just have to make it to the street. Princess, do not leave my side, and do not stop or speak to anyone, no matter what they might say."

I nod. The instructions are familiar. I follow Philip and Thomas out into the now empty hallway. Philip leads us down the hallway and through a door to the right. A short flight of steps later, he pushes open a metal door, revealing the rear of the brick building. We exit the building in single file, but Thomas and Philip fall into a protective formation on either side of me as soon as we emerge outside into the daylight.

The press isn't visible yet, but I can hear the commotion coming from the front of the building.

"That's our car right there." Thomas points to a black sedan idling alongside the curb a few hundred feet away. "Let's go."

I spot Julie and Steve standing next to it. An assortment of campus security and police cars are haphazardly parked along the street as well.

We only make it twenty feet before we're spotted. Bright flashes and questions surround us. Thomas places a hand on my back, simultaneously urging me forward and grounding me. The paparazzi fade to the background as I focus on the black car ahead of us as it slowly draws closer and closer. Finally, we reach it.

The campus police and Lincoln police have formed a

perimeter around our car, so that the press are unable to follow us past the sidewalk. I slide hurriedly into the back seat, letting out a loud sigh of relief when I'm behind the tinted glass. Thomas and Philip remain outside as they talk with one of the police officers along with Julie and Steve.

I pull out my phone. The screen is devoid of notifications now. I pull up a new message and stare at the empty "To" field for a moment, deliberating. Finally, I type a "K", and hit Katie's name when it appears.

I type and delete a few different messages before finally sending *I'm sorry I didn't tell you. Hope you understand why.*

Immediately, an error message pops up saying *Phone Disabled.*

The front passenger door opens, and Thomas climbs inside the car.

"Can I use your phone, Thomas?" I ask. "There's something wrong with mine."

"I know." Thomas looks at me apologetically. "Whoever shared your identity here also thought to leak your cell number. I had the phone deactivated as soon as you called me, so no one could track your location or hack it."

"But without my phone, I won't be able to…"

The door across from me opens, and Philip gets in. Julie and Steve climb into the police car parked in front of us. It pulls away from the sidewalk. Thomas instructs our driver to follow. I turn in my seat and look out the back window to see another two police cars are pulling out after us.

I feel a fresh surge of panic as we drive toward the main entrance.

"What about all my stuff? My classes? I rented a car. It's parked in the lot and has to be returned tomorrow."

Thomas looks back reassuringly. "We'll send someone to

collect all your belongings and straighten things out with the university for your final exams and grades. They can return the car as well."

"So that's just it?" I ask in disbelief, leaning forward. "We're leaving? It's over?"

Thomas's face is apologetic. "Your cover has been completely blown. We can't guarantee your safety here anymore, especially with just four agents. We've been instructed to get you back to the palace as soon as possible. They want to make a plan immediately to manage the public response to all this and make a statement."

I lean back against the plush seat and rest my head against the cool glass window. The cold seeps through my entire body, leaving me numb.

I stare blankly ahead into the driver's side mirror and watch as the campus grows smaller and smaller until Lincoln University fades from view entirely. Suffocating despair smothers me.

Four months too late, I realize why I truly wanted to leave Marcedenia for this glimpse of normalcy. So I would stop yearning for it. So I could experience it and move on. I never expected to encounter something—someone—I craved even more.

It's not normalcy that just disappeared behind me.

It's Jace.

And now I'll have to spend the rest of my life knowing I'll never see him again.

PART 2

TWO DECISIONS, ONE DUTY

CHAPTER TWENTY

JACE

She's engaged.

At least according to the half dozen tabloids tossed carelessly across my new front porch. Ever since I moved in a month ago, they've been delivered to the front door each morning without fail. Either the rookie the Sharks put up here last had some strange obsession with gossip magazines, or it's retribution from the teams' publicist for my unremitting disregard of the nightclub openings and other events she's constantly trying to force me to attend to "elevate my profile."

The first time Vivienne was featured on one of the covers, I called the magazine directly, asking to be removed from their list. The glossy pages still appear daily.

I've never bothered to read any of the articles, but today's cover is impossible to ignore. The photo is mostly Viv, her supposed fiancé is just a shadowed blur to her right. She's glancing over her shoulder, her stunning features on clear display through the swirl of strawberry blonde hair that still looks foreign to me.

I stare at the obnoxious black words printed across the glossy cover. *SHE'S ENGAGED! Soon to be Queen of Marcedenia set to marry son of Duke Vanderbilt, long-time royal insider*, it reads.

Ever since Viv's true identity was revealed, interest in Marcedenia's royal family has skyrocketed. It figures the entire country would become obsessed with the girl I'm trying to forget.

The thought of Vivienne marrying anyone, much less the over-privileged, stuffy son of a duke, makes me want to punch something. Since I've just signed a multi-million-dollar contract that depends upon my ability to throw a football, that's not an option.

So, I do the next best thing.

I tear the shiny pages to shreds and then walk out the front door, slamming it behind me.

I have practice later, so I force myself to keep a slower pace as I jog past the rows of mansions that fill the gated community the team has put me up in. Angry thoughts swirl through my head, and I embrace the vitriol, knowing the pain that lurks beneath is infinitely more dangerous.

It's been almost seven months since I last saw her, yet any reminder of her existence still sears just as painfully as it did the Monday morning I realized I would never see her again.

One day I hope I'll be able to laugh about the fact I went to a school with over fifteen thousand willing and available girls for three years, yet managed to fall in love with the only one I couldn't have in just a couple of months. When Anderson brought up the same sobering statistic, I didn't speak to him for a week. I've made it quite clear to both my friends and family the subject of Vivienne is one I won't discuss. I know they all think it's due to anger, or regret, but the truth is, I already think of her often. Too often. I don't need the additional reminders.

I didn't think Viv would be easy to forget, but I didn't think it would be this hard.

Anderson is the only one who still dares to mention her to me. I know it's because he thinks I'm miffed every journalist and photographer within a fifty-mile radius descended on campus to announce an actual celebrity was in our midst before I knew. He thinks I need to get over my grudge and move on. When I'm feeling particularly petty, I wish that was actually the case.

That I'd been blindsided.

That I hadn't known and chosen her anyway.

That I could hate her.

I run for longer than I intend to, and by the time I arrive back at the cookie-cutter mansion that is my temporary home, it's already time to leave for practice. I don't bother changing out of my sweaty clothes before grabbing my practice bag, phone, and keys off the counter and heading into the connected garage. The shiny silver sports car gleams under the automatic lights, a fresh slash against the wound opened by that glossy cover.

Like the girl who gave it to me, my feelings toward the Porsche are complicated. As complex as feelings toward an inanimate object can be, at least. It's the car I always dreamed of having, the car I never would have bought myself, given to me by the girl I can never have. In my most bitter moments, I view it as a bribe. In my most desperate moments, I view it as the most thoughtful, extravagant gift I've ever received. Like I said; complicated. I've considered selling it, but I know doing so would haunt me in its own way.

Despite my thorny feelings toward the car, I can't deny it's a dream to drive. The winding streets leading from my gated neighborhood to the Sharks' stadium fly by underneath the purring engine.

I enter the parking lot reserved for players, unsurprised to find it mostly empty. Most people assume I coast by on my natural talent, but the truth is I'm usually the first to arrive and the last to leave practice. I still have something to prove, even now. Especially now.

I walk through the parking lot and into the luxurious locker room. Lincoln's facilities were nice, but they pale in comparison to the amenities provided by my new team. Everything looks brand-new, and there's a faint citrus scent always lingering in the air that makes it difficult to believe the building is frequently filled with dozens of sweaty football players. I arrive at my gleaming wooden locker and change out of my still-damp t-shirt into my practice jersey.

My new teammates nod at me as they trickle into the locker room. The Sharks' longtime quarterback and team captain, Chris Jackson, slaps my shoulder as he heads to his locker. Rumor is this is his last season, and I'm his natural successor.

I've yet to encounter any of the animosity or hazing most rookies face. Worn down after years of last-place finishes in the league, every Sharks player is looking to me to resuscitate the weary franchise. The unfamiliar challenge is exhilarating. I've never been the underdog before.

I head out of the locker room as soon as it gets crowded, opting to clear my head out on the freshly mowed field instead. Football has always been a constant. It's never beguiled me and then disappeared.

Practice is exhausting, but I welcome the physical and mental strain as a temporary escape from the residual ache left by the cover I can't seem to forget, no matter how hard I push my body. After practice ends, I follow one of my new teammates to Jackson's mansion. Apparently, it's tradition for the team captain to host a barbecue the week before our first preseason game. Based on the Sharks' previous season's records, I'm not sure if it's a tradition worth continuing, but I keep the pessimistic thought to myself.

I'm one of the last to arrive. Most of the team is already eagerly devouring the massive spread of food after a grueling practice. Once I've said hello to Jackson and the coaches, I head in the direction of the buffet at the insistence of my growling stomach. Halfway there, I hear my name called. James Cooley, the Sharks' rookie wide receiver, is standing next to the pool with a couple of the other younger players. Cooley calls my name again once he has my attention. I amble over to them.

"What's up, guys?" I greet.

"Hey, Dawson," one replies.

"You played for Lincoln, didn't you?" Cooley questions.

"Is this about how we decimated you guys last year?" I reply, grinning. "Don't feel too bad. We did it to everyone else we played, too. It's how you become national champions, you know."

Cooley flips me off. "No, it's about the princess chick." He turns his phone around, revealing a photo of Viv on the screen. My grin freezes in place. "This article says the school she spent a semester at was Lincoln. Did you ever see her?"

It takes a Herculean effort to keep my face blank and voice calm. "Lincoln is a huge school," I tell him. "The only person everyone knew there was me." I flash them all a cocky smirk, hoping that will be the end of it.

"Surprised you managed to overlook a girl who looks like *this*," Cooley remarks, shoving the phone screen closer to my face as though I'm unfamiliar with the features burned into my brain. "I can't believe no one from Lincoln's announced they screwed her royally yet. She probably came here to have some fun before shacking up with this bore." He zooms out on the photo to show the blond guy walking next to Viv, looking every bit as groomed and pompous as one would expect the son of a duke to be.

I don't reply, determined to keep my face neutral. I don't have the same clout here I did at Lincoln yet, and I can't afford to give any of my new teammates the slightest indication of my true feelings regarding this topic.

"I wouldn't have pegged you guys as regular readers of..." I squint at the phone screen. "*Star Sightings Today?*"

Cooley laughs. "One of my younger brothers sent me the link. He's got a massive crush on Princess Vivienne and can't believe she's off the market now." He rolls his eyes. "Kid almost went to Lincoln, and he's convinced if he had been there last year they would have been soul mates."

Not fucking likely is my first thought, but I keep it to myself.

The conversation moves on from Viv to other subjects. I leave as soon as I can to head to the buffet, feeling like I was just sucker-punched in the stomach. It's harder to forget someone when their existence is constantly shoved in your face.

I spend the rest of the evening being pulled from one group to another, making small talk with teammates and meeting their families. Our crusty head coach looks uncomfortable in the domestic atmosphere, which I can relate to. Few of my teammates at Lincoln even had girlfriends, let alone wives and children, the way many of my new teammates do.

The backyard gathering finally begins to die down, but as soon as I try to head out, I'm drawn into a group eager to continue the evening. I'm tempted to beg off, but the realization I have nothing waiting for me besides an empty house results in me agreeing to join the group traveling to the most exclusive club downtown.

Even after all the attention I received at Lincoln, it's still strange to arrive someplace and have everyone stop and stare. I know the scrutiny is partially due to the fact I'm with several of my teammates, but there's no doubt my name is the one being screamed the most as we exit the car and walk along the cordoned off carpet inside the dimly lit club. As soon as we enter the main area, we're surrounded, mostly by scantily clad women. They're all gorgeous, but I barely spare them a glance.

Instead, I push through the crowd to the closed off VIP section and make a beeline for the private bar. I order a drink and lean against the sleek metal counter to watch the bartender make it.

"You're Jace Dawson, aren't you?" A statuesque blonde wearing a tight red dress has joined me at the bar.

"Yup," I reply briskly, then turn back to watch the bartender pour a stream of amber liquid over one perfectly square cube of ice. He slides the tumbler in front of me, and I give him a brief smile of thanks before handing him a bill that includes a hefty tip.

"I grew up here, and I've never seen people this excited for the start of the football season. They were giving away tickets for the pre-season games last summer, but my roommates and I paid a hundred bucks apiece for the game next week. I've heard you're an incredible athlete." Her final sentence drips with unveiled innuendo. "That final throw in Lincoln's championship game? Truly incredible."

I don't experience the slightest twinge of attraction in response to the pretty smile she flashes me following the flattery. Instead, I hear *You get sick of people telling you what an amazing football player you are? I'm shocked.*

My memory captures her saucy voice perfectly.

I down the glass of bourbon in one gulp, barely feeling the burn of the expensive liquor as it traverses down my esophagus.

"Thanks," I tell the blonde, then brush past her without another word.

Cooley catches my eye as I walk toward the exit. He abandons the three women he's chatting up to come over to me. "You're leaving already?"

"Yeah, I'm not feeling too great," I reply. It's true, at least.

"Sure you don't want a 'nurse' for the night?" Cooley suggests, nodding to the eager groups of women eyeing us.

"I'm not in the mood tonight. I'll see you tomorrow." I clap him on the shoulder, and head for the back exit.

CHAPTER TWENTY-ONE

VIVIENNE

I've lost count of how many times I've re-read the same sentence. The persistent clicking makes it impossible for me to focus. I set the heavy textbook down on the steel patio table and reach for the sweating glass of iced coffee sitting in front of me.

Charles looks up from his own work and gives me a sweet smile. The tempo of the clicking quickens as the cameras pointed at us rush to capture the moment. It will undoubtedly be splashed across every paper in Marcedenia by the morning.

The Royal Press Office will be thrilled. The more articles featuring Charles and me, the fewer mentioning the fact I snubbed Marcedenia's most elite academic institution to pretend I was an American for four months.

I give Charles a quick smile in return, and he goes back to typing the assignment he's working on, allowing me a chance to study him from behind the shield of my sunglasses.

His short blond hair is neatly combed, and his handsome, angular face is clean shaven. He flips a page in the book he's looking through, and the lean muscles in his exposed forearm shift below the rolled-up sleeves of his button-down shirt, empha- sizing the definition from his time spent playing for Edgewood's polo and crew teams.

I drop my gaze back down to my textbook, wishing I had insisted we work in the library instead. While I've readjusted to the relentless scrutiny in public, the attention feels particularly oppressive when I'm with Charles. I don't let myself linger on why.

A half hour later, I down the final remnants of my watered- down coffee.

"I'm ready to go," I tell Charles. "I can't focus out here." I gesture around the stone patio we're sitting on that's bathed in warm sunlight, pretending it's the pleasant weather distracting me, rather than the horde of cameras.

Charles nods in understanding and begins packing up his work. I slide my textbook into my leather bag and stand, prompting the four agents seated at the table next to us to rise as well. Two more hover along the periphery of the patio.

Charles maintains several feet of distance between us as we walk back toward the line of black cars, which I'm grateful for. I've drawn the lines regarding our relationship very clearly, despite Charles's repeated suggestions he's interested in more and the press speculating we're already engaged.

Since my father's illness has become public knowledge, my coronation has been set for next spring. I'll have to be married by then, and Charles is by the far the most logical candidate. Our repeated sightings together have done nothing to discourage that conclusion. There's no real reason why we shouldn't already be planning our lives together, except that every time I contemplate committing to that inevitable future, a pair of gray eyes haunt me.

"Catherine asked me to invite you to her party tonight," Charles tells me.

"How nice of her to invite me herself," I retort.

"Apparently, I'm more approachable than you. Surprising, I know." Charles smiles teasingly.

Charles is more than approachable. He's an enigma in the upper echelons of the Marcedenian society circle that's comprised the same noble families for centuries. His prolonged time at school in Germany makes his presence at Edgewood now a novelty, despite his automatic acceptance among the traditionally impenetrable horde of students whose great-grandparents gossiped about each other.

He's wealthy, but not spoiled.

Noble, but not pretentious.

Handsome, but not devastatingly so.

Paired with his friendly charm, he's undoubtedly become the most coveted guy on Edgewood's small campus. Despite the lack of encouragement I've given him, he seems utterly devoted to me, which I find more annoying than flattering. It hasn't done me any favors amongst the female students at Edgewood. If I weren't untouchable, I have no doubt I would have been on the receiving end of more than one practical joke or cruel prank by now.

I contemplate the secondhand offer. Spend the night in the company of most of Edgewood, or watch the American reality show Katie got me hooked on alone in my room?

"Fine, I'll try to overlook the fact she invited me as an afterthought."

He smiles broadly in response, not bothering to hide his excitement that I've finally agreed to attend a social event outside of my royal duties.

"It starts at ten. What time should I pick you up?"

"I'll just meet you there," I reply, pretending not to see his disappointed expression as I climb in the car. "See you tonight!" I call before the SUV's door is closed behind me. I attempt to infuse some enthusiasm in my tone to temper my rejection. I'm sure Charles has noticed I avoid being alone with him when we're not in public, but he has yet to broach the topic with me directly. *I* certainly won't be the one to bring it up.

As the car begins to move, I lean against the soft leather seat. With nothing to distract me, the bothersome burden of melancholy reappears.

I've been back home for nearly twice as long as I was a student at Lincoln University. Everything in my life has returned to how it was before I left. I had the chance to experience normalcy, and now I'm living the life I always knew I was destined to.

Memories of walking around campus unaccompanied and sleeping a few feet away from Katie in our tiny dorm room still cause a twinge of nostalgia, but I've become re-accustomed to having heavily guarded men constantly surround me and sleeping alone in my enormous room.

It's *him* I can't seem to shake.

The difference is that I now know Jace Dawson exists, and that knowledge has infiltrated every cell of my body and permanently altered me in a way neither time nor distance has managed to revert.

I arrive back at the palace in a sour mood despite the beautiful weather outside. I hustle up the left staircase as soon as I enter the residence, where I immediately encounter my mother.

"Vivienne! How was your afternoon?" she asks, smiling in a way that suggests she's spoken to Charles's mother recently.

"Fine," I clip, continuing up the stairs.

"Did you have a nice time with Charles?" she persists, confirming my suspicions as she follows me upstairs.

"Yes, we had a lovely time posing for the dozens of photographers camped out across the street," I reply dryly. "I'm sure you'll be able to read all about it in the papers tomorrow."

My mother lets out a deep sigh. "Honestly, Vivienne, I don't understand what's gotten into you since you returned. Your father moved heaven and earth to give you what was your heart's desire, and then we had to deal with the massive media fallout from it. Now, you act like you're being tortured because you're spending time with a well-mannered, kind young man who happens to be a Vanderbilt and likely will become your husband?"

All the fight drains from my body. "I had a nice time with Charles. Everything is fine," I state passively, too exhausted to keep up the combative tone.

My mother sighs again. "Fine." She turns and heads back down the stairs, leaving me to make the rest of the trip back to my room solo.

I drop my bag on the gleaming wooden floor and wander across my room over to the window seat that stretches below the bay windows. I flop down on the cushions, only to stand again minutes later, restless.

Although I already went for a run this morning, I change back into a pair of athletic shorts, then rifle through the shelf of neatly folded t-shirts. When I see the worn gray material at the bottom of the stack, I freeze. I pull it out slowly, running my fingers across the cracks that have appeared in the white letters. I forcibly swallow the lump in my throat and leave the shirt in a rumpled heap next to the rest of the stack, opting to grab a plain white cotton tee out instead.

The moment my feet touch the gravel outside, I start running. I don't bother to stretch or jog, accelerating my pace to a flat-out sprint immediately. Footsteps patter forcefully behind me, and I hear a few grunts as the agents try to keep up with my desperate pace.

I run until my thoughts are drowned out by burning pain in my muscles. When I finally slow, my legs wobble slightly. I'm tempted to collapse in the grass, but I force my muscles to keep cooperating until the gardens are in sight again. I haul myself along the gravel path and up the stairs to my room, where I slump on the hardwood floor as a drained, depressed mess.

The last streaks of orange are fading from the sky when I finally haul myself up. After showering, I put on a pair of faded jeans and a black shirt. I know most of the girls will be wearing dresses tonight, but I don't care enough to put any further effort into my appearance. I take a painkiller before I hobble down the stairs to the dining room, already beginning to feel the effects of my second run of the day.

My parents are already seated when I enter the dining hall. As soon as I take my seat, the first course is brought out.

"You showered before dinner?" My mother looks at my damp hair with surprise.

"Yup," I reply, stabbing at an errant piece of carrot.

"Helga said you were in the shower this morning when I was trying to summon you."

It's not a question, so I don't answer, opting to continue to eat my salad silently.

"Showering twice in one day is terrible for your hair," she chastises.

"It was sweaty," I reply.

"I thought you went for a run this morning?"

"I felt like going again," I tell her, exerting more force against my vegetables. "Can we discuss something else?"

My parents exchange a loaded look I act like I don't see.

My father intervenes. "I had a meeting come up that can't wait until tomorrow, Vivvi. But we can still play our match right after it ends, if you'd like."

"Fine," I respond. "I'm headed out at ten."

The surprised faces of my parents are a sad testament to my total lack of a social life.

"You're going out tonight?" my mother asks, not bothering to hide her shock.

"Yes. Catherine Lennox is having a party and asked Charles to invite me."

"Duchess Lennox's niece?"

I shrug. "I guess so." I don't keep up with the intricate web of Marcedenian society the way my mother does.

"And Charles is friends with her?" My mother's tone holds a touch of concern.

I smile to myself, knowing she's likely concerned she's going to lose her first pick for son-in-law.

"I guess."

"Don't you see who he socializes with?"

My irritation grows. "Not really."

"And that's what you're wearing?" She eyes my casual attire. "You have so many beautiful dresses."

"It was the first thing I came across."

"You could put a bit more effort into your appearance, Vivienne."

"There's no one I'm trying to impress," I tell her truthfully.

My mother huffs, but drops the subject for the remainder of the meal.

I head straight to my father's study after dinner, pouring myself a generous splash of whiskey before sinking into my usual armchair next to the fireplace.

My father bustles into the room about twenty minutes later.

He eyes the empty glass next to me but doesn't say anything as he takes a seat across from me in the matching armchair.

I opt to preserve the silence. I simply move the first piece, and he follows suit. We've barely started playing when there's a loud knock on the door of my father's study.

"Come in," my father calls.

One of his many aides opens the door and bows. "My apologies, Your Majesty," he says. "But the Council would like your input on one more matter."

"It can't wait?" my father asks.

I glance at the clock above the fireplace. It's already almost ten.

"No, I'm afraid it can't, Your Majesty."

My father sighs.

"It's fine, Papa. I need to go anyway."

"Okay, Vivvi. Have some fun." My father kisses the top of my head as he walks out of his study.

I head to the front entryway to discover Michael is already waiting for me. Three other members of my security detail linger behind him.

"Ready, Princess?" Michael asks.

"Yup," I reply, then follow him out to the waiting convoy of cars. Two more agents climb in.

A half hour later, we pull up in front of a house that would look opulent to anyone who didn't live in a palace. There's a long row of limousines and town cars parked in front of the mansion, dotted with uniformed drivers loitering around, waiting to be summoned.

I stride up the front walkway, flanked by four agents. The other two remain by the car. As we near the front door, I see Charles leaning against one of the columns.

"You actually came," he says. Surprise is evident in his voice.

"My other plans fell through." I grin at him before I stroll past him into the house.

The house is crowded with groups making polite conversation, but an audible hush falls as I enter the foyer. I continue walking forward, not bothering to stop and talk to anyone. I was right; every other girl I see is wearing a dress. I even spot a couple of guys in suits. I head into the kitchen first to survey the spread of expensive liquor. Despite our luxurious surroundings, I know my security team won't let me drink anything that's not sealed.

I end up with a bottle of water.

I stand in the kitchen, sipping at the cool liquid with my agents standing nearby. It's a stark contrast to the last party I attended, where I got drunk and played poker with a group of raucous football players. I halt the train of thought before I can recall any of the other events that transpired that same night.

Sick of standing around, I inform my security team I'm heading to the restroom. I've never been to the Lennox estate before, so I wander down the long hallway aimlessly.

Finally, I open one of the doors. It turns out to be a bedroom, and I swing open the door of the dimly lit room. A thick cloud of smoke envelops me. I step back, coughing. Two guys are sitting on the bed, with lit joints dangling from their fingers. They stare at me, wide-eyed.

"Open a window," I choke out before backing out of the room.

I close the door and open the next one. It's a wood-paneled study similar to my father's, but much smaller. A bar cart sits in one corner. Several bottles of expensive liquor are on it, two still sealed. *Bingo*. The bottle unseals when I yank the cork, making a satisfying *pop*. I take a long swig from the clear liquid encased in the glass container. I hate vodka, but the burn as it scorches its way to my stomach, followed by the welcoming warmth that begins to pump through my veins, is worth the abhorrent taste. Before I replace the cork, I take several more pulls of the clear alcohol.

Already, I feel looser. Lighter. Numbed.

I open the door. One of my agents is standing in the hallway. He looks behind me into the empty room.

"I can't find the restroom," I tell him, glad the burst of liquor coursing through my system hasn't impacted my improvisation skills yet.

"It's at the very end of the hall, Your Highness."

I nod and continue down the hallway until I reach the correct door. Once inside, I walk over to the expansive granite sink and stare into the mirror that covers most of the wall. I grip the edge of the cold, unyielding stone tightly as I study my reflection. I look more put together than I feel. My hair has dried in loose waves, and I'm not wearing any makeup, so my smattering of freckles are clearly visible against my pale skin.

I look calm.

Regal.

Poised.

But there's an ineffaceable sorrow in my eyes that I study closely, trying to discern the exact flecks conveying woe.

I jump when there's a knock on the door. I expect it to be one of my agents checking up on me again. Instead, a female voice calls out, "Hey! Can you hurry up?"

I walk over to the bathroom door and pull it open, grateful for the interruption. A brown-haired girl I don't recognize is standing there. She's wearing a short silk dress, and has a hip cocked, seemingly waiting to further berate the bathroom's leisurely occupant.

Her bravado falls away as soon as she sees my face. "Shit—I mean, sorry!" She straightens, wobbling on her heels before dropping into the saddest attempt at a curtsy I've ever seen.

"No need for that," I assure her, stepping through the doorway. "It's all yours."

I take my time walking back down the long hallway, but eventually return to the living room aided by a slight buzz. My classmates are standing around in small groupings, chatting politely. Most of them try to subtly stare at me when I enter.

An expensive looking pool table sits in one corner of the room. I walk over to it and pick up a cue stick.

"Anyone want to play?" I call out to the room. It falls silent at my words.

"I'll play." Brett Adams steps forward. He's one of the few members of Marcedenia's elite willing to incite trouble, since his inner circle status is insulated by the fact his father's an earl. It hasn't kept him from being expelled from almost every school in the country, however. I'm surprised he's lasted at Edgewood this long.

He's perfect for my current mood; I'm looking for a challenge.

I gesture toward the green felt table after he picks up his own cue stick. "Gentlemen first."

Brett gives me a devilish grin that probably would affect a girl not already in love with one guy and practically engaged to another.

"So, is that what Americans wear to party?" he asks, glancing over my casual attire as he lines up his first shot.

"I guess so," I reply, taken aback by his question. "There certainly weren't any guys wearing suits."

"Did you go to parties there?"

I look at him, surprised. No one at Edgewood has ever asked me about my time in the States. Even Charles avoids the subject.

"Yeah, I did."

"Is that what you wore?"

I let out an uncomfortable laugh, finally realizing where he's going with this line of questioning. "No."

279

I tell him the truth just as Charles enters the room and comes over to me. I'm surprised it's taken him this long to track me down.

"Vivienne, what are you doing?"

"Playing pool," I reply, feeling a flash of déjà vu. I know my voice conveys an unsaid "obviously." A few whispers sound around the quiet room.

"Are you sure that's a good idea?" Charles asks, looking at Brett with a hint of apprehension. He glances to my agents for back-up, and I smother a laugh. I doubt Charles will be encouraging me to attend any more Edgewood parties anytime soon.

"I'm sure," I say.

Brett has finished his first few shots and is leaning against the edge of the table, watching Charles and me closely. I leave Charles standing alone to take my starting shots, easily knocking out several more balls than Brett managed to.

He raises his eyebrows. "The future queen can play. Who knew?"

He goes again, then it's my turn. I round the table, looking for the perfect angle. Suddenly, my foot slides along the floor. I grab the edge of the table to keep myself vertical. Charles rushes to my side, along with two agents.

"I'm fine!" I hold my arm out to keep them back as I look down at the small puddle of liquid I slipped on. Probably someone's spilled drink.

They follow my silent command and back up. I need a minute. Because suddenly, I'm not playing pool in a Marcedenian mansion. I'm in the kitchen in the blue house, being caught by Jace.

This is why I shouldn't chug vodka. Because I can picture the worry in his gray eyes when he caught me.

"Vivienne..." Charles starts, approaching me cautiously, like I'm a wounded animal.

"Don't touch me," I snap, moving away from his touch. I feel nauseous and unwieldy. The only person I want right now is Jace, and that angers me. I've never been anything but independent. I don't need him. I *can't.*

One of my agents appears at my side. "Are you ready to leave, Your Highness?"

"Not yet."

The last thing I feel like right now is being left alone with my thoughts. I take a deep breath and walk over to the same spot I was headed to before, taking care to avoid the small puddle. One of the maids is already cleaning it up.

Brett proves to be a worthy competitor, but I still win easily.

"I'm impressed, Your Highness," he compliments when I sink my final striped ball.

"You exceeded my expectations as well," I reply. "I thought your only talent was getting kicked out of every school in the country."

Brett laughs loudly, attracting even more attention.

"Let's go," I call to Michael, who's standing closest to me. He nods and straightens. The rest of my agents quickly fall into formation as well. Brett gives me a mock salute, and I can't help but smile as I turn on my heel and walk out of the room.

I know Charles will follow even before I hear his footsteps. I climb into the car as Michael holds the door open, and glance back at him.

"Do you want a ride?" I offer.

He nods. I look behind him to see a number of our classmates are staring out the massive front windows at us.

Charles climbs into the other side of the car, and we begin to drive along the cobbled stones back toward the main street. We sit in silence for a while, until I manage to get my discombobulated words under control and know what I need to say to him.

"I know I can be difficult," I tell Charles, breaking the silence between us. "It's not you. I'm still—I'm having trouble adjusting to everything that's about to change in my life, and I'm taking it out on you, which isn't fair. I promise I'll work on it."

"I'm not going to lie. You're not that easy to get to know," Charles replies. "But I would like to. I know your situation isn't ideal, but... I like you, Vivienne. A lot."

Unbidden, Jace's voice sounds in my head. *Has anyone ever told you that you're difficult to get to know?*

I let Jace in. I let him know me. I don't regret it, but I didn't realize letting him in would mean I wouldn't want to open up to anyone else.

"I'm working on it; I promise," I reply, choosing to ignore the end of his statement. "I just need a little more time to come to terms with everything."

Charles nods.

We pull up in front of the Vanderbilts' estate and pause for the gate to open. It slides back slowly, the same way the one at their house in South Carolina does. The thought sobers me more than the cool night air did.

We pull up in front of the house, and Charles takes off his seatbelt, then turns to look at me. I don't move. I've given him all I can tonight.

"Good night, Vivienne."

"Good night," I reply.

He lingers for a moment longer, but I still don't move, so he opens the door and steps out. As soon as the door shuts, we begin moving, headed back through the dark to the palace.

CHAPTER TWENTY-TWO

JACE

"Was it this difficult to assemble last year?"

"It's probably that fancy new tent you bought," I call out, grinning. "Camping is not supposed to include an air mattress and an electrical outlet."

Anderson, Owens, and I are lounging around the campground, watching with amusement as Kenny struggles with the slippery material.

We've gone on this trip together for the past three years, ever since Kenny and I met Anderson and Owens the summer before our freshman year at Lincoln's preseason camp. The four of us melded easily, forming a tight unit within Lincoln's already close team.

We spent our first weekend off from preseason training in the Michigan woods together, and it's become an annual tradition. This year Anderson and Owens are the only ones who will be returning to campus. Kenny and I were both drafted, and are set to make our professional football debuts next week.

"We'll see how you feel tomorrow after spending the night on the ground without a fan, Dawson," Kenny retorts, zipping up the side of the fabric structure that could easily sleep ten.

I roll my eyes, settling deeper into the comfortable chair I'm lounging in. I take a long sip from the cold beer I'm holding and enjoy the peaceful sounds of nature surrounding us, feeling relaxed for the first time in weeks.

～

"How's the pro life treating you, Dawson?" Anderson asks me as we're sitting around the campfire eating dinner.

"Good," I reply, taking a large bite of chicken. It's surprisingly tasty, and I'm glad Kenny also sprang for some fancy new portable grill. Not that I'll tell him that.

"Don't spare us any details." Anderson rolls his eyes.

"It's not that different from Lincoln. Longer practices, better facilities. Still football."

"What are the girls like?" Owens asks, shooting me a sly grin. "I hear southern girls are super hot."

"Yeah, they are." I think back to the girl at the bar. The one I barely glanced at.

"I'd bet your pro contract you haven't touched one of them though, right?" Anderson asks.

I scoff and take another bite of chicken.

"We're still not allowed to talk about her?"

"There's nothing to talk about," I clip.

"And you're still pretending you're not in love with her?"

"I'm not in love with her," I state, injecting as much resolution in my voice as possible in hopes Anderson will decide to drop it.

"So...you're turning down models and refusing to talk about her because...?"

Owens and Kenny are silent as Anderson and I stare each other down. I'm surprised he's pushing the topic as much as he is; normally he mentions her once and then drops the subject.

"I'm focusing on football."

"Why can't you just admit you still have feelings for her? That you're pissed about what happened?"

"Why can't you just drop it?" I shoot back, taking a long swig from my beer. All traces of relaxation have long disappeared. I'm tense, edgy, and annoyed.

"I liked her," Anderson replies. "Obviously not as much as you did—or do—but still. And I can see how it bothers you. Just admit it and do something about it. Or else move on."

"There's nothing to do. She's a fucking *princess*, Anderson."

"Plus, there's that duke's son in the picture now," Kenny adds.

I snap my gaze over to him. "How do you know that?"

Kenny is one of the last people I would expect to follow tabloid gossip. He glances at Anderson and Owens instead of answering me.

"Flores sent it to the team group chat," Owens informs me.

"What are you talking about? I didn't get anything."

"I know—Thompson set up a separate one. We didn't think you'd want to be included."

"What? Why?"

Anderson is the one who answers. "Because it's mostly about her."

I glance between the three of them, expecting one of them to burst out laughing at any moment and tell me this is some sort of joke. None of them do.

"You're telling me that the entire Lincoln football team—with the exception of me—is part of a group chat discussing my *love life*?"

"More like your lack of one, but aside from that…yes."

I open my mouth, but Anderson keeps talking. "You're a legend, dude. Even if she wasn't royalty, and you hadn't been basically dating her, people would still be curious. She's literally the hottest—"

"Watch it," I growl.

Anderson lets out a dry laugh. "Yeah, you could really care less, huh? My point is, people talk, and you made it clear it wasn't a topic you'd discuss. Which only made people talk more. We figured it would be better to stay in it, so we knew what people were saying, at least."

"And?" I prompt, curious despite myself.

"Lately it's mostly making fun of the fact her new flame plays polo and rows crew. Before that, there were a few mentions of how you dodged a bullet with the marriage law."

"What marriage law?" I ignore the mention of Vivienne's supposed fiancé.

"There's some old law that means Vivienne has to be married before she can become queen."

"That can't be true. She would have told me." I say the words without thinking them through.

"Told you? When would..." Kenny starts, but Anderson jumps on my unintentional admission first.

"She told you who she really was, didn't she? Before it came out on campus?"

"Yeah, she did," I finally admit.

"What did you say when she told you?" Owens asks.

I shift uncomfortably. No way am I telling them the truth about what transpired between us on that trip. "None of your business."

"Meaning you either did something you regret, or you fucked her," Anderson interjects. "Or both."

I glare at him. "Listen. I met a girl, we hung out a few times, she told me she's royalty, and then everyone found out she's royalty. She left, I got drafted. That's all there is to it, okay?" My voice is unyielding. Steely.

None of my friends look convinced, but they all drop the subject. We return to discussing football.

The following morning, I wake up to the sound of chirping birds and a fresh breeze wafting through the vents in the side of my tent. Despite the idyllic surroundings, my muscles are protesting the hard dirt I spent the night lying on. Or rather tossing on, thanks to the unwelcome conversation about Vivienne.

I stretch and groan before crawling out of my sleeping bag and pulling on a pair of athletic shorts. I unzip the front and wriggle my way out of my small tent.

Kenny is already sitting next to the remnants of last night's campfire, sipping on a steaming mug of coffee. I help myself to my own cup and take a seat beside him.

"Morning," I greet.

"How'd you sleep?" Kenny asks, grinning.

"Later than you," I retort. "Air mattress didn't live up to the hype?"

Kenny snorts. "No, it was comfortable. Just have a lot of my mind."

"Yeah." I sigh. "I know the feeling."

"I'm sorry about last night. I should have backed you up with Anderson more." He hesitates. "The truth is…I was curious about it too."

"It's fine." I stare at the pile of charred wood.

We sit in silence until Anderson and Owens stumble out of their own tents. After eating breakfast, we all change into swimsuits and head in the direction of the lake we stumbled across last year. It's an arduous climb. I embrace the strain of my muscles as I laugh and joke with three of my best friends.

Thoughts of Vivienne finally fade away.

We reach the top of the tallest peak. The lake is spread out before us, glistening in the sunshine. After taking a moment to appreciate the view, we start the trek down the other side toward the water lapping across the shore. As soon as we near the edge of the lake, Anderson drops his gear and starts running toward the shallows. Water sprays everywhere, disturbing the pristine surface, as he submerges himself.

"You're such a child, dude," I call, as the rest of us lazily shed our own packs and sneakers.

Anderson just grins, shaking his shaggy head of hair like a dog so that he sends droplets of water flying everywhere.

Owens wades into the water. Kenny and I follow. The water's just cold enough to be refreshing, and the chilly temperature soothes my tired muscles. We swim out to the small island in the center of the lake and climb ashore, exploring along the craggy rocks and mossy ground.

The sun is shining overhead by the time we swim back to the sandy shore to retrieve our lunch.

I'm spread out on the warm sand, drying off after devouring my sandwich, when Owens says, "I think you should go on a date, Dawson."

I squint over at him. Anderson and Kenny are back in the water, so it's just the two of us on shore sunbathing.

"That's why Anderson keeps bringing her up. He's worried about you—we all are. You're not the same. I thought you were just worried about the championship, or getting drafted at first. But it's not. It's her."

I sit up and begin dragging my fingers through the sand. "I don't want to date another girl," I admit. "I keep waiting to want to. But I don't."

"I get it, Dawson. Well, maybe not totally. Jen and I dated for a couple months and crashed spectacularly. And I barely cared. But I also didn't want to go through that again, so I just started hooking up with random jersey chasers. But you're not even doing that, are you?"

I shake my head.

"Just think about it. You said you two are done. She's getting married. You should move on."

Owens' words stick with me through the rest of the trip and the flight home. I'm swarmed with fans when I land at the airport in South Carolina, and I end up with an entourage of airport security agents the escort me to a waiting car.

As the driver heads towards my neighborhood, I study the palm trees and thirsty grass. I know I'll talk myself out of this if I wait for too long. I pull my phone out of my pocket and tap on the number for the team publicist.

She answers on the third ring. "Hello?"

"Hi Ellie, it's Jace Dawson."

"Hi, Jace. Is everything all right?"

"Yes."

There's a pause. "So, what can I do for you?"

"Yes. To what you asked me last week. I'll do it."

"The dinner with Miss South Carolina? You'll do it?"

"Yes."

"Okay, I'll make the arrangements for the end of next week. The press is going to love this!" She sounds thrilled, exuberant that the months of pestering me about how I'm not visible enough are finally paying off.

I hang up, wishing I could share her excitement.

CHAPTER TWENTY-THREE

VIVIENNE

I'm sitting out in the gardens, working on a paper, when one of the butlers appears.

"Your Highness, there's a young woman here to see you," he informs me. "In the front foyer of the residence."

I look at him with confusion. I don't have any idea who he could be referring to; I'm not expecting anyone. Curiosity propels me to my feet and inside.

Katie stands in the center of the marble floor, mouth agape as her gaze bounces between the twin sweeping staircases.

"Katie?" I ask, my surprised voice echoing along the marble. "What are you doing here?"

She looks over at me and smiles widely, rushing over to give me a big hug. I hug her back automatically.

"Surprise! It's so good to see you!"

"I can't believe you're in Marcedenia," I say, looking her over. She's grown out her chestnut hair, but aside from that she looks exactly the same as the night she welcomed me to Lincoln.

"Me neither! I was visiting my mom's great-aunt in Paris, and she happened to mention her trip to Marcedenia. So then I thought how cool it would be to come see where you live. Or rule, rather."

I smile at her bubbly babbling.

"So I called the palace, and I got transferred like ten times— how many people do you have working for you? And then finally this one really serious guy got on the phone and started asking me all these questions."

"That was probably Richard," I surmise.

"Yes! That was his name! Anyway, he asked me all this stuff about myself and Lincoln and how I knew you. And then finally he said I could see you. So I bought a flight to come here, and they had a car waiting for me at the airport and brought me here and…do you seriously live here? Like this entire giant museum is your *house*?"

I laugh. "I missed you, Katie."

"I missed you too." She gives me another hug.

"How long are you here for?"

"I have to leave tomorrow afternoon. I got into this theater program in New York City, and it starts on Monday."

"That's amazing! Congratulations!"

Katie blushes, but looks pleased.

"What else is new with you?" I ask.

We've managed a few phone conversations over the past eight months, but knowing Katie, I'm sure there's a lot I have yet to hear about. She can make a story about a five-minute interaction last an hour.

"Oh no, we're not talking about me right now. We're in your literal palace! I want to see everything!"

I laugh. "Okay. Do you have any bags?" I glance at the bare floor.

"One of your butlers already took them," Katie says, and then grins. "I can't believe I actually just got to say that."

I roll my eyes. I already feel lighter, more buoyant in her happy presence. Katie's enthusiasm is infectious.

I show her around the entire main residence, and she's appropriately dazzled by the endless stream of luxurious rooms.

"Can we go outside now?" she asks.

"Sure. Did you bring a bathing suit? There's a pool."

Katie shakes her head.

"Come on, you can borrow one of mine." I lead her to the wing that houses my room and a couple of guest suites. "They probably put your things in one of those rooms," I tell her, gesturing down the hall when we enter the new wing. "I'll have someone find out."

I open the door to my room and step inside. Katie is right behind me.

"Holy shit," she says, looking around the massive room. Then she claps her hand over her mouth. "Can I swear here?"

I laugh. "Yes."

Katie walks over to my window seat and looks out the bay windows at the gardens spread below. "Wow," is all she says.

"Come on, the closet's this way," I instruct her.

She follows me into my walk-in closet. She looks around at the endless racks of clothes with awe. "I thought you brought a lot to Lincoln," she says. "Who knew it was like two percent of your wardrobe?"

I smile as I walk over to the portion that houses my swimwear and open the series of drawers.

"Here, take your…" I turn back to Katie to see she's staring at the gray t-shirt I left pulled out of the stack yesterday. She looks over at me, but doesn't say anything.

"These the suit options?" she asks, coming to stand beside me.

"Yeah," I reply. "I was already going to swim later, so I'm wearing a suit. I'm going to grab some towels. Be right back."

I duck out of the closet and into my bathroom. There are already towels piled by the pool, but Katie doesn't know that, and I need a minute.

I knew the moment I saw her, the topic of Jace would come up. No matter how often I find myself thinking about him, I haven't had to discuss him with anyone. Not once. Not a single person in Marcedenia knows he exists outside of me and my security team. I was worried Thomas might say something as part of the investigation into who leaked my identity, but since the Royal Guard immediately determined Philip was the one who shared it, there was no reason to look into anyone else who might have known my true identity at Lincoln. Jace would have been at the top of that list. The *only* name on that list.

I grab a couple of fluffy towels and re-enter my closet to find Katie's already changed and put her shorts and t-shirt back on.

"Ready?" I ask.

"Yup!" Katie replies, following me out of my room, down the side staircase, and out onto the patio. My laptop's still sitting on the table where I was sitting earlier.

I lead Katie off the patio and onto the gravel path to the pool. Her gaze bounces around the carefully manicured greenery and colorful flowers that surround us as she smiles broadly. I see the surroundings differently, with her next to me. If we'd gone to a place like this while I was pretending to be a normal teenager, I'd be marveling right alongside her. It's funny—how perspective shifts.

I drop the towels on one of the chaises and pull off the green sundress I'm wearing before laying down on the soft cushions. Katie follows my lead, tugging off her shorts and shirt before flopping down on the chaise next to me.

"Wow," she says, looking over at me and shading her eyes

against the sun. "I am *super* grateful we got paired as roommates right now."

I laugh, for what feels like the thousandth time since Katie arrived. I thought being at Lincoln, thousands of miles away from my inevitable duty, was responsible for the lightness in my chest I haven't experienced in months. But I feel it now, sunbathing with someone I know likes me for more than my clout. "You should have thanked Richard when you talked to him. He was the one who selected you."

"The one who let me visit?"

I nod.

"You're right, I owe him big." After a pause, she adds, "I'm so glad I came."

"Me too," I reply truthfully. "And I'm sorry I haven't been better about keeping in touch these past few months. It's just that talking to you reminds me of Lincoln. It reminds me of..."

"I know." Katie says softly. "I get it, Vivienne."

We're both silent for a while.

"Can I ask? What happened to Philip? I saw in the paper he was the one who talked to the press."

"Yeah, he was." I sigh. "He told the Guard it was because he heard rumors about my true identity on campus and was trying to protect me. There was a private hearing, and he was found guilty of treason. I'm not sure where he got sent."

"So, he told the press who you were because he thought other people might? That doesn't make any sense."

"I know. Thomas thinks he did it because he had feelings for me," I admit.

Katie nods. "He was jealous of Jace."

His name causes a painful twinge I make sure to keep off my face. "Probably." I drop her gaze and look at the serene surface of the pool instead.

"Do people here know? About Jace?"

I look back at her. "No, nothing ever came out about us—miraculously—so once everything with Philip was resolved, I just figured…" I let my voice trail off when Katie drops eye contact. "What?"

"I think Jace had something to do with that," she blurts.

"What?" I ask, once again ignoring the sharp twist the sound of his name procures. Hearing it is more painful than thinking it.

"It's the only thing that makes sense. Practically every journalist in the state shows up to report on the most exciting thing to ever happen on campus? And yet everyone just seemed to know not to say anything about you to the press? Good or bad? Only one person had—has—that type of power at Lincoln."

I don't say anything in response. Was he trying to protect me? Embarrassed by me? Angry at me?

"Have you talked to him?" Katie asks hesitantly.

"No," I reply. "There's nothing left to say." Bleak, but accurate.

"Don't you think you should at least explain? Just tell him…" Her voice fades away as she looks at my face. "You'd already told him, hadn't you? The truth. Before it came out in the press."

I shift under the warmth of the sunshine. "I'm sorry, Katie. I should have said something to you too. It's not that I didn't trust you, I just—"

"It's okay. I wish you'd told me, but I get it," Katie replies. "You guys had an…intense relationship. I've never seen two people so comfortable and confident in who they are as separate people, yet also so completely different together."

"What do you mean?"

"You're both so self-assured, and charismatic, and intimidating on your own. When I saw you guys together, you were both more so, but also less so, if that makes sense."

"Not really," I say, laughing uncomfortably.

"You both acted like each other was all that mattered," Katie replies softly. "And I say that as someone who's pretty jaded when it comes to love."

Her words intensify the ache. "I'm pretty jaded, too."

We spend the rest of the day lounging by the pool, watching trashy television, and gossiping. I fill her in on Edgewood and the little drama I've paid attention to among my classmates. I can tell she's awed by the casual way I use their titles. She fills me in on all the latest gossip from Lincoln—with the exception of anything that concerns the one person I actually would want to hear about.

I hope he's not miserable, but I also don't want to know if he's happier without me.

We have dinner with my parents that night, and they're both amused by Katie's bubbly personality and her description of our time at Lincoln.

I've been less than forthcoming with details about my time in the States, and I can tell they're surprised by how much I withheld as Katie describes our shopping trips, movie nights, and solitary trip to a football game.

"I thought you hated football?" my father asks when Katie mentions it.

The last time the two of us discussed the sport was when I was complaining to him about having to study it. Katie shoots me a quick look of apology, clearly realizing why I left my parents with that impression.

"It's fine," I reply, eager to drop the subject. "I only went to the one game."

"You should mention it to Lionel the next time the Vanderbilts are over," my father suggests. "You know he's a big fan of the sport."

"Yes, I know."

"Who are the Vanderbilts?" Katie asks.

"Vivienne hasn't mentioned them?" my mother replies, sounding surprised. "They're some of our oldest friends. Their son is the same age as Vivienne. Charles."

"Oh," Katie says, putting the pieces together.

She gives me a sympathetic glance. We haven't discussed the marriage law, but I'm not surprised she already knows about it. Along with the rumors regarding who I'll end up marrying.

Katie and I exchange an emotional goodbye the following afternoon. I promise her that I'll call more often, and I actually mean it. Now that the topic of Jace has been broached, it also feels more settled.

I've been simultaneously clutching my memories while also trying to forget about him, and it's gotten me nowhere. There's only a handful of months before I need to be married. I can't keep holding on to him.

The resolution resulting from Katie's visit carries me through the week. I make an effort to be more talkative with my parents and invite Charles to attend a formal fundraising gala with me one evening. I can tell he's thrilled by the invitation, and I end up enjoying myself more than I expected to.

On Thursday, my father informs my mother and me he's planned for us to take a trip with the Vanderbilts for the weekend. I agree to go, figuring it will be an opportunity to bridge the gap with Charles more. My excitement grows when I overhear my mother telling her assistant Helga we'll be staying at the Vanderbilts' German estate. I've never been to the country before.

Early Friday afternoon, my mother and I board a plane with the Vanderbilts. My father travels separately on his own plane. I end up sleeping for most of the flight, but wake up to look out the window of our private plane as I start to feel it descend. To my surprise, I realize I recognize the small hangar sitting next to the runway we're rapidly approaching.

The plane's wheels hit the asphalt with a jolt, and I look over at my mother accusingly.

"This is not Germany."

"Believe me, that would have been my preference. Charles told your father he thought you would prefer to return to the States rather than visit their German estate. That you've been missing it here. Lionel and Margaret graciously offered for us all to stay at their beach house."

Panic swirls within me as the meaning behind her words begins to fully register. The door to the plane opens, and the Vanderbilts exit first. It seems like a cruel twist of fate I'm being forced to face the most potent reminder of Jace since I left Lincoln mere days after resolving to forget him.

Charles smiles at me as he walks past, pulling a pair of sunglasses out of his pocket to slip on before disembarking into the hot air already infiltrating the plane. My mother follows after them. I reluctantly do the same, trailed by the six agents that traveled with us.

We all walk over toward the line of four black SUVs parked alongside the hangar to watch as my father's plane lands. Charles and his mother Margaret climb into one of the cars to escape the oppressive heat.

"I can't stay at their house," I whisper to my mother.

She laughs in disbelief. "What are you talking about? Of course you can. They're some of our oldest friends, and you'll likely marry their son."

"No, I can't." The alarm building inside me fills my voice with urgency.

"Vivienne." My mother's voice is sharp, leaving no room for argument. "I don't know what has been going on with you lately, but it ends now. I won't have you embarrass us, especially in front of the Vanderbilts. Do you understand me?"

I refuse to wither under her harsh look. Desperation doesn't let me. "I will get on that plane and fly back home right now."

"Vivienne, you're being ridiculous, not to mention extremely rude. They invited us here as their guests. And your father took the time to fly us all the way here just to make you happy."

Lionel is the only Vanderbilt who hasn't climbed into one of the cars yet, and I see him watching our whispered argument closely out of the corner of my eye.

My father exits his plane and walks over to us, followed by another six agents. "Is something wrong?" he asks, looking between our two tense faces.

"Vivienne is refusing to stay at the Vanderbilts' house here for some reason," my mother informs him. "Maybe she'll listen to reason if it's coming from you."

The confused and disappointed look on my father's face guts me, but I can't fathom the thought of driving up the beach house's tree-lined driveway. I know the second I see that house again I'll lose it, which will be even harder to explain.

"I'm sorry, Papa," I tell him. "I need to stay someplace else." My words are final. I can't yield. Not about this.

My father holds my anguished gaze for a long moment, testing my resolve. Then he turns and beckons Richard forward. As per usual, he's just a couple feet behind my father.

"Richard, you'll need to arrange new accommodations for us. Whatever you think is most appropriate. Make certain you're discreet. And tell the Vanderbilts to go ahead, that the Princess isn't feeling well."

Richard nods and turns back toward another agent. They begin talking intently. My mother huffs in disbelief, but I know she won't make a scene now that my father has decided.

"Thank you, Papa." My voice is filled with gratitude.

He nods once, studying my distressed expression a little longer before turning to speak with Richard again.

We end up staying at a beach house not far from the Vanderbilts'. I recognize the upscale neighborhood as we drive through it. I don't know who the house belongs to, and I don't ask. I spend the remainder of the afternoon in my bedroom and fake a stomachache when my parents ask me to come with them to a French restaurant for dinner.

Neither of them argue with me once I decline the invitation.

I end up heating a frozen pizza, ignoring the glances from the agents who heard me beg off from dinner. I go to bed early and am grateful I fall asleep quickly.

The sunrise wakes me early the following morning. I slip out of the silent house and go for a long run before I stop and sit on the beach to stare at the crashing waves. The rhythmic battering against the sand is comforting. Despite everything that's so drastically different in my life from the one and only other time I've been here, the aquamarine ocean still looks exactly the same.

Eventually, I head back inside to eat breakfast and shower, ignoring my parents' puzzled looks.

I'm sitting on the deck reading when my father comes outside.

"Hi, Papa," I greet him, glancing up from the book.

He's scrutinizing me closely, the skin between his eyebrows creased.

"I'm sorry if I've ruined the trip," I apologize. "I know you were just trying to do something nice for me. It's just…" I falter. "It's just difficult being back here. This country represents some things I'll never get back, and it's challenging to be here again, as Princess Vivienne."

My father nods slowly. "I should have consulted you first before changing our destination. Charles was certain coming here is what you would prefer…"

"I may have led him to believe my reluctance to get engaged is because I'm having trouble readjusting to being back in Marcedenia," I admit.

"And it's not?"

"Not entirely." I waver on how much I should reveal.

"Is that why you didn't want to stay there?"

"Yes," I lie.

My mother appears in the open doorway. "The Vanderbilts are here," she tells us.

"I didn't think we were seeing them until dinner?" my father questions.

"Lionel called, said he's set up some sort of surprise outing."

"Where?" I ask.

"He didn't say. Hurry up now. You've caused enough problems this weekend." My mother sends me a pointed look that makes it clear all is far from forgiven when it comes to my recent behavior.

I sigh, but rise out of the chair and smooth the wrinkles in my navy sundress before I follow her outside to where three black cars loiter. Charles waves to me out the window of the first one, and I smile back, resolving to be friendlier to him today.

My parents settle into the middle car and I climb inside the last one, settling against the cool leather with a deep sigh. I wonder what type of outing Lionel planned as we drive along the quiet street. I've narrowed it down to a garden tour or a sailing trip when a massive structure looms up ahead, surrounded by thousands of cars.

My stomach drops.

"Where are we going?" I ask the agents traveling with me, trying to keep my voice neutral.

"I'm not sure. It looks like some sort of sports complex," one replies.

I clamber out of my car and onto the sidewalk as soon as we pull up alongside a large door labeled *VIP Entrance.* "Where are we?" I ask urgently as everyone else climbs out onto the sidewalk as well.

"I thought we should check out a football game!" Lionel says jovially. "Immerse ourselves in the local culture." He winks at me.

"What?" I ask, hoping I somehow misheard him. There's a clear note of panic in my voice I hope no one else can detect. This entire trip seems to be shaping up as some sort of cosmic joke meant to punish me for thinking I could forget Jace. "Isn't it too early for football? It's only August."

"It's the first preseason game," Lionel replies as we approach the tinted glass door.

The doors glide open in a anticipation of our approach. I trail at the very back of the group, ignoring the concerned glances being sent my way. Evidently, I'm once again not reacting to a surprise the way my companions hoped.

"Are you okay?" Charles asks as we walk inside. "Your father said you weren't feeling well yesterday and thought you might be coming down with something."

"I'm feeling much better today, thanks," I respond, although the statement couldn't be further from the truth at this particular moment.

The lobby we enter is buttressed by an elaborate security set-up we're quickly waved past; one of the few perks of traveling with your own team of agents. We're all ushered inside a large carpeted elevator. An older man stands in the corner. Once we're inside the surprisingly roomy space, the elevator attendant pushes the button, and we ascend rapidly. With each foot we rise, my feeling of foreboding grows.

Eventually, the doors open to reveal a carpeted hallway. Straight ahead, a couple rows of cushioned chairs sit, with the closer row elevated to allow a view beyond the first. A long, gleaming bar top sits to the right. The surface is spread with an array of finger food and a long shelf filled with expensive liquor stretches behind it. Several high-top tables with matching stools are pushed against the opposite wall. Two black and white clad waiters stand behind the bar top, waiting to serve us.

"Not bad, huh?" Lionel walks ahead of our group and spreads his arms to showcase the plush suite. "The team owner is an old friend. He owns the house next to ours."

We all walk over to the two rows of seats that provide the perfect vantage point over the massive stadium. The sight of the lush green grass and straight white lines is familiar, and it sends a pang of sadness through me as I think of the other three times I've looked at a football field. I claim one of the available seats quickly, needing to ground myself in this present moment somehow.

My father and Charles sit on either side of me.

"I told Lionel you watched a football game while you attended Lincoln," my father tells me, looking over at my face curiously. I wonder what he sees as I scramble to paste on a smile. "I assume that's why he set this up."

"That makes sense," I respond woodenly.

I've spent every moment since I left this country trying to forget my time here, but everyone else seems to have interpreted the melancholy as homesickness. I school my features. I can do this. I can sit through one football game and keep Jace banished from my mind.

"Thank you for setting this up. It was very thoughtful of you," I tell Lionel, finally finding my manners. He's sitting on the other side of Charles, and leans forward to reply to me.

"You're welcome. Although my motives were partially self-ish. John's been going on about their new quarterback for months. The team has been waiting for a first-round draft pick for a while. This is their first sold-out preseason game in years."

"New quarterback?" I echo.

A horrifying possibility is dawning on me.

"Yes. He's garnered the most excitement the league has had in years. Incredibly talented. He's quite handsome as well." Lionel winks. "Was with some of his teammates at the same restaurant as us a few weeks ago, and Margaret was enamored," he teases his wife.

She elbows him good-naturedly in response.

"Come on," Charles groans.

"What's his name?" I ask. I attempt to sound nonchalant. I'm not sure if I succeed, since I can hardly hear my voice over the pounds of my thundering heart while I wait for his response.

"Lawson?" Lionel answers. "No, Dawson. Jace Dawson."

My breathing stutters. The sound of whooshing blood fills my ears. Heat floods my body.

I sit frozen in my seat, unable to move even if I wanted to. The prospect of watching a football game and acting normal was daunting. The thought of watching Jace play football and acting normal seems impossible. I take deep breaths, trying to regain control over my overwhelmed body.

He's here.

Not just in the same country, not just in the same state, but somewhere in this stadium beneath me. That knowledge is more than I can process after having spent the past eight months resigning myself to the fact I'd spend the rest of my life at least an ocean apart from him.

"Vivienne, are you all right?" Charles asks. He raises a hand to touch my face, but I flinch away.

My father looks over at me as well, twin lines of worry forming between his eyes.

"I'm fine. My stomach is bothering me again," I reply, staring straight ahead and hoping they'll both buy it as an excuse for my increasingly odd behavior.

"Would you like to leave?" my father asks.

Fleeing is tempting, but there's a larger part of me that's rooted in place. That's rejoicing.

Jace will never know I was here, but I'll know. I'll get to see him live his dream, if only for the four quarters the game lasts for. It's more than I ever expected I might have. I assumed he was drafted, but the knowledge he was not only drafted but is already viewed as a star hits me with an unexpected emotion.

Pride, I finally realize.

I'm proud of him.

The announcer begins speaking, but I'm not paying attention to a word he's saying. A pack of players clad in white jerseys appear on the field, and then a few minutes later, a horde of navy jerseys jog out as well. Their appearance draws roaring cheers and applause from the spectators, including Lionel, suggesting they're the home team.

I scan the navy players anxiously, but they appear as nothing more than one giant blob of blue from this distance. Two navy players make their way over to the referee, along with two white jerseys. They confer for a moment, then return to their respective benches.

"Yes!" Lionel exclaims. "We won the coin toss."

One of the navy players kicks the ball down the field, and a white jersey is tackled.

The game moves along slowly, and soon there are only a few minutes left in the third quarter. I've relaxed slightly, amidst a growing confidence I can, in fact, make it through this unscathed. At least visibly.

Just then, the voice over the loudspeaker announces, "And it looks like Coach Taylor is going to test out the Sharks' new superstar, rookie Jace Dawson, for the first time." A loud and enthusiastic roar greets this announcement.

A solitary navy figure jogs out onto the field from the group assembled along the sideline. My breath hitches as he's surrounded by his teammates on the field.

I stand shakily and walk over to the buffet of food on autopilot. I order a glass of ice water from the waiter standing behind the bar, taking advantage of the opportunity to rein in my churning emotions away from the prying eyes of my father and Charles.

My eyes are glued to the television mounted above the bar and buffet as the players all assemble on either side of the line. Jace easily catches the ball he's tossed. He pivots on the grass for an extended moment, looking for someone to pass to.

The camera zooms in on his face, offering me my first glimpse of Jace in eight months. Streaks of black are smeared underneath his gray eyes, clearly visible through the bars of his helmet in the high definition image. They scan the field as he tries to decide where he should throw it. He sends the ball flying up the field after a brief moment of indecision. The camera follows the brown ball spiraling rapidly through the air. It drops between the waiting hands of one of his receivers. The player begins to run, cradling the football like a baby.

"What an arm on Dawson," is the commentary.

Most of the stadium seems to agree. I can hear the jubilant background noise on the television echoed around the cheering stadium as the player who caught the ball runs into the end zone. I walk back over to my seat, wanting to see Jace's reaction to the touchdown without the glass proxy of a screen.

I expect the noise in the stadium to continue growing, but the sound of applause dies off abruptly instead. I hasten my steps until I arrive at the edge of the suite. I look down at the field, scanning it anxiously for the source of the sudden hush.

A solitary navy figure is lying on the bright green grass. A bulky white-clad player stands a couple feet away. He's pulled off his helmet, and the cameras project his distressed expression on screens around the entire stadium.

I don't register that I've dropped the glass I was clutching until I feel a spray of icy water against my bare legs. I don't react, numb to the cold liquid dripping down my shins.

"Who is that?" I ask. "Which player?"

No one in the suite replies. They're too busy craning their necks in morbid fascination along with the rest of the stadium, but I already know who it is.

"And we've got a South Carolina player still down right now. Looks like it's the rookie quarterback, Jace Dawson."

I don't think.

I run.

I sprint back toward the hallway we entered from, passing first my mother and Margaret, and then the six agents who are sitting and enjoying the food.

All six leap to their feet as I rush past, scanning the room for some invisible threat. I hear my parents and Charles calling my name behind me, but their shouts don't deter me. The need to get to Jace has overridden everything else.

I jab the elevator button several times, but nothing happens.

307

Glancing around wildly, I spot an emergency exit door and rush toward it. One of the agents grabs my arm, trying to stop me. I whirl and elbow him in the stomach, which he clearly isn't expecting. He doubles over, and I spin back toward the door. I've almost made it when I'm grabbed again. I employ another one of the self-defense maneuvers I was taught, this time kicking the agent in the knee. His leg buckles. I'm through the door before he hits the ground.

I race down the endless flights of stairs, until I finally reach the bottom and emerge at the same security checkpoint we passed when we entered the stadium. Only one young woman stands next to the metal detector now.

"The team locker room? Where is it?" I demand. I know agents are only seconds behind me.

She looks startled, both by sudden appearance and urgent tone.

"The team locker room? Is that where they take injured players?" I ask desperately.

This time she answers me. "Sometimes. If it's more serious, they'll just take them straight to the hospital."

"How would they do that?"

"There's a side entrance that connects to the tunnels. They'll have the ambulance pull up there."

"How do I get there?"

She looks at me cautiously.

"Please, it's an emergency," I beg.

"Head through that door." She points to one off to the right. "And just stay straight through the hallway. It will bring you to the tunnel, and the entrance will veer off from that."

"Thank you," I tell her fervently before rushing to follow her instructions. I've just emerged into the tunnel when I hear footsteps behind me. I increase my already rapid pace, and am rewarded when I see light off to the right that suggests I'm close to the entrance.

Up ahead, a stretcher suddenly appears. It's being rolled along by four paramedics and closely followed by a couple of other figures. The pain of my burning muscles and the sound of footsteps behind me disappear as my world narrows to nothing else but reaching that gurney.

The small crowd of people gathered around Jace all glance up at me in surprise as I barrel toward them. I reach them just as they're wheeling Jace out through the open entryway.

An ambulance is parked just outside the large opening in a small area surrounded by chain-link fence. A couple of stadium security agents stand beside the open gate. Several reporters hover on the other side, watching the events closely. I come to a screeching halt once I'm alongside the stretcher. Jace's eyes are closed, but his breathing is even.

The cold fist of fear around my heart relaxes slightly.

"Is he okay?" I ask one of the paramedics frantically, my voice breaking as I take inventory of his still body.

He looks at me with surprise. "Who are you?"

Another one of the paramedics looks back at the man and woman walking behind the stretcher. They're both wearing navy polo shirts embroidered with the Sharks' team logo.

The woman steps forward. "Ma'am, I'm going to have to ask you to leave this area. I'm not sure how you got back here, but it's restricted access."

"I'm not leaving," I state. I don't leave any room for argument in my tone.

The woman looks startled by the authority in my voice, but recovers quickly. "I'll have to call security," she threatens. As she does, two of my agents appear, breathing heavily as they stop behind me.

The woman eyes them skeptically.

"Call them," I tell her.

The paramedics begin moving the stretcher forward again, lowering it when they reach the ambulance to load Jace inside. I follow after him.

"Princess, what are you doing?"

I turn and realize Michael is one of the agents who followed me.

"I'm going to the hospital."

"What? Why?" Michael asks, coming to stand in front of me. "What on earth is going on?"

"I don't have time to explain. Move," I snap.

"I'm not letting you leave here on your own in an ambulance."

"Get out of my way," I repeat, louder this time. "That's a direct order."

Michael moves to the side, but follows me as I climb into the back of the ambulance, ignoring the paramedics' wide eyes as they bounce between me and Michael.

"I'll go with her."

I turn to see Thomas has appeared, along with two more agents who were supposed to stay with the cars. Clearly, they've already called in reinforcements. Thomas climbs into the ambulance next to me.

"Why are we still here?" I ask the paramedics sharply. "Let's go."

They listen to me, closing the door on the confused expression of the woman who spoke to me and the annoyed faces of my agents.

I stare down at Jace's handsome face as I feel the ambulance lurch forward, silently cataloguing the changes. His dark hair is shorter, and his ordinarily clean-shaven face sports a hint of stubble. Twin black lines are still streaked across his face. Otherwise, he looks exactly the same as he did the last time I saw him.

"Can I touch him?" I ask the paramedic.

He nods. "He's sedated."

I lace my fingers with Jace's larger ones, noting the green staining the skin. I lean forward, so that I'm close enough to him no one else in the close confines of the ambulance will be able to hear the words I've wanted to say to him for a lot longer than I care to admit.

"I love you, Jace." I lean back, but continue holding his hand, feeling the tears slip silently down my cheeks. I thought I was protecting us both by holding those words back, but keeping them contained brought about their own pain. And they're words he deserved to hear.

We arrive at the hospital to a flurry of activity. More reporters are lingering outside the emergency room entrance, but I ignore them as I rush after Jace's gurney into the hospital.

"Twenty-two-year-old male with head trauma…"

I tune out the medical jargon that follows, turning to one of the doctors that's come over to examine Jace. "Is he going to be all right?"

"Ma'am, we're going to take him to do some tests. Are you family?"

"Yes," I lie.

The doctor eyes me dubiously, but decides not to argue with me. It's a wise choice. I can be unpleasant to deal with when I'm in the best of moods. I'm far from that right now.

"Okay, we'll have someone come find you as soon as we know more," the doctor tells me before following the nurses wheeling Jace farther into the hospital. A sob bursts out of me, and I feel a gentle hand rest on my back.

"He'll be fine, Princess," Thomas comforts. "I'll be right back. I'm just going to see where we should wait."

Thomas walks over to the front desk, where I see the woman from the Sharks has arrived and stands speaking with a couple of nurses. The man who was with her previously has also arrived and looks over at me. Thomas joins their conversation for a few minutes, then returns and guides me down the hallway into a carpeted room lined with about twenty chairs. I sink into one and rest my head in my hands.

I hear Thomas take the seat next to me as I study the fibers that comprise the faded carpet.

"I didn't—I never—I never told him how I felt...how I feel," I admit in a whisper. More tears streak down my face, coating my hands with salty liquid. "Now he might never know."

"I'm sure he knows, Princess," Thomas comforts me. After a moment, he adds, "You're quite skilled at hiding your emotions regarding everything...except him."

We sit in silence, until the door opens and I glance up to see my parents enter the room along with their entourage of security. The Vanderbilts follow them inside, glancing around the waiting room.

"What on earth is going on, Vivienne?" my mother demands as soon as the door shuts. I've never heard her sound so angry, and the Vanderbilts all shift uncomfortably at the sound of her furious voice. They choose to take seats against the far wall of the waiting room. "This behavior is absolutely unacceptable. Are you having a sort of nervous breakdown? You can't just run off like that, and then to come here of all places? In front of the American press? We had to pass through dozens of them to get in here. Is there something wrong with you? Do you need medical attention?"

"Is it your stomach?" My father looks at me with concern. "Where is the doctor? Shouldn't you be in a hospital bed?"

I look over at Thomas and realize he must have told my parents we traveled to the hospital, not the reason why. He gives me a small nod.

I look to the Vanderbilts. "Would you mind giving me a moment alone with my parents?"

Lionel and Margaret quickly stand, seeming eager to escape the tense room. Charles gives me a look of concern, which I disregard.

Just then, the door to the private waiting room opens, and Ellen Dawson walks in. Her eyes are wide as she takes in the crowded room, especially all the black-clad agents. Jace's father and Mike stand just behind her. Her confused gaze shifts to me as Claire and the twins appear in the doorway as well.

"Vivienne?" she asks. "What are you doing here?" I brace myself for anger or derision, but her voice is as warm as I remember it, albeit filled with worry.

I walk over to her. "I was there," I explain. "At the game. It wasn't intentional—we were here anyway, and I thought we were going sailing, but instead we ended up at the game—I didn't even know where, or if, he got drafted." I take a deep breath to quell the flow of irrelevant details. "I came in the ambulance. He was unconscious. Sedated. They haven't told me anything." My voice sounds hysterical even to my own ears, and my cheeks are damp again.

Jace's mother steps forward and opens her arms. I collapse into them, comforted by the scent of fresh baked goods and spices that remind me of happier times.

"I'm sorry," I whisper to her. "I'm so sorry. I can't even imagine what you must think of me. I wanted to write, or call, but I didn't even know where to begin."

Mrs. Dawson tightens her grasp. "It's okay," she tells me. "We understand. Jace told us why he had to lie at Thanksgiving."

I pull back in surprise. Jace told his family he lied to them? Purposefully? I'm too confused to respond, but my mind continues trying to make sense of her words as I'm passed through the rest of Jace's family. They all give me warm hugs despite the fear on their faces.

Claire looks at me with amazement after I hug her last. "Jace said you're a real-life princess?" she asks me.

I nod, smiling slightly at her awestruck voice.

"Can I come visit your castle?"

The smile disappears from my face, but I'm saved from having to reply. The door opens again, and this time a nurse enters.

"You're all here for Jace Dawson?" she asks, looking around the crowded room. An awkward silence descends, since the majority of the people in the room have never so much as met him.

Ellen steps forward. "I'm his mother."

The nurse nods. "He's conscious now, but still has some moments when he's delirious and somewhat dazed. He keeps saying 'She's here.'" The Dawsons all glance over toward me, but no one says anything as the nurse continues speaking. "He won't answer any basic neurological questions to see what the extent of any brain damage might be. Now that you've all arrived, we're hoping that might change. The doctor is ready to speak with you about his preliminary findings, but I can take you to see Mr. Dawson first, if you'd like?"

Ellen looks over to me. "Go ahead," she instructs.

"What? No, you all should go. He doesn't need to see me. I just needed to make sure he wasn't..." I let my voice trail off, not sure how to finish the sentence. Dead? Paralyzed? Alone?

"He knows you're here already. Go. We'll talk to the doctor," Mrs. Dawson urges.

I risk a glance toward my parents for the first time since the Dawsons' arrival. My mother looks shocked; my father looks concerned.

I walk toward the door. "Which room?" I ask the nurse as I pass her.

"He's in Room 128," she replies. "Just down the hall on the left."

Thomas is the only one who follows me as I make my way down the hallway and pause outside the wooden door that has *128* emblazoned on the plastic plaque next to it. I take a deep breath and walk inside the room, shutting the door behind me.

I didn't know what to expect based on the nurse's words, but Jace looks alert and aware as he leans against the partially raised bed, his gray eyes bright and clear. He doesn't seem surprised to see me, but I'm completely unprepared for the sudden swell of emotion that hits me when I see him awake.

Wracking sobs leave my body as I hurry over to his bedside. I perch on the edge of the bed, careful not to disturb whatever injuries the white blanket might be concealing.

"Jace," I heave out brokenly. "I thought—it seemed like— you were—" I can't manage to string more than a few words together.

Jace watches me closely, his face completely blank as he listens to me stutter. I take a deep breath, and rest one of my trembling hands on the tan, calloused one resting on the sheet. Jace inhales sharply as our skin makes contact.

"I love you," I whisper to him. "I told you in the ambulance, but I want to make certain you know that."

Emotion flickers across his face for the first time since I entered the room. His eyes look down to my left hand, and I realize what he's looking for when he quietly asks, "Aren't you engaged?" His voice is measured and carefully controlled.

"What? No!" I reply. "Where did you hear that?"

"I saw it in a magazine," Jace admits. He shifts in the bed, looking slightly sheepish.

"Those aren't the most reliable sources," I tell him gently.

"So you don't have to get married before you can take over for your father?"

It's my turn to shift uncomfortably. "No, that part is true."

"You left that out before," Jace accuses.

"I know. It wasn't supposed to happen until after I graduated. I didn't think it—I—would matter to you by then."

"And now?" Jace questions.

"Sometime next spring."

Jace curses. "Fuck, Vivienne. What are you even doing here?" His tone has changed from accusing to angry.

"You could have *died*, Jace," I reply, letting some aggravation seep into my voice. "What was I supposed to do? Sit there and wait for the official statement? You expect me to have just stayed and watched the rest of the game?"

"Why do you always insist on making this more difficult?" Jace questions. "Why are you even in South Carolina? I don't know what you were thinking, coming here. Rushing to check on me and acting like I'm all you care about, consequences be damned."

"Care about? Jace, did you not hear me before? I love y—"

"Don't." Jace's voice cracks through the small room like a whip, sharp and fast. "You don't get to say that to me now. Not here. Not like this. You said you couldn't say it and leave before. Don't say it now."

"Jace..." I whisper, my voice breaking. My heart feels as though it's being slowly torn from my chest, bloody and barely beating, as I study his handsome face for what I now know will be the last time.

He's right. I didn't think this through. For him. For me. I didn't think about how reuniting would mean I'd have to say goodbye all over again. Mean I'd know I'm saying goodbye this time.

"Leave," he demands harshly. Meeting my pained gaze, he softens his voice. "Please, Viv." I wince at the familiar nickname. "Please, just go."

I stand and turn around. I rush for the door and fumble with the knob, frantically trying to leave his room before I lose the battle I'm fighting with my tear ducts. I finally open the door, revealing the surprised expression of the nurse about to enter the room. Thomas stands just to the right of the door, staring ahead impassively. I brush past the nurse, ignoring the puzzled look she gives me before walking into Jace's room.

"Mr. Dawson, your family has arrived..." I hear her say.

Her voice fades as I rush down the busy hallway, not looking or caring to see if Thomas is following me. Every room I pass is crowded with people. I search for anywhere that will allow me a moment to myself.

Finally, I spot a door ahead that reads *Stairs*. I open it and duck into the silent, empty stairwell. As I turn, I see Thomas has followed me. Thankfully, he remains in the hallway as I close the door. I sit on one of the cold cement steps and press a palm to my mouth. I scream against it for a few moments, trying to expel the swirling mass of pain, panic, anger, and relief currently churning inside me. Then, I start to cry again, releasing heaving sobs that slowly wring the emotion from me further.

When I left Lincoln, I regretted the fact I hadn't known the last time I saw Jace, it was the last time. It feels like the final in a series of cruel jokes that wish would be fulfilled now, like this.

I'm not sure how long I've been sitting on the cement when I hear voices on the other side of the door. I stand, taking a few deep breaths and wiping the tears from my face with my fingertips.

I walk over to the door and hear Thomas say, "If you could just take the elevator..." I pull the door open to reveal Thomas standing protectively in front of the doorway, arguing with a couple of white coat-wearing doctors. The two physicians both look at me with surprise when I walk out of the stairwell.

"It's fine, Thomas," I tell him. "I'm all set." I continue down the hallway and back into the private waiting room. It's exactly as I left it, except that the Dawsons are nowhere to be found. I heave a sigh of relief I won't have to face them again.

No one speaks as I enter the room.

I walk over to the corner where my father is seated. "I'm ready to leave now."

He looks at me for a long moment, his expression downcast.

"I'm sorry, Papa," I add quietly.

He nods slowly and then calls, "Richard?"

Richard appears at his side immediately.

"What are our options?" my father asks.

"It's gotten even worse since we arrived. The hospital has been swarmed by the press," he informs my father. "I have no way to get you out of here unseen. It will be a struggle to keep you safe, even with twelve men."

"What about more men?"

"We don't have any jurisdiction here. I can put in a call to the local police requesting they set up a barricade, but it will be just that, a request. There's no guarantee they'll comply."

"Anyone else we can call?"

"The Duke offered to call a friend, the Sharks' team owner. But, in my opinion, that won't do anything at this point. Even if the owner wanted to help us himself, the team just hit a publicity gold mine, as far as they're concerned. The coverage on this will be astronomical. It's already a national story. There's no way they'll want to help us shut it down."

"Make the call to the police," my father instructs. "See if they're feeling generous. And call the airport too; I want to be in the air within the hour."

Richard nods and pulls out his phone.

I take a seat in one of the empty chairs, staring ahead. No one in the room speaks except for Richard, who mutters into his phone urgently. A couple minutes later, he hangs up.

"We're leaving," he announces. "Cars are outside."

He turns to Lionel. "Are you and your family traveling back with the royal family?"

Lionel looks to Margaret. She shakes her head. "No, we'll stay here for a few more days. Can someone bring us back to our house?"

Richard nods, then leads the way out of the waiting room into the hospital hallway. Our sudden appearance causes a wave of commotion, but Richard and the rest of the agents take it in stride, ushering us along quickly.

We emerge outside the hospital into a sea of flashes and clamoring. The agents form a ring around us, pushing through the crowd toward the waiting cars. I close my eyes as my name is called again and again.

"Princess Vivienne!"

"Over here, Princess!"

"Princess!"

"Are you involved with Jace Dawson, Princess?"

"How do you know Jace Dawson, Princess Vivienne?"

The calls are relentless as we hustle toward the waiting cars. As soon as we're all loaded inside, the agents climb in as well.

We peel away from the curb, leaving the calls from the press behind. Thomas ends up sitting next to me, and he gives me a series of concerned looks as we race along.

I'm still drowning in heartache and pain, but beneath it there's a fresh stirring of anxiety as the implications of the press suspecting a relationship between Jace and me begin to set in.

Our entourage stops briefly at the beach house for the Vanderbilts to disembark. The parting is awkward; I refuse to look at their house, keeping my gaze on my hands resting on the fabric of my navy dress.

We pull up at the airport to see only one plane parked on the runway.

"Where's the other plane?" Richard asks as soon as we've all climbed out of the cars.

"There was a fuel leak," the attendant answers. "It was scheduled to be resolved by tomorrow morning, so we didn't think we needed to inform you."

My mother looks at me accusingly. Yet another problem I've caused on this trip.

"We need to leave today," Richard replies. He looks to my father. "We'll have to risk it."

My father nods. It's against protocol for the two of us to travel together, but we've obviously crossed into extenuating circumstances at this point.

We all climb up the stairs and inside the small aircraft, which is packed to capacity between me, my parents, and the dozen agents traveling with us.

The flight crew begins rushing around, hurriedly preparing for the unexpected takeoff. Richard pulls out his phone to answer a call. I sink into one seat in the first row, leaning my head back and closing my eyes. I wish I had turned around and left as soon as we arrived, just as I threatened to.

The sound of Jace's name causes my eyes to fly back open.

Richard has hung up the phone and is now standing in front of the television that's mounted in the front of the plane, currently set to an American news station.

"Dawson was a first-round pick for the South Carolina Sharks and made his professional debut today. The Sharks have released a statement saying Dawson is stable and expected to make a full recovery, and the league has suspended the Panthers player who made the illegal tackle for three games. The Sharks even pulled out their first preseason victory in five years, but it's what happened after Dawson was tackled that has them in the headlines. The Crown Princess of Marcedenia, a small European country, was revealed to be secretly attending Lincoln University last December. Aside from her undercover arrangement and true identity, very little came out about her time there. That may have all changed today."

The screen changes from the pretty blonde woman speaking to a video of me outside the stadium, standing next to Jace's stretcher, and then climbing inside the ambulance after him. The screen freezes on my face. The pain and panic in my expression are readily visible.

"As you can see in this video footage we obtained, the first person to rush to Dawson's side after he was injured was none other than the Princess herself. Before making his hotly anticipated debut as a Shark today, Dawson was the best quarterback to come out of Lincoln, leading them to a championship in his final season there for the first time in twenty-five years—"

Richard changes the channel. Another video is playing, this time of me rushing out of the ambulance and into the hospital after Jace's gurney. *THE PLAYER AND THE PRINCESS* is the headline prominently displayed beneath it. A reporter is speaking in the background.

"—Princess Vivienne was rumored to be dating the son of a duke in Marcedenian tabloids, but we now have multiple sources reporting she's actually in a secret relationship with Jace Dawson, who was injured earlier today, that started during their time at Lincoln University together last year. Now—"

Richard flips rapidly through three more news channels, all of which are reporting on Jace and me. I rest my head in my hands, feeling nauseous.

"Vivienne Marie Elizabeth, start talking," my mother announces. "*Now.*"

"We're not in a secret relationship," I tell my knees.

"Would you care to explain why we just spent the last couple hours in an American hospital after you rushed to his side, then? You've never even mentioned this boy before."

"We were…involved when I was at Lincoln," I admit. "It ended before I left. I still—I was just worried about him."

"And you didn't think there might be these sorts of consequences? Forget the American news. This will be all over the press back home. We've only just started to repair the damage from the media fallout after your semester in the States was revealed! This coverage is already dredging all of that up again!"

"I know. I'm sorry—I wasn't thinking. I'll do whatever I need to do to fix this."

My mother huffs. "I don't know *how* we'll fix this. Accusations of a secret relationship go against everything we've been trying to accomplish with you and Charles."

"Is that why you've been so resistant to an engagement, Vivvi? This boy?" my father asks, breaking into the conversation for the first time.

I shake my head. The true depth of my feelings toward Jace is all I have left of our private relationship now, and I have no intention of sharing them. Not even with my father. It won't change anything. "No, like I said, things have been over between us for a while."

Jace's angry face flashes in my mind.

"So you haven't been carrying on a secret relationship?" my mother asks.

"Of course not."

"Don't act like it's such a ridiculous notion after what happened today."

I don't reply.

"How do you know his family?" she presses.

"They came to Lincoln for a game." The lie comes easily.

The revelation of my relationship with Jace will dredge up enough questions about my time at Lincoln. Admitting to my parents I deceived my security team to spend Thanksgiving with Jace's family in Nebraska is not something I can drop on them now.

It's early morning by the time we arrive back at the palace, but one wouldn't think so based upon the flurry of activity that greets us. I'm immediately whisked to the office of the head of the Royal Press Office, Anne Riley.

This is far from our first interaction, although I'm sure she wishes it was our last. We spent a protracted amount of time together in the wake of the media bombshell consisting of my undercover status and father's illness, and I doubt she's pleased to learn I withheld details that have now been spun into an even juicier story.

Sure enough, she's pacing circles around her desk and muttering to one of her many assistants when I enter the office. My mother follows after me, still sporting the glower she managed to hold for the entire five-hour flight.

Anne snaps to attention as we walk in, dropping into a deep curtsy. "Your Highnesses," she greets before rounding her desk and taking a seat, gesturing for us to do the same. She takes a long swig from a mug sitting next to her keyboard.

I wonder if there's something stronger than coffee inside.

"I already have a statement prepared for release, but first we need to make sure it's completely airtight. No more leaks. We've barely mitigated the last scandal. Another misstep could cause irreparable harm to this office and the monarchy itself. No one will listen to what we say if they're revealed to be half-truths." She takes another sip from her mug. "Now, Princess, what is the current nature of your relationship with Mr. Dawson?"

It's strange, hearing Anne ask about Jace. In some crazy way, today has served as affirmation that we really existed.

"We don't have a relationship anymore," I tell her. "Before the hospital, I hadn't seen or talked to him since I left Lincoln last December."

"You're certain about that? No contact whatsoever. Nothing that could link the two of you in any way since then?"

"I'm certain," I affirm. "There's nothing."

Anne visibly relaxes. "Well, that's a relief."

"So, we'll deny any ongoing romantic relationship and say Vivienne rushed to the side of a good friend?" my mother asks Anne.

"I'm not sure 'good friend' is quite accurate," I hedge.

"Will Mr. Dawson try to allege there was more?" Anne asks me.

"Jace? No, of course not."

"All right. Let's try to spin this as platonically as possibly, then. Vivienne, you'll need to make an appearance with Charles as soon as possible. An engagement announcement would be even better."

"Fine," I agree, eager to end the conversation and get to bed.

It doesn't even take twenty-four hours for that decision to backfire spectacularly.

I arrive at Edgewood College Monday morning to rampant stares and speculation. I'm unsurprised by the attention in the wake of the media coverage surrounding Saturday's events. I am surprised by the sight of the abandoned magazine laying on top of one of picnic tables I normally sit at.

The cover is two photos of Jace and me. We're standing against a wall I recognize as belonging to Lincoln's athletic facility. In the first one, I'm smiling up at Jace and he's grinning down at me. We look happy, oblivious, in love. In the second? We're kissing. Bold white letters spell out *Just Friends?* above Jace's head.

I mutter a long stream of curses. Had the possibility of other students at Lincoln taking photos of us occurred to me? Of course. Had I thought anyone actually had? No. Did I imagine they might sell them to the press for who knows how much money? Absolutely not.

I feel angry, violated, and naïve as I stare down at the glossy cover. The full weight of my spontaneous actions yesterday hits me. Jace will see this. His family will see this. His teammates will see this.

In one panicked moment, I completely upended his life. Again. His words from yesterday echo in my mind, and I'm oddly grateful he's already angry with me. It tempers the blow, somehow. But I still experience a sharp stab of pain at the knowledge Jace likely hates me even more now. And I know what I need to do to try and fix this—for me, but more so for him.

Several hours of stares later, I end the call with Anne and

walk over to the bench where Charles is sitting, taking a seat next to him.

"Hey," I greet, setting my backpack down next to me.

Charles closes the book he's reading and looks over at me. His usual easy-going expression is glaringly absent. "Is it true? What everyone is saying? About you and that American football player?"

I'm expecting the question, but uncertain how to answer it. "Some of it," I finally say. "We had a relationship when I was there for school, but that's long over now."

Charles eyes me. "You're certain?"

Jace's angry face flashes in my mind yet again. His expression will haunt me for a long time. "Yes. I'm certain."

"Okay." Charles lets the subject drop.

"I need to get married in the spring," I say after a brief pause. "Which you know. They want me to announce my engagement now. Clear up some of the bad press."

"Is this your idea of a proposal?" Charles asks me after a long pause. Some of the good humor has returned to his face.

I huff out a laugh. "Yeah, I guess so."

"Okay," Charles states.

"Okay?" I echo.

"Yes. Let's get married."

CHAPTER TWENTY-FOUR

JACE

Dead silence greets me when I walk inside the Sharks' locker room. Despite the annoyance of having my mom flutter around me constantly while ensuring I'm following every component of the concussion protocol to the letter, I almost wish I had stayed home. Even the concerned looks my mother cast me each morning that another tabloid about Vivienne's engagement arrived were better than this.

I wish I knew another guy who was knocked unconscious during his first professional football game, only to have his ex-girlfriend—who happens to be an actual princess—rush to his side and reveal their formerly secret relationship to the global media.

Unfortunately, it seems to be a rare occurrence, so I have no metric for how best to handle this. I settle for denial as I stride over to my locker, ignoring the stares.

Unsurprisingly, Cooley is the first one to approach me. "Never met her, huh?"

I heave out a sigh. "I'm sorry I lied, man. It was—is—complicated. Not something I exactly like talking about."

"Dude." Cooley laughs. "Don't apologize. You're a fucking legend, Dawson. And you weren't exactly struggling in that department before. Most of the guys I know have crushes on Princess Vivienne, and she's in love with you."

"No, she's not," I dispute automatically, although I can't help but think of her words in the hospital. She said love, not loved. Present tense.

Cooley looks doubtful.

I finish changing and start shoving my gear back into my locker. "She's not. It was a long time ago."

"Are you sure your head's okay? It was less than a week ago."

"What are you talking about?" I ask.

"You haven't seen the video?"

"What video?"

"There were reporters filming when you got taken to the hospital and arrived there."

I groan. "It's bad?"

"Well…you were passed out for all of it. So, I guess it's only bad if you're bothered by the fact a hot girl was literally chasing after your unconscious body. I would be thrilled if any girl did that, and you managed to get Princess Vivienne." He shakes his head. "Talk about life being unfair."

I snort. "Whatever you say."

By the time I return home from practice, my mom has scoured every surface of the entire mansion I'm living in. Each visible plane gleams.

"Hey, honey," she greets when I walk inside the kitchen.

"Hi, Mom," I reply, opening the fridge and gulping down half of a chilled bottle of water. "You didn't have to do this, you know?" I gesture to the immaculate house.

"I know. I wanted to. Also, I didn't have much else to do," she admits. "You're a lot easier to take care of than the farm, your siblings, and your father."

Guilt eats at me. "Mom, you don't need to stay with me. I feel totally fine."

She gives me a dubious look I pretend not to see. "Okay, I'll only stay for one more day…if you promise you'll come home next weekend. I know you have it off. I checked with Ellie when she dropped some stuff off earlier."

"Okay, I will." I promise. "I'm going to shower."

"Okay, honey." My mom glances at my damp hair from the shower I just took at the stadium, but doesn't say anything else as I head upstairs.

I walk into my bedroom and grab my laptop from the bedside table. Taking a seat in the armchair nestled in the corner of the room, I open the computer, studying the blinking cursor in the search bar for a long moment before I finally type *princess vivienne*.

As soon as I press enter, millions of results immediately appear. To my surprise, the articles listed first aren't about her engagement; they're about us. I click on the third one, which has a headline that reads: *'Good Friends?' Footage of Princess Vivienne and Jace Dawson Suggests Otherwise!* The article loads quickly, displaying a video showcasing a still frame of an ambulance parked outside one of the stadium's side entrances under the headline. I hover the mouse over the play button and then finally press it.

The image is frozen at first. There's just the whispers of the reporters coming through the speakers. "Is that him? Are they coming out?" someone speculates.

Another voice adds "I hope this is the right side. Sometimes they send them to the other one."

I watch as Ellie and Adam appear alongside a stretcher surrounded by paramedics.

"There he is!" One of the reporters whisper-shouts. The rapid click of a camera sounds nearby.

Suddenly, a new figure arrives on the scene in a flurry of strawberry blonde hair. I watch as Viv comes to a sudden halt next to my stretcher and looks down at me. The expression on her face collides forcefully against the wall I've carefully constructed around my heart. She looks gutted. Wrecked.

"Holy shit! Isn't that the princess? The princess who was at school here? Joe, get out your phone!" The reporter's commentary cuts into the dramatic scene.

Vivienne turns to speak to one of the paramedics, waving her hands urgently. I watch Ellie step forward and say something. Viv replies, and for the first time ever I see Ellie look a bit cowed. Two men in black suits arrive on the scene, and both stand behind Viv protectively while they scan the surroundings. I watch myself be rolled closer to the ambulance, and then disappear from view as I'm loaded inside. It's bizarre.

Viv tries to follow me, but one of the suit-clad men steps in her way. The camera zooms in on her face. Terror and alarm are clearly displayed across her face. I watch her blue eyes flash as she says something to the man blocking her way that causes him to move to the side. Several more men in black suits arrive and watch as Viv climbs inside the ambulance. One of the new arrivals says something to the man who tried to stop her and then also climbs in the ambulance. To my surprise, I realize I recognize him. He was one of the agents with Viv at Lincoln. Her supposed stepfather.

The ambulance doors are closed, and the vehicle begins moving toward the gate.

"It was definitely her," I hear a reporter say. "I can't—" The audio and recording cut out at as the video ends.

I let myself think back to the heart-wrenching conversation in my hospital room for the first time. It's difficult to muster the same rage I drew on then, especially after having just seen her fear-filled face. Her words come back to me. *What was I supposed to do? Sit there and wait for the official statement?* I wonder how it would feel if she had. If it had come out after the fact that the Marcedenian royal family had attended our first game. If I'd learned she was there but hadn't reacted. Hadn't cared.

It's a long slog through the next week. I don't leave the house aside from going to practice. The press is waiting every time I leave the gated neighborhood I live in. I'm sure my new neighbors love me. The press also loiters around the stadium. I'm grateful the season hasn't officially started yet, so I don't have to participate in any post-game interviews. I'm forced to sit out the next preseason game, but cleared for the first game of the regular season the following week.

As promised, I fly home for the weekend. It's a relief to step off the plane in Nebraska and only receive a couple of side glances, rather than the mob I left behind in South Carolina.

My entire family is there waiting when I walk out of the baggage claim, and I can't help but smile at the sight. I'm passed through them all for hugs of greeting. Aside from my mother, I haven't seen any of them since the hospital, and that was a brief interaction, considering I was dazed from the hit and from seeing Viv.

I feel myself de-stress further when my dad starts up the long dirt driveway that leads to the farmhouse I grew up in. The media and its endless speculation feel distant now that I'm surrounded by rolling fields. One thing that doesn't feel distant? Vivienne. I've only been back home once since we were here together, and I'm immediately reminded why as my dad parks next to the faded red truck we drove here together in.

I lived here for eighteen years before leaving for Lincoln. I returned for countless breaks once I had. But in the five days she was here, she somehow managed to brand everything. There's the cart she got stuck that's parked next to the barn, the stairs she shucked corn with Max on straight ahead, the black horse she rode grazing in the pasture. It's even worse in the house. I've made a point not to enter the laundry room where she stayed.

My mom sends me a concerned look as we head indoors, as though she's aware of the direction my thoughts have taken.

I spend the day throwing myself into every task around the farm I can find. I chop wood, mow the lawn, scrub buckets, harvest crops, and generally do everything I can to stay occupied. No one mentions her. Not even Claire. Since she doesn't have much of a filter, I'm guessing my family had a conversation before I arrived.

The following morning, Mike and I head into town to pick up the paper. It's early enough we only encounter a few of Fulton's other residents.

I leave Mike chatting with a high school friend at the general store and head across the street to get us coffee. I've just grabbed the steaming cups of liquid and am turning to leave when I encounter Gretchen, who's just entered the small shop. She looks startled to see me.

"Jace!"

"Hey, Gretchen," I reply. We exchange a brief hug.

"How are you doing? I was so worried when I saw the reports you were injured..." Her voice trails off as she undoubtedly recalls the other topic prominently featured in the reporting. She doesn't bring the subject of Vivienne up, however, which I'm grateful for.

"I'm okay. Thanks for asking."

Gretchen nods awkwardly. "I'm glad." A brief pause ensues as I try to come up with an excuse to leave.

"I have to get to work," she tells me, glancing at the clock on the wall. "But would you want to catch up tonight? We could meet up at Jerry's?" she asks, referencing the only bar in our small town.

I'm not thrilled by the invitation. Gretchen and I have never hung out alone together. However, it certainly beats sitting at home getting sympathetic looks from my mother and little sister.

"Yeah, sure," I reply.

She smiles. "Okay, I'll text you when I'm finished with my shift."

"Okay."

She smiles at me again before heading over to the counter. I walk outside and head for the car to wait for Mike. He appears minutes later.

"Sweet!" he crows, grabbing the cup I hold out to him. "Thanks, Jace."

I nod, taking a sip from my own cup. Gretchen walks out of the coffee shop clutching a pastry bag and waves as she walks past us.

"Is that Gretchen Williams?" Mike asks.

"Yeah, I ran into her inside."

"Bet she was thrilled about that," Mike mutters.

"What?" I ask.

"Jace, she's always had a thing for you."

I scoff. "Maybe in high school. I'm sure she's over it now."

Mike sighs. "I hate saying this because your ego is already healthy enough. But girls don't seem to just get over you, Jace. I'm still scarred by the shit I saw at Lincoln. Remember that one girl who gave you her bra? At that diner?"

I shake my head, chuckling. "Yeah, I do."

"My point is, those were girls who didn't even know you. Gretchen does know you and still seems to like you."

I roll my eyes.

"I know. It baffles me too," Mike adds.

I laugh.

"Come on, you must have noticed how she acted with Vivie —" Mike stops speaking, and there's an awkward pause between us. We've never discussed her. He clears his throat. "You had to have noticed Gretchen didn't exactly seem thrilled you brought her home. Here."

"No, I didn't notice," I reply. "I was...distracted." Meaning I barely paid attention to anything but Vivienne that entire trip.

Mike snorts. "Yeah, you were." There's a long pause between us. "I still can't believe you carried her across that field. Guess that's the shit you have to do when you're dating a princess, huh?"

I look out the window. I didn't know Viv was royalty then, and I'm still not sure why I told my family I did. I guess I was worried they might resent her. I couldn't have been more wrong. They all still love her, and in some ways that's even worse.

After dinner, I tell my parents I'm going to meet Gretchen for a drink. They exchange a loaded glance and then proceed to give me the same lecture I've received since high school about the dangers of drunk driving. I'm a professional athlete who's currently more famous than most movie stars, and they tag team me for twenty minutes about blood alcohol content and how, if I have more than one drink, I should call them. My siblings all mouth along the words, and I try not to laugh.

I arrive at Jerry's to find Gretchen is already there. She's wearing a tight top and jeans. Her hair and makeup suggest she spent some serious time on her appearance. My stomach sinks. I've been around enough girls to know what that means.

She smiles widely when she sees me and saunters over. "Hey! Should we grab a table?"

"Sure," I reply, rubbing a hand across my face as soon as she turns and heads toward one of the open ones. This was a mistake.

A waitress arrives at our table as soon as we sit down.

"What can I get you?" she asks me, ignoring Gretchen entirely. "It's on the house for our hometown hero." She leans over in an obvious attempt to flash me the view her low-cut shirt offers.

I pull the plastic menu that lists the limited options from behind the napkin dispenser. "I'm going to need a minute," I inform her.

"No problem." She flashes me a flirty grin before back-tracking to the bar.

"Wow, I forgot what it's like to be around other girls with you," Gretchen remarks. She laughs, but there's a clear note of possessiveness lurking underneath. How did I miss that before?

I don't reply, surveying the short list of beers they offer.

"So, what's it like being a professional football player?" Gretchen asks. "You did it. You really made it. I still remember you talking about it in middle school after you watched that Jerry Lewis documentary."

"Yeah, I did make it." I smile at the memory.

"So? What's it like?"

"It's fun." My voice sounds flat. "I like the team, and we've melded well. It's been an intense couple of weeks lately."

"Yeah, I saw," Gretchen admits.

The waitress reappears. "Did you decide?"

"I'll just take whatever you recommend on tap," I reply.

She smiles and nods.

"I'll take a vodka cranberry," Gretchen adds.

The waitress heads back to the bar to put in our orders.

"So this is your last year at Jameston, right?" I ask, eager to change the subject to anything but me.

"I just have one semester left. I'm graduating early." Gretchen sounds displeased by my question. Was I supposed to know that? We've only talked sporadically since the end of high school.

"Congrats," I offer, suddenly glad our waitress is disregarding all the other patrons and chooses this moment to return with our drinks. I take a greedy gulp of the cold beer.

Our conversation turns to more neutral topics, discussing our mutual high school friends, our families, and future plans. I take slow sips of my beer, but Gretchen downs two more refills after she finishes her first vodka cranberry.

"So, are you dating anyone?" Gretchen asks once we've exhausted the neutral topics.

I shift uncomfortably. "No. I've just been focusing on football."

She smiles. "You know, I was thinking maybe I could come visit you. Before I have to head back to school."

I take a deep breath. "Gretchen, I don't think that would be the best idea."

"Why not? Things are just going to keep getting crazier for you, Jace, and I can help handle it. I know you. I can support you. We would be perfect together. I've always had feelings for you, and—"

"Gretchen, I don't know where any of this is coming from," I interrupt. The abrupt turn our conversation has taken is giving me whiplash. "I mean, yeah, we grew up together and were friends in high school, but I never realized—I didn't know...I'm not looking for a relationship right now."

Gretchen stares at me, then lowers her head to her hands. "Fuck," she groans. "I need another drink."

"I think you're good," I say, eyeing her empty glasses. "Let me take you home."

The waitress suddenly appears again. "Can I get you anything else?"

"Just the check, please," I respond.

"I told you, it's on the house." She smiles at me.

"Uh, right. Okay. Thanks," I tell her, standing. "Let's go, Gretchen."

She still has her head on the table and raises it slowly. She looks confused. And drunk. The only other time I've helped a drunk girl was when Viv showed up at a football party, but I don't feel the same surge of protective possessiveness I felt watching Viv chug whiskey in an effort to avoid talking to me. I just feel exhausted.

"Come on." I hold out my hand, and she uses it to haul herself to her feet, wobbling unsteadily in the heels she's wearing.

We make our way to the door, and I'm grateful it's a slow night. I'm sure there are enough rumors circulating through Fulton about me already. I don't need to add to the list.

I help Gretchen into the passenger seat of the truck and start driving toward her house. I can feel her eyes on me as I drive along the empty streets.

We're about halfway to her house when she finally speaks. "It's because of her, right?

I tighten my grip on the steering wheel and exert a little more pressure on the accelerator. "Gretchen, I just don't think of you that way."

"But you think of her that way? Vivienne?"

I sigh. "Yes."

"That figures," Gretchen replies bitterly. "I think I knew when I saw her in the store with your mom. No girl who looks like *that* just shows up in Nebraska."

I grit my teeth at the insinuation I only care about Viv's looks. "That's not why I was with her."

Gretchen snorts. "Sure."

"I mean it. Am I attracted to her? Yes. But our relationship was about a lot more than that. We just…got each other. One day you'll meet someone, Gretchen. And you'll understand. It's just not me."

She doesn't say anything else until I pull up outside her house.

"Thanks for the ride, Jace." She climbs out of the cab and runs inside.

I continue driving back to the farm, parking my truck in its usual spot and turning off the engine. The house is dark. Mike was planning to go out shortly after I did, and everyone else has clearly gone to bed.

I pull my phone out of my pocket and tap on Sam's name.

"Hey, what's up?" he answers.

"I just met up with Gretchen for drinks at Jerry's," I inform him.

Sam groans. "And? I doubt you're calling me because it went well."

"She started spouting all this crap about how we'd be perfect together, and—"

I'm cut off by the sound of Sam's laughter. "What did you expect?"

"What do you mean?"

"Jace, Gretchen's been in love with you since we were eight. You seriously had no idea?"

Mike's never going to let me forget this.

"How would I know that? She's never said anything before tonight!"

"But she's always trying to get your attention, and she laughs at your lame jokes."

"Every girl does that." With one glaring exception.

Sam scoffs. "Okay, that's mostly fair. I still thought you had some idea. I can't believe she finally said something to you."

"I think alcohol may have factored in. She got wasted."

"Well, your last girlfriend did turn out to be a princess. That's a lot of pressure for a first date."

"I'm having trouble remembering why I called you."

Sam just laughs.

CHAPTER TWENTY-FIVE

VIVIENNE

The cover of this morning's tabloids displays two photos side by side. One is the official engagement portrait Charles and I took last week. The other is a picture I've never seen before. It's of me and Jace in Lincoln's dining hall. *Who Should She Choose?* is the headline splashed across the front. I toss the papers to the side and turn on the television.

"—and in an additional twist in the story surrounding Jace Dawson, new photos were released last night of Princess Vivienne with him during her time at Lincoln. The most notable part of these photographs is what the princess is wearing."

"I didn't exactly expect to end up on national television," I mutter in response to the commentary.

"In these new photographs, Princess Vivienne is wearing a *Fulton Football* sweatshirt. Now, according to Lincoln University's website, Jace Dawson's hometown is Fulton, Nebraska—"

I let out a series of swears.

"Your Highness? Anne would like to see you," one of the maids utters nervously as she enters the room. I let out a long breath, still uttering obscenities. I leave the sitting room and head for the wing that houses the Royal Press Office.

I enter Anne's large office and walk into the connecting conference room to find she's already sitting at the round table in the center of the room. My mother, my father, and Richard are all seated as well, along with a couple of Anne's assistants.

I heave out another sigh and take the solitary remaining seat.

"You wanted to see me, Anne?"

"Yes, Your Highness." Anne and her assistants all rise and curtsy.

"Well, what is it?" I ask.

"I assume you've seen the news this morning?" Anne inquires.

I nod.

"Simply put, no one seems to be interested in the fairytale engagement story while rumors about you and the American football player are still consuming the press. The official statement and the engagement announcement were meant to kill the story. Instead, it's still gaining traction. We need an outright denial that you two are still romantically involved to salvage the publicity around the wedding. From both of you."

I start. "Both of us?"

"Yes. Mr. Dawson will need to deny the relationship as well. He hasn't made a single statement to the press. And there are new reports you were in his home state of Nebraska for the American holiday of Thanksgiving. No one wants to look at a stiff photo of you and Charles—pardon the characterization, but that seems to be the general consensus—rather than read about that. If the media continues to spread romantic, false stories, it will draw out the coverage for longer and longer. We'll be battling against it until the wedding itself. High-profile stories like these take on a life of their own. Think of it like a tree. You need to remove the roots or else it keeps growing and growing."

"Can't we just deny this false story?" my mother asks. "Reemphasize it was not a serious relationship? It seems like a statement will just draw more attention to it. Indulge and reward the press."

Anne opens her mouth to reply, but I speak first. "The story isn't false."

"*What*?" My mother and Anne sport twin expressions of horror.

"The trip to Jace's hometown for Thanksgiving. It's not a lie. It really happened. We can't deny it."

"Security reports state you spent the Thanksgiving break on campus," Richard says, raising his eyebrows.

"I know. I lied to my agents." I look to my parents. "It's how I really met Jace's family. I didn't think there was any way the press would find out about it. That's why I lied to you. I didn't want to upset you even more. I'm sorry."

Silence follows my announcement.

"Then it's even more important we get ahead of this," Anne finally states. "We need to get him here by next week, if possible."

"Get who here?"

"Mr. Dawson," Anne replies.

"Have Jace come here?" I ask, shocked. "Why?"

"I can't control the American press. Any interview needs to take place here, so I can make certain it goes smoothly."

"He can't come here. He's just starting his first season! The last thing he needs is to come here and be subjected to more media scrutiny."

Anne raises her eyebrows. "We don't have a choice at this point. If we don't kill this story, you won't be able to do a single interview again without a mention of Jace Dawson. There's hardly a paper in the country that hasn't made some mention of you two, and that's based off a video that's less than two minutes long!"

JACE

I'm just about to leave the locker room when I'm pulled aside by one of the equipment managers.

"Mr. Fairfax would like to see you," he tells me.

"The team owner?" I ask, surprised. I've only spoken to him once before, after I was first drafted and arrived in South Carolina.

"Yes."

"Okay." I follow him upstairs to the plush offices that house the Sharks' management. We stop in front of the corner office. I knock, and a man's voice calls out, "Come in." I open the door to reveal John Fairfax sitting behind an elaborate wooden desk.

"Ah, Jace, wonderful. Take a seat." He gestures to one of the chairs across from him. "How are you feeling?"

"I'm good, sir," I reply, sitting in the chair.

"Glad to hear it. I'll get right to the point. You've been requested for an interview," John states. "Given the sensitivity of the matter, I wanted to speak to you about it myself."

"Respectfully, sir, I'm not interested in doing any interviews before the season starts." I reply.

"I understand, Jace," John says. "I'm asking you as part of a personal favor, however." Noticing my confused look, he continues. "Lionel Vanderbilt is a good friend of mine. I've known him and his family for years, including his son, Charles." I experience a sinking realization at the sound of the name. "He's engaged to the Princess of Marcedenia."

"I know who he is," I reply stiffly.

John nods. "Then you may also know their wedding is supposed to take place this spring."

I nod.

"The press is being less than kind toward that announcement in light of the continuing speculation regarding your own alleged relationship with the princess. They'd like you to do an interview that puts that speculation to rest."

"I'll repeat, I'm not interested in doing any interviews. Especially not as a favor for the Vanderbilts," I reply. "No offense," I tack on.

John smiles. "Sorry, I wasn't clear. While the Vanderbilts obviously have a vested interest in this interview, the request for it isn't coming from them. The Marcedenia Royal Press Office called our publicity team personally."

"The Royal Press Office?"

John nods.

"Did they say who the request had come from there?"

"No."

"I need to know that before I make a decision." I stand, expecting that to be the end of the conversation.

"Just a name?" John asks.

"No. I want to talk to them directly."

"All right," John replies. "I'll let you know when I hear back."

I nod again and leave the room.

VIVIENNE

I'm sitting by the side of the pool reading when I look up to see my mother and Anne whispering together on the terrace. Anne glances over and sees me watching them. She walks over to the pool. My mother follows.

"We heard back on the interview request," Anne tells me, stopping next to the edge of the water.

"And?" I ask, my heart pounding.

"He wants to talk to the person making the request. Something tells me you should be on the call if we want this to actually happen."

"Now?" I ask, my voice anxious.

"Yes. Time is still of the essence here."

I rise from the stone patio that surrounds the pool. "Okay."

I follow after Anne, my anxiety rising with each additional step. Jace and I parted on far from good terms. He has no reason to do this, and I'm not eager to relive the tone of our last conversation.

We enter the same small conference room off Anne's office where we met two days ago. A couple members of the press staff are already in the room, bustling around. I take a seat at the round table, with my mother on my left and Anne on her other side. The staffers settle down into chairs after they all curtsy.

"Ready?" Anne asks.

I nod once.

She pulls the conference phone closer and begins dialing. The only sound in the room is the long rings coming through the speakers. After four of them, I think he isn't going to answer.

"Hello?" Jace's deep voice suddenly fills the room. I dig my nails into the palm of my hand to keep my face expressionless.

"Is this Mr. Dawson?" Anne asks.

"It is," Jace replies. "And this is?"

"My name is Anne Riley. I'm the head of the Marcedenia Royal Press Office. I was told you wanted to speak personally rather than going through your team's publicist. I'm calling regarding the request we made that you complete an interview to answer some questions about your past relationship with the princess."

"Diminish it, you mean?" Jace's tone is cold.

Anne glances at me. I know I've given her the impression there's nothing about my relationship with Jace to belittle, and I can tell she's thrown by his choice of words and their tenor.

"Yes," Anne finally replies. "As you may know, the princess's upcoming nuptials are not receiving the most positive of press coverage. Mostly due to speculation you are involved in an ongoing relationship with her."

"I'm aware of that," Jace states emotionlessly.

"To be frank, it's terrible," Anne continues, seeming to sense Jace's apathy, "and at a time that's already very uncertain for the monarchy due to the King's condition and the Princess's young age. We need to be spinning a fairytale, and the press can't leave the speculation regarding you two alone long enough to write it. This story needs to die, and quickly. An interview with you explicitly denying any ongoing relationship is the only way to do it. Your silence is only fueling conjecture."

She pauses, but Jace doesn't reply. Anne continues speaking.

"We would need you to come to Marcedenia next week, so it can be conducted with our journalists."

"Come there?" Jace asks. "Absolutely not. I've got practice during the week, and I don't see any reason why I should be the one to make the trip. If I agree to this—and to be clear, I haven't —it would have to take place in South Carolina."

"I'm afraid that's just not possible," Anne replies. "It has to happen in Marcedenia."

There's a long pause on the other end of the line. Anne glances to me and then nods her head toward the phone. It's obvious Jace is far from amenable on this topic, and I'm her Hail Mary.

I keep my mouth closed, hesitant to speak. I'm the one who created this media mess in the first place. Jace made it clear the last time we spoke he wants a life free from me, and all I've done since is to turn his into a circus. Now I'm inadvertently asking him to halt his life to come fix mine.

Self-loathing keeps me mute.

"Does Vivie—does the princess know about this? That you're asking me to do this?" Jace asks.

Anne looks to me. I clear my throat; it's now or never.

"Jace…" I start, then stop. "Jace," I say again, relishing the feeling of saying his name. "It's me. Vivienne."

"I know what your voice sounds like, Viv," Jace replies, a hint of amusement in his own now.

I let out a strained laugh. I feel eyes on me, and know that I'm blushing.

"You know about this?" he asks. Though his tone is no longer amused, it's lacking the cool indifference that was present when he was speaking to Anne. I watch her and my mother exchange a glance, suggesting they've noticed the same.

"Yes, I know," I confirm. "I didn't suggest it," I clarify quickly. "But I did know they were going to ask you to do this."

"And you didn't tell them not to?" Jace's voice isn't accusing, just resigned.

"No." The self-loathing returns.

"And it will help you if I agree to do this?"

"Mr. Dawson, as I told you before—" Anne starts.

"I know what you told me," Jace interrupts. "I want to hear it from Vivienne, not some random public relations person."

I half-smile at his arrogant tone. Few people dare to interrupt Anne, but of course Jace would be one of them.

"Viv?"

"Everything Anne said was true," I reply, avoiding his question.

Jace notices. "That's not what I asked you."

I remain silent. One answer would be the same as asking him outright; the other would be a lie.

There's another long pause. Then, "I'll do it. Send the team publicist the details." There's a click, and the line goes dead.

"Well, having you in the room was certainly the right decision, Princess," Anne remarks, attempting to lighten the mood. "For a while there, I didn't think there was any chance he would agree."

I nod stiffly.

"I'll set up the travel arrangements and call a hotel," Anne says.

I open my mouth to protest, but to my surprise, my mother speaks first.

"No, he'll stay here."

Anne and I both look over at her in surprise.

"I don't think that's the best idea. If it gets out to the press that he's staying here, it'll send entirely the wrong message." Anne replies.

"Like he said, he's the one doing us a favor. He'll stay here." My mother's tone is final. Anne doesn't argue further.

"I'll just arrange the travel, then."

CHAPTER TWENTY-SIX

JACE

They send a plane that's already waiting at the same small private airport Viv and I flew to and from when I arrive. A stoic man dressed in a black suit is the only other passenger on board, aside from the flight crew. I settle into one of the oversized chairs after I board, dropping the suitcase I brought at my feet.

We're in the air within minutes. I stare out the window as we travel over the blue of the ocean. The never-ending stretch of water is pacifying, and my eyelids quickly begin to feel heavy. Anxiety about this trip kept me up most of the night.

"Mr. Dawson, we've arrived," is how I'm woken up by one of the flight attendants. I look outside to see a small airport, similar to the one I departed from. I follow my single companion off the private jet.

The temperature outside is similar to the climate I just left, and I'm comfortable in my shorts and t-shirt. He leads me over to a black SUV and opens the door before rounding the fender and climbing into the front passenger seat. I get in and toss my bag on the seat next to me before pulling the door shut. The driver glances back, and I'm surprised to realize I recognize him.

"You're Thomas, right?" I ask, almost certain he was one of Vivienne's agents at Lincoln.

The driver smiles. "Yes, I am. It's nice to see you again, Mr. Dawson."

We pull away from the airstrip, and I look out the window at the scenery of Vivienne's home country. It's gorgeous. There's no way to deny that. The greenery is lush, and the scenery is dotted by open-air villas surrounded by tall, thin trees. Turquoise water suddenly appears to the right, and I look to the left to see a series of white-washed cottages rising out of the cliff that overlooks the sparkling sea.

The countryside eventually gives way to more concentrated neighborhoods and then we drive past a series of stores, restaurants, coffee shops, churches, and museums. Every place we pass is packed with people.

The buildings abruptly stop as we drive up a slight incline. Massive wrought-iron gates rise before us, melded into a metal fence that runs out to the left and right as far as I can see. Crowds of people mill about on the stone sidewalk that stretches on either side of the road.

A severe-looking man steps out of a booth to the left, and Thomas hands him a badge. The man returns to the booth and the gate opens. We drive through and roll along a tree-lined drive toward the imposing stone facade of a building up ahead. We round a massive fountain before Thomas drives underneath an overhang that sits in the very center of the building, supported by elaborately carved columns on either side.

"Where are we?" I ask, although I'm fairly certain I already know.

"The palace," Thomas replies.

"What are we doing here? I thought I'd be staying at a hotel or something?"

"I was told to bring you here. I've got to park the car, but feel free to head right inside. Someone will be waiting to greet you."

I grab my luggage and climb out of the car, glancing around at my surroundings with awe. The grass and landscaping are immaculate and the alabaster stone that comprises the outside of the opulent building in front of me gleams in the sunlight.

Thomas pulls the car away as I walk up to the ornate doors, wondering if I should knock. I'm saved from deciding when a middle-aged man opens the door.

"You must be Mr. Dawson," he greets me.

I regret my choice of casual attire as I take in his coattail and white gloves. I feel as though I've stepped into one of the period dramas my mom likes to watch as I stare at who seems to be an actual butler.

"Yes, that's me," I respond.

He smiles and steps aside for me to enter. I should have expected it from the extravagant exterior, but I still stare around at the entryway in shock. I'm fairly certain my entire childhood home could fit inside it. The ceiling is soaring, allowing for the twin set of staircases that curl around each wall to meet in the center, covered with red carpet. The walls are white, but covered with subtle carvings with a gold accent. The marble floor is so well-polished I can practically see my reflection in it.

I'm studying the table that rests in the center of the room, holding a massive arrangement of colorful flowers, when I hear footsteps. I glance up to see Viv appear on the balcony that joins the tops of the stairways. She's wearing a white strapless sundress, and her strawberry blonde hair is down in its usual messy waves.

Our eyes lock, and I can see the tentativeness in her light blue ones. I feel another pang of regret about how I acted in the hospital as she holds my gaze. I give her a smile, trying to convey my apology wordlessly.

She stands frozen for another moment and then suddenly begins running down the stairs. She's wearing heels, but doesn't falter when she reaches the gleaming floor, sprinting effortlessly across the glassy surface toward me. I barely have time to drop my bag before she hurls herself into my arms.

"Jace," she breathes.

Her scent surrounds me, floral and fresh. I breathe deeply, savoring the feel of having her in my arms again. Too soon, she draws back so she can look up at me. I study her features, even more stunning in person than on the airbrushed pages of the tabloids I've been haunted by.

"I was hoping you might be a little more excited to see me," I tease.

She smiles, but then her expression dims slightly. "Of course I'm excited to see you. It was you I wasn't sure about."

I deserve that. "I'm sorry for how I acted at the hospital. You caught me off guard."

"It's fine. I understand." she replies quickly. Too quickly. Her blue eyes won't meet mine.

"Viv, I mean it. I'm sorry. It wasn't fair to lash out at you like that. I know—I know you didn't do it to hurt me. And I know it's done nothing but complicate things for you." I don't elaborate on what those things are, unwilling to bring up the fact she's engaged to someone else when things are already so strained between us.

Viv finally looks at me. "Thank you for doing this."

"You would do it for me," I state confidently.

"Yeah, I would," she confirms. "But you're the one actually having to do it."

The sound of a throat clearing interrupts our conversation. I look away from Viv for the first time since she appeared, expecting to see the butler who initially greeted me.

Instead, I see a middle-aged couple standing between the staircases who I immediately realize must be Viv's parents. The king and queen. Her father is as distinguished looking as I expected. His eyes are the exact same shade of cornflower blue as Vivienne's. Her mother is poised and elegant. She's dressed formally, as though she's on her way to an important meeting. They're both studying me curiously, and I shift uncomfortably. I'm not sure what Viv has told her parents about me, if anything, and the fact that they're royalty only complicates things further. I expected to be staying at a hotel and interacting with their publicists. Instead, I'm standing in a palace with Viv face to face with the king and queen without another person in sight.

I experience another dilemma when I realize I have no idea how to greet them. Desperately, I try to recall how people greet royalty. Do I bow? Use titles? No one gave me any guidance, and I didn't expect I'd need to know.

Viv seems to sense my quandary. To my shock, she grabs my hand and walks over to the couple, who look equally surprised by our casual contact.

"Mother, Papa, this is Jace," she tells them. "Jace, these are my parents, Robert and Evelyn."

Her father raises his eyebrows slightly and her mother purses her lips. I glance over at Viv, unsure if she's serious about me addressing them so informally. We have a brief silent conversation where I shoot her an "are you serious?" look she returns with a "just trust me" one. Since I do, I reach out and offer my hand to Vivienne's father.

"It's nice to meet you, Robert," I say. "Sir."

He shakes my offered hand firmly. "It's nice to meet you as well, Jace. We really appreciate you coming all this way."

I smile and turn to Vivienne's mother. Her shrewd eyes are bouncing between me and Vivienne.

"You have a lovely home, Evelyn," I compliment, since I can't come up with anything to say about her pantsuit.

"Thank you, Jace," she replies.

Another butler appears in the entryway, dressed just as formally as the first one. He's picked up my abandoned suitcase and bows deeply as he approaches us.

"Your Highnesses, Your Majesty, where should I place Mr. Dawson's belongings?" he inquires.

I flash Vivienne a look, but she just smiles sanguinely in response.

"Any of the guest suites will be fine, Joseph," Vivienne's mother replies. "Perhaps the Hamilton Suite?"

The butler nods and departs with my bag in hand.

"I have to head to a meeting. I'll see you all at dinner," the king says before heading off to the right.

"I have a few things to take care of as well," the queen adds. "Jace, I'll have someone show you to your accommodations so you can get settled."

"I'll show him, Mother," Vivienne replies, rolling her eyes.

"I thought you had some obligations to take care of this afternoon," the queen replies.

"Nope," Vivienne responds. "We'll see you at dinner."

"Very well." Vivienne's mother heads off in the same direction as her father.

"Sorry about that," Viv tells me. "My mother finds most tasks to be ones best handled by the staff."

"Feel free to pass me off to a butler if there's something you need to do," I reply.

Vivienne laughs. "I definitely don't. My mother's just trying to keep us apart."

I raise my eyebrows. "Why is that?"

"I think they're a little unsure how to act around you. I was pretty vague about our relationship, ergo the 'good friends' controversy."

"I'm familiar with it. Nothing tells your ex it's over quite like the friend zone, followed by getting engaged to another guy."

Viv looks startled, so I hold my serious expression for a few more seconds before relaxing it into a grin.

"I'm kidding, Viv."

"I think you've gotten less funny. I didn't think that was possible," she shoots back.

I laugh as I start to follow her up the stairs. The varnished banister feels as smooth as glass. I let out a low whistle as I survey the elaborate entryway from this new vantage point.

"So...this is where Princess Vivienne grew up, huh?" I ask, echoing her words from when I brought her to my home.

She laughs. "Yes. What do you think?"

"It's...nice." Understatement of the century.

Viv smirks. I follow her down a series of long carpeted hallways lined with expensive looking paintings. Finally, we reach a more modern hallway with marble floors and white walls.

"Is there any way I can get a map of this place?" I ask. This time I'm not joking, but Viv smiles anyway.

"I'll be your tour guide," she promises.

We finally arrive outside a wooden carved door Viv stops at. She opens it to reveal a massive four-poster bed made out of dark lacquered wood. The thick navy bedspread spread across it matches the hanging velvet drapes. Frames filled with expensive, fancy artwork hang on the walls. I can't believe Viv stayed in my parents' laundry room when she visited. I've never felt ashamed of my upbringing, but the level of decadence that Viv grew up surrounded with is both astounding and intimidating.

She seems to sense my trepidation. "It's pretty over the top, I know."

"Are you sure there's not a laundry room I can stay in instead?" Even that's probably luxurious.

"It's just a bunch of expensive stuff my family inherited, Jace," Viv says softly.

I look over at her, and understanding pulses between us. This. This right here is what I was trying to convey to Gretchen. Gretchen may have grown up with me, but Vivienne has always had some uncanny sense of my true feelings. She read the underlying insecurity in my joke.

"Did you bring a swimsuit?" is how she breaks the poignant moment.

"Why do you always ask me that? Trying to get me shirtless?" I tease, belatedly realizing it might not be the most appropriate comment to make since she's currently engaged to someone else.

Viv just grins. "We have a couple hours before dinner if you want to go swimming."

I may have just teased her about it, but I'm equally eager for the opportunity to see her in a bikini again. Before she dropped the princess bomb on me out at sea during our ill-fated sailing trip, I was having difficulty stringing a coherent thought together.

"Sure," I reply.

"Okay, I'm going to change. I'll come back to grab you so that you're not wandering around until dinner trying to find the pool."

"You joke, but it would likely happen."

She smiles. "Okay, I'll be back."

"Okay."

She seems reluctant to leave, but eventually she turns and exits the room. I stay rooted in place, trying to readjust to the rapid change of events that's taken place over the past twenty minutes. I take a seat in a chair that looks like it's several centuries old and pull out my phone.

"Wassup?" Anderson answers.

"You seriously answer the phone like that?"

"I knew it was you, Dawson. I'm much smoother with the ladies."

"I've yet to see that happen," I refute.

"I think She Who Will Not Be Named might disagree with you there. I did get her to a football party."

I'm silent, and Anderson misreads it.

"I know, I know. I'm sorry I brought it up. So, what's up? Did you just leave practice or something?"

Fuck it. "No. I'm in Marcedenia. At the palace."

Anderson bursts out laughing. "Glad you've finally gotten your sense of humor back, dude. Where are you really?"

"I'm serious."

"*What*? You're actually in Marcedenia?" Muffled exclamations come through the other end of the line following his words.

"…tell him…" I hear Owens' voice for a brief second.

"Wait, where are you?"

"I *did* just finish practice. I'm in the locker room right now."

Shit. "Why didn't you tell me that before?"

"How the hell was I supposed to know you were going to bring her up? You haven't done so in almost a year. And it's not my fault the guys are all gossipy fucks."

Laughter and shouts come through in the background.

"So? What the hell are you doing there? You're actually at the palace? Have you seen her?"

A knock sounds on my door.

"Shit, hang on a minute. There's someone at the door. Probably the butler."

"There's fucking butlers?" Anderson yells.

I laugh before I set down the phone on the embellished table sitting next to the door.

I open the door to not a butler like I'm expecting, but rather Viv wearing a sheer sundress that more than hints at the light blue bikini she's wearing underneath. She's pulled her hair up in a bun, but a few wayward strands have already fallen around her face. I simply stare at her for a moment.

She smirks in response to my ogling. "I thought you said you packed a swimsuit?"

I glance down at the shorts and t-shirt I'm still wearing. "Give me two minutes." I shut the door and pick my phone back up. "I'm back."

"How many butlers are there?" Anderson asks.

"I've already lost count," I reply. "But it was a false alarm on that front. It was Vivienne, so I've got to go get changed."

"She's at your room? What do you mean, you need to get changed?"

"We're going swimming," I admit.

"Dawson, I don't even know where to fucking start—"

"I know, I know. I've got to go, though. I'll call you later." I hang up before Anderson responds, which is probably for the best. I'm sure I'm going to regret telling him anything. I pull on a pair of black swim trunks and leave on the same gray t-shirt I was already wearing. I set my phone back down on the same table. It's already lighting up with messages. I open the door to find Viv is still standing in the same spot, looking amused.

"Finally ready?"

"That wasn't even two minutes," I retort, shutting the door behind me and following her down the hallway.

CHAPTER TWENTY-SEVEN

VIVIENNE

J ace shrugs off his gray t-shirt once we reach the edge of the pool, and I'm dumbstruck by the amount of tantalizing, tan skin suddenly on display. His muscles are even more defined now than they were in college, something I hadn't thought was possible. Jace catches me staring and grins, clearly pleased by my close appraisal.

"Something on my face, Princess?" he teases.

"I don't know what you're talking about," I retort. I'm certain my biting tone is rendered irrelevant by the burning heat I can feel in my cheeks, which Jace confirms when he does nothing but laugh.

I pull off my sundress and feel a surge of satisfaction when I notice Jace is having as much trouble looking away from my body as I'm having keeping my gaze from his. I saw what the girls who flocked to him at Lincoln looked like, and I have no doubt he attracts a lot of female attention in South Carolina. Vainly, I'm glad I still appeal to him.

Then again, physical attraction was never one of our issues.

I let my hair down from its bun and walk over to the diving

board, suddenly grateful for the summer I spent teaching myself how to somersault off it. Jace watches me closely as I climb the short stretch of stairs to reach the firm surface. I walk to the very end of the bouncy board and perform a couple of tentative jumps to get a feel for the motion. I haven't bothered to try this in years.

I flash Jace a quick smile. "You'll jump in if I knock myself out, right?"

"Isn't there a royal lifeguard for that?" Jace calls back.

I roll my eyes, then propel myself up into the air. I spin and twist twice before neatly slicing through the cool, clear water. I swim back to the surface and wipe the water off my face with one hand as I tread water.

"How the hell can you manage to do that but not catch a football?"

"I caught it once!"

Jace shakes his head as he walks over and climbs onto the diving board. I swim over to the edge of the pool to watch him. He walks out to the edge of the board and then dives cleanly into the water, swimming the full length of the pool and emerging at the other end. He flips around and swims back to the opposing end. I roll onto my back, floating on the surface of the water as I stare up at the cloudless sky and listen to Jace's rhythmic strokes.

I eventually swim back to the edge of pool and pull myself out of the water once my fingertips begin to prune. Jace swims a couple more laps and then does the same. My mouth goes dry at the sight of the water sluicing off his arms and dropping down the chiseled planes of his abdomen.

We sit in near silence side by side on the stones that surround the pool, warmed by the late afternoon sun. The only sound is the slow drip of water off our bare legs back into the pool.

"What's he like?" Jace suddenly asks.

I glance over, but he's staring at the clear water. I don't need to ask who he's referring to.

"He's fine," I reply. "Nice, friendly, easygoing. I've known him since we were kids." I pause. "We'll never be an epic love story, but we get along fine."

"It sounds like he'll be your bitch."

I laugh, startled. After months of deference, I've forgotten how blunt Jace can be.

"I'll be queen," I tell him, winking. "Everyone will be my bitch."

"So, why's he doing it?" Jace asks. "I know why you have to get married, but why is he?"

"He'll be my consort. There are a lot of privileges that comes with. Money. Power. Influence."

"Isn't his family already rich and powerful?"

"Yes, but not to the same extent."

I feel Jace's eyes on me. "He has feelings for you, doesn't he?"

I sigh. "He's said some things that suggest that. And he was pretty upset about the inferences the press is making. About us."

Jace returns his gaze to the water.

"What about you?" I voice the one question I promised myself I wouldn't ask him. "I'm surprised a cheerleader or model hasn't caught your eye yet. Or has one?" I try to lighten the questions with a teasing tone.

"There's no one." Jace's response is brisk.

"I saw what it was like at Lincoln. It must be even crazier now."

Jace doesn't reply, which makes me even greedier for information I have no right to know.

"You don't—"

"Excuse me, Princess?" One of the younger maids appears on the patio next to us.

"Yes?" I turn away from Jace reluctantly.

"She told me—I was asked to—you're supposed to—" The maid stammers, her gaze locked on Jace. More specifically, his impressive physique.

"What is it?" I snap, more harshly than I intend to.

The girl jumps, and Jace smiles slightly before looking away.

"The Queen needs to see you. Immediately."

"Fine," I stand. "I'll be right back," I tell Jace, starting to walk toward the terrace. The maid remains standing in place. "Aren't you going to take me to her?" I ask, unwilling to leave her alone with Jace.

He smiles knowingly.

"Right, yes," the maid says, scurrying toward me. I follow her inside the palace, and she leads me to the butler's pantry where we store all the silver and china. My mother stands at the center counter where the maids usually polish the silver, flipping through a thick cookbook.

"What are you doing?" I ask as I walk into the small room, puzzled by the scene before me. I've never seen my mother with a cookbook in my life.

"Oh, good, she found you," my mother says, glancing up. "What is Jace's favorite meal?"

"What?" I ask, completely thrown. "Why?"

"So that I know what to tell the chef to make!" my mother exclaims, as though it's obvious.

"This is why you summoned me?" I ask in disbelief. "To ask me about Jace's diet?"

"I don't know what Americans eat!" My mother throws her hands up in the air.

I stifle a laugh. "You ate while we were in South Carolina," I remind her.

"At a French restaurant!"

"Okay, let me see the cookbook." I walk over to the island. She slides it over, and I flip through a few pages.

"Here, he'll like this." I show her a recipe for chicken pot pie. She studies it for a moment.

"Okay, I'll tell the chef." She spins to head toward the kitchens.

"Mother," I say, and she stops, turning back around.

"Yes?"

"Thank you," I tell her. "For letting him stay here—for making him feel welcome. It means a lot."

Her expression softens for a moment. Then she nods and sweeps out of the room.

CHAPTER TWENTY-EIGHT

JACE

I stand in the massive entryway, looking around in confusion. Earlier, the palace was crawling with uniformed staff, and now I can't find a single person to help me navigate my way to the dining room. I peek inside another drawing room that looks like it belongs in a museum.

"What are you doing?" Vivienne's voice sounds behind me.

I close the door and turn around, relieved. I suck in a sharp breath when I see her. Her strawberry-blonde hair has been carefully curled and falls in loose ringlets down her back. She's wearing a navy dress that's made out of some loose, airy fabric that gathers tightly around her torso and then flares and tumbles to the floor. I've never seen her look more like a princess, and I'm immensely grateful I decided to wear a suit to dinner. Clearly it won't be a casual affair.

"Viv—wow. You look..." I stumble over half-formed compliments.

In typical fashion, she deflects my attempt at flattery. "You don't look too bad yourself." "Now, let's get some food." She grabs my hand again, surprising me.

For some reason I expected her to be colder, more aloof here. To act more like royalty and less like the bold, sassy girl who calls me out every chance she gets.

I relied on that assumption more than I realized. Because the Vivienne who's giggling as she tugs me through yet another magnificent hallway, the same one who told me off in front of all my friends, who boldly snuck into my room in an outfit I still fantasize about, is not someone I expected to encounter. Or someone I can imagine saying goodbye to again.

I'm pulled from my thoughts when Viv yanks me to the right suddenly. A double set of elaborately carved wooden doors, twice as tall as me, stand before us, flanked on either side by two more men in tuxedos. They both bow as we approach.

"Good evening, Your Highness," one of them greets Viv. She nods in acknowledgment as they pull the doors open to reveal a cavernous room.

The ceiling is arched, showcasing thousands of intricately carved patterns carefully sculpted into it. In its very center, a huge chandelier hangs over a polished wooden table that stretches the entire length of the extensive room. Every couple of feet a carved wooden chair lines the edge of the table, cushioned with cream-colored upholstery that's embroidered with golden thread. One huge fireplace sits at each end of the room. Between them are glass-paned doors that overlook an impeccably maintained courtyard.

I don't realize I've stopped walking until I feel a squeeze on my hand.

I look over at Viv. She's smiling at me reassuringly, but I also detect a hint of nervousness, as though she's afraid I might flee from the grandiose space. I start walking again. Viv drops my hand as we approach one end of the lengthy table.

Belatedly, I realize her parents are already seated. Her father is at the very head, while her mother is in the chair to his right. Both have changed since I saw them earlier. The queen is now dressed in a pale pink dress, and the king is wearing a full suit. Vivienne's mother studies Viv's outfit closely as we approach, a strange expression on her face.

"Good evening," the king greets as we approach. There are two place settings to his left, and I let out a small sigh of relief, glad I won't have to face another etiquette dilemma regarding where to sit.

"Good evening," I repeat, taking the seat farther away from him so Vivienne can sit next to her father.

The queen gives me a small smile as I sit down, then shifts her gaze to Viv. "Is that a new dress, Vivienne?" she inquires.

"Yes, it is, Mother," Vivienne replies. "How kind of you to notice." The words are polite, but there's a clear undercurrent of challenge in them as well. I glance over at her.

"When did you get it?" the queen presses.

"Evelyn," Vivienne's father chastises quietly.

"A few days ago," Vivienne replies firmly, holding her mother's gaze.

"Hmmm," the queen muses. Viv glances to me, and a light blush colors her cheeks. I'm uncertain what exactly is happening. Is the queen trying to imply Vivienne chose her outfit for me? I'm lost amidst the unfamiliar dynamic. The queen drops the subject, although I'm less than enthused when she turns her sharp attention toward me.

"So, Jace, you play football for a living?" Evelyn asks me.

I shift nervously. "Yes, ma'am, I do."

A small group of waiters enter the dining room from a hidden doorway to the left of the fireplace and set small plates of salad in front of each of us.

"And you live in South Carolina?"

"Yes, I moved there when I was drafted." I keep my voice calm, but I'm sweating under the scrutiny.

"Do you like living there? I found it to be rather humid."

I'm tempted to mention how Marcedenia's climate feels remarkably similar, but I refrain. "It's definitely warmer than I was hoping for."

"Had you never been there before?"

"Uh…" I glance to Viv. She's fiddling with her silverware. "Once. Viv took me."

"You two went to South Carolina together?"

"We spent a weekend there, yes."

The queen pauses, and I take the opportunity to shove my mouth full of lettuce.

"How long have you been playing football for?" Vivienne's father jumps into the conversation.

I swallow hastily. "Since I was four," I respond. "It's sort of a rite of passage where I'm from."

Another server enters the room and begins pouring white wine in each glass. A second server follows him around the table, carefully pouring water in the second crystal goblet in each place setting. I'm fairly certain it's the same girl who retrieved Viv from the pool earlier; although I've seen so many new faces today, I can't be certain. The number of people who work here is overwhelming. The female server fills the king and queen's glasses and then moves to Vivienne's side.

I'm certain it's the same girl when I see her hands shaking nervously, recalling Vivienne's possessive tone at the pool earlier. She fills the glass with sparkling water but jerks nervously as she moves to set it down in front of Viv's place setting, sending a few droplets of fizzy liquid flying onto her arm and dress. Vivienne starts in surprise, so I lean over and wipe the water off her bare skin with my napkin.

"I'm sorry—sorry, Your Highness—" the girl stutters.

"It's fine," I jump in. "Could you please bring me a glass of still water instead of sparkling?"

The girl jumps to attention, taking the request as an opportunity to scuttle from the room.

Vivienne sends me an amused glance before grabbing her own napkin to dab at the damp spots on her dress. "She already has a crush on you. There was no need for that," she whispers to me.

The girl reappears, clutching an identical goblet filled with flat water. She sets it down carefully in front of me.

"Thank you," I tell her.

She gives me a small smile and then hurries away again. Vivienne lets out a small scoff, and I look at her as I quickly switch our water goblets.

"I didn't do it for her," I whisper, smirking.

She blushes.

"So, Jace, do many people end up playing football professionally where you're from?" Vivienne's father asks, continuing our previous conversation.

"No, not too many, sir," I reply truthfully.

"It's more competitive than making it into the Royal Guard, Papa," Vivienne adds. "There are thousands of players who try to play professionally, but only a couple hundred are selected each year. You have to be incredibly talented and hardworking to even be considered. Jace broke almost every record when he played at Lincoln, not to mention he was the very first player chosen at the draft. It's a tremendous honor."

Pride saturates her words, and it wrecks me. I've listened to my parents brag about me, I've gotten countless compliments from teammates and friends over the years, but I've never heard Viv boast about me before. The closest thing to a compliment I've ever received from her is when she said she admired me in my parent's kitchen. Witnessing Viv vaunt about me knocks down every defense I erected around my heart in anticipation of this visit.

"That's very impressive, Jace," Vivienne's father says. There's a new layer of respect in his voice. "Congratulations."

"Thank you, sir." I respond.

"Your family must be very proud."

I shift in my chair, uncomfortable with the accolades. "Uh, yes. I believe they are."

"Your family lives in Nebraska, Jace?" Vivienne's mother asks, rejoining the conversation as our salad plates disappear and are replaced by individual pot pies.

"Yes, that's right," I reply, surprised she knows that detail about me. Vivienne's mother does not look like the type of person who would know Nebraska exists.

"And what do your parents do?"

"They're farmers. The land has been in my family for generations."

A new server enters the room, distracting me again. How many people work here? Dozens? Hundreds? I'll have to ask Viv. This server is carrying a glass chalice of water and a fresh goblet that he sets down next to Vivienne.

"Your Highness, my apologies. I just realized you were served sparkling water by mistake."

"It's fine," Viv replies. "Thank you."

A brief silence descends as both of Vivienne's parents eye the extra water glass.

"This dinner is delicious," I finally jump in with. "I wasn't sure what to expect from Marcedenian cuisine, but pot pie is one of my favorites."

For some reason, Evelyn looks miffed by my compliment. I'm certain she wasn't the one who actually made it, so perhaps that's the reason why. I glance at Viv for some clue, but she's studying her plate.

Robert asks me about football again, this time about my training schedule and role on the team. The topic guides us through the end of dinner. Evelyn and Viv stay mostly silent, although Viv does chime in after her father incorrectly asks about the downs.

She summarizes the four opportunities perfectly, and I look at her in astonishment, not bothering to hide my amazement.

"How did you know that?"

She rolls her eyes at me. "You explained it to me five times during Mike's game."

"And you remembered?"

"I thought there might be a quiz later," she sasses me.

I laugh. "You passed."

Once dinner ends, Robert asks if I'd like to have a drink with him in his study. I'm worried this is his way of getting in his own interrogation, but there's no way I can turn him down. He's literally a king.

"Sure," I reply, hoping no apprehension has leaked into my voice.

Evelyn leaves the dining hall after saying good night, but Viv lingers.

"Are you good?" she asks.

"I'm fine, Viv," I reply, noticing Robert watching our whispered conversation.

"Okay. If he asks to play chess, try to get out quickly after the first game," Viv murmurs to me. "Or he'll have you play best of three."

I nod, smiling.

"Good night, Papa," she calls to Robert.

"Good night, Vivienne," he replies.

I follow Robert down another unfamiliar stretch of lavish hallways and into a dark-paneled study. A massive window is centered behind an imposing mahogany desk. A spiral staircase leads up to a second level.

"Bourbon?" Vivienne's father asks as I gaze around. I look over to see he's standing at a table with several glass canisters of brown liquid lined up along the surface.

"Sure."

"If you'd prefer something else, we have it all. Vivienne prefers—"

"Whiskey," I finish.

"Yes, exactly." Robert looks surprised by my response.

He fills two glasses with amber liquor and hands me one before walking over to the plush armchairs sitting next to the fireplace. He takes a seat. I follow his lead and sit down in the matching one opposite him. An antique chess board sits on the small table between the two chairs.

"This must be where the matches happen," I observe, nodding to the checkered board.

"It is," the king replies, studying me intently. "Vivienne's mentioned our games to you?"

"Um—yes," I reply, suddenly unsure. It seems like an innocuous enough detail, but something in Vivienne's father's expression makes me second-guess that.

"Would you like to play?"

"Sure," I reply, apprehensive. This feels like a test, and I wish chess was ever part of my family's Friday night game rotation. I have no doubt I'm about to embarrass myself. In front of a king and Vivienne's father.

Robert sets up the board while I take a few more sips of the bourbon. It slides down my throat easily, leaving a smoky burn in its wake.

"You seem to know my daughter quite well," Vivienne's father remarks as he moves his first pawn forward a square. "Much better than I expected."

I gulp down another swallow of bourbon nervously before moving a pawn of my own. I have no idea how to respond to his statement.

"Vivienne has always been fiercely independent," Robert continues as he moves another pawn forward. A grudging, proud smile crosses his face. "She holds people at arm's length. She doesn't care what anyone thinks of her. Useful traits in a monarch, but they make for a lonely life."

"She'll have Charles," I choke out.

Robert laughs once, but it's devoid of genuine amusement. "Vivienne couldn't care less what Charles thinks about anything, much less her."

"I know she cares what you think," I offer, eager to drop the subject of Charles. "It means more to her than anything."

"I appreciate that," he says, chuckling. The sound is authentic this time, and I relax slightly in response. "But that's not true. Not anymore." He takes in my confused expression, then continues. "When we were at that football game, and you were injured, Vivienne ran from the suite like her life depended on it. We were in a public venue. She knew it would upset her mother, she knew it would disappoint me, she knew what the consequences could be, and she ran to you anyway. I've never seen her so panicked. When the doctors told her my diagnosis, she sat there calmly and started asking questions. She accosted two of her own agents to get down to you that day."

I drop my eyes to study the glass tumbler I'm gripping.

"I thought she was just missing her time in the States when she first returned home. She was so withdrawn, so lifeless. Lackluster about everything. We went to South Carolina just for her, because Charles convinced me she was missing America. But nothing changed when we landed—if anything, she was even more despondent. Until Lionel said your name. When you arrived earlier, she was the happiest I've ever seen her. And at dinner, I couldn't believe…she listens to you. She cares what you think. She relies on you. I've never seen her act that way before—with anyone."

I look at the chess board and move one of my pieces as I avoid Robert's probing gaze. I can't even begin to sort through the myriad of emotions his words are provoking.

"You came here, even though you have nothing to gain from it. Why?"

"Because she needed me to. If Vivienne needs to get married, I'll make sure she gets her wedding so she can fulfill her duty here," I reply, staring him straight in the eye.

Vivienne's father nods sadly. "There's nothing I can do about the marriage law," he admits. "I've tried everything. It's no longer in effect, but Vivienne was born before the date of the official record. There's no way to change that now. I hoped she wouldn't have to take the throne until she's older and would have already chosen to marry voluntarily. Then it would be a moot point. Things changed suddenly, as you know."

"Wasn't she always destined to have an arranged marriage, though? There can't be that many options who are close to her age."

"What do you mean?"

"Doesn't Vivienne have to marry someone from a noble family?"

"Of course not," Robert replies. "What gave you that idea?"

"Movies, I guess," I mutter.

He chuckles. "Vivienne is entitled to marry anyone she likes. Royalty marrying other nobility is certainly a tradition, but not a requirement. Vivienne's mother was a subject when we married."

"She can marry anyone?" I ask, shocked.

"They just have to be a Marcedenian citizen."

"How do you become a Marcedenian citizen?"

"Same as in the States, I believe. You're born here, or you apply for citizenship," Vivienne's father replies.

I don't say anything, trying to process this newest revelation.

He seems to understand the direction of my thoughts. "Vivienne was insistent you two couldn't marry."

"I didn't know it was even an option."

"Royal life requires a great deal more sacrifice than most people realize," Robert advises. "Like a career, for instance. It's difficult enough to navigate having never known anything else, but a wholly other thing to choose it."

I nod, understanding his meaning.

CHAPTER TWENTY-NINE

VIVIENNE

I sit cross-legged atop my bed, staring at the pages of the book I'm trying to read, but not actually registering a single word. Suddenly, there's a knock on the door to my room. I toss the book down, and clamber eagerly off my bed, tightening the knot on the silk robe I put on after changing from dinner.

I open the bedroom door, and Jace is standing there in his same clothes from dinner. His tie is loosened and is slightly askew. When our eyes meet, he sends me a crooked grin that makes my heart begin to race.

"*Three* games of chess," he informs me, stepping inside my room. I close the door behind him. He glances around the bedroom, letting out a low whistle at the size and decadence. "I also got lost."

"I warned you," I tell him.

"What was I going to do, turn the man down? He's a king, not to mention your father."

I laugh.

"He said some things…and he asked me some questions," Jace continues. "About me—and about us."

"What did you tell him?" I ask. My heart's pounding for a different reason now. Jace doesn't sound upset, but what could my father have possibly asked him? I tried to make certain there was nothing to ask him about.

"The truth," Jace replies simply. We remain standing just inside my bedroom door.

His answer does nothing to alleviate my curiosity, but he doesn't elaborate. "Do you want to watch a movie or something?" I ask tentatively. "Or are you too tired?"

It's a bad idea.

Him in my room; me offering for him to remain here. We're truly alone for the first time in almost a year.

Jace studies my face for a moment. "I'm not too tired," he eventually answers.

I'm both thrilled and worried he said yes, so I turn to grab the remote from one of the side tables to give myself a moment to collect my emotions. I face Jace again and point the remote toward the wall opposite my four-poster bed. Two panels slide away, exposing the television behind them.

"Fancy," Jace remarks.

I dim the chandelier and walk over to the massive bed.

Jace follows me, kicking off his shoes and climbing up on the plush white bedspread. I pause to stare at the surreal sight of him sprawled across my bed. It's not something I ever thought I would get to see. As he settles against the heap of decorative pillows, I lean across the bed to grab the book I tossed earlier when he knocked. As I stand back up, I notice Jace is now looking at my chest.

"What?" I ask, glancing down to realize my movements have opened the front of my robe, exposing the lace I'm wearing underneath. I re-knot the scrap of silk holding the robe shut.

Jace doesn't say anything; he just rubs a hand across his face.

I turn out the lamp on the bedside table before I climb on top of the bed next to him. Electricity hums between us.

"What do you want to watch?" I ask, grabbing the remote to flip through the options.

"What were you really asking me earlier?" Jace asks abruptly, instead of answering my question.

"What do you mean?" I reply, only half-listening as I scroll through the movies.

"At the pool. When you asked about other girls."

That catches my full attention. I lower the remote. "You know what I was asking."

"If I've fucked anyone?"

I cringe at his crude choice of words but answer truthfully. "Yes."

"What about you and your fiancé? Have you fucked him?" Jace asks belligerently.

My short temper flares. "How could you ask me that?"

"Have you?" Jace presses.

"It's none of your business," I retort.

It's a weak argument, but I don't want to reveal to Jace how empty my relationship with Charles really is. How I'm barely friendly toward him most days, never mind how far I am from being a doting fiancé. That I've barely let him touch me, much less be as intimate as Jace is suggesting.

I don't want Jace to realize how much I still mean the three words I finally told him at the hospital.

His gray eyes are tempestuous. "None of my business? Are you kidding me? I—"

"Fine, no, I haven't!" I snap. "I haven't even kissed him! We held hands for the engagement photos, and that's the only time I've even touched him. Are you happy now?"

"Yeah, that makes me pretty happy," Jace says, his voice back at a normal volume. The calm after the storm.

"What about you?" My voice is hesitant, small. I'm not certain if I want to know the answer.

"I haven't been with anyone else since you bumped into me the first day of the semester," Jace admits.

I look over at him, completely floored by this new revelation. "What?"

"I told myself it was because it was my last season at Lincoln, and I needed to focus on that. Finally winning the championship. Getting drafted. But I'm pretty sure it's actually because I fell in love with you when you told me you were out of cocktails."

I freeze. I've told him twice now, but Jace has never said it to me before.

"You love me?" My voice breaks on the last syllable.

Jace's smile is bittersweet. "You know I do. I wouldn't be here if I didn't."

"I wasn't sure...after the hospital. It seemed like you might not care anymore."

"How the hell could you think that, Viv? I only asked you to leave because it hurt too much to see you again. And it only hurt that much because there hasn't been a day that's gone by since you left Lincoln that I haven't thought about you."

I can feel the tears threatening to spill, so I do the only thing that will prevent that from happening. I lean over and kiss him.

He kisses me back. Desire, delight, and despair war within me. It's been almost a dozen months since we last kissed, but the time melts away as his tongue traces along my bottom lip. I shiver and shove my hands into his disheveled hair, rolling my weight on top of him. He grunts at the impact, wrapping his arms around me to pull me closer.

I slide my hands down along his shoulders and over the ridges of his stomach to his waist. I fumble with his belt as blind need overrides everything else.

Jace pulls away.

"Viv, we can't…"

"I want you," I tell him. Lust coats my words.

His eyes flare with heat, but he doesn't move. "It'll just make things worse."

"How could things possibly get any worse?" I whisper. "Consider it payment for coming here." I run my fingers enticingly through the trail of dark hair and along the sharp V just above the waistband of his suit pants.

Jace snorts. "You're a princess, Viv, not a prostitute."

"I'll be whatever you want me to be. I'm yours," I remind him.

"That's not fair to say," Jace replies. His expression is pained.

"I know," I admit. "But it's true. It will always be true."

He surrenders, pulling my lips back to his. His fingers trail down my sternum and pass between my breasts, resting on the knot holding my robe together. He deftly unties the thin piece of fabric barely holding my silk robe together and pulls the flaps apart. He pulls back to gaze down at the set of lingerie I put on earlier in foolish hopes of this very moment.

"You always wear this to bed, Viv?" he asks, quirking an eyebrow as he surveys my scanty choice of attire.

"Only when you're staying in the same building," I pant before tugging his mouth back to mine.

We don't exchange any more words after that; both too desperate for each other to draw things out. Jace removes my lacy outfit in seconds, and I unbutton his dress shirt and pull off his undershirt. Jace helpfully pulls off his pants and socks, lying before me in just his black briefs.

Suddenly he stills. "Do you have a condom?" he asks.

"No," I tell him. "The only guy I'm interested in having sex with was in another country. You didn't bring one?"

"No." Jace curses. "I figured I'd be staying in a hotel."

"I'm on birth control," I suggest, after a pause. "I trust you."

Jace studies my face for a moment, then pulls down his briefs.

He thrusts inside of me, and I moan at the exquisite sensation. Unlike our first time together, he doesn't treat me like I'm fragile. He immediately starts moving, rutting into me forcefully enough that we bunch up the fabric of the comforter. I dig my fingernails into his broad shoulders, spurring him along. He nibbles and sucks along my neck and breasts. The sensation sends additional frissons of pleasure shooting through my already overstimulated body.

It doesn't take long until I feel the beginnings of my release building. I let out a low cry as the pulsation of pleasure increase. Jace brings his mouth back to mine, smothering my moans.

My skin turns feverish as sweat accumulates between our naked bodies. I push against him, and he complies, rolling over onto his back. I sit up with him still inside me. The new angle creates a fresh surge of pleasure as he slips even deeper inside.

"Viv," Jace groans. I lean over and kiss him deeply as I rotate my hips. My strawberry blonde hair falls around his face, curtaining us off from the rest of the world. His warm hands slide up my thighs and rest on my waist, helping to propel my body against his.

Ecstasy rockets through me as wave after wave of pleasure consumes my body. I moan loudly, still kissing Jace hungrily. I feel warmth seep inside me as he finds his own release.

I collapse on top of him, resting my head on his chest and listening to the steady beat of his heart. Our first time together, I thought nothing could be better. I was wrong. Jace traces light patterns on my back with his hands, and I hum with contentment. My eyes start to grow heavy.

"Viv?"

I groan, already half asleep. Jace carefully moves my body off of him and slips out of me. I groan again at the loss of warmth and snuggle against the comforter, but my eyes fly open when I'm suddenly lifted off the bed.

"Did I wear you out?" Jace asks, giving me a proud grin.

I roll my eyes. He carries me into the large marble bathroom and turns on the shower with one hand while supporting my weight with his other. He steps into the large tiled shower, still holding me. A warm spray of water hits my legs. I startle before sliding out of his arms and finding my footing on the shower floor. I take a generous pump of shampoo and quickly work it through my long hair, watching as Jace rinses himself off. For the first time, I get to see his chiseled body on display in full light. The sight of him wet and naked sends heat pumping through my body again.

I finish sudsing my arms and torso and lean down to wash my legs and feet. I step closer to Jace, letting the jets of water rinse the soap from my body. His body immediately reacts to my proximity. I glance down and take his long length in my hand, stroking it.

"Viv," Jace groans.

He sounds tortured, and I feel heady with power. I sink down to my knees and relish the reverential look he gives me as I take him in my mouth. He threads his fingers through my wet hair as I alternate between stroking and sucking his thick shaft.

"Viv, I'm going to come," he warns a few minutes later. I quicken my pace, and a warm, salty liquid fills my mouth.

Jace pulls me up and pins me against the wall, moving his hand between my legs to rub the nub of nerves there. I'm already aroused, so it only takes a few seconds before I'm hit with another toe-curling surge of sheer bliss. Jace leans his forehead against mine, both of us sated for the moment.

I turn off the faucet and step out of the shower, drying myself off with the plush towel hanging there, then wrapping the soft fabric around my body. Jace steps out after me. I pull a fresh towel from the cabinet for him to use. He dries off and then ties it around his waist. I quickly brush my teeth and hand Jace one of the extra toothbrushes stored under the sink. I lean against the wall next to the sink, watching as he spits and rinses off the toothbrush.

"What?" he asks gruffly, catching my stare as he turns toward the door.

I shrug, grinning. "I just like looking at you."

Jace smiles. I turn off the lights and walk back into my bedroom. I drop my towel and slip under the crisp sheets. Jace follows suit, and I snuggle up against his side.

I'm warm and content, rapidly losing hold of consciousness, when Jace says the last thing I ever expected him to.

"Why didn't you tell me we could get married?"

"What?" I open my eyes, wondering if I somehow misheard him.

"Your father told me tonight we could get married if I apply for citizenship."

"He did *what?*" I exclaim, sitting up in bed. "He had no right to do that."

"You let me think we could never have any future."

"We can't."

"We could. We could get married, and you wouldn't have to marry him."

"I told you I'd never ask you to choose me. I meant that.

You'd have to give up everything, Jace. Your career, your family, your friends, your country. I could never ask you to do that."

"I know you're not asking me to. But it's my choice. I didn't even know there is one."

"There's *not*," I insist. "It's not an option, Jace."

"Because you don't want to marry me?"

I huff out a dry laugh. It's a ridiculous question. Almost as ridiculous as my father suggesting to Jace this is an option.

"Because you would be miserable. You would be stuck here all day, every day. No privacy, no freedom, endless obligations. You would hate me for all you had to give up. You're meant to be playing in front of thousands of fans and visiting your parents' farm and…" My voice threatens to fail, but I forge on, needing to make certain Jace drops this subject permanently. I won't be able to muster the strength to discuss it again. "And to marry someone like Gretchen, who can support you and do those things with you."

Jace doesn't say anything.

"I'm sorry," I say softly into the darkness. "You know I wish things were different. More than anything."

Jace lets out a long sigh. "I know."

Neither of us say anything after that, and eventually I drift off to sleep.

CHAPTER THIRTY

JACE

I wake up to an empty bed. I roll over to see Viv perched on the loveseat in the corner of the room, tying her shoelaces.

"Hey," she greets once she sees I'm awake, giving me a hesitant smile.

"Hi," I reply. We stare at each other, gauging the other's mood.

Viv breaks the silence first. "I grabbed your bag for you," she says, nodding to my suitcase, which is sitting on the armchair by the windows. "I thought I'd save you the walk of shame." She winks, acting more like her usual self as she finishes tying her shoelace and stands. She's dressed in a pair of running shorts and a bright pink sports bra.

"How thoughtful," I tease, smiling.

Viv relaxes visibly at my response. I sit up in bed, stretching my arms above my head. I have no idea if Marcedenia has some special type of mattresses, but I seriously feel as though I just spent the night on a cloud. I have a feeling the girl shifting her weight back and forth between her feet while staring at me deserves most of the credit, though.

Vivienne's gaze drops to my exposed torso as I stretch, and I watch her cheeks redden as she realizes I'm still naked. My own body reacts to her blatant admiration.

"How come you didn't wake me up?" I ask. I mean for more than just retrieving my bag, and she knows it.

Viv bites her lip. "I'm always the one who initiates it," she admits, not meeting my gaze. "And I wasn't sure if you would…"

She stops talking when I climb out of bed and walk over to her.

"I always want you, Viv. Always, okay? Even at inconvenient times, like when you play charades with my mom and sister, or when you were there at the hospital. Whenever I've stopped you —or let's be honest, tried and failed to stop things—it's never been because I didn't want to. Okay?"

She nods. I kiss her as soon as her blue eyes finally find mine. Hungrily, greedily, desperately. We've already blazed past all the physical boundaries I was so certain would be in place, and I can't muster the necessary restraint to keep myself from doing so again, especially when Viv is kissing me back just as eagerly.

It's another half hour before the two of us emerge out a side door into the palace gardens. It's still early, but the temperature outside has already risen to warmer levels than it reached yesterday. Viv's strawberry blonde hair is adorably mussed as she stretches her hamstrings.

"You ready?" she asks, beaming at me.

"Ready as I'll ever be," I reply, returning her smile as I stretch my own leg. "My muscles have purposefully forgotten what it's like to run with you."

Viv rolls her eyes as she starts jogging. "You're a professional athlete, Jace. Keep up."

We only make it a couple hundred feet before I hear the sound of footsteps behind us. I glance back to see two men dressed in black running behind us.

"We have an escort?" I ask Vivienne, raising my eyebrows.

"Yup," she replies. "My security team is kind of overprotective. People have tried to climb in before." She gestures to the towering iron fence that runs along the edge of the trail we're on.

"What?" I reply, suddenly panicked. Threats to Vivienne's safety have never even occurred to me. "Are you safe here?"

Vivienne has the audacity to laugh at my worried expression. "There's no place in the country that's better protected," she promises me. "An army couldn't invade this place. The only trespassers we've ever had were either journalists or mentally ill, but harmless." Her expression softens. "Thanks for caring, though."

We keep running in companionable silence. Beads of sweat roll down my face as the wooded trail stretches on and on. I let out a loud sigh of relief when I see the gardens appear again, and Viv laughs. The temperature has increased even more, and we're both drenched in sweat. We draw closer to the gardens, and I spot the pool we swam in yesterday. Vivienne follows my gaze and immediately guesses my intention.

"Jace, don't you—"

I don't allow her a chance to finish the threat, swinging her up and over my shoulder in one smooth motion. She waves her arms and legs wildly but is laughing too hard to keep protesting as I jog toward the pool.

I leap into the deep end, submerging us both in the cool liquid, fully clothed. I push off the cement floor and shoot myself back to the surface. Vivienne bobs up a couple seconds later, slicking her hair back out of her face. She splashes me in the face immediately.

"You're the worst," she informs me, but is grinning too broadly for the words to have any bite.

"That's not what you were saying earlier," I tease, laughing as her cheeks grow even more flushed. "Or last night."

She splashes me again, making me laugh harder.

"Vivienne!"

I glance over to see the queen is standing along the edge of the pool. She doesn't look angry, but I still start guiltily.

"Yes, Mother?" Vivienne calls back as she treads water, managing to look composed despite being sopping wet.

"I told you Anne wanted to meet with you and our houseguest at nine this morning to prepare for the interview tomorrow. It's quarter of now."

Vivienne groans under her breath. The humor recedes from my face as Evelyn's words register. I almost forgot why I'm here.

"Okay, Mother," she replies. She starts swimming for the ladder, and I follow. She hauls herself out and begins wringing out her hair. I grab two towels, passing her one before I twist the hem of my shirt to shed the excess water from the saturated fabric.

"You'll both need to change," the queen states as we stand there dripping.

"How come?" Vivienne asks with a straight face.

I rub the towel across my face to conceal my grin.

The queen sighs. "I'll let Anne know you'll be running late and have a breakfast buffet set up in the conference room."

"Thank you," I'm quick to say.

The queen nods in acknowledgement. "Vivienne, may I speak to you?"

I glance over at Viv, but she looks unperturbed.

"Do you know how to get back to your room?" the queen asks me.

I don't, but I don't need to get back to my room. I need to get back to Viv's. I see her reach the same conclusion I do.

"Stephen?" Viv calls. One of the butlers hurries over.

"Yes, Your Highness?" he asks, bowing in front of Viv.

"Can you show Mr. Dawson to the entrance of the east wing? I'm sure he can find his own room from there."

"Of course, Your Highness."

I nod at Viv once, and she winks at me.

"It was nice to see you, Evelyn," I offer to Vivienne's mother.

"You too, Jace."

I follow the butler back inside through a series of winding hallways covered with a resplendent blue carpet I'm certain I've never traveled through before. He stops at the start of a stretch of marble hallway I recognize.

"Thanks, Stephen."

He smiles. "My pleasure, Mr. Dawson." He turns and heads back the way we've just come.

I wander down the hallway until I come to Viv's door. I open it and slip inside, feeling like I'm on an incognito mission. Do they have cameras inside this place? Something I probably should have considered before kissing Viv in the hallway this morning. She didn't stop me, but she was distracted.

I look around her immaculate room. I didn't pay much attention to my surroundings last night. The hardwood floor is gleaming, a long stretch of varnished boards that's only interrupted by a few fluffy rugs.

The room is decorated in soothing shades of light blue and gray. I think back to how Viv teased me about the childhood photos on my bedroom wall. There aren't any such sentimental touches in her room. Pencil-drawn, framed sketches are artfully hung across the walls. I peer at the signature in the corner of one, shocked to realize I recognize the name. And it must be an original.

Walking past the stretch of bay windows, I enter the white

tiled bathroom. My t-shirt and shorts cling to me as I peel them off and step under the pulsing spray of water. After washing and rinsing, I grab the same towel I used last night and dry myself off. I step back into the bedroom just as Viv walks in the room. I study her face carefully. She doesn't look upset. Just resigned.

"Everything okay?" I ask as I open my suitcase and pull on a clean t-shirt.

She nods.

"What did your mom want?" I can't help but ask.

Viv sighs. "Engagement stuff."

"Oh." The word hangs awkwardly between us. Relief I wasn't the topic is swarmed with jealousy.

Viv sends me a small smile before heading into the bathroom. "I'll be quick."

I finish getting dressed and pull out my phone as I wait. Hundreds of missed notifications cover the screen. I shove the electronic device back in my pocket without replying to any of them. The only person I want to talk to right now is on the other side of the bathroom door. Anyone who has questions about our relationship can watch our interview tomorrow like the rest of the world.

I sit down on the window seat and stare out at the sea of color spread before me. Uniformed gardeners mill along the gravel paths that wind between the flowerbeds, watering and weeding.

"Two more minutes," Viv tells me, stepping out of the bathroom in a towel and rushing into her closet.

"Take your time," I call back. "I'm not in a rush for this inquisition."

Viv emerges from her closet wearing a blue dress patterned with tiny white flowers a minute later. A couple of thin straps reveal the smattering of freckles across her shoulders. She yanks a hairbrush through her long hair a couple of times.

"Okay, I'm ready." She looks at me questioningly, and I realize I'm just staring at her. "Jace?"

"Yup, let's go."

This meeting is going to be painful in more ways than one.

I've given up on learning my way around the palace. I simply follow Viv as she leads me through one decadent room after another. Finally, we emerge into a new hallway. I know I haven't been in here before, since the sight of it almost makes me stop in my tracks.

The ceiling is arched the same way the dining hall was, but this time it's completely white, composed of hard stone that has a diamond pattern carved into it. The floor is a gleaming pattern of white and black tiles. Arched windows run the length of the hallway on both sides, situated between white columns. To the left, an emerald carpet of green grass stretches as far as the eye can see. To the right, I see the tree-lined driveway I entered the palace through yesterday. The elaborate fountain sits right in the middle of the gravel driveway, and the imposing front gates are just visible in the distance.

"Wow," I say. The word doesn't do the view justice.

"This connects the residence to the rest of the palace," Viv explains. "Where the Press Office and all the other official business takes place."

Her heels click against the shining tiles as we pass through the hallway and back onto carpeted floor. It suddenly feels as though we're inside an upscale office building. We pass several men and women in suits carrying stacks of paper and binders. They all stop to bow or curtsy as soon as they see Viv approaching.

Viv stops outside a nondescript wooden door. She opens it and steps inside. I follow after her, glancing around curiously. The floor is dark wood that matches the molding that frames the cream-colored walls. There's a small oval table in the center of the room. A middle-aged woman with a sleek blonde bob is already seated at it. She rises and curtsies.

"Your Highness," she greets Viv. Her gaze shifts to me. "Mr. Dawson, I'm Anne Riley. We spoke on the phone previously."

"Yes, I remember," I reply.

She appears just as brisk and efficient in person as she sounded on the phone. "Wonderful. Queen Evelyn asked for some breakfast to be brought up." Anne gestures to a buffet of food that's been set up on a table along the wall. "She said neither of you have had a chance to eat yet. So, help yourselves and then we'll get started. Let me just grab an assistant, then we can begin as soon as you're both ready." She smiles and leaves the room.

I make a beeline for the array of food, my stomach grumbling loudly at the sight of the spread. I load a plate high with eggs, French toast, fruit, bacon, and toast. Viv raises her eyebrows at my overloaded plate as she starts to fill her own with food.

"What?" I ask. "I'm a growing boy." I wink, and she rolls her eyes.

"I'm not sure boy is the right word."

I smirk. "I don't know what you're insinuating, Viv. I'm just hungry. I had two workouts this morning."

She blushes.

"Is that why you don't think of me as a boy? Because—"

"Stop it," she hisses, glancing wildly toward the door.

"Stop what?" I reply, grinning at her as I take a large bite of toast.

"Talking about sex! You're going to make Anne suspect something is going on."

"Only if you keep blushing all the time," I inform her.

Viv sticks out her tongue at me.

"Okay, I'll stop," I promise. "But for the record, I fucking love when I make you blush," I whisper against her ear.

She shivers, and it's a serious test of my willpower to leave her side and walk over to the table. Vivienne is a dangerous addiction. No matter how much I get, I always crave more.

I set my plate on the table, then return to the buffet to grab a cup of coffee. The door opens, and Anne reenters the room with a brown-haired girl who looks my age in tow. She curtsies to Viv and looks at me curiously before taking a seat at the table. I add some milk to my coffee and glance over at Viv. She's holding her own overloaded plate and a glass of orange juice.

"Coffee?" I ask her.

"Yeah, thanks," she replies, grabbing a few napkins and then heading over toward the conference table.

I follow after her, setting down both mugs. As Viv sets down her plate and glass, I pull the chair next to me out slightly so she can sit down. I take a large bite of eggs and glance up to see Anne staring at me intently. Her lips are pursed.

"Okay," she says, opening her notebook. "Are you both ready to get started?"

Viv and I both nod.

"The point of this meeting is to prepare you both for any questions that may come your way in the interview and go over anything else that could come up as a surprise. I have some control over the press, but if anyone has anything they consider juicy enough, they may go off-script. We need to ensure that doesn't happen, got it?"

I nod, glancing over at Viv. It probably would have been a good idea to discuss our strategy going into this, but it's too late now. I'll just have to follow her lead.

"Cara will be recording this session, just in case we need to review anything later, all right?"

I look at Viv, who seems nonplussed, so I nod my agreement again.

"Okay, let's start at the beginning. You'll most certainly be asked this. How did you two meet?"

I grin automatically in response to her question, recalling the moment Vivienne literally crashed into my world. I glance at Viv, who's already looking at me. I tilt my head in a silent indication she should go ahead.

"We ran into each other on campus," she says.

Anne holds a pen poised over her notepad, clearly waiting for Vivienne to elaborate. When neither of us say anything else, she glances up expectantly.

"It was a brief conversation," I contribute.

Viv snorts, and I wink at her.

Anne jots something down on the paper. "Okay then. When was the next time you saw each other?"

"We happened to run into one another a few weeks later," Viv answers. "Also on campus."

"Stalker," I cough. Viv elbows me sharply.

Anne makes another note. "Did anyone witness this interaction?" she asks.

"I don't think so. We were out in the open on campus, but it was early in the morning. There wasn't really anyone else around."

"Okay," Anne replies. "When was the first time you were seen together?"

"Uh...probably when Jace took me to the football stadium. He was trying to show off—"

I scoff at that, although it's true.

"—and the whole team saw us together."

"Could there be any photographs or recordings of that interaction?"

"I don't think so," Vivienne replies, looking to me.

"There are security cameras in the stadium," I state. "But I don't know if Lincoln keeps the recordings."

Anne nods. "It shouldn't be an issue. Any other public interactions?"

"We were at a party together," Viv admits.

"And people saw you together?"

"Yes," I respond this time.

"Photos or videos?" Anne questions.

"It's possible," I acknowledge, recalling the stares when I caught Viv in the kitchen. "But I imagine they would have come out by now if there were any."

"You might be surprised by what people can be convinced to come up with for a few thousand dollars."

"A few thousand dollars?" I laugh. "You're joking."

"I can assure you I'm not, Mr. Dawson."

"For a grainy video of me carrying Viv up the stairs?"

"You carried her upstairs at this party?" Anne asks. "In front of other students?"

I falter. "Uh, yes."

"To your bedroom, I presume?"

"It wasn't like that," I defend. "She was—"

"I'm not asking you to divulge any details regarding your private interactions with the princess, Mr. Dawson," Anne interrupts. "My job is simply to ensure the public narrative doesn't involve any more surprises and assure the media your brief relationship is long over. I'm sure you can appreciate why a photograph or video of you carrying the princess to your bedroom wouldn't be helpful for either of those goals. Regardless of what may or may not have happened behind closed doors."

Vivienne bristles beside me. "We're both well aware of the current situation and the goals for this interview, Anne. There's no need to lecture Jace about them." Her voice is sharp.

"My apologies, Your Highness," Anne replies. While she does look remorseful, surprise and confusion also flash across her face before she schools it into a neutral expression again. "Let's move on."

I eat the last bite of my breakfast and set my plate to the side.

"Were there any other events on campus you attended together?"

"No," Viv replies. "Jace came to my dorm once. That photo was already leaked to the press. We left campus right after that for the Thanksgiving break."

"Ah, yes. The break when you traveled to Nebraska while your security team believed you were still on Lincoln's campus?"

"Yes," Vivienne replies curtly. I can feel the tension radiating off her.

I grab her hand underneath the table and give it a light squeeze.

She relaxes. "We spent most of the time at Jace's family's house."

"Did you drive anywhere together?"

I seize the opportunity to lighten the tense mood. "We didn't let Viv drive anywhere after the cart incident."

To my relief, Vivienne laughs, just as I hoped. "Of course you would bring that up." To Anne, she adds, "He's kidding, that was on the farm. No one saw."

"What was the cart incident?" Anne looks between us in confusion.

"Vivienne got our farm vehicle stuck during her visit," I elaborate, grinning at Viv.

She rolls her eyes. "I told Max I hadn't done much driving. He insisted, so I decided I'd impress you by driving around the farm like a native Nebraskan."

I chuckle at this new revelation. "You blew me away with

your ability to get the cart stuck on a dry, flat road. My dad, too. It's one of his favorite stories to tell."

"Really?" Viv asks, looking both surprised and sad. "I didn't think he would… I mean, I figured I wasn't—"

"They didn't just forget you," I assure her. I both love and hate the fact Vivienne fits so perfectly in my family.

Viv swallows a couple of times rapidly. "Jace…"

"It's fine, Viv. They understand."

Anne clears her throat, startling me. I completely forgot she was in the room. Viv jumps as well, indicating she did, too.

"How about we take a break?" Anne suggests, rubbing her forehead.

I let out a sigh of relief. "Sounds good to me." Vivienne nods in agreement.

"Cara, you can stop the recording." Anne's assistant rushes to comply with her instruction. Anne closes her notebook. "I'll see you both later," she says, standing and leaving the room. Cara follows her.

As soon as the door shuts behind them, Viv drops her head to the table. "Ugh," she groans.

"You didn't think that went well?" I ask, smirking.

She turns her head to look at me. "I'm so sorry, Jace."

"It's not your fault."

"Yes, it is." She raises her head and traces her finger in circles on the table. "I didn't tell them. When I got back, I should have told them about us, that it could come out, but I didn't. And then, by some miracle, no one at Lincoln talked about us to the press. But I made a huge scene at the game. I might as well have announced I was in love with you on national television."

"I would have been offended if you told some reporter you're in love with me before you told me," I reply.

She laughs. "Better than never saying it all." Her voice holds a hint of regret.

"You don't have anything to apologize for, Viv," I tell her softly.

She smiles at me. "You know, it was easier to argue with you when you were being an inconsiderate asshole."

I chuckle. "It was easier to argue with you when you were acting like an ice princess."

Viv grins. "That's what the staff used to call me."

"Used to?" I tease. "Anne's probably uttering those words at this very moment. Her assistant didn't say a single word, she's so terrified of you."

"Anne is the one who suggested making you come all this way. She should at least treat you like you're doing us a favor, not causing problems. And her assistant didn't say anything because she was too busy staring at you."

I shake my head.

"Come on, I want to show you the library," Viv says, rising from her seat.

I follow suit. "What about all this?" I ask, gesturing to our dirty plates and the remaining food.

"Leave it," Viv instructs. "I'm sure there's staff waiting outside to clear it."

"Seriously?" I ask, marveling. "I'm not sure how you survived Lincoln's dining hall."

"Honestly, it was a relief," Viv admits. "No protocols or procedures."

"Speaking of which, what the hell am I supposed to be doing?"

"What do you mean?" Viv asks, puzzled.

"Everyone we encounter is bowing and using titles and holding doors, and I have no idea how I'm supposed to act."

Viv stifles a smile. "You're asking me if you're supposed to bow to me?"

"It's not funny!" I reply. "But yes. And your parents."

"You're right, it's not," Viv sobers. "But no, you don't."

"Are you sure? Because I don't mind. I mean, it would be a little weird, at least with you, but I don't want anyone to think I'm disrespecting your family."

"No one thinks that," Viv assures me.

"Fine," I reply. "I'll trust you on the local customs. Just remember I shunned the time-honored American tradition of pumpkin pie on Thanksgiving if you're lying to me about this."

Viv's still laughing as she pulls the door open. As she predicted, several uniformed staff members stand in the hallway, along with Anne's assistant Cara. She begins stammering when Viv and I enter the hallway.

"Uh—Princess—I mean, Your Highness—"

I give Viv a meaningful look.

She sighs. "What is it, Cara?"

"Anne would like to see you now," Cara replies nervously.

"That wasn't much of a break," Viv states. She glances to me. "Are you okay to keep going?"

Cara starts speaking again before I can answer. "She specifically asked for just you, Your Highness. Not Mr. Dawson."

Vivienne frowns slightly. "Fine," she agrees. "I'll stop by after I bring Jace to the library."

"It's fine, Viv," I tell her, not wanting to incite further conflict. "I'll find it on my own. I've got playbooks I should study anyway."

"The same way you 'found' the dining hall last night?" Viv questions, looking amused. "The library's all the way in the North Wing."

"I can show Mr. Dawson the way, Your Highness," Cara offers.

Viv looks at me, and I nod.

"Okay," she relents, then begins walking down the hallway.

"It's this way," Cara instructs, nodding her head in the opposite direction from Viv's retreating figure.

I follow her as she begins walking. "So, have you worked in the press office for long?"

Cara looks startled I'm speaking to her. I notice she glances behind us before answering. She relaxes slightly once she confirms Viv is out of view. "No," she replies. "I'm just an intern here for the summer."

"Oh, really?" I respond. "So you're still a student?"

Cara nods. "I'll be starting my final year at Edgewood in September."

"Edgewood?" I repeat. "Isn't that where Vivienne goes now?"

"Yes. The princess will be entering her second year."

"But you two don't know each other?" I ask. I didn't sense any familiarity between her and Viv. "Isn't it a small school?"

"I'm quite certain Princess Vivienne has no idea who I am," Cara answers wryly. "But yes, it is a small school."

I let the subject drop. We turn a corner and walk down another long corridor in silence.

"I didn't believe them." Cara breaks the quiet. "The news reports. I couldn't figure out why everyone here was so panicked. But I get it now. She's different with you. Really different. I mean, with Charles, she—" Cara glances over and stops talking when she sees my tense expression at the mention of Vivienne's fiancé.

We make another turn, and I'm grateful I have a guide. There's no way I could have found the way myself.

Cara stops outside a pair of ornately carved doors. "Here's the library."

"Thanks for helping me navigate, Cara."

"No problem," Cara replies. "I can ask someone to retrieve whatever it is you need to study. Playbooks?"

"Thanks, but I'm all set," I reply, belatedly realizing they're still in Viv's room, along with the rest of my belongings.

"You're sure?" Cara asks. "It's no trouble."

"Positive," I confirm.

"Okay, Mr. Dawson."

I laugh once. "Please, call me Jace."

Cara smiles. "Okay. Jace." A slight flush colors her cheeks. She turns around, only to pivot back toward me and complete the circle.

"Can I ask you a favor, Jace?"

"Yeah, sure."

"Could you not mention anything I said to Vivienne? She, uh —you seem to be the one person she listens to...not that she should listen—I know she's almost queen—"

I cut off her awkward babble. "I won't say anything."

"Thank you," Cara replies, looking relieved. She turns to leave again, this time not turning back.

I open the door to the library and step inside. Towering metal shelves line the walls. Several stories of wrought-iron walkways provide access to volumes that stretch to the domed ceiling that's covered with intricate, detailed paintings. I grab a random book from a reachable shelf and sprawl out on one of the leather couches scattered throughout the large room. I start to fall asleep before I reach the second page.

CHAPTER THIRTY-ONE

VIVIENNE

It only takes me a few minutes to arrive at Anne's office. I hover outside the ajar doorway, steeling myself for another confrontation. I'm about to push the door open when I hear voices.

"How bad was it?" my mother asks.

"Unsalvageable," Anne's voice replies, followed by a long sigh. "There's no way they can do the interview together. Even separately, it's going to be a challenge."

"Are you certain?" My father joins the conversation. "They both seem committed to doing the interview and extinguishing the story."

"Their commitment to it is not the problem," Anne answers. "It's the two of them together. Watch the video of them from our session. If we air anything similar to that on national television, this story will never go away. Their body language, the way they look at each other, talk about each other. I lost track of the number of times they touched. You both must have noticed the way they interact. You've spent time with them. You can't fake chemistry like that, and you can't hide it, either."

"It is…interesting," my mother replies, sounding as though there's a different word she'd prefer to use. "I hoped it would come across differently in an interview setting."

"There was no way of knowing until we saw them together in person," Anne replies. "Although, based on their rapport, I'm guessing the princess underplayed their past relationship pretty drastically when we first discussed it. We're far beyond that now, though. Bottom line: we cannot air a joint interview with Jace Dawson. The two of them answering live questions together will make our current publicity problems look like a cakewalk."

"But we've already announced a joint interview," my father responds. "Won't changing that now raise questions?"

"Probably," Anne admits. "But I don't see any other alternatives. I'm receiving reports the American media is paying six figures for copies of the interview. We can't risk that type of widespread coverage of the princess exchanging inside jokes and holding hands under the table with someone other than Charles if we want anyone to believe their impending marriage is the least bit genuine."

"You're certain more preparation won't solve things?" my mother asks.

"Your Highness, with all due respect—I'm very good at my job. But even I cannot make two people in love appear as if they're not. That's the situation we're dealing with here. I'll have my team start working on a statement about the separate interviews immediately."

There's a long stretch of silence.

I school my expression before knocking on the door and pushing it open. Anne's sitting at her desk, with my mother across from her. My father's standing by the window.

"You asked to see me?" I try to look surprised by the sight of my parents.

"Yes, Your Highness," Anne states. "I wanted to inform you that I've decided against doing the joint interview, and that we should have you and Mr. Dawson answer questions from the media separately instead."

"Why is that?" I ask, hoping I look convincingly perplexed. I'm curious about how honest Anne will be.

"After meeting with the two of you today, I've decided a joint interview will give the press too much to speculate about. You're obviously very"—she pauses—"familiar with one another, and the media will analyze not only what you say, but how you interact with each other. Speaking separately will give them less to work with and hopefully help this die out sooner, which is our goal."

I nod. "Fine."

"All right, I'll be there tomorrow for your interviews to make certain things go smoothly. I'd also like to meet with you both separately before then to discuss some general guidelines. We'll be releasing a statement tonight, likely citing some sort of scheduling issue as to why you're no longer going to be appearing together."

"That's fine about the statement, but I'd like to be there for your discussion with Jace."

"With all due respect, Your Highness, I'm not sure that's the best idea."

"Jace came all this way. The least I can do is be there for his prep sessions."

"Considering you'll be the topic of our conversation, I think you being there might be counterproductive." Anne continues, "I can assure you our interests are entirely aligned when it comes to preparing Mr. Dawson to speak to the press."

I study her for a moment. "Fine," I agree. "As long as Jace is all right with it."

"I'll send for Mr. Dawson shortly and update him on the change of plans."

"That won't be necessary," I reply. "I'll let him know."

Anne looks like she would like to argue, but simply nods.

"What are you and Papa doing here?" I ask my mother.

"We just wanted to see how things were shaping up for tomorrow," she replies neutrally.

"Hmmm," I respond. "And?"

"It seems like Anne has everything under control," she replies. "We'll leave you to it, Anne," she says, standing from the chair.

"Thank you, Your Highness," Anne replies, bowing her head respectfully. "Your Majesty," she adds, nodding to my father.

He smiles, then follows my mother and me out into the hallway.

"You were listening, weren't you?" my mother accuses.

"The door was open!" I defend. "I can't believe she made him come all this way for a glorified press release. I thought the whole point of asking Jace to come here was so we could appear in person together."

"It was!" my mother snaps. "None of us knew you'd act like some love-struck schoolgirl around the boy!"

"Evelyn," my father reprimands.

She sighs. "I'm sorry, Vivienne."

I nod in acknowledgement of her apology, but the words still sting. "I'm going to find Jace," I tell my parents. "Is the boat back at the marina?" I ask my father.

"Yes, they finished the repairs last week," he replies. "Why?"

"I want to take Jace out on the water," I respond. "He's never been sailing before—well, I did try to take him in South Carolina, but it didn't go very well…"

"I'm not sure if that's the best idea, Vivienne," my mother

cautions. Her voice has calmed. "If anyone managed to get photographs of you…"

"We'll be careful," I promise. I turn to go, and then reconsider. "Do you two want to come?" I offer hesitantly.

My parents both look floored by the invitation. We rarely spend any time together during the day unless it's for an official engagement.

"We would love to." My father is the one who responds. "It's been too long since I was out on the water."

My mother looks more hesitant, but she doesn't refute my father's words.

"Okay, let me go grab Jace. We'll meet you in the front foyer in fifteen minutes."

I turn to head toward the library. My parents whisper behind me, but I'm too buoyant to worry about what they might be saying. Jace will be gone by tomorrow afternoon, and I'm determined to make the most of our time together.

I enter the library to find him fast asleep, his tall frame splayed across the length of one of the leather couches. He stirs when the door creaks shut behind me.

"Viv?" he mutters sleepily.

I grab the book that's resting on his chest and climb on top of his relaxed body. "Yeah, it's me," I whisper.

"I didn't think anyone else here would be this presumptuous," he mumbles with his eyes still closed, wrapping his arms around me.

I laugh. "Wake up. We're going sailing."

Jace opens his eyes. "What? I thought I have another session with Anne."

"She wants to have individual meetings instead. She decided we shouldn't do an interview together, after all."

"We're not going to be interviewed together?"

405

"Nope. Just answering questions separately." I study his face. "Are you mad?"

"Mad?"

"After you came all this way."

"Why would I be mad? I came here to help. If they don't want us to appear together, that's fine with me. Honestly, I was a little worried about it."

"Worried?" I ask. "Why?"

"That I might do or say something to make things worse."

"That's why they decided against it." Seeing his dismayed expression, I quickly add. "I mean both of us. Anne said our chemistry is too obvious." I run my fingers through his hair. "Our body language is too familiar," I whisper, kissing him once.

I pull away to see he's watching me dubiously.

"Seriously?" he asks. "Or are you messing with me?"

"'You can't fake chemistry like that, and you can't hide it either,' is a direct quote," I tell him. "We've got to get going. My parents are waiting."

"Your parents are coming sailing with us?"

"Yeah, I invited them. Is that okay?"

"Of course. I'm just surprised they'd want to come. I don't think your mom likes me very much."

"I think she actually likes you more than she wants to," I reply. Seeing Jace's confused expression, I add, "She's wanted me to marry Charles since I was a toddler. She sees you as a threat to that."

Jace scoffs. "Not according to you."

It's the first reference he's made to last night's conversation, and I still in response. I'm not sure what emotions are displayed across my face, but Jace studies my expression for a long moment before rolling over and pulling us both upright.

"Come on, let's go get stranded at sea again," he tells me as we head out of the library.

"I won't be the one sailing, so that likely won't happen," I inform him, relieved he's changed the subject.

We arrive in the front foyer to find my parents are already waiting.

"Good morning, Jace," my father greets, holding out his hand.

"Good morning, sir," Jace replies, shaking it.

"I asked for your car to be pulled up, Vivvi," my father says. "Since it's so nice out."

"Thank you, Papa."

Michael enters the foyer. "Your Majesty, the cars are ready."

"Excellent," my father replies, heading outside. The bright yellow convertible I received for my most recent birthday is parked in the drive between two black SUVS.

Jace lets out a low whistle of appreciation at the sight of the expensive car. "That's yours?"

"Yup," I reply, grinning. Given his fascination with sports cars, I had a feeling he would appreciate it.

All four of us walk toward the line of cars.

"Are we supposed to ride in the back?" Jace whispers to me.

I'm about to open my mouth to inform him my father and I can't travel together when my father shocks me by saying, "No, we will," and grabbing my mother's hand. She and I both stare at him, flabbergasted. He chuckles. "I'm not old and senile yet."

"Your Majesty—" Richard begins.

"I'll be traveling with my daughter, Richard," my father interjects. His voice is casual, but there's an underlying layer of steel I rarely hear.

Richard doesn't say anything else, he just nods.

We approach my convertible, and I watch in amazement as

my parents climb into the rear seats. I'm even more surprised to see them both smiling and laughing.

I walk to the driver's seat and pluck the keys from the ignition. I toss them at Jace's surprised face and round the front of the car to climb in the passenger's seat. I don't look behind to see what my parents' reaction is.

Jace climbs into the driver's seat carefully and grins over at me. I smile back, relaxing under the warmth of the late morning sun. With a jolt of surprise, I realize I feel happy. For the first time within this iron fence, I feel free. Unconstrained. Normal.

I lean over so I can read the screen mounted in the dashboard and start scrolling through the car's musical library. "Any requests?" I ask Jace.

"Something you can't sing along to?" he suggests.

I hear my father's distinctive low chuckle sound from behind us. "Hilarious." I stick my tongue out at Jace.

He grins in response before shifting the car into drive.

The trip to our private marina is a short one, and I find myself wishing it was longer as we pull up in front of the boathouse. I hardly travel anywhere with my parents unless it's for an official event, and I know that's part of the light-hearted feeling of normalcy I'm experiencing.

But if I'm being honest, I know it's mostly because of Jace. And that's a dangerous feeling to have. Because Jace and I are temporary. Fleeting. The complicated pattern of dominos that tumbled to create this perfect moment won't do so again. After Jace leaves tomorrow, our paths won't cross again.

They were never really meant to.

Jace parks my car at the edge of the dock, and we climb out. I watch with amusement as my father fumbles his way out of the back seat and then turns to help my mother out. They head toward the boat, a horde of agents behind them. Jace and I follow.

"I probably should be used to the fact that everything here is extravagant and over the top by now," Jace tells me, staring at the massive, eighty-foot sailboat we're walking onto. "But I'm not."

"It's a lot, I know."

We step on board next to one of the raised sails. The canvas flutters and flaps in the wind, proudly displaying the Marcedenian flag.

"This is way bigger than I was picturing. I thought we might be on a boat the same size as in South Carolina."

I laugh as we walk across the teak floor out to the hull of the boat.

"Don't forget to put on sunscreen, Vivienne," my mother instructs as she and my father head inside the cabin.

I roll my eyes at the reminder, but grab one of the bottles that's already been set out and begin lathering my arms.

"Can you do my back?" I ask Jace, handing him the tube.

He nods. I don't think anything of the request until I feel his warm hands make contact with my skin. He's touched me much more intimately than this, but something about the feel of his calloused hands smoothing the oil along my bare skin is surprisingly erotic. Goosebumps appear on my skin, despite the heat. I hear Jace chuckle softly.

"I'm regretting inviting my parents on this outing now," I admit, as I tamp down the relentless lust I've only ever felt around him.

Jace laughs. "It was worth it just to see your mom climb into the backseat of a convertible."

I can't help but smile in response. It's not an image I'll forget anytime soon.

"Plus, we'll have all night." His eyes turn molten, and I shiver despite the warm breeze.

The boat lurches away from the dock and forges through the

choppy waves closest to shore. I grab Jace's hand and pull him toward the bow.

"Come on, the best view's up here." I don't stop tugging until we've reached the farthest edge of the deck. From this vantage point, the boat behind us is invisible, providing the illusion we're flying across the sparkling blue water untethered.

"I feel like I'm overusing it this trip, but *wow*." Jace says.

The heat of his body radiates as he comes and stands directly behind me. I lean back, and the solid steadiness of his body is there waiting. I let him support my weight, and he rests his chin on the top of my head. We both stare out at the endless spread of saltwater.

"I never thanked you," Jace says suddenly.

"For what?" I twist to try to see his expression, but all I can see is the sharp line of his jaw.

"For the car," he explains. "You didn't need to do that."

"I know I didn't," I reply, turning my gaze back toward the water. "I wanted to. So you can finally beat Chris Morgan."

Jace laughs once. "I can't believe you remember that."

"Of course I remember. I was worried you'd think it was some sort of bribe...or worse. Because of the timing." It's easier to admit it without looking at his face.

"I'd be lying if I said the thought never crossed my mind," Jace admits. "But I never really believed it. Plus...I saw afterwards, that he was the one who leaked everything. Philip."

"Yeah." I sigh.

I expended a lot of energy toward resenting Philip when I first returned home. Hating him for taking me away from Jace, for revealing my father's illness, for making my inevitable future all the closer. Now, I simply accept it. All of those things would have happened eventually.

"I told you he was jealous," Jace states.

"Thomas thought the same. I'm not sure...he never admitted to anything."

Jace is silent, which I know is his way of disagreeing with me without upsetting me.

"Katie visited. Right before the trip to South Carolina. She thought—thought that you had something to do with why the stories about us never came out when I left. Is that true?"

Jace doesn't answer right away. Finally, he does. "I thought it might make things more difficult for you if they did."

"Thank you," I reply softly.

I'm tempted to apologize again for the actions that made it a wasted effort, but I don't. I'm not sure I would still mean them. Do I wish the media never found out about me and Jace? Of course. But them finding out and forcing us to reunite is the only reason I'm leaning against him right now. Why I got to hear him say he loves me. I can't think of anything not worth enduring for this stolen time together, and that's terrifying.

The lapping of salty water against the wooden hull is the only sound between us for a while.

"I was supposed to go on a date with Miss South Carolina," Jace suddenly says. "The day after the game where you..." His voice trails off. "The Sharks' publicity team, they want me to be more visible..." He stops speaking again. "It got rescheduled for a week after I return. Just in case you happen to see anything about it. I want you to know it was—is—planned. Happening."

"Oh," is the only response I can come up with. Not a quip about girls who compete in beauty pageants, not a joke about how Jace isn't going to wait even one week to move on from this, not a question about what exactly being "more visible" means.

The realization Jace is going to move on from this respite from reality where we get to flirt and kiss and touch is expected.

It's also devastating.

CHAPTER THIRTY-TWO

JACE

The boat trip ends sooner than I'd like, and we disembark onto dry land.

"I might now be a fan of sailing," I inform Viv. "Because that was an entirely different experience than the last time."

"So you wouldn't go out on a smaller boat again?" Viv asks, arching an eyebrow.

"With you sailing it? No."

Viv rolls her eyes.

"This trip was an effortless glide. Last time was all..." I attempt to mimic the flapping motion Viv did to the sails to return us to shore, and she bursts out laughing. I laugh with her, relieved to hear the sound. She's been more reserved since I mentioned my upcoming date with Miss South Carolina. I'm still not sure why I told her. I felt obligated to, which is incredibly stupid considering Viv is currently engaged to someone else.

We turn the corner around the boathouse, and Viv abruptly stops laughing. I follow her gaze. As though I've conjured him with my thoughts, I see a blond guy who I'm certain is Charles

Vanderbilt standing in front of us. His brown eyes bounce between me and Viv as we both stop walking.

"You're Jace Dawson," he states.

"Sure am," I breeze, surveying his pressed shorts and polo shirt. "And you are?" I add, just to be a jerk. I'm not going to admit to having seen tabloid photos of the guy. Plus, I'm feeling confrontational.

A flash of annoyance crosses the guy's face. Viv gives me a quick glance but doesn't say anything. I quirk an eyebrow at her.

A muscle jumps in the guy's jaw as he witnesses our exchange. "I'm Charles Vanderbilt," he announces. "The Princess's fiancé."

I'm certain I would find it impossible to like any guy Viv was engaged to, but Charles certainly isn't doing himself any favors.

"Thanks for that clarification," I respond. "Because I know a lot of Charles Vanderbilts, and I really wasn't sure which one you…" This time Viv does intercede, swatting me on the arm.

"Jace," she hisses.

"Oh, I'm sure you just assumed I hadn't heard your name before," I continue, enjoying watching Charles's face darken with anger. Viv glares at me, but it also looks like she's trying not to laugh.

Vivienne's parents round the corner after us, and Charles's haughty glower falters.

"Your Majesty, Your Highness," he greets, bowing.

"Charles!" Vivienne's mother greets. "I didn't realize Vivienne was expecting you." She shoots Viv a questioning glance.

I take a great deal of pleasure in the uncomfortable expression that crosses Charles's face.

"She wasn't," he admits. "I just thought I would stop by and check on her before the interview tomorrow. One of the butlers said she was down here."

"Oh," Evelyn replies. "That was considerate."

Or overbearing.

We all stand in awkward silence for a protracted moment. No one seems to know what to say.

"Robert, I'd love to take a look at that catamaran now," I finally offer.

He spent the latter half of the trip describing all his boats to me while Viv rolled her eyes at the lengthy descriptions.

Vivienne's father shoots me a grateful glance, and the queen takes the opportunity to excuse herself from the uncomfortable situation as well.

"I'd better get back to the palace. Good to see you, Charles," she says before heading toward the line of cars waiting just past the boathouse.

I glance to Viv, and she gives me a small nod. I know she's more than capable of handling herself, so I follow Robert inside the boathouse. A massive boat sits on stilts in front of us.

"Wow," I repeat for the umpteenth time. "This is quite a boat."

"Isn't she a beauty?" Vivienne's father replies. "She needed some restoration, but she'll be back in the water next week."

"She?" I ask.

The king nods to the rear of the boat, where *Queen Vivienne* is painted in an elegant, scrawling script.

"I had that done when she was only two years old," Robert remarks.

"She's exquisite," I respond. I'm not just referring to the boat, and Vivienne's father seems to understand that. He nods, then proceeds to show me several other boats in his collection. Eventually, we end up back by the main door we entered through.

"Charles is a good kid," Robert states. I take this to mean he overheard some of our conversation.

I sigh. "I'm sure he is."

"He's threatened by you."

"He shouldn't be. After tomorrow, I'll be gone. She made it clear I shouldn't change any plans."

Vivienne's father nods. "I see." His expression is unreadable as he glances outside. "Looks like we're good to go," he informs me.

I follow him outside to see Viv leaning against the side of her convertible, staring out at the water we just returned from. Charles is gone.

"I'll take one of the other cars back," Robert tells me. I nod.

I walk over to Viv, and her gaze meets mine. Her face is completely neutral, purposefully so. Her hand twitches, and a flash of silver flies toward me. I catch the car keys easily and walk around to climb in the driver's seat. Viv settles beside me.

"Are you okay?" I ask as I insert the ridged metal into the ignition.

"I'm fine," Viv replies.

"Do you want to talk about it?"

"Nope."

"I'm sorry about before. I was…jealous," I admit.

"I know," Viv murmurs. She looks out toward the ocean again. "The fucked-up part?" I look at her in surprise. She hardly ever swears. "I liked that you were. Even worse? The whole time you were being an asshole toward Charles, I was thinking about all the awful things I would want to say if I ever met Miss South Carolina."

"It's just a publicity thing, Viv."

"I know. But one day it won't be."

"You can't say shit like that to me, Viv. You can't—" I huff out a sharp breath.

"I know. I'm sorry, okay? I'm sorry."

She casts her gaze down at her knees when I look at her.

"I'm sorry," she repeats softly, and I know she's talking about more than just her words now.

"I might not like sailing after all. It seems to come with a lot of emotional turmoil," I reply.

Viv smiles sadly. "Good thing you're from the only triply landlocked state then, huh?"

My brief laugh is bereft of any real humor. I'm too drained. "Yeah, good thing."

I turn the key, and the engine roars to life. I shift into gear and twist the wheel as I begin to drive back the same way we came. Reaching out to the dashboard, I turn down the volume of the music. Viv reaches out and tangles her fingers with mine before I have a chance to return my hand to the wheel. I drive one-handed the whole way back.

When we arrive at the palace, Cara is waiting in the entryway.

"Anne would like to meet with you now, Mr. Dawson," she informs me, glancing at Viv a couple of times nervously.

"Do you want me to come with you?" Viv asks.

"Not unless you feel like you need to," I tell her. "I can handle it."

She nods. "Okay, I'll see you after."

To my surprise, she gives me a kiss on the cheek before strolling toward one of the twin staircases that leads to the upstairs residence. I look over at Cara, who is quickly schooling what looks to be a shocked expression.

"Uh—this way, Mr. Dawson," she instructs.

I don't engage her in small talk this trip. It's only late afternoon, but I'm completely depleted from this rollercoaster of a day. Cara stops in front of the same conference room Viv and I met with Anne in this morning.

"Anne should already be in there," Cara tells me.

I nod and head inside. I feel a flash of déjà vu as Anne rises from her seat at the table. She doesn't curtsy this time, just smiles at me before sitting again. I take the same seat I sat in earlier.

"Hello, Mr. Dawson."

"Hello, Anne," I respond, mimicking her formal tone.

"I take it Princess Vivienne filled you in on the change of plans for tomorrow?"

"Yes, she did," I confirm.

"And why?"

"Yes."

"All right, then. Based on our conversation earlier, I don't think there's going to be anything new that comes out the press is going to question you about. Rather, they'll focus on how you respond to their questions. Body language, facial expressions, etcetera. The calmer and more detached you appear, the better. Now, my suggestion is for you to imagine each reporter who questions you as someone you don't particularly like but have to interact with in a somewhat civil manner. It could be a former teammate or coach, whoever you like."

"Charles Vanderbilt?"

The words slip out unbidden, a product of the phrase "the Princess's fiancé" I can still hear echoing around my head.

To my shock, Anne actually laughs at my response. She looks as surprised about it as I am as she quickly regains her serious expression.

"As I said, whoever you like. Now, make sure you're not being too curt or overly short in your responses. Stick to the facts about your relationship with the Princess, but make them sound as uninteresting as possible. Understood?"

I nod.

"Good, now I'm going to ask you a couple of questions. Try to respond the way we just discussed, all right?"

I nod again, settling back in the chair.

It's at least another hour before Anne is satisfied enough with my responses to let me leave the conference room. She offers to have one of her assistants show me back to the residence, but I decline, wanting some time to myself.

I take a few wrong turns, but eventually manage to find the same hallway I passed through with Viv this morning. The sun is just starting to set. Swirls of pink and orange reflect off the glassy floor as I pass through the hallway and into the residence. I round the corner and almost collide with the queen. She looks startled by my sudden appearance.

"Jace!" she exclaims, holding a hand to her chest. "I didn't expect to see you here."

"I just finished my meeting with Anne," I explain. "I'm trying to find my way back to Vi—I mean, my room."

"I was coming to see when you might be wrapping up. We're planning to eat out on the terrace tonight. The staff is just starting to set things up now."

"Okay, let me just change," I say, glancing down at my shorts and t-shirt. Vivienne's mother is wearing a calf-length silk dress.

"Your attire is fine, Jace," Evelyn replies.

"Okay, then I'm ready for dinner now, I guess." I laugh awkwardly.

Vivienne's mother makes me nervous. I want her to like me, and I can't tell how she feels about me at all. It's disconcerting.

I try to come up with something to say as we walk along, but the queen speaks first.

"How did your session with Anne go?"

"She seemed pleased by the end. I just hope someone actually asks me how Viv and I met, since we spent twenty minutes on that question alone."

"How did you two meet?" Vivienne's mother asks. I glance

over at her, but her gaze is fixed forward, not providing me with any indication of her expression.

"Uh... I was walking to practice. There's this one central path that runs through the middle of Lincoln's campus. It's smooth and flat, unlike the other walkways on campus, so there are a lot of students who like to skateboard there. Anyway, I'm walking along, and a couple guys on skateboards ride past me. All of a sudden, this girl slams into me, trying to get out of the way of another skateboarder." I smile. "I told her she should watch where she was going. I've never seen someone go from confused to indignant so fast. She informed me she would rather get hit by a skateboarder than talk to me again, then strode off. I walked that same route at the same time for the next week, hoping I'd see her again."

The queen smiles as we turn down another hallway. "And what did Anne instruct you to say?"

"That we ran into each other on campus and had a brief conversation."

"It took twenty minutes to come up with that?" the queen asks. I'm surprised to hear her laugh. I'm on a real roll with phlegmatic women at the moment.

"I'm a slow learner, I guess."

"I don't think that's the case," the queen replies, which I *think* is a compliment, but I'm too taken aback to respond right away, and she continues speaking before I have the chance to say anything. "Vivienne said you two decided to...end your relationship before she left. Do you mind me asking why?"

"Uh..." I stall. "That's all she said?"

"Yes." Vivienne's mother looks at me expectantly.

"We realized we had some...irreconcilable differences," I hedge. I'm guessing the queen already suspects the truth, but I'm not going to rat out Vivienne directly.

"She told you the truth," Evelyn surmises.

I nod once.

"I was less than enthused about our trip to South Carolina over the summer. Robert and Charles insisted returning to the States was what Vivienne needed. That she was missing it there. We landed, and she acted just the opposite. The only part of the trip I was looking forward to was seeing the Vanderbilts' beach estate. Margaret—Duchess Vanderbilt—has been going on about it for years."

I frown, unclear on what her point is and unenthused it involves the Vanderbilts.

"The moment Vivienne found out we would be staying at their beach house? She threatened to climb back on the plane and fly home if we didn't find other accommodations. She's always been obstinate, but I'd never seen her put her foot down like that before." She pauses. "Your loyalty seems contagious. I would hardly characterize Vivienne as the sentimental type."

"Why would you tell me that?" I can't help but ask. Vivienne's mother is the last person I expected to share anecdotes of Viv's feelings with me.

"Vivienne's always struggled with being royal. I expected your relationship with her—her feelings toward you—to be an extension of the freedoms she enjoyed during her time in the States. A reminder of happier times for her that would become tarnished by reality. Instead? You arrive here at the palace, where she's a princess again, and she dresses up for dinner! She laughs at dinner! She invited Robert and me sailing! Do you know the last time the three of us went on an outing that wasn't part of an official engagement? I'm not sure if we ever have. And even if we did? The only reason Vivienne was laughing and smiling today was because you were there with us."

I take a deep breath. "I think Vivienne believes she can never meet your expectations. And so she's given up on trying to. Maybe try talking to her more like her mother, and less like a queen. She's funny. Ask her to tell you about the treehouse she built in the woods. Or ask her to go shopping. She loves to shop, mainly to buy gifts for other people. She went shopping with my mom and sister, and a sweater my mom liked showed up at the farm a week later. She's thoughtful. And Katie got her hooked on some reality television show. I forget the name of it. She'll go on about it for hours, mostly about how terrible she pretends she thinks it is. You could watch it together."

The queen is staring at me, eyes wide, and I panic.

"Those were just a couple of suggestions. I didn't mean to overstep, or…"

"Jace!" Vivienne appears through the terrace doors we're approaching. "I went to Anne's office, and she said you left almost twenty minutes ago. I figured you got lost." She looks over at her mother.

"Partly, but then I ran into your mother and she showed me the way."

"She did?" Viv's vivid blue eyes dance between us, filled with confusion.

"Yup." We approach the door. I pause to let Vivienne's mother pass first. She still looks shell-shocked as she walks past me out onto the patio. I follow after her to see Vivienne's father is already seated at the wood slatted table. Viv comes up to my side as I emerge outside.

"Did it go okay with Anne?" she asks.

"Our juicy love story is about as interesting as a history documentary if you listen to my version of events."

Viv laughs. "Good to know."

"I also managed to make Anne laugh," I inform her. "Unfortunately, this session was not recorded by Cara, so I have no proof."

"Cara?"

"Anne's assistant from this morning?"

"Oh, right," Viv acknowledges.

"She goes to Edgewood too, you know."

"She does?" Viv looks surprised. "How do you know?"

"She mentioned it when we were walking to the library."

"Hmmm." The sound drips with disapproval.

"She's nice, Viv." I roll my eyes. "Scared stiff of you, but nice."

"Whatever you say. So, what did you tell Anne to make her laugh?"

"I don't want to tell you," I admit.

Viv raises her eyebrows.

I sigh. "I made a joke about Charles."

Viv's lips quirk.

"Vivienne! Jace! Come eat," Robert calls.

We both glance over from our spot just outside the patio doors. The slatted surface of the table has been completely covered by platters of delicious looking food.

Dinner passes quickly. I feel more comfortable with Viv's parents after the individual conversations I've had with both of them, and sitting outside feels more relaxed than the massive, formal dining hall we ate in last night. It's been dark out for a while by the time Robert and Evelyn say good night and head inside.

Viv and I sit underneath the muted lights of the patio in silence after they leave.

"Viv…" I finally start.

"Shhh," she scolds. "Come on." She stands and holds out her hand.

"I'm not allowed to talk?" I raise an eyebrow.

"There are other things I'd prefer you do with your mouth,"

she challenges. The smirk slides off her face, replaced by despondency. "I don't want to talk, okay?"

"Okay," I acquiesce. I'm not sure what I would have said anyway.

Viv leads me back inside, up the stairs, down the hallway, and into her room. And we don't talk.

CHAPTER THIRTY-THREE

VIVIENNE

I wake up with a heavy coil of dread in the bottom of my stomach. Jace is leaving today, and I'll never see him again. I'll have no reason to see him again. These past two days, I've allowed myself to live in a fantasy world, one where I get to touch him, and kiss him, and love him. As soon as he gives his interview and denounces our relationship, that will be it. He'll return to football, to his family, to his friends, and to his date with Miss South Carolina. I'll remain here. It's the way things have to be, and I'm thankful Jace hasn't brought up the topic of us getting married again. I'm weak right now. Vulnerable.

I meant everything I said to Jace when he brought it up. But I didn't say it because I wanted to. Because I don't want him.

I slip out of bed, glad Jace doesn't wake up when I do. I can't face him yet. I shower quickly and dress in a black dress and blazer for the interview later. For once, I don't feel like running. I'm not angry or upset. I'm sapped. An emotionless void.

I head downstairs into the sitting room where I ordinarily eat breakfast. One of the maids appears immediately. "Would you like your breakfast brought in, Your Highness?"

"Yes, please," I respond.

She curtsies and leaves.

Absentmindedly, I turn on the television. Maybe some background noise will tune out my incessant thoughts. The noise doesn't; the topic of conversation does.

I turn to watch a pretty blonde woman discuss my love life on the morning news. "…and there's rampant speculation around the country this morning, as the Royal Press Office released a statement late last night announcing the hotly anticipated interview featuring Princess Vivienne and Jace Dawson will not be taking place as scheduled. The statement cites scheduling complications as the reason for the last-minute change, despite the fact Dawson is rumored to have arrived in the country two days ago and there is currently nothing else on Princess Vivienne's official calendar. She is now set to answer questions two hours after Mr. Dawson finishes his interview later this morning. Stay tuned for live coverage of both interviews. We'll keep you posted on updates from the palace if and when we receive them. Now, we're taking you to…" I turn the television off.

I eat breakfast and then head to Anne's office for my preparation session before my interview. I'm distracted the entire time, which makes it easier in some ways. My voice is lacking any emotion as I repeat Anne's suggested phrases and responses.

My apathy disappears when I leave Anne's office and am confronted by a pair of troubled gray eyes.

"Hey," Jace greets me.

"Hi," I reply softly.

He's dressed in a suit, and he wears it well. Very well. Jace glances behind me before stepping closer. "I woke up, and you were gone."

"I thought it might be… easier," I reply. "You're leaving, and—"

"Mr. Dawson, wonderful. You're right on time." Anne's voice sounds behind me. She greets Jace more enthusiastically than she's ever spoken to me. Maybe he wasn't lying about the laugh.

I summon a smile. "I'll see you after. You'll do great."

Jace looks like he wants to say something in response, but Anne interrupts. "We'd better head down, Mr. Dawson. The media has already assembled."

"Okay," Jace replies. He walks past me, and I continue down the hallway.

I end up back in the same sitting room I watched the news in this morning. I turn on the television and watch as it broadcasts the live feed of Anne walking toward the table that's been set up, with Jace close behind her. An audible murmur ripples through the assembled reporters as he appears, followed by the rapid clicking of cameras. Jace and Anne take seats at the table, then Anne leans forward to speak.

"We only have Mr. Dawson here for a limited time," she says. "So, we'll go ahead and get started. Cedric, you have the first question."

"Thanks, Ms. Riley. Mr. Dawson, do you have any comment on the last-minute change that means the princess is not here with you?"

Anne leans forward with a disapproving frown. "I'll be directing any questions about the interview format to the statement the palace released last night. Next question, please."

"How long did your relationship with Princess Vivienne last?" the next reporter asks.

"About three months."

"How did you meet the Princess?" another shouts.

"We ran into each other on campus and had a brief conversation."

Anne must be thrilled. Jace is calm, cool, and collected as he fields the barrage of questions. Anne gives up on calling on reporters individually as Jace answers the questions as they're called out.

"Is it true the Princess stayed with your family over one of Lincoln's breaks?"

"Yes."

"When did your relationship with the Princess end?"

"Shortly before she returned here."

"Why did it end?"

"We made a mutual decision to end our relationship."

"Do you have any thoughts about the royal wedding?"

"I wish Vivienne nothing but the best."

"Have you met Princess Vivienne's fiancé?"

There's a brief pause. Then, "No, I haven't."

"Did you know the Princess would be attending your football game?"

"No, that was a complete surprise to me. I believe it was to Vivienne, as well."

The press continues pelting Jace with questions about our past relationship, and he continues to field them easily. Finally, Anne intercedes and announces they'll only entertain a couple more. A disgruntled-looking Cedric calls out, "Do you think Princess Vivienne shirked her responsibilities by attending college in the States under false pretenses?"

Raw emotion flashes across Jace's face for the first time. "I think it's awfully easy to pass judgments and incredibly difficult to shoulder the responsibilities Vivienne is taking on," he clips, eyes flashing.

His terse response sends fresh energy through the assortment of reporters, most of whom seemed to have begun to write the interview off as a waste of time.

Anne seems to sense the same. "I'm afraid that's all we have time for," she says. "Mr. Dawson has a flight home to catch. Refreshments are being served in the next room. The interview with Princess Vivienne will start in two hours." She stands and walks off the stage. Jace follows her.

I rush back to the conference room we had our interview with Anne in yesterday. The room is full of people when I arrive. Anne is there with several of her assistants, and my parents are both standing in the corner. Jace is leaning against the wall, sipping from a mug. Everyone looks over as I burst into the room. Anne and her assistants curtsy.

"Ah, Princess, wonderful. I wasn't sure where you'd gone. I was just telling everyone how well Mr. Dawson did. I think we're on our way to becoming a dying story."

"That's wonderful." I say, although I know my tone conveys the exact opposite.

"Well, it's been a pleasure, Mr. Dawson," Anne says, shaking Jace's hand. With a stab of panic, I realize this is it. He's leaving. "Your luggage has been loaded and is in the car outside. Cara can show you the way when you're ready."

"Okay, thank you." Jace responds evenly. He seems to be holding it together much better than I am. He turns to my father and holds his hand out to shake. "It was a pleasure to meet you, sir. I'll work on my chess strategy."

My father laughs. "It was wonderful to meet you, Jace. I wish you the best with everything. I can't tell you how grateful we are you made the trip."

Jace turns to my mother. I'm shocked to see her step forward and give him a quick hug. "Thank you," she tells him. "Travel safe."

Jace smiles and nods, then turns to me expectantly. I'm frozen. I stare at him, and he stares back, and everyone else in the room stares at us.

"Perhaps we should wait in the hallway," my father suggests tactfully.

Suddenly, everyone can't get out of the room fast enough. We're standing in an empty room in seconds. Jace takes a few steps closer, until he's only inches away from me. I let myself fall forward until I'm met with the comforting support of his chest.

We stand like that. Him upright, me leaning against him. I should have had him stay at a hotel. I should have acted cold. I should have done everything I could to keep him at arm's length. Instead, I let him in all the way this time. Not just into my heart, but into my family, into my home, into my world. And now I have to remain in it. Without him.

I know I should thank him for coming. Tell him to travel safe. Wish him luck in his game this weekend. Make a joke. Do anything to let him know I'm okay. That I'll be okay.

Instead?

I whisper, "I love you," against the starched cotton of his dress shirt.

His chest deflates as he lets out a sigh. "I love you too, Viv."

I scrunch up my eyes tightly, trying to memorize this moment. I never want to forget the sound of Jace Dawson saying those five precious words to me.

There's nothing left to say, so I pull back. I can't look at his face. One glimpse of slate-colored concern, and I'll break. I'll beg him to stay, and I love him too much to let him do that. So instead, I study the grooves in the hardwood floor as I listen to Jace walk away. The door opens and closes, and then there's total silence. I take several unsteady steps back, until I encounter the sturdy wall. I let myself slide down against it, staying partially upright even though I want nothing more than to just curl up in a ball on the floor.

I imagine Jace getting into one of the SUVs, driving through town, back along the coast, arriving at the airport, flying back over the ocean. Arriving back home. I wonder what his new house is like. I never asked. His new coach, his new teammates? They felt like details I would learn one day. Now? They'll forever be a mystery.

The door opens again. I have no idea how much time has passed since it closed.

"Your Highness?" Anne asks, glancing around the room. "Are you—oh." She stops speaking when she sees me sitting on the floor. "Your interview is supposed to start in ten minutes, but I'll, uh, let them know you aren't feeling well."

I've never seen Anne look so uncomfortable. I wonder what my face looks like.

"Don't be ridiculous," I snap, standing and pasting on a neutral expression. "Let's go." Jace did his part. The least I can do is follow through on my end. He deserves to move on with his life without further reminders of me.

Anne looks skeptical, but doesn't protest as I walk out of the room and down the hallway toward the media room. I enter the cavernous room ahead of her. All chatter ceases. I hear heels clacking as Anne hurries after me. I take a seat in the chair Jace occupied earlier and lean forward into the microphone. "Hello, everyone."

Anne hurriedly takes a seat beside me. "Hello again. We're running ahead of schedule for once, so we can get started whenever you're all ready to."

The questions come immediately, and I let Anne field them for me. Most of them are the same ones Jace was asked, and I paid close enough attention to his responses I'm able to mirror them almost exactly. Approval radiates from Anne as the press grows increasingly bored by my nonchalant answers.

The topic shifts to my upcoming wedding. Anne announces

Charles and I will be giving a joint interview in three weeks with a prominent Marcedenian network. It's news to me, but I keep my face neutral as I dodge questions about the flowers and venue, saying those are all still being planned. The only time I falter is when I'm asked about an engagement ring. Anne quickly steps in. "Her Highness will receive a family heirloom at her wedding."

We're nearing the end of the interview when Cedric strikes again. "Princess Vivienne, do you have any response to allegations Mr. Dawson is profiting off his association with you, and agreeing to this interview was an attempt on his part to do so even further?"

Anne leans forward to respond, but I beat her to it. I don't want any confusion on this topic, and I don't bother to hide the ire in my voice as a result. "Jace Dawson is the most loyal and considerate person I've ever met. I'm not sure what part of having your private life splashed across the front page of every major paper you consider 'profiting,' but I can assure you Jace only agreed to participate in an interview here as a favor to me. It was entirely void of any personal gain."

My response prompts a new flurry of questions, but Anne stands and announces the time for questions has ended.

"You did well, Princess," she tells me as we exit the media room.

The brief flash of emotion drained me even further. "Thank you," I reply bleakly. "I'm sorry about the last question. I just couldn't... after everything he did."

"We'll handle it," Anne assures me. "The wedding segment will play well. They should focus on re-airing clips from that."

"Okay," I respond.

"We'll need to start preparing for the interview with Charles," Anne says hesitantly. "But that can wait for a few days."

"Okay," I say again.

I trudge upstairs to my room, pausing just outside the door. Finally, I push it open. He's everywhere. Sprawled out on my bed, perched on the window seat, emerging from the bathroom.

I shed my clothes and step under a hot spray of water. Pulsing liquid eases some of the stress from my muscles. I emerge from the shower and change into a pair of pajamas. I don't bother to brush or dry my hair. I just climb under the covers, spreading my sopping wet hair across the pillow Jace slept on. I lie there until the silence becomes defeating.

I grab the remote from my bedside table and turn on the television. It's set to the news, and I groan as I see they're playing a video clip of me sitting at the table with Anne. Reluctantly, I unmute the television.

"Princess Vivienne, the only child of King Robert and Queen Evelyn, has had little public exposure over the years aside from scheduled public appearances or prepared speeches. She's always appeared cool and collected. However, over the years, reports from her school instructors have described her as 'spirited,' and multiple classmates have characterized her as intimidating. Today we may have seen our first glimpse of the real Princess Vivienne. Despite repeated reports her relationship with the American football player Jace Dawson has ended, the princess did not take kindly to accusations Mr. Dawson may be using his association with her to further his own interests. We'll show you the clip of her heated defense…"

I switch the television over to an episode of my favorite show. A few minutes later, I hear a knock on my door.

"Yes?" I call out.

My mother opens the door, and I sit up in shock. "Mother? Is everything all right?" I can't remember the last time she's come to my room.

"I was going to ask you the same," she replies.

"Oh. I'm fine," I respond. "Just tired."

She nods. "Okay." She glances over at the television. "What are you watching?"

"Just some reality show I stumbled across. It's terrible."

"Really?" My mother looks amused for some reason. "Well, I'll let you get some rest, then."

She lingers for another moment before finally leaving the room, shutting the door quietly behind her.

I flop back down against the pillows and try very hard not to think.

CHAPTER THIRTY-FOUR

JACE

The realization I'm never going to see Vivienne again sinks in slowly. My time in Marcedenia was an ending, even though it didn't feel like one.

The Sharks' owner, John Fairfax, summons me to his office the morning after I return to South Carolina.

"I'm hearing some fantastic buzz following your interview in Marcedenia," he tells me. "I'm so pleased you decided to go. And I heard a rumor you're going on a date with Miss South Carolina. Princesses, beauty queens, it's not too terrible being a pro quarterback, huh?"

He gives me a wink, which I return with a tight smile.

"Thank you, sir," I respond.

None of my teammates mention my absence over the past several days, or the reason for it. Not even Cooley. I'm grateful.

I talk to my parents once, to let them know I'm back safely. There were several long pauses in between their questions, making me think there was an extended side conversation going on between them. I never called Anderson back, and I haven't spoken to any of my other friends. I don't know what to say. What to divulge, what to retain.

Because what's worse than knowing I'll never see Vivienne again? The knowledge that I could. Six words that haunt me. *Vivienne is entitled to marry anyone.*

It was one thing not to have any options. It's worse to know that I do.

Do I love her enough? To give up my dream of playing professional football to attend museum openings and fundraisers and whatever else royalty does? To leave my friends and my family and move to an entirely new country?

I know that I do, and that's terrifying in its own way. I know there's not another person in the world who I'd be able to say the same about. Who I'd be willing to sacrifice so much for.

But there are other factors to consider besides my own feelings. For one, I just signed a five-year contract a few months ago. For a lot of money. Money that's security for my family. I know Vivienne's family is wealthy, but I don't want to have to rely on her.

She was also adamant we can't get married when I broached the topic. I know she doesn't feel the same way about Charles as she does about me, but he's part of her world. He already knows how to navigate everything I'd be entirely clueless about. Is that more important?

The cycle of thoughts is relentless. I play better than ever on Sunday, relieved to finally have something else to focus on. We win easily. Our post-game interviews last longer than usual as a result. The crowd of reporters belabor every play and begin mentioning our chances of making it to the championship for the first time in franchise history.

I'm running late by the time I get home. I quickly shower and pull on slacks and a button down before rushing outside to the waiting limousine. I slide across the rear seat, and we begin to move immediately. Ten minutes later, the car stops in front of a townhouse. The limo driver opens the door for a stunning blonde in a short black dress. She smiles at me as she slides onto the seat next to me.

"Hi Jace, it's nice to meet you," she greets. "I'm Megan."

I return her smile. "Nice to meet you, Megan."

Discussions of the unseasonably cool weather and favorite spots around the city last us the short drive to the restaurant. Our limousine pulls up in front, directly in front of the horde of paparazzi snapping photographs. Their presence is expected. Doesn't make it any less annoying.

"Should we go face the sharks?" Megan asks, and I like her more for it.

"Let's do it."

She climbs out first, and I follow. I'm blinded by the flashes, but I smile and wave as though I'm having the time of my life as we pose before heading inside the Italian restaurant. It's small and intimate, with lots of exposed brick and unfinished wood and soft lighting. We're shown to a back table that's cordoned off from the rest of the diners.

Megan is easy to talk to, but I struggle to stay focused on our conversation. Instead, I keep recalling how Vivienne stiffened when I told her I was going on this date. The waiter comes to take our drink order, and I can't help but think about how she would have ordered whiskey instead of the fancy cocktail Megan selects.

What's worse? I like Megan. She doesn't act like I'm simply a football player. She asks about my family, my time at Lincoln, and my interests. And I can tell she's genuinely interested in my answers. This doesn't feel like a publicity stunt. It feels like an actual date.

And all I can think about is when Viv asked me about going

on a date in Lincoln's dining hall and wish I hadn't assumed we'd have the following semester. Wish she was the one sitting across from me.

Our waiter returns with Megan's cocktail and my bourbon and asks for our dinner orders.

"Chicken bucatini, please," I request. It's the first thing I spot on the menu.

"I'll have the pumpkin ravioli, please," Megan orders.

I close my eyes and take another long pull of bourbon.

The reporters are still waiting for us when we leave the restaurant. I smile and wave, ignoring the reporter's shouted questions. Megan and I climb into the waiting limousine. Before I know it, we're back in front of Megan's townhouse.

"I had fun tonight," she tells me.

"I did, too," I reply. For the few minutes I managed to pay attention.

Megan smiles and leans forward. I know what's about to happen, and I let it. She kisses me softly, and I don't feel even the slightest stirring of desire.

I pull away first. "Good night, Megan."

"Night, Jace." She climbs out of the limo, and it pulls away from the curb as soon as she's inside.

Twenty minutes later, I sink into one of the few comfortable armchairs that came with this house, cold beer in hand. The silence feels claustrophobic instead of relaxing, so I pull out my phone.

"I'm in the pantry," is how Anderson answers the phone after six rings.

I laugh. "What?"

"You haven't talked to me since the last time you called and I didn't immediately inform you of my surroundings. Just trying to keep the only famous friend I have." The words are joking, but I detect an undercurrent of hurt in them.

"I'm sorry, man," I reply. "It's not just you. I haven't felt like talking to anyone lately."

"But you do now?"

"Not really. I'm just…bored, I guess," I admit, looking around my empty, bare living room.

"Well, I feel much better about our friendship now, Dawson. Thanks."

I laugh again. "You know what I mean."

"Wait, wasn't tonight your date with Miss South Carolina? I mean, at least according to the ten or twelve articles I saw about it…"

"Ten or twelve, Anderson? Seriously?"

"I had to set up a Google alert on you. I got mobbed by all these girls asking about the interview with Vi—the interview you did—and I had no idea about it, so I've had to make sure I'm updated so I don't have to make shit up. Wish I could rely on you, but that's unpredictable at best, so… I was going to stop after eight, but then there was this one article that described the way your hair looked with your gray eyes during your interview so beautifully I had to see if anyone else did it justice."

"I can't tell if you're kidding or not, and that worries me."

Anderson chuckles. "That's the beauty of humor, my friend." After a brief pause, he asks, "So…wasn't your date tonight?"

"Yeah." I sigh. "It was."

"I'm going to take the fact that you're calling me at ten thirty as a sign it was not a smashing success?"

"No, it was fine. She was nice. Pretty."

Anderson snorts. "Please, don't stretch your vocabulary on my account."

"She didn't fawn all over me and pretend she's watched every minute of every game I've ever played in. She didn't mention a boy band. She wants to be a kindergarten teacher. And she was more hot than just pretty," I elaborate.

"Okay, I actually knew all that except the lack of fawning. Owens read her pageant interview to us on the way home from the game yesterday. And showed some photos."

"Of course he did." I roll my eyes, even though Anderson can't see me.

"So…what happened? What horrible act did Miss Nice and Pretty commit? Did she insult Nebraska?"

"She ordered pumpkin ravioli."

Andersons laughs. "Seriously? What the fuck does that—oh."

"I spent the whole night comparing them," I admit.

"I don't see how that could become an issue," Anderson replies sarcastically. "Oh, wait…"

"I know. It was just—I couldn't help it." I pause. "I miss her. I just left, and I already miss her so fucking much." It's a relief to say the words out loud.

"Yes, I'm definitely getting that vibe from you, Dawson," Anderson jokes. Then his voice sobers. "I'm really sorry, dude. I wish there was some way it could work out for you guys."

"Thanks," I reply. "I'll be fine. I just need some time, and I'll refocus on what's important."

Anderson scoffs. "Cut the shit, Dawson. There's nothing more important to you than her."

He's right, but I push back anyway. "There's a lot of other things I care—"

"I know you care about other things, Dawson." Anderson sighs. "Okay, look. I got knocked out my sophomore year of high school, the same way you did. When I came to, do you want to know what my first thought was? Trisha Adkins. I was planning to ask her to Homecoming after the game. Been planning it for weeks. It was all I thought about. If your first thought was

439

anything other than her, then you're right. She's not the most important thing to you."

"She was there. For the first time in months. I'm not sure that's an objective test."

"It would have been different if she wasn't?" Anderson challenges.

I'm silent. "This call hasn't cheered me up much."

Anderson laughs. "That's kind of my point. All we talk about —or avoid talking about—is her. Call the beauty queen. Go out with her again. Avoid anything that could involve squash."

I laugh.

"You're not going to get over her unless you try to, Jace."

His use of my first name emphasizes his serious tone more than anything. He hardly ever calls me by it.

"I know. Thanks for talking, man."

"Anytime, Dawson."

I hang up the phone and slouch further on the couch. Anderson is right. About how I feel; about what I should do. The problem? I don't want to get over Viv. I don't want to forget about her. And I might not have to.

The following morning, I wake up with the same resolution I fell asleep with. I want to do this. I just don't know if I can. While frying some eggs for breakfast, I call my agent and ask him to meet me at a local coffee shop.

"How's my favorite client doing?" my agent, Jeremy Michaels, asks as he sits down, smiling widely.

"I bet you say that to all your clients, Jeremy."

"I do," he admits. "But I only mean it when I tell you. Not only have you turned out to be incredibly lucrative, your only 'scandal' involved a princess that portrayed you as a complete gentleman and resulted in you becoming the best-known player in the entire league."

I shift uncomfortably at the mention of Vivienne. Jeremy notices.

"Fuck, I knew you were too good to be true, Dawson. What is it? Drugs? Prostitutes? Gambling? Don't be shy, I've seen it all."

"It's nothing like that," I assure him. "I just want to know my options."

"Regarding?"

"Exiting my contract early. Now, to be specific."

Jeremy's jaw literally drops. "Exiting your contract now? Your multi-year, extremely generous contract we negotiated for weeks over? The one that's ensuring you're making millions? Every little boy in this country dreams of becoming a professional football player. Forget that. Do you know the percentage of successful college football players that make it to the pros? Never mind being the *first* pick? People would kill for the opportunity you've been handed. You're only months into your contract, and the Sharks are undefeated. You..." Jeremy heaves out a breath and takes a large gulp of water. "Is this some sort of power play because of the recent publicity? Are you trying to play elsewhere? Earn more?"

"No, it's nothing like that. It's just—I..." I pause to collect my thoughts. "I always wanted to play football. More than anything. My priorities may have shifted, that's all."

Realization dawns across Jeremy's face. "This is about her. The princess."

I don't answer.

"Dawson, women don't last. What does last? Your name in the Hall of Fame. You could be one of the greats. Don't toss this dream away on a whim. You're going to wake up bitter and angry one day that you gave up this opportunity."

I ignore his bleak prediction. "All I asked was for you to tell my options. I'm only—"

"You wouldn't have called me here if you weren't seriously considering it, Dawson."

I sigh, frustrated. "And I didn't ask you to comment on my personal life. I asked you here so I know what my options are."

Jeremy heaves out an exasperated sigh of his own. "You'll have to buy yourself out. That's the only way to exit your contract barely into the first year."

"How much?"

"Five million."

Fuck.

CHAPTER THIRTY-FIVE

VIVIENNE

I stare out the window at the falling leaves. It's chilly today, colder than it's been in months. It reminds me of Michigan.

"Vivienne? Vivienne!"

"Yes?" I ask, turning to look at Anne.

"I was trying to update you two on our media strategy."

"Oh, right. Sorry," I reply, glancing at Charles. He's grinning at me, and I smile back automatically. "Just admiring the nice weather."

I receive twin expressions of confusion for that comment. Any time the temperature drops below mild is typically not considered very pleasant here.

"I was just saying how well the interview of you two is playing in the media. Especially the story you told, Charles, about handing the Princess flowers when you two were little. Someone dug up old footage of it, and it's getting coverage everywhere. We need to shift toward the wedding next…"

I tune her out again, glancing back at the leaves dancing in the wind.

"…been six weeks since any mention of the Dawson story…"

That regains my attention. I look to Anne. "What did you just say?"

"I said we'll wait a couple more weeks, but any mention of your past relationship with Mr. Dawson has been absent from the media since six weeks ago."

"It's been six weeks?" I ask. My stomach sinks.

"Yes."

"You're certain?"

"I can assure you I've been keeping very close track," Anne replies. "Now, there's the photo shoot for the magazine article later this week, but aside from that, there's nothing we need to prepare for yet. Any questions?"

Charles shakes his head and looks to me. I shake my head as well.

"Okay, wonderful." Anne closes her binder and rises from the table in the corner of her office before walking back over to her desk.

Charles stands up as well, stretching. He starts toward the door, then realizes I'm not following.

"Vivienne?" he asks.

"Go ahead," I instruct. "I thought of something I'd like to discuss with Anne, after all."

Charles pauses, clearly expecting me to offer that he can stay. I don't.

"Okay," he finally says before leaving the room.

I remain sitting, and Anne comes back over to the table. I look back out the window.

"Your Highness?" she asks expectantly.

I don't say anything. Out of the corner of my eye, I watch Anne shift awkwardly as the silence stretches out.

"I need a pregnancy test, Anne," I finally manage. I keep my gaze trained outside. I don't want to see her reaction.

There's an even longer pause than there was before I spoke. Then, "Of course, Your Highness. I'll send someone immediately. I'll make sure they're discreet."

I look at her. "Anne, it's not—it wouldn't be Charles's."

She pales even more. "I'll go myself. Stay here."

I watch as she puts on a felt fedora and sunglasses and then rushes out of the room.

Two hours later, I sit on the edge of the pool, dangling my feet in the heated water. The wind whips my hair around my face.

Movement to my right startles me. I glance over to see my mother standing beside me. I move to stand, but to my surprise, she kicks off her heels and lowers herself next to me. She hikes up her silk trousers and tentatively dips her toes in the warm pool.

She doesn't say anything at first. Finally, she speaks. "Anne mentioned you might want to talk."

"Did she also mention I'm pregnant?" I ask the water.

My mother is silent for a long moment. "There's no chance it's Charles's?" she finally asks.

"No, there's not," I admit.

There's a pause, and then my mother says one of the last things I expect her to. "I guess he should have stayed at a hotel after all."

I turn to look at her for the first time. "Are you seriously making a joke out of this?"

My mother looks sheepish for maybe the first time in my life. "It seems it's a little late for anything else. Do you want a baby?"

"I never thought about it before. I knew—one day, I knew that I would need heirs. It always seemed like a long ways off. But—this isn't just *a* baby. It's…his."

445

My mother nods once. "You have options. I'm sure Charles would…" she trails off without finishing the sentence, but we both know what she's suggesting. "It wouldn't be the first time it's happened," she finishes quietly.

"No, I can't do that. Jace knows things aren't like that between Charles and me. He knows we haven't—he would know it's his. Even if he didn't, I can't keep something like this from him. It'd be wrong. He deserves to know."

"So why haven't you told him?"

"Because he would come back. He would give up his career, his family, his dreams, and come back."

"Isn't that what you want?"

"Selfishly, yes. But not for him. And certainly not because he feels obligated to me because of a baby."

My mother looks hesitant to voice the obvious question.

I sigh. "I know. I can't have it both ways. I just need some time to think."

She nods. Then she reaches out and squeezes my hand. It's one of the most maternal things she's ever done. "We'll support you, whatever you decide."

Tears prickle at my eyes. "Thanks, Mother." I look back out at the smooth water before she can see them.

We remain sitting there for a while, and for the first time in years, I'm disappointed when she finally stands and leaves me alone.

I employ a brilliant and flawless portrayal of denial over the next several days. I go to class, I go to meetings, I act completely normal. The only time my facade falters is when I meet the concerned gazes of Anne or my mother.

I've started sneaking into my father's study every night and sitting upstairs among the shelves of musty books the same way I did when I was a child. It's one of the few places in the palace that's devoid of memories of Jace. That's when I allow my mind to swim in answerless circles. I imagine telling Jace. Watching our child run through the gardens. Despite what I told my mother, I also picture telling Charles I'm pregnant. Admitting I betrayed him. Asking him to lie for me. I know he would do it. He would forgive me, and he would be a devoted father. But would I be able to live with myself? The only option I've definitively ruled out is ending the pregnancy. I've never been a believer in fate, but this pregnancy seems fated somehow. A piece of Jace I get to keep, no matter what.

This evening I'm pulled from my thoughts by the sound of a door opening downstairs. I peek over the edge of the metal walkway to watch my father enter his study with Lionel Vanderbilt right behind him.

"I wasn't expecting you, Lionel." My father speaks first. "What did you want to discuss?"

"I would like you to tell me what is going on here," Lionel states as they sit in the pair of armchairs next to the fireplace. His tone is filled with anger.

"I'm not sure what you're referring to," my father replies politely.

"I just got a call from John Fairfax. He owns the Sharks football team. Old friend of mine. He tells me Jace Dawson met with his agent to ask what his options are for getting out of his five-year contract."

My heart stops.

"John's incensed. I asked him to help get that boy here as a personal favor to me in order to smooth out the mess with the press before the wedding. John convinced him to come here, and now he's potentially going to lose his star player who's delivering an undefeated season. Neither of us are under any illusions as to why that might be happening."

"I didn't get the impression from Mr. Dawson that his team's owner factored in his decision to come here. At all," my father replies evenly.

"Then what did? This entire engagement is making my family look like a laughingstock. That is completely unacceptable. I would like some answers." Frustration leaks from Lionel's voice.

"I don't have any for you. As far as I know, Vivienne has every intention of marrying Charles in the spring. However, who Vivienne marries is her decision, and I certainly don't know anything about the nuances of professional football contracts."

Lionel lets out a loud huff. "I understand." His voice has calmed. "It's not just my family's reputation. Charles is quite invested in this relationship."

"I know nothing Vivienne has done was meant to hurt Charles or your family in any way," my father responds.

My heart sinks as I rest a hand on my stomach. My father and Lionel shift to discussing more neutral topics, and I tune them out entirely. Jace is considering quitting football, and he doesn't know I'm pregnant. Charles is upset with me, and my father's oldest friendship is being affected.

I wait until my father and Lionel leave his study, and then I stand and tiptoe down the spiral staircase. I cross his study, opening the door slightly. The hallway is empty, and I make my way back to my room without encountering anyone.

I change into pajamas and climb into bed as soon as I'm inside the sanctuary of my room, grateful for the opportunity to be oblivious for the next six hours. Despite my troubling thoughts, I feel myself start to fall asleep immediately.

Subconsciously, I feel the dread before I really wake up. I

slowly sink through layers of awareness, until I gradually notice my surroundings. I'm in my bed. My room is dark and quiet. But something is wrong. I roll over, and alarm ricochets through me. I fumble for the light and sit up in bed. Before I pull the covers back, I take a deep breath. All I see is red. I start shaking.

I feel for the phone that sits next to my bed, unable to look away from the blood. I pick it up and say the extension code robotically when I'm prompted to.

"Hello?" my father's sleepy voice answers.

"Papa, I need you to put Mother on."

"Vivienne?" Confusion and concern replace any drowsiness in my father's voice. I've never called my parents' room in the middle of the night. Not once.

"I need you to put Mother on," I repeat. There's fumbling on the other end of the line, and then my mother's voice comes through.

"Vivienne?" Her voice is panicked.

"I need you," I admit. "There's blood…" I let my voice trail off, unable to say anymore.

"I'll be right there."

The next few hours pass in a blur. My mother appears, then Anne, then one of the maids who has been with us the longest. My bed is stripped, I'm helped into the shower and then examined by my personal doctor. She confirms what I realized as soon as I woke up.

Once all the commotion has ended, I lie in bed again, trying to come to terms with the fragility of life. I hadn't expected this baby, but I wanted it. And now it's simply gone.

I finally fall into a troubled sleep. When I wake again, it's to the sound of a quiet knock. I glance at the clock to find it's already late morning.

"Come in," I call.

449

My mother enters the room. The expression on her face is foreign. I'm used to exasperated indifference when she looks at me, not sympathy and pity. She's been different with me since Jace left. Warmer. The shared secrets over the past ten days have cracked our previously strained relationship wide open.

"Are you doing all right?" she asks me.

I shrug. "I'm sad."

"I know. There were a couple times... I know what it's like."

A lump forms in my throat as I realize what she's trying to tell me.

"I'm sorry, Mother." I say softly. "I didn't know."

She nods once in acknowledgement. "I was thinking we could head to the cottage for a couple days. Get away for a bit?"

"That sounds wonderful."

She smiles. "Can you be ready in an hour?"

"Yes."

"Okay, I'll go get ready." She leaves, and I immediately climb out of bed. Suddenly, there's nothing I would like more than to be as far away from this room as possible. It's seen too much.

I shower again and dress in sweatpants and a fleece jacket. I pack a bag with toiletries and a random assortment of clothes, and then head down to the main foyer, avoiding eye contact with everyone I encounter.

My mother's already standing in the foyer. She's rattling off a long list of items to be taken care of in our absence to her assistant, Helga. She pauses when I appear in the entryway.

"The car's all ready, Vivienne. I'll be right out."

I nod and head outside, handing off my bag to one of the butlers. He deposits it inside the trunk. I climb into the backseat of the car and relax against the buttery smooth leather, slipping on a pair of sunglasses. It's only a couple more minutes until my mother emerges from the palace and climbs in the back seat with me.

"We're ready," she instructs the driver. We start rolling forward. A car filled with agents follows closely behind. Neither my mother nor I say anything as we drive along the familiar route. The scenic landscape fades to a swirl of blue and green as I stare out the window unseeingly. We arrive at Glendale Cottage. The scent of salty air inundates the car as soon as I open my door.

"I'm going to walk down to the water," I tell my mother.

She nods.

I cross the clamshell driveway and start toward the worn path that winds through the rugged shore and beach grass down to a narrow strip of sand. I take a seat on one of the larger rocks scattered along the private beach. The wind combs through my long hair. I pull my fleece jacket closer around my torso, grateful for the warmth it provides. I stare out at the roiling, churning water, trying to make sense of the crushing calamity that just took place. I know it will take time to come to terms with it, but that's not a luxury I have right now.

I'm no longer pregnant. Whatever remaining thread, however tenuous, that tied me to Jace is now fully severed.

I can't keep waffling. I can't let Jace waffle. I need to let him know that I'm fine. Not the wobbling mess who could hardly hold it together when he left. Charles is a good person. He'll be a good husband and a good king. That's what I need. That's what Marcedenia needs. It doesn't matter what I want. Not if everyone else will be the better for things remaining as they are.

CHAPTER THIRTY-SIX

JACE

I don't know what to do, and it's eating at me. I can't talk to anyone about it. I don't want to hear what they'll say.

I'm too afraid they'll tell me to do it. Too afraid they'll tell me not to.

Five million dollars.

It's a lot of money. But I haven't spent much of my advance. I'm living in a house owned by the Sharks for free. I don't spend thousands of dollars each weekend buying random women drinks the way many of my teammates do. I was saving it for my family. And I'm still short. I'd have to take out a loan for the rest of it.

I'm paralyzed. I've always been a decisive person, but this isn't just a decision. It's the path of the rest of my life. And I'm worried if I try to talk to Viv about it, she'll tell me no again. When I realize it's been two months since I last saw her, the vacillation becomes too much. I have to talk to her. Her opinion is the only one that counts regarding this topic.

I can't get through to the palace on any of the public numbers I find online. After sitting on hold for what feels like hours, I finally dial the one direct number I have.

"Anne Riley."

"Finally! I haven't been able to get through to anyone. I need to talk to Viv, Anne. I can't reach her any other way."

"Oh, no," Anne says. Her voice is morose. "I'm so sorry, Jace. I didn't realize she ended up telling you. I thought she was going to wait until she was further along."

"What are you talking about? Further along on what?"

Anne sucks in a sharp breath. "Nothing. She'll be back tomorrow. I'll have her call you as soon as she returns, okay?" Anne hangs up before I have a chance to say anything else. I sit there, puzzled.

How would Anne know I needed to talk to Vivienne? Not only needed to, but was expecting I would call? Why would she think there was something Vivienne needed to tell me? I'm more confused than ever, but finally give up on trying to solve the mystery. I'll call Viv tomorrow and straighten things out.

Sam calls as I'm eating dinner.

"Hey, how's it going?" I answer.

"Pretty good. I'm going to be an uncle!" he informs me. "I was just home for the weekend. Tim said they weren't going to tell anyone yet. She's not very far along, and I guess people usually wait…" He keeps talking, but I've stopped listening. Anne said Viv was waiting to tell me something until she was further along. Did she mean Viv is…pregnant?

"I've got to go." I tell Sam before I hang up. I race upstairs and hastily shove a few things in a duffle bag before I go out to the garage. I'm at the airport in twenty minutes. There's no direct flight to Marcedenia, but there's a flight to France with a connection there.

I tap my foot anxiously as I board first one flight, and then another. It's early morning in Marcedenia by the time I land. Instead of a private airfield, this time I emerge into a bustling airport. No one seems to recognize me beneath my baseball cap and sunglasses as I make my way through the busy building and flag down a taxi.

"Can you take me to the palace, please?" I ask.

The driver scoffs. "Sure, kid."

He makes good time and stops in front of a familiar set of gates about twenty minutes later. "I can take you to your hotel after you've snapped a few pictures."

"I'm good here, thanks," I respond.

He shrugs. "All right, suit yourself."

I walk up to the guard booth, ignoring the other tourists milling about. I'm relieved to see Thomas is the one sitting there.

"Mr. Dawson?" He looks stunned to see me. "What are you doing here?"

"I need to see Vivienne—the Princess," I reply. "Please, it's an emergency."

Thomas appraises me and then finally nods. "She's out in the gardens with Charles, I believe." He looks hesitant to share that information, and I feel a glimmer of anger start to form. Was she even going to tell me?

The walk up the tree-lined drive and past the fountain does nothing to calm me down. I attract a lot of stares from the landscapers and other staff milling about, but I don't pay them any attention.

I stride angrily around the side of the palace and into the gardens. Immediately, I spot Viv sitting at one of the patio tables alongside Charles, her mother, and two women I've never seen before. Samples of cake, floral bouquets, and piles of stationary sit on the table, and my temper rises further as I realize they must be in the midst of wedding planning.

Viv glances up as the crunch of gravel announces my approach. She freezes. Charles follows her gaze. His face contorts in irritation when he sees me. I gain Vivienne's mother's attention next, closely followed by the two other women. The queen looks worried, the other women puzzled.

I stop about ten feet away from the table. Vivienne has half-risen from her chair.

"Jace," she gasps. "What—how—what are you doing here?"

"Can I talk to you?" I ask. She flinches at the animosity in my tone, but leaves her seat and walks over to me.

"What are you doing here?" Her gaze is wide-eyed and disconcerted.

I don't answer as I continue walking over to the pool. I don't want anyone overhearing us. The click of her heels on the stone patio sounds from behind, indicating she's following me.

"Jace, you're freaking me out. What's going on? Is everything okay?"

I whirl around to face her. "Are you pregnant?" I planned to show up and give her a chance to tell me, but being here—seeing her—it's more than I was prepared for. I'm barely holding it together; drawing this conversation out will only make it worse.

The expression on her face tells me everything I need to know.

"And you're planning your wedding? With Charles?" I accuse. Betrayal courses through me. "How could you not tell me something like this? After everything?"

Viv looks panicked. "I don't understand. How did you even find out?"

"That's what you're worried about?" I ask, my voice cutting. "How I found out?"

"No—Jace—I—" I've never seen Viv so flustered, but I'm too mad and hurt to care. "I would have told you, it's just—"

"Is it not mine?"

Anger flickers across Viv's face for the first time. "How could you ask me that? You know—"

"I don't know anything, apparently!" I shout.

"I would have told you, okay? I found out I was pregnant, and I was going to tell you, but then—"

"But, what? It was too inconvenient for you?"

Viv's eyes flash. "I'm not pregnant anymore, okay? That's why I decided not to tell you."

An unexpected wave of loss hits me.

Sympathy dawns across Viv's face. "No, Jace, that's not what I—"

"I'm done. I'm fucking done," I spit out. "I wish you never came to Lincoln. I wish we never met." I've thought the words before, but this is the first time I've ever said them out loud. I regret them immediately, even before I see the spasm of pain cross Viv's face. But I also know if I stay, I'll only say more things I'll later regret. Especially now that my reason for making this trip is gone.

I turn around and start to walk back toward the main gate. There's a pause, and then I hear Viv call my name.

I keep walking.

VIVIENNE

I collapse on the hard patio, resting my head against my knees. I know I should go after him, tell him the truth. But what then? He'll comfort me, he'll apologize, he'll leave. Maybe it's better this way. Cleaner.

Footsteps sound, but I don't look up.

"Vivienne?" my mother asks quietly.

I don't respond.

"What's going on? What's wrong with her? What was he doing here?" Charles asks. Derision drips from the last question.

"Can you let Maria and Joan know we'll need to reschedule?" is my mother's only response.

I hear Charles's retreating steps a few seconds later.

"Vivienne?" my mother says again.

I can't respond, too busy trying to smother the waves of pain. I gave Jace the power to hurt me a long time ago; I just never thought he'd do so purposefully. "He found out."

My mother is uncharacteristically silent.

"He thinks I chose to...he hates me," I whisper.

"Vivienne, that boy loves you."

"Not anymore." My voice breaks.

"Let's get you inside," my mother instructs, hauling me up from the hard stones. I lean heavily against her as we walk along the terrace toward the palace.

Anne rushes out as we reach the sliding doors. "There you are, Your Highness. I was hoping to catch you as soon as you returned. I got pulled into something. Mr. Dawson called last night, and I really think you need to speak to him as soon as possible—"

"Mr. Dawson just left, Anne," my mother states.

Anne's silent as she looks at me, seeming to register my expression for the first time.

"I'm so sorry, Your Highness. I had no way to contact you at the cottage. I never imagined he would come all—"

"It's fine, Anne," I reply woodenly before continuing my trek inside.

Days pass. I can't shake Jace's horrified face from my brain, but the pain dulls. It helps that this time there's no media speculation involved. This is a private battle I'm waging within myself.

Charles never asks me about Jace's visit, and I'm grateful. I don't know how I would respond. I show my gratitude by making an extra effort toward him. Tonight is our engagement party. I'm fawned over for hours by a makeup artist, then a hair stylist, and finally one of the royal dressers. It's been over a year since I attended an event this formal, and I feel like an authentic princess by the end of the process. I feel regal.

I mill around the assortment of dignitaries, politicians, dukes, and lords in attendance, making small talk. Our engagement party is being held at Marcedenia's parliamentary building, which is almost as ostentatious as the palace.

Charles gives a brief speech after dinner. "On behalf of Vivienne and myself, I'd like to thank you all for being here tonight to celebrate our engagement. And thank King Robert and Queen Evelyn for not only hosting this event, but also welcoming me into the family with open arms. I know a lot of you believe our engagement has always been a forgone conclusion, but the truth is far from it. Princess Vivienne is a shining emblem of everything Marcedenia stands for. She captivated me from the very first time we met. All I did was hand her a bouquet of flowers, and I can still remember how nervous I was."

Charmed chuckles fill the room. Charles finishes his speech and then leads me out onto the dance floor. We begin twirling in time with the slow music playing.

"Are you having fun?" he asks me.

"Yes, I am," I respond, surprised to realize it's true.

"I'm glad." He smiles down at me.

"Thank you for what you said in your speech. It was very thoughtful."

"I meant every word, Vivienne." His expression is earnest.

"I know you did." I smile at him as we continue spinning under the glimmering lights.

CHAPTER THIRTY-SEVEN

JACE

Scalding coffee burns my throat as I take another sip. The farmhouse is dark and silent around me. Tomorrow's Thanksgiving, and everyone went to bed long ago. Except for me. I've barely slept since the fifteen hours I spent on three planes following the fifteen minutes I spent at the palace.

A creak sounds behind me. I glance back to see Mike walking toward the kitchen, rubbing his eyes. He comes to an abrupt halt when he sees me.

"You're still up?" he asks.

"Couldn't sleep," I respond, taking another searing gulp.

"I'm sure some caffeine will help with that." Mike fills a glass with water and takes a seat across from me at the kitchen table. "Do you want to talk? Before you answer, Mom's talking about going back to South Carolina with you. She *hates* South Carolina."

"There's no reason for her to do that." I state.

"I've got to disagree with you on that. You look like shit, Jace."

"I haven't been sleeping."

"So you mentioned. Why?"

"I went to Marcedenia last week."

Mike lets out a low whistle. "Now we're getting somewhere. Want to know what my guesses were for what you were upset about? Or rather, my one guess."

I roll my eyes.

"So? What happened?"

I haven't told anyone what happened, not even my best friends. It's too personal, but Mike is family. "Vivienne was pregnant."

"You knocked her up?" Mike gasps loudly.

"Shhhhh," I scold him, glancing behind me to make sure none of the rest of our family is loitering in the doorway. "Tell the whole house, why don't you?"

"You said *was*. So, she…"

"Ended the pregnancy."

"She told you that?"

"Essentially."

"And what did you do?"

"I left," I admit. "Well, I said some other things first."

"You yelled at her and split?" Mike surmises. "You're an ass."

This is far from the sympathy I was looking for. "What? How am *I* the bad guy in this scenario?"

"Jace…" For the first time, my little brother looks older than me. "Think about things from her perspective. She's royalty. She's got a whole country following her every move, relying on her. She's about to get married because her father has Alzheimer's and she has to. She gets pregnant while she's engaged to someone else and a few months before she's supposed to become queen. Does that seem like a simple and straightforward problem to you?"

"I know it's not simple and straightforward," I hiss. "Nothing about our relationship has *ever* been simple and straightforward. But she could have reached out to me—she could have at least told me."

"When? Between your practice schedule and dates with models?"

I glare at Mike. "That's not fair."

"But it's true. You don't even live in the same country. Does she know your new address? What was she supposed to do? Jump on her private jet and show up at a Sharks' practice with a 'you're the daddy' banner?"

I grit my teeth, hating that he's right.

"More importantly, why do you care?" Mike asks.

"What?" I ask, shocked. "How can you ask me that?"

"You guys broke up, right?"

"You know we did. The whole world does at this point."

"You've known for almost a year you guys can never be together. I get why you're upset, but it's probably best things worked out this way. Otherwise you would have—what? Had to watch some other guy raise your kid with her?"

"Of course not!" I exclaim indignantly. "I would have made her marry me."

"Wait—what? I thought you guys can't get married?"

"Well, apparently we can. I'd have to quit football, move there, and become a Marcedenian citizen."

"So…why haven't you?" Mike questions.

"I'm glad you think it's so simple, Mike," I snap. I'm beginning to regret having told him anything.

"It *is* simple, Jace. When you brought her home last Thanksgiving, it was the happiest I've ever seen you. You barely cracked a smile when you got the call you'd been drafted. Doesn't that tell you all you need to know?"

"It's not that easy, Mike," I insist.

"What's so complicated about it? Have you even tried?"

"Yes," I retort, angry now. "I asked about my contract, okay? I'd have to buy myself out, which is five million dollars I do not have. The last thing I need is more debt to worry about. The whole reason I even entered this season was—"

"Mom and Dad?" Mike guesses.

"What do you mean?" I ask carefully.

"Come on, Jace, I'm seventeen, not seven. We all know how tight things have been over the years. But I just got my scholarship, and things are better for the farm too. Mom and Dad have been getting checks from a small farm grant that have helped a lot. They've almost paid everything off."

"What? A grant?" My mind begins spinning. "Since when?"

"I don't know, the checks started coming right after last Thanksgiving…" Mike trails off, having come to the same conclusion I have. "She wouldn't…would she?"

"She absolutely would," I reply, both annoyed and touched.

"And your plan is still to do nothing?"

"She asked me not to."

"Because she doesn't want you or because she thought it was what you wanted?"

"I don't know," I admit.

"You love her, right?"

"You know I do."

"Enough that it would be worth it? To give everything up? Even if it doesn't work out? *Especially* if it doesn't work out?"

I stare at my brother. "When the hell did you become some sort of love guru?"

My brother shrugs, smirking. "Girls can't resist me. The other guys come to me for advice a lot."

I scoff loudly.

"So?" Mike asks. "Is it worth it?"

I've known the answer for a while, but the fear of what the repercussions could be have always haunted me. "Yeah, it is."

Mike smiles widely. "Damnit, I was just getting used to having a brother who made it to the pros. Guess you being a king will have to suffice."

"Don't jinx anything," I tell him. "She might have meant it. And we didn't exactly part on great terms. She might not say yes."

"Jace, she's a literal princess. And she came to *Nebraska* to spend Thanksgiving with you on our family's farm. She stayed in our laundry room and went plowing with Dad. And the whole time she was here she looked at you like you'd just come back from hanging the moon. She'll say yes."

I feel lighter after my late-night talk with Mike, and I can tell it shows. My mother's expression is relieved when she studies me across the table during dinner. I'm not plagued by memories of last Thanksgiving as we sit and eat. I know I'll get to see Vivienne at least one more time, and that eradicates any pangs I normally would have experienced recalling her time here last fall.

I arrive back in South Carolina to a massive stack of mail, including the persistent tabloids. I'm glad to see the covers are absent of any mention of me or Vivienne, but I still toss them all in the recycling right away.

An envelope made of thick, expensive-looking paper catches my eye. I inspect it more closely and see that my name and address are written out across the front in calligraphy. A wax seal is holding the back flap shut. I pull it open and wrestle out the piece of paper folded inside. I open it, and a smaller piece of paper flutters to the floor. The full sheet of paper only has five words written in the same fancy script as the address. It reads *In case you need it.*

I reach down and pick up the smaller paper that fell out. I suck in a sharp breath when I see that it's a check made out to me. For five million dollars. I pull out my phone and tap on a name.

"Anne Riley."

"Hi, Anne, it's Jace Dawson."

There's silence on the other end of the line. I'm guessing Anne's recalling our catastrophic last conversation.

"I need to speak with Robert...er, the king," I add.

"Is he expecting your call?" Anne finally asks.

"I think so."

"All right. One moment."

There's a long pause on the other end of the line, then finally a click.

"Hello?" I ask.

"Jace? How are you?" Robert's voice comes through the line.

"I'm all right, sir. And you?"

"Fine, thanks." There's another pause.

"I just received my mail," I state.

"Ah. Anything interesting?"

"One thing."

"I had a visit from Lionel Vanderbilt the other day. He heard you expressed some interest in leaving your football team. I just wanted to ensure you have the means to do so, if that's what you want."

"That's very thoughtful of you. And generous," I reply, trying to decide how to phrase my response so I don't sound ungrateful. "But I can't accept it. It's too much."

"Jace, what I sent you was the money set aside to renovate our summer cottage. I can assure you my daughter's happiness is worth much more to me than a new library and patio. But, like I said in my note, the decision to use that money is yours. One of a few choices you'll need to make soon."

"I'm aware, sir."

"Good. Take care, Jace." The line goes dead.

I can't use the money Robert sent. But the fact that he sent it fortifies the decision I've already made.

The following morning, I make my way to John's office as soon as I hang up with Jeremy. Who will no longer be my agent as of midnight.

John's secretary waves me past after giving me a flirty smile.

"Could I speak to you for a moment, John?" I ask as I pass through the doorway. He looks up from the binder he's reading.

"Dawson! Of course! I've always got time for my star player."

I try not to grimace. He is going to change his tone very quickly, I'm guessing.

"I wanted to let you know personally, sir. I'm leaving the league."

The jovial smile falls off John's face immediately. "What?"

"I've enjoyed my time as a Shark immensely. I promise I never had any intention of leaving the organization before my contract ended. However, my personal circumstances have changed."

John forms words silently, but no sound emerges.

"My agent will be putting out a statement tomorrow. In the

meantime, please keep this between us. Any *old friends* of yours will hear soon enough."

John's mouth tightens, and I receive confirmation of where Lionel Vanderbilt received his information.

I stride out of his office and head for the airport.

CHAPTER THIRTY-EIGHT

VIVIENNE

I can't quite place the expression on my mother's face. She looks…apprehensive? Uncertain?

"Vivienne, you need to go out to the front foyer," she tells me again.

"What is it?" I grumble, irritated. I wave to the papers spread across the table. "Joan and I were just about to get started on the seating arrangement, and you know how long that will take. If we start now, we'll be lucky to have it done by dinner. And I've got to approve the bouquet now or else—"

"Vivienne, you need to go out there. Now."

I heave a sigh and stand. "Is there some sort of problem?" I ask, walking toward the doorway. "Because I seriously cannot handle—" I swing the door open and freeze.

Jace is standing in the middle of the front foyer next to the center table that always holds a fresh floral arrangement, no matter the time of year. His hands are shoved deep in his pockets as he studies one of the paintings on the wall. He looks over, and his eyes meet my stunned gaze. The random assortment of butlers, maids, and agents currently in the foyer glance between us uncertainly.

I don't say anything, and neither does he. My mind can't process his presence. Is he here to apologize? Yell at me again? Did something bad happen? I'm angry at him. But happiness is the emotion that hits me first. And I'm mad about that, too.

Jace shifts his weight and pulls his hands out of their pockets. "Can I talk to you?" he asks quietly. "Outside, maybe?"

I don't move or speak, and he shuffles again.

"What are you doing here, Jace?" I finally ask.

"I came to talk to you."

"You flew for five hours across who knows how many miles to talk to me?" I state emotionlessly.

"Yes."

"Why?"

He hesitates, so I finally voice my biggest fear.

"Are you okay? Did you get hurt again? Did your family—"

"Nothing's wrong, Viv. I promise."

The use of his nickname for me startles me. Even more surprising? The tender way he's looking at me. I feel like I've stepped into some strange alternate universe.

"Can we go outside?" Jace glances around at the many people listening to our conversation. If I'm reading his expression correctly, he's nervous.

Based on our last private conversation in the gardens, I'm not thrilled by the prospect of heading outside with him again, but he's definitely not as angry as he was last time. And I'm no more eager to have people gossiping about us than he seems to be.

I nod and follow him out the terrace doors and over to one of the benches that sits on the periphery of the garden. The air is crisp, but the sun is warm. I shiver slightly as I sit down beside him in my navy dress and matching blazer.

"I'm quitting football." Jace drops this bomb on me as I'm buttoning up the front of the blazer for some additional warmth.

I turn to stare at him, utterly flabbergasted. It's one of the last things I ever expected to hear him say. "What?" I gasp.

"Actually, I already did. Bought out my contract yesterday. There's a press release coming out tomorrow. I didn't want to tell you until I'd already done it. I didn't want you to think I don't mean this."

"You quit football? For me?"

"I know you told me not to—that you didn't want me to give it up for you. And yeah, okay, I wouldn't have had to walk away from football if I fell in love with some other girl who didn't happen to be a princess. But I didn't fall in love with some other girl. I fell in love with you. And if giving up football means we can be together, then it's worth it to me. You're worth it to me, Viv."

"I thought you hate me," I whisper. "After what you said…"

Jace glances down at the gravel path and sighs. "I'm sorry about what I said. I was hurt and upset, and I took it out on you. That wasn't fair. It was your decision to make, and I shouldn't have reacted that way."

"Jace, I didn't decide to end the pregnancy. I lost the baby."

"What?"

"I was going to tell you. I don't know what I was going to do after that. But I was going to tell you. Afterwards…well, it seemed pointless and selfish to tell you then."

Jace's face is fiercely emotional. "Viv…" he starts, looking lost. "I'm—"

I shake my head and collapse against his chest. He wraps his arms around me tightly. I close my eyes, letting myself remember that horrific night. How the only thing I wanted was him holding me the way he is right now.

469

"I'm sorry I wasn't there," he whispers to me. Silent tears slide down my cheeks.

We sit like that for a long time. Long enough for my tears to stop and my cheeks to dry. Finally, I pull away, straightening my blazer and smoothing my dress in an attempt to pull myself together.

"I'm all in, Viv," Jace states. "If you want me, I'm all in."

"I need some time," I tell him, looking away at the gardens. "This—you—it's a lot."

"I get it," Jace says. "I have to fly back in…" He checks his watch. "Shit. I've got to go now, actually."

"What? You just got here!"

"I know. I left as soon as I could get away, but I still have a bunch of paperwork to sign and some other odds and ends to take care of. Plus, I have to move out of the house they gave me."

A new thought occurs to me. "Jace," I say urgently. "Your contract. The money. You can't—"

"I can and I did," he replies calmly. "Let me worry about the money. My family will be fine, especially since they've been receiving money for the past year from some anonymous grant. You wouldn't know anything about that, would you?"

I blush for the first time in a couple of months. "I couldn't just do nothing," I mutter.

"Thank you," Jace tells me earnestly.

"So, what are you going to do after you move out?" I ask.

Jace looks to me. "That's up to you."

"You'd really do it? Give up everything and move here? Get married?"

"Yes," Jace replies simply.

I shake my head in disbelief. It can't be this easy. I've hardly let myself even dream of this possibility, and here it is. Suddenly sitting right in front of me.

"You don't really know what you're getting into. What you'll be sacrificing." I can't help but warn Jace again.

"I know what I'm gaining. And I know I'll spend the rest of my life regretting not doing this if I don't. I want to marry you, Viv. I want to have kids with you. That's part of why I was so upset. Because when I thought you were pregnant, I was shocked, but I was also excited."

I stare at him, completely overwhelmed. It must be obvious, because Jace lets out a low laugh.

"Well, I'm glad I didn't follow Mike's suggestion and just surprise you with a proposal."

My heart races at the suggestion. I've conditioned my body to cringe at every thought of marriage, but the thought of Jace on one knee, looking up at me? It fills me with happiness, not dread.

I let out a small smile. "This is…a lot," I tell him. "And very unexpected."

"I know," Jace replies. "Take all the time you need." He leans forward and gives me a kiss on the cheek. "I'll understand. Whatever you decide."

He stands and strides back inside the palace.

I hide out for the rest of the night. If I let Jace do this, it will be the most selfish thing I ever do. But am I really *letting* him do anything? He was right; it's his decision too. And he's made it. It's my turn to make mine.

I turn on the television when I wake up, and the story is already being covered in Marcedenia.

"We've just obtained a copy of a statement released in the United States today by the South Carolina Sharks. For those of you who are wondering why we're covering this, they're the football team Jace Dawson plays for. Or rather played for, since he is the subject of the press release. It states Dawson is leaving the Sharks for 'personal reasons,' but doesn't elaborate on what those might be. The vague language is the topic being discussed on every sports station in the States right now, since Dawson seems to be voluntarily walking away from a contract worth millions after being heralded as the best American football player in decades. Of course, the leading theory on this is that it may have something to do with his former relationship with Princess Vivienne, despite the fact she is expected to wed Duke Vanderbilt's son Charles in just a few months. When asked for a statement, the palace refused to comment, only spurring further speculation."

I turn off the television and get dressed. I'm eating breakfast in my usual room when one of Anne's assistants appears. "Anne would like to see you, Your Highness."

I nod. "Do you know where my mother is?"

"She's in Anne's office, Your Highness."

"Perfect." I rise and make my way to the press offices. I knock on Anne's shut door.

"Come in," she calls.

I walk inside to see she's seated at the table, along with my mother and another assistant. I recognize her from my session with Jace. Cara.

"Have a seat, Vivienne," my mother says.

"We need to know what you want us to do, Princess," Anne states. "We can't keep saying 'no comment.' There's no such thing. By refusing to comment, we're saying a lot, and the story is already out of control. The president of Italy is scheduled to arrive this afternoon, and do you know how much time she got on the morning shows? Five minutes! Out of an hour long segment! I need to write a statement, and I need to know what to say."

I nod and stand. "Can I talk to you and Papa?" I ask my

mother. "Privately?" I've made my decision, but this doesn't just affect me.

She stands as well. "He's in his study," she tells me. "Let's go there."

We make the trip in silence. I knock when we arrive at the heavy wooden door.

"Come in," my father calls. I open the door, and my mother and I step inside before I close it.

My father looks up from his desk. "Well, this is an unexpected surprise."

I walk over to his desk and take a seat in one of the chairs angled in front of it. My mother follows.

I take a deep breath. "Jace quit football."

"Really? I hadn't heard," my father says cheekily.

"Robert," my mother admonishes. "Now is not the time for jokes." She's hardly one to talk, considering how she reacted to my pregnancy announcement, but I don't bother to bring that up now.

"He says he wants to give everything up. Get married."

My father's face turns serious. "And how do you feel about that?"

"I'm scared. Scared to let him. Scared to let myself believe it could actually happen."

"Vivvi, this is your decision. Whatever you do, I'll support you. But for what it's worth, you've always been an excellent judge of character. I had my doubts, when you first told us about a relationship with an American football player, I'm not going to lie. But I shouldn't have."

I smile, recognizing the approval of Jace hidden in his words.

"Mother?" I ask, looking to her.

She smiles at me with a touch of sadness. "You know how I feel about Charles, but I'm not sure if he would fly ten hours to hold you in the gardens for twenty minutes. That should tell you everything you need to know. But you don't need us to make your choices for you. You never have."

I raise my eyebrows at her admission.

She looks sheepish. "I was worried about what was taking so long."

I laugh. "Okay, I'll need to speak to Charles." I sober. I'm not looking forward to that conversation. "And then I'm going to need the plane."

My father smiles. "Go get him, Vivvi."

I pack in a flurry. Jeans, dresses, and jackets are tossed in a pile, only to be carefully folded and packed by a group of maids. Once I'm certain I have everything I might need for Nebraska or South Carolina, I instruct them to zip the bags up and load them in the car.

I take a final glance around my room. I've changed into jeans and one of the sweaters I wore in Nebraska. I'm wearing Jace's t-shirt underneath. It's silly, but it makes me feel closer to him.

When I arrive downstairs, my bags have already been loaded inside one of the SUVs. My security team stands next to the car.

"Let's go," I instruct them.

"Yes, Your Highness." Thomas is the one who replies and climbs in the back seat next to me. Michael climbs into the passenger seat, and we're moving.

"I need to stop at the Vanderbilts' first."

"Understood, Your Highness," the driver replies.

It doesn't take long for us to arrive at the Vanderbilts' manor. I tap my fingers against my thigh anxiously as I wait for the gate to their mansion to open. Finally, it does, and our small procession of cars starts up the driveway. I climb out as soon as the car comes to a stop. Michael and Thomas flank me as I walk up to the front door.

One of the Vanderbilts' butlers opens the door.

"Your Highness, how can I help you?" he asks nervously, bowing.

"Is Charles home?"

"Yes, come in, please." The butler replies. He leads me into one of the sitting rooms. "I'll ask Mr. Vanderbilt to meet you in here."

"Thank you," I tell him. "Wait out here, please," I instruct Michael and Thomas.

They both nod.

I take a seat on one of the linen couches to wait for Charles. He enters the room only a couple of minutes later. His expression is guarded. Tense.

"Hi," I greet.

Charles smiles, but doesn't say anything as he takes a seat on the identical couch across from me.

I take a deep breath. "Charles, I hope you'll believe me when I tell you that I never expected this to happen. Any of it. My father's illness. The marriage law. My time at Lincoln. I went to the States to escape things for a little while. And I fell in love. I came back, and suddenly I had to get married right away. And I couldn't—"

Charles interrupts me. "You don't have to explain, Vivienne. I saw the news this morning. You're going to marry him, right?" His face is blank. Carefully so.

"I'm so sorry, Charles. I never meant to hurt you, and I truly planned to marry you—"

"It's fine, Vivienne."

"No, it's not. Charles, I'm really sorry. I can't tell you how sorry. It's—"

"Vivienne. Our engagement is over. I get it."

"You're an amazing guy, Charles. Truly."

Charles scoffs, his first hint of emotion other than indifference. "Yeah, we'll see how many girls want the Princess's castoffs."

"Charles..."

"I wasn't under any illusions you would pick me over him, Vivienne. I just didn't think you'd *be able* to pick him."

I nod once, understanding what he's really saying. He didn't expect Jace to choose me. To give everything up for me.

"Just go, Vivienne. Please."

"Okay," I whisper. There's nothing else I can say, except, "I really am sorry, Charles."

He doesn't say anything as I walk out of the room back to the waiting car.

It only takes twenty minutes to drive to the airport. The plane is already sitting on the runway, waiting. I jump out of the car as soon as we pull up to the airstrip. My entourage of agents follows closely behind as I climb the stairs onto the plane.

"Welcome aboard, Your Highness." The pilot bows as I emerge inside. "Where is your destination?"

Shit. I don't know. "Head toward the States," I reply. "I'll let you know more details shortly."

He nods and heads into the cockpit. The door is closed, and we're airborne in minutes.

I pull out my phone. It's childish, but I don't want to call Jace and ask where he is. I'm not sure exactly what I'm going to say to him, but I know I don't want it to be over the phone. That means I have to track him down some other way. I try to come up with ways to do so, and press the first name I think of.

"Hello?"

"Katie! It's Vivienne."

"Vivienne! Is everything okay?"

"Yes, everything's fine." I reply quickly. "But I need a favor.

Can you get me Joe Anderson's number? Or Owens's? I forget his first name—everyone just calls him Owens. Either of them."

"The football players? Uh—yeah, I can try." Katie sounds bewildered. "Are you sure everything is okay?"

"I'm trying to find out where Jace is," I admit.

"Jace? He's here."

"What?"

"Jace is at Lincoln right now."

"He's at Lincoln?"

"Yes."

"What is he doing there?"

"It's the last game of the regular season today. The last game for everyone his year. He's the guest of honor."

"Shit," I groan.

"Um, do you mind me asking why you're looking for Jace? Aren't you about to marry someone else?"

"Not anymore," I reply. It's the first time I've said the words out loud, and they're remarkably freeing.

I expect Katie's answering squeal will do permanent damage to my eardrums. "ARE YOU KIDDING ME?" she shouts when she finally stops screeching.

I laugh.

"You're coming after Jace? That's the most romantic thing I've ever heard."

"Can you meet me on Lincoln's campus? By the stadium? And bring a hat or something?"

"Yeah, of course, but the game doesn't start for four hours."

"Katie, I'm still flying over the Atlantic."

"Oh." She laughs. "Okay, I'll see you soon, then."

"See you soon," I repeat before I hang up the phone.

I glance to Michael. "Can you let the pilot know we're headed to Lincoln, Michigan?"

He nods and heads up front.

Several hours later, I meet Katie underneath one of the towering trees that surrounds the football stadium. She gives me a big hug and then hands me a *Lincoln* baseball cap.

"This is all I could find," she tells me apologetically.

"Think it will be enough?" I ask, putting the hat on and pulling my hair forward so it falls on either side of my face.

Katie studies me doubtfully. "For someone who doesn't know what you look like? Maybe. Unfortunately, everyone here does. It doesn't help that you look like a supermodel. Did you seriously just get off a five-hour flight?"

I roll my eyes. "Let's do this."

"We'll sit up at the very top and we can plan how to find him after," Katie tells me.

"Okay, let's go."

Most of the students have already made their way inside the stadium, which I think is a good thing until Katie and I emerge inside to discover there's not an open seat in sight. Jace's voice is echoing around the stadium. It gives me chills, but I don't look down at the field, keeping my gaze trained on the cement floor in an attempt to avoid drawing attention to myself.

"Claudia said she saved some seats down below..." Katie suggests.

I sigh. "Okay, let's go." Wandering around the stadium aimlessly isn't going to help anything.

We make our way down toward the very edge of the field.

I give Claudia and Katie's other friends a small wave as I slide into the seat at the very end of the row. They all looked stunned to see me. I settle in the seat and finally glance around the field. Both teams are standing on the sideline. A podium and short row of folding chairs has been set up in the middle of the field. Jace stands at the podium, still speaking. I finally focus on what he's saying.

"I know most of you have probably heard my football career is ending much sooner than I planned. I won't get into the decision, since I made it for personal reasons, but it was my time here at Lincoln that allowed me to have that opportunity in the first place. I'm incredibly grateful for that, and insanely lucky to have played with such an awesome group of guys who pushed me every day to perform better. I feel honored to be here today, and…"

Jace stops speaking. Murmurs and movement ripple around the packed stadium as thousands of students crane their necks to see what he's looking at. I don't need Katie's whisper of "The hat is not working!" in my ear to realize why. He's seen me. I can feel his eyes on me.

Whispers echo around the packed stadium as Jace stands there, staring. The girl sitting across the aisle from me has pulled out her phone and started filming. I curse under my breath.

"You brought security, right?" Katie asks as spectators sitting in the upper levels of the stadium leave their seats and trickle down to the lower section we're seated in to get a better look.

"They're outside the stadium. I thought they'd be too conspicuous," I groan.

More phones appear around us. "I don't think they're the only conspicuous ones," Katie observes.

"What should I do?" I ask her wildly.

"Vivienne, this was your plan!"

"This was *not* the plan! We were supposed to sit up top, and no one was supposed to see us!" I panic.

"Go Lincoln!" Jace finally finishes his speech. He hands the microphone back to a man I recognize as the college president. I expect Jace to take a seat on the empty folding chair waiting for him, but instead he begins walking over toward the edge of the field. Toward me.

"Oh my God, oh my God, oh my God," Katie chants next to me. She's practically vibrating with excitement.

I glance behind me. The cement aisle and walkways surrounding my section have completely filled with people. I have no emergency exit.

There's someone else speaking now, but the entire stadium's attention is focused on Jace and me. I keep my head down in a ridiculous attempt to avoid the scrutiny. I expected to have the entire game to plan out what I was going to say to him. Now I have a matter of seconds. What if he's changed his mind? What if I'm ruining his life—agreeing to this?

Jace reaches the partition at the edge of my section, and I'm out of time. The whole stadium is looking between the two of us expectantly, trying to discern whether this is some sort of pre-planned spectacle. As if. Just poor planning, people.

Profanities run through my head, but I'm out of options. I'm at the edge of a cliff, and the painful, grueling climb to reach this point is about to pay off or crash spectacularly.

I pull off the baseball cap that served as my sad attempt at a disguise, and stand. Fresh noise floods the audience as I walk down the cement stairs to the edge of the field.

For the second time, I step out onto the perfectly manicured grass of Lincoln's football stadium. Jace stands about ten feet away. His face is carefully expressionless, but his jaw ticks a couple of times as I approach, indicating he's not as indifferent as he appears.

I stop when I'm a couple feet from him. "My plan was for no one but you and Katie to know I was here."

A reluctant grin tugs at Jace's lips. "How's that working out for you?"

I heave out a breathy laugh. I'm nervous. Incredibly nervous. More nervous than I can ever recall being.

It was daunting enough imagining saying this to Jace, but to know we're in front of thousands of people who worship him? Even if they can't hear what we're saying—which I really hope they can't—I'm not looking forward to having to slink out of here if this doesn't go well.

Jace seems to come to the same conclusion about my choice of venue. "I didn't expect for you to be here."

"Really? It didn't seem to catch you by surprise," I tease.

Banter between us has always been easy. It's everything else that is hard.

I jump. "By the way, my answer is yes."

Jace doesn't react at first. "Yes to what?"

"Anything you might decide to ask me. Whether I want you. It will always be a yes. I knew my answer as soon as you told me you'd quit. I just needed some time—to believe you. To let you change your mind. To convince myself there could actually be an us."

Jace takes a step forward. Flickers of emotion start to cross his face. "You're saying yes?" he asks.

I'm shocked to hear he sounds surprised. I laugh. "This can't come as a surprise to you."

"And Charles?" Jace's voice is strained.

"I ended our engagement."

Jace takes another step closer to me. We're only inches apart now. I feel my heart begin to race from both our proximity and the anticipation of how he'll respond.

"I love you," he offers.

Tears fill my eyes. Joy—pure, unfiltered, potent joy—permeates every crevice and cell of my body.

"I love you, Jace."

I close the distance between us and kiss him, wrapping my arms around his neck tightly. It's not enough contact, so in a very un-princess like manner I leap up and wrap my legs around his waist.

Jace stumbles from the unexpected impact, but quickly recovers to begin kissing me back. Our kiss is explosive and passionate, but there's something missing. Uncertainty, I realize. Every other time we've kissed, I've known it was fleeting. Temporary. Possibly the last. There's no trepidation as Jace's mouth moves hungrily against mine. Heat pulses through my body, and I wish we were alone.

But I've completely forgotten just how far from alone we are until I become dimly aware of the sound of cheers. The volume in the stadium continues to rise the longer we kiss.

"The football team's going to have a hard time topping this show," I whisper to Jace.

I feel him smile against my lips before pulling away to beam down at me. I feel a giddy smile spread across my own face in response.

"I'm supposed to help Joseph warm up," Jace tells me. "We can leave right after."

"It's fine. I can sit through a football game," I inform him.

"That's not what you said after your last Lincoln game."

"Well, I had to spend it listening to twenty girls going on and on about how hot you are after you had just ditched me for a week."

Jace flashes me his signature cocky grin. "Only twenty?"

I roll my eyes. We walk closer to the divider.

"Do you have agents with you?" Jace asks, looking at the large crowd that's congregated around the section I was sitting in.

"Yes, but they're outside. I thought my attempt at an inconspicuous entrance might be difficult with an armed escort."

Jace snorts once, but then sobers. "Call them, get them inside here. Now."

"Jace, I really—"

He skewers me with one hard look. "Viv."

I relent. "Fine."

We stare at each other for a moment, reconciling the fact that the past few minutes just forever altered the course of both of our lives.

"I'll come find you after the game, okay?" Jace finally says.

"I'll be the one surrounded by big men with guns," I respond.

Jace smirks. "Very reassuring." He gives me a quick kiss that leaves me breathless before he strides back toward his abandoned chair. I turn to climb back over the partition and take my previous seat next to Katie. She looks over at me expectantly as I settle down next to her.

"It seemed like that went well," she suggests, smiling broadly.

I nod and smile, biting my lip.

She squeals and begins bouncing in her seat. "Thank God that security guy picked me as your roommate. I mean, you snagged Jace fucking Dawson. I felt like I couldn't really freak out about it before, because you were upset, and then you left, and then you were engaged to that other guy, but now..." She breaks off her enthusiastic speech. "Why does he look annoyed?"

I glance over at Jace to see he's already looking at me. When I meet his gaze, he raises his eyebrows expectantly. I roll my eyes but comply with his silent request, fishing my phone out of my jacket pocket.

"He wants me to call in my security team," I inform Katie, unlocking the phone and pulling up Michael's number.

I don't miss Katie's "Aw."

"Yeah, yeah, it's super sweet," I grumble. "He's not the one who's going to get a twenty-minute lecture about how I should have let them come along in the first place."

Michael picks up the phone after a single ring. "Princess?" His tone is urgent.

"I'm fine," I reassure him. "But I think a few people might have an idea about who I am…"

Katie lets out a guffaw at the understatement.

"And by that, I mean the whole stadium knows I'm here."

The distant sound of car doors slamming comes through Michael's end of the line.

"We'll be right there," he assures me. "What section are you sitting in?"

I glance behind me. "102 H. Three rows back from the front."

"Okay," Michael replies. The line goes dead.

"I don't think they'll have much trouble figuring out where you're sitting," Katie remarks after I've put my phone away.

"I know." I sigh.

It doesn't take long for my security team to cut through the crowd of wide-eyed students that surround us. I grimace when I see all eight of them made the trip inside. Michael crouches down next to my seat.

"You were worried we might be too conspicuous, so you decided to reunite with Mr. Dawson out on the field in front of the entire stadium?"

"How did you know that?"

"Princess, this game is being broadcast on live television." Michael nods to a small horde of video cameras in one corner of the field.

I groan. "Do I need to call Anne?"

"No, she had a statement put out as soon as I let her know we landed."

"Okay," I reply, relieved.

"I'm happy for you, Princess," Michael adds.

"Thank you, Michael," I reply, smiling.

The game passes quickly. Lincoln wins. The sound of jubilant cheers fill the air as students slowly filter out of the stadium to celebrate. "I've got to get out of here," I tell Katie. "But I'll make sure to say goodbye before I actually leave." She nods and gives me a hug.

I'm placed in the center of a protective formation of my agents. I can't see over their broad shoulders, but our progress is brisk along the walkway and outside the stadium. We stop at a tree close to where the two black cars loiter. Half of my agents climb back inside the cars, while the other four remain close by as I lean against the tree to wait for Jace. I don't have to wait long.

He strides confidently over to where I'm standing minutes later, attracting everyone's attention, including my own. He doesn't stop until he's standing in front of me.

"Nice sideline standing," I compliment him.

He grins.

I smile back. "So...um, how long are you here for?"

"I'm supposed to leave tomorrow. All my stuff's in storage in South Carolina, so I was planning to head to Nebraska from here and have everything shipped. And then basically just wait," he admits, giving me an endearing smile. "What about you?"

"In case you hadn't already figured it out, this wasn't exactly a carefully thought out trip, so...I was kind of just planning to go wherever you go."

A fresh smile dawns across Jace's face, crinkling the corners of his gray eyes. "Really? You don't have to get back right away?"

"I don't have to go back right away."

We agree to go get some food, so I slide into the back of the SUV. Jace climbs in next to me. Even though the middle seat is

485

long enough for three people to comfortably sit across, we remain close enough to touch. Heat sears through me as we sit side by side with our thighs pressing together.

"So, how does this work?" Jace whispers to me as the car starts moving. His breath tickles my ear.

"How does what work?" I murmur back.

"Ditching your small army. Do I have to kidnap you?"

"Why? Is there something you don't want them around for?" I smirk as Jace gives me a heated glance before leaning down to kiss the small strip of skin exposed by my jacket.

"Peter, can you actually take us to the hotel first?" I ask, not allowing myself to linger on the tingling sensation Jace's lips left behind. I know it will come through in my voice if I do. I don't let myself look at Jace's smirking face either.

"Of course, Your Highness," Peter replies.

Minutes later, we pull up in front of the nicer of Lincoln's two hotels. Jace climbs out of the car. I look at Michael, who's sitting in the passenger seat. "I'm going up with him," I inform him. "We have a lot to talk about. I'll text you the room number, and I won't leave the room without informing you first. Get checked in and wait to hear from me? Understood?"

Michael scans the front of the hotel. One elderly couple is climbing inside a sedan the valet has just pulled up for them.

"All right."

I nod and slide out of the car to join Jace. I grab his hand and start to tug him inside.

"What was that about?" he asks, glancing behind us at the two cars of agents.

"I was getting permission to be kidnapped."

We walk through the lobby quickly, trying not to draw attention. Thankfully, late afternoon doesn't seem to be a popular time to hang out in the lobby. No one spares us a second glance as we slip inside one of the elevators. Jace hits 5 and the doors slide shut.

We emerge into a carpeted hallway that's completely empty. I'm glad. I imagine most of the other hotel residents are also here for Lincoln's last game of the season, and I'm sure anyone we came across would recognize Jace.

Jace stops in front of room 523. I quickly text the room number to Michael and assure him I've ascended the five stories safely. He replies, reminding me to let him know when I'm planning to leave.

A beep draws my attention away from my phone. The green light on the doorknob flashes, and the hotel door swings open. Jace flips on the lamp and walks inside, and I follow closely behind. The heavy door swings shut automatically behind us, effectively sealing off the rest of the world.

I glance around the room curiously. It's neat and clean, with a rich red carpet and what looks to be a king-size bed with a plush cream-colored comforter. A small black suitcase sits on the table in the corner of the room next to an overstuffed duffel bag. I take note of a series of inconsequential details: the nondescript paintings on the walls, the white door leading to the bathroom, the remote resting haphazardly next to the television.

I look over and meet Jace's eyes. "I'm kind of nervous," I admit, laughing at the absurdity of it.

His face relaxes into a tender look I've never seen him give anyone else.

Jace opens his arms when I step closer. I relax into his embrace, breathing in the familiar scent of his cologne. His lips are right there, waiting, as I turn my head. We kiss softly, slowly, languidly, which feels like a luxury all of its own. I grow impatient first, sliding my hands down Jace's chest to tug at the hem of his shirt. He helps me pull it over his head and then stands before me in just a pair of khakis, his dark hair adorably mussed.

"Are you sure, Viv?" Jace asks, scanning my face for any hint of hesitation. "We can wait."

"I don't want to wait." I pull off my sweater, revealing the t-shirt I'm wearing underneath. His t-shirt.

I watch his eyes darken before I kiss him again. He responds eagerly, running his fingers under the soft material and across the bare skin of my back. I shove against his hard body, trying to move him closer to the massive bed. He chuckles.

"From bashful to bossy," he remarks.

I wrinkle my nose at him before I pull my t-shirt off, and he laughs outright.

"That's my girl."

The words settle around me like a warm blanket as he picks me up and carries me over to the bed. Sinewy ropes of muscle shift in his forearms as he sets me down on the soft mattress. I unzip and pull off my leather boots, then undo the button on my jeans so I can shimmy the tight denim down my thighs. Jace laughs as I wriggle around.

"You could help, you know," I suggest.

"You're doing such a great job, though," Jace replies. His gray eyes swim with humor as he watches me struggle.

I stick out my tongue at him. "My ego is insulted you're in no rush."

Jace grins. "We've got time."

There's nothing hanging over us. My impending departure. His impending departure. My engagement to someone else. The realization is freeing, but it doesn't do anything to abate the lust coursing through my veins.

"Well, I'm ready to bang now," I inform him.

Jace looks on the cusp of laughter again. "Bang?" He quirks an eyebrow at me.

"Yup." I pop the P for emphasis.

Jace shakes his head, smiling, but walks over between my legs and seizes the dark blue material. He begins tugging it down, revealing inch after inch of skin. I'm grateful for every mile I've ever run as I watch the amusement fade from Jace's face. His gaze returns to mine, hungry now. I wrap my long legs around him, forcing him to step closer to the edge of the bed. To me. He leans over me, taking his time as his gaze trails along my exposed skin, leaving goosebumps in its wake.

"Fuck, Viv," he breathes when he's inches from my face.

"We can do that, too," I whisper.

Jace huffs out a laugh before he kisses me. His tongue eagerly explores my mouth. I bite down on his bottom lip, spurring him on. He growls in response, lowering more of his weight on me so our bodies are flush. I trace my fingers down the length of his back and use his belt to pull him even closer to me. He deftly unsnaps my bra and begins to kiss his way down my sternum. I arch against him as the stiff fabric of his khakis rubs against me.

"Off," I pant.

Jace doesn't bother with a quip about my bossiness this time. He rolls off me and pulls down his pants and boxer briefs in seconds. I take the opportunity to slide off my underwear.

I marvel at the exposed view of his golden skin, but Jace doesn't give me the chance. He leans back over me, and I let my knees fall apart in a silent invitation. He brings his lips back to mine, kissing me lazily, yet skillfully. It's a stark contrast with the rest of his movements, as he quickly rolls a condom on and sinks inside me. We both groan as he fills me over and over again. I meet every motion, pushing back against him and urging him deeper. Sweat beads on my skin.

The pleasure intensifies. I bite Jace's neck as every cell experiences the heady rush of bliss. Jace curses and thrusts into me twice more before I feel him find his release. We lie there for a moment, catching our breath and soaking each other in. Jace seems as unwilling to move as I am, but eventually he shifts and slips out of me to dispose of the condom. He lies right back down on the bed. I muster enough energy to crawl over and lie down on top of him. My soft curves meld to the hard ridges of his chest.

"I could get used to this," I mumble against his warm skin. I feel his lips brush against my hair.

"Good."

I lie there for a while, just on the brink of unconsciousness.

"Viv?" Jace finally says. I groan in response. "Do you want to talk about it? The baby?"

"I'm okay," I whisper, even though it's just the two of us. "It will always hurt, but I'm okay. There was nothing to be done. It just wasn't right." I almost drop the subject, but then I admit, "I thought it was my only chance with you. Our only chance. Knowing it's not now—that helps."

The feel of Jace's lips against my forehead is the last thing I register before I sink into unconsciousness.

CHAPTER THIRTY-NINE

JACE

The annoying sound of my phone buzzing is what wakes me up. I glance down at Viv, half-shadowed in the light cast from the one lamp we have on in the room. Her face is peaceful, and her hair is spread out across the pillow in a reddish-gold curtain. My phone buzzes again, and I reach over to grab it. Anderson's face flashes across the screen.

"Hello," I answer. My voice is thick with sleep.

"Dude! Are you fucking sleeping? Get your ass over here! Where are you?" Anderson shouts. Loud music pounds in the background.

"What? What time is it?"

"It's almost midnight. Everyone's wondering where you are!"

I groan.

"Get your ass over here with Vivienne. Or else I'll just keep calling!" Anderson threatens before he hangs up. I look at my phone. Sure enough, it's quarter to midnight.

I look over at Viv, still sound asleep. She may be an early riser, but she sleeps like the dead.

I lean over and start kissing my way along her arm. She rolls against my body and lets out a soft moan that's much more effective at waking up my body than Anderson's shouts were.

"What time is it?" she mumbles, opening one blue eye.

"Almost midnight," I reply. "Anderson called. He wants us to come to his party."

Viv groans, and I laugh. "I had the same reaction. But he said he'll keep calling until we show." On cue, my phone buzzes again.

Viv grunts, but then rolls over me and off the bed. "Okay, but I need to shower first. Can you call Michael and have an agent bring my bag up? They'll also want to tag along to this shindig."

It takes me a while to respond as I watch her enter the bathroom, still completely naked. I'm not sure I'll ever get used to the sight. Belatedly, I call back, "Sure."

Water starts running, and I have to force myself to focus and comply with Viv's instructions. I pick up her phone and call Michael. It doesn't even ring before he answers. He must keep it glued to his hand.

"Princess?"

"Uh—no, it's Jace," I inform him.

"Is the princess all right, Mr. Dawson?"

"She's fine," I rush to assure him. "She asked me to call you and have her bag brought up. And also to let you know we'll be leaving in about fifteen minutes."

"I'll have her bags sent immediately," Michael responds. "Might I ask where we'll be heading to at this hour?"

"A party," I admit.

Michael heaves out a sigh. "I see." His voice is heavy with disapproval. "Let us know when you're ready to depart."

There's a knock on the door only a couple minutes later. I pull on a pair of athletic shorts and open it to reveal two of Viv's agents, carting three large suitcases. I grin. "These all Viv's?"

One of them smiles. "Yes."

"Okay, I've got them from here," I tell them both, realizing one look inside of our room would make it pretty clear how we spent the afternoon and evening. Neither of them argues with me, seeming relieved to abandon the heavy suitcases. I drag them one by one into the room and shut the door.

Viv steps out of the bathroom with a fluffy towel wrapped around her, a cloud of steam trailing behind.

"Your 'bag' arrived," I inform her, nodding to the stack of suitcases.

She grins. "You didn't leave an itinerary for where you would be and what you would be doing. I wanted to be prepared for anything."

"How many places did you think I could be?"

"Well, one bag is for Nebraska and the other for South Carolina. I didn't think you'd be here."

"So, the third is for…?"

"Shoes," she admits.

I chuckle. "Michael's on standby. I'm going to take a quick shower."

Viv nods and unzips a suitcase. I step into the bathroom, dropping my shorts and stepping into the shower under the warm spray of water. It washes away dried sweat as I scrub my hair. I step out of the shower and wrap a towel around my waist before brushing my teeth and spraying some cologne on my neck.

Emerging from the bathroom, I find Viv is ready to go. She's leaning against the bed, scrolling through her phone. I let out a low whistle as I enter the room and take her in. She's wearing a short black dress made of some smooth, slippery fabric with a black leather jacket over it. Her strawberry-blonde hair falls in messy waves, the ends still damp. She looks absolutely stunning, and I'm floored she's somehow mine.

She smirks as she takes in my awestruck expression. "See something you like, Dawson?" She brushes past me, trailing her fingers across my abs as she walks into the bathroom.

I shake off the temptation to follow her and change into jeans and a faded red Henley as I listen to the whir of the hair dryer.

Viv steps out of the bathroom a moment later. "Ready?" she asks, digging through one of her suitcases and pulling out a pair of black heels.

"Ready," I affirm, walking over toward her. Her heels place her just a few inches lower than my six-foot-three frame. Viv pulls her phone out of her jacket pocket and types something.

"They're meeting us in the lobby."

I double-check I have my own phone, then follow Viv out of our hotel room and into the hallway. My phone rings as we walk down the hallway. I pull it out of my pocket and glance at the screen. It's Anderson again.

"You seriously don't have anything better to be doing?" I grumble to Anderson.

He simply laughs.

"We're on our way," I inform him, and hang up.

My phone rings as soon as I shove it into my pocket. I groan and answer it without even glancing at the screen.

"What?"

"Jace?" My mom's voice comes through the phone.

"Mom? Is everything okay?" I ask. The sound of crying comes through the phone. "Mom?" Panic fills me.

"I'm fine," she tells me. "I just saw the video."

"What video?"

"The one of you and Vivienne earlier!" My mom sniffles.

I laugh, relieved. "That's what you're calling about?"

Viv hits the elevator button and glances over at me. "Everything okay?" she mouths. I nod.

"Mom, I'm glad you're so…happy," I tell her. The word doesn't seem to fit as I listen to the sound of her cries still coming through the phone. "I've got to go, but we'll be there tomorrow, okay?"

"What? You're still coming?"

"Yes. We both are," I state. "I've got to go, okay? I'll let you know when we leave."

"Okay." My mother's voice is giddy now. "See you then."

"Bye, Mom," I say as the doors open. "She's thrilled," I tell Viv as she steps inside the elevator. I follow her in.

She walks over to me until we're only inches apart. "I'm glad." She smiles up at me, and I slip my hands underneath her jacket and along her back. Heat burns through the thin fabric of her dress; it's reflected in her cerulean eyes.

"Viv, I already don't want to go to this party," I whisper. "You can't keep looking at me like that."

She kisses me until the doors ding, indicating we've arrived at the ground floor. I groan as she pulls away.

"Let's go." She grabs my hand and pulls me out of the elevator after her. All eight of her agents stand in the hotel lobby. Viv strides past them and out into the cold air, tugging me along with her.

The ten of us pile into the black SUVs and pull away from the hotel.

"Address?" Michael asks, glancing back from the front passenger seat.

"34 Fourth Street," I rattle off.

The trip to my former home only lasts minutes. The blue house is more crowded than I've ever seen it when we pull up in front. If all of the neighbors weren't in attendance, I have no doubt there'd be noise complaints.

"You ready?" I ask Viv.

495

She nods.

Michael glances back at us. "We'll escort you up to the house and then remain outside. Call if you need anything, okay?"

Viv opens the door and steps outside. I follow. Our appearance sparks a wave of activity among the crowd assembled on the front lawn of the blue house. I place my hand on the small of Viv's back and guide her up the brick pathway and onto the porch in the midst of her security team. They melt away when we reach the front door. I don't bother knocking, just open the door. One freshman rushes over as it swings open. He stops as soon as he sees my face.

I walk inside the front room, Viv alongside me. Every person in the room is staring at us. I pull her to my side as we walk through the crowded room into the dining room. Predictably, Anderson is huddled around the table with a bunch of other football players.

"Dawson!" he shouts when we appear in the doorway. Immediately, he stands and comes over to us. He gives me a slap on the back and then shifts his gaze to Viv. Anderson lets out a low whistle of appreciation, and I glare at him. He meets my hard look with a smirk.

"Vivienne, how set are you on Dawson?" he asks brazenly.

Viv rolls her eyes. "You couldn't handle me, Anderson."

I grin.

"I'm going to find Katie," she informs me.

"Okay. Go easy on the whiskey this time," I tease.

She scoffs before strolling away into the kitchen.

"So…you left a few things out of our last conversation, huh?" Anderson asks me once she's out of sight.

I chuckle. "Yeah, sorry. I didn't know what exactly I was going to do, and I had to straighten things out for myself first."

"I'm happy for you."

"Thanks, man."

"Although, I have to ask. You're going to be…what? A king now?"

"I guess," I respond. "To be honest, I don't know how any of the royalty stuff works. We haven't had a chance to discuss any of it."

"Ah, didn't do much talking after the game, then?" Anderson grins.

I flip him off, and he's still laughing when Owens suddenly joins us.

"Dawson!" he crows.

"Hey, man," I greet. "Nice job out there today."

"I could say the same to you," Owens replies, waggling his eyebrows. "That was quite the show you and the princess put on."

"You guys need to find a new hobby besides gossiping about my love life."

"I've already got bets going on how many of us get invited to the royal wedding. Odds on Owens and me are 2-1, by the way. Don't let us down or it'll be fucking embarrassing," Anderson informs me.

I choke on a laugh. "Are you serious?"

"I never joke about bets. You know that, Dawson," Anderson replies.

"You *are* getting married, right?" Owen asks.

"Yes," I confirm.

"Thank God," Owens replies. "My mom already told all of her book club friends, so if she finds out I was wrong, she'll be…"

"Wait, what?" I interject. "Why was your mom asking if I'm getting married?"

"I guess you didn't bother to watch the news after the game, either," Anderson remarks dryly. "You and Vivienne are the lead story everywhere."

Owens nods. "Even the sports networks are covering it. Which makes sense, because you're—you know, you—but they don't normally report on celebrity gossip. My mom heard about the wedding from my dad, who's never watched anything but a sport channel in his life."

I rub my forehead. "I need a drink." They both laugh as I follow them in the direction of the kitchen.

"Grab a beer and then let's play some pong," Anderson suggests as we reach the doorway.

"Holy fuck, Dawson," Owens comments as we enter the crowded kitchen. Viv is standing with her back to us amongst a group of girls, gesturing with her hands. She's taken off her leather jacket, revealing her short dress dips even lower in the back than the front. Every guy's gaze in the room is glued to her, including two of my best friends.

"Yeah, I'd tell the Sharks to fuck off for that too," Anderson offers.

I ignore them both and head over toward Viv. The only person I recognize in the group is her former roommate Katie, whose eyes widen as I walk over.

I don't stop until I'm directly behind Viv. I drop my chin on the top of her head and wrap my arms around her waist. She relaxes against my body, turning her head to grin up at me. I drop a quick kiss on her lips. They taste like whiskey, and I look down to see she's clutching a red cup filled with the amber liquid.

"Hello, ladies," I greet the group crowded around Viv. They all look too startled by my appearance to reply.

"Are you limiting Viv's whiskey consumption?" I ask Katie. "Last time, you didn't do the best job." I wink at her so she knows I'm kidding.

Katie opens and closes her mouth several times but doesn't make any audible response to my teasing.

"Pretty sure that was your fault," Viv informs me when it becomes clear Katie's not going to speak anytime soon.

"Are you forgetting who carried you upstairs and forced you to drink water?"

"I'm sure your intentions were completely honorable."

"Too bad you can't say the same." I smirk at her. She blushes, and I laugh.

"Dawson, quit flirting!" Anderson says as he strolls over and passes me a beer. "We've got a fourth for pong. Let's go!"

Owens is close behind him. "We're flipping for it," Owens adds, tossing a quarter in the air and catching it neatly. "And then we'll switch."

"You guys are flipping for who gets to play against Jace?" Viv asks, amused.

I grin, and Anderson laughs.

"No, with him." Owens explains.

"They're both sore losers," I tease.

"Then they should just beat you," Viv contends.

"We've tried," Anderson replies, rolling his eyes and looking disgruntled at the admission.

Viv scoffs. "I haven't."

Anderson crows with delight at this development. I look at Viv, brows raised. She meets my gaze, smirking. I don't find any hint of apprehension in her expression.

"Did you miraculously gain some hand-eye coordination?" I ask. "I've seen you play football, you know."

"I had a better beer pong teacher." Viv challenges.

"Okay, you're on." I gesture for her to leave first, and she rolls her eyes, likely thinking I'm trying to soften her up by acting like a gentleman when really I'm just trying to keep my friends from staring at her ass.

Anderson's already cleared away the remnants of the poker game and set up the cups. One of the wide receivers is filling the cups with beer. Viv and I take our places at either end of the table. I expect the confident expression she's wearing, but I study it carefully, looking for any trace she's bluffing. I find none.

For her sake, I hope she actually does know what she's doing, or else this will be a short game. If she's expecting me to take it easy on her just because I'm in love with her, she's going to be sorely disappointed. You don't get selected as the first overall pick without a healthy competitive spirit.

"Ladies first." I gesture to Viv once the cups are filled.

She tosses the ball into one of the furthest cups, taking the most difficult shot first and executing it perfectly. Shouts and cheers fill the room. I keep my expression blank but raise one eyebrow at Viv. She winks at me.

I pull her ball out of the cup and drain the contents before passing it off to Anderson. He looks like a five-year-old kid on Christmas morning. I roll my eyes at him before turning back to the table to take my own shot. I usually start with the front cups, but Viv upped the stakes. I sink the white ball into the same cup she chose. I grin at her; she narrows her eyes before fishing it out and drinking from the cup. She passes the empty cup to Anderson and then turns back to the table. Viv sends the ball flying into the cup directly in front of the empty space her last shot created. I drink, then copy her.

We match each other shot for shot until we both only have two cups remaining. The number of people in the dining room has tripled, drawn to the cheers and yells our performance has garnered. I'm focused on the game. Viv has a matching expression of concentration. I've run with her enough to know she's got a serious competitive streak in the final stretch.

She shoots and misses for the first time, the ball just glancing off the rim of the plastic cup. Her features don't give anything away as I catch the errant ball before it hits the floor.

I toss the ball immediately, not letting myself think about it. There's a satisfying splash as it lands in the cup of beer. Vivienne's poker face is impressive. She drinks the cup and tosses the ball back. It lands in the center of the cup this time. She quirks a brow at me as I drink.

We're down to one cup each. She misses. I miss again. The crowd grows restless, impatient after our previously rapid pace. She misses. I miss again.

She doesn't.

I stare down at the white ball bobbing in the solitary cup in front of me, genuinely surprised.

"I love you?" Viv calls out from the other side of the table, grinning.

I shake my head as Anderson spins her around.

"You were already one of my favorite people, Vivienne, but I think you just topped the list," he tells her.

She laughs and comes over to me. "We good?" she asks, biting her lip adorably.

"I might have to retire some of my uncoordinated jokes. Let's hope your driving skills don't improve as well, or I'll be completely out of material."

Viv laughs before giving me a quick kiss. "I'm going to run to the restroom."

"Okay, I'll be here," I reply.

As soon as she's out of sight, I seize the opportunity to sneak out one of the side doors and through the neighbors' yard until I reach the two SUVs parked across the street. Michael climbs out as soon as he spots me. "Is everything okay, Mr. Dawson?"

"Everything's fine," I assure him. "I just want to ask you about something. But, uh—I'm not really sure how this works," I admit. "Since I'm pretty certain you have more authority than me."

"I do, sir." Michael nods.

I shift awkwardly and catch a twinkle in his eye.

"I'd like to take Viv—the princess somewhere tomorrow morning. Alone."

Michael sobers. "Mr. Dawson, I'm aware the royal protocols are all still quite new to you, but the princess's safety is of the utmost importance. You're asking me to put the entire future of the Marcedenian monarchy at risk—"

"Look, I just want to propose to her!" I blurt.

Michael stops speaking.

"Preferably without a group of eight men surrounding us," I add.

He smiles outright. "Okay, I suppose we can make that work."

"Really?"

"Yes."

I smile, buoyant. "Okay. Thank you."

I head back inside and see Viv talking with another group of people. I keep walking out onto the back deck. Joseph, my former back-up, is sitting in one of the lawn chairs set out. I take a seat in the one next to him. The air is chilly, but it feels refreshing in comparison to the stuffy house.

"Congrats on the game earlier," I tell him as I sink against the cold plastic. "Hell of a way to end the season."

"Thanks. Congrats on the girl. I'm happy for you guys."

"Thanks." I smile.

More of Lincoln's football team comes out to join us, and I'm drawn into an analysis of plays and strategy from the game earlier. I'm talking with one of the juniors when I see his eyes widen. I glance behind me to see Viv walking out on the deck. She's put her leather jacket back on, but I can still see her shivering as she makes her way over to me.

"I'll talk to you later, Dawson," the junior tells me.

I nod.

Viv takes a seat on my lap and leans against my shoulder.

"I forgot how cold it gets here," she admits.

"This dress was from the South Carolina bag, then?"

"Mm-hmm," she mumbles, nuzzling her cold face against the hollow of my throat.

"Are you ready to go?" I ask.

"I guess. I told Anderson I'd play poker, but I don't really want to move."

I huff out a laugh. "I'm sure he'll get over it. You *are* his favorite person now."

I stand, pulling us both vertical. Viv leans heavily against me. I say goodbye to my teammates, then lead her out the same side door I snuck out earlier. As soon as we're clear of prying eyes, I pick her up bridal style and carry her over to the waiting SUVs.

We slide into the backseat and then speed off into the night, back to the hotel.

CHAPTER FORTY

VIVIENNE

"Viv, wake up."

I groan groggily and roll over, hearing a low laugh. "Viv, c'mon."

I open my eyes. "What time is it?" I feel like I went to sleep minutes ago. I glance at the clock next to the bed to discover I did. One hundred and ninety-three, to be exact. "Jace, it's only six. Why the hell are you waking me up?"

"I have a surprise for you."

"Can it wait until daylight?"

"It will be daylight by the time we get there. Come on." The sheets rustle as he climbs out of bed.

I want nothing more than to burrow back under the warm covers, but curiosity has me reluctantly peeling them back and climbing off the soft mattress. I stand and yawn widely.

"Ready?" Jace asks. I look over to see he's already dressed in jeans and a fleece jacket. All I'm wearing is one of his t-shirts.

"Yeah, sure, I'll just wear this."

Jace laughs. "Come on, hurry up!"

I roll my eyes. "This better be a really great surprise," I

inform Jace as I pull on a pair of leggings and my heavy black wool coat. "And I look ridiculous, so we better not be going anywhere there's paparazzi."

Jace grins and hustles me out of the room. My curiosity grows as we emerge from the empty lobby to see a black SUV already waiting. Jace opens the door, and I climb inside. Michael is sitting in the driver's seat. None of my other agents are anywhere to be seen.

"What the hell is going on, Jace?" I ask.

"Have a little faith." He throws my words from our trip to South Carolina back at me.

I arch an eyebrow, but don't say anything as we drive through Lincoln's deserted downtown area and approach a familiar collection of buildings. We roll past the stone sign announcing we're on Lincoln University's campus. Michael pulls the car off on the shoulder of the road and comes to a stop. I look at Jace. He smiles at my obvious confusion.

He opens the door and climbs out, turning around to offer me a hand. I grasp it and jump out of the SUV onto soft grass. Jace shuts the door behind me and begins tugging me farther onto Lincoln's campus.

"You dragged me out of bed to come to campus?" I finally ask.

"Astute," Jace compliments.

I roll my eyes as I'm towed along the gravel path barely visible in the beginning streaks of morning. Brilliant splashes of pink, yellow, and orange appear on the horizon.

We round a curve in the path, and I stumble in surprise. A familiar shape is silhouetted against the pastel sky. My breath catches as Jace and I near the enormous elm tree where we used to meet every morning.

"Jace…" I breathe, unable to get more words out past the

505

lump in my throat as we stop underneath the gnarled, bare branches.

"Now, I know this part might not come as much of a surprise," Jace says, looking at me. "Seeing as most of our relationship has been defined by the fact you have to get married in the next few months, but I figured, since we're here..." He sinks down on one knee.

I rake one hand hastily through my hair, partly because I didn't spend *any* time on my appearance this morning, which is not how I would have chosen to look during this moment, but mostly so the tugging on my scalp can assure me this moment is really and truly happening. I feel the pain, but Jace is still kneeling in front of me.

He pulls a small black box out of his pocket. "Viv, I love you more than I thought it was possible to love another person. From the first second I saw you, I knew you were unlike anyone I'd ever met. Not because you're a princess, but because you're bold, and brave, and stubborn, and you light up every room you enter. I've spent more time thinking about you than anything else. Every time something embarrassing or silly or frustrating happens, you're the first person I want to tell. For most of the past year, I've had to imagine what you might say in response. Hopefully, I'll never have to do that again."

He pauses. I don't realize I'm crying until I watch a rapid succession of shimmering droplets fall to the grass between us.

"Vivienne, will you marry me?"

I start nodding before he even has the chance to finish the question. "Yes!"

He opens the box, and I gasp. A massive, round diamond is nestled in the silk cushion, surrounded by a halo of smaller diamonds that continue along the length of the platinum band.

"Jace..."

He takes the stunning ring out of the box and slides it on my finger. I tilt my hand to the side, watching the gemstones glimmer in the early morning light.

"Do you like it?" he asks tentatively. "You can get something different."

"I love it! But how…"

Jace grins. "Once my agent realized I was serious about leaving the league, he became remarkably amenable to helping me book as many advertisements as possible while he was still earning a commission. It was enough to pay off my contract, and a lot more."

I'm completely overwhelmed. "I can't believe this is happening," I admit. "That we're engaged!" I half-laugh as I exclaim the last word, glancing down at my left hand to assure myself the gorgeous ring is still there.

Jace grins. "Not what you expected to happen one day when you first tried to outrun me here?"

I laugh, thinking back to the moment I saw Jace for the second time in this very spot. "Definitely not. Although, I wasn't actually trying to run away from you. If I had been, you wouldn't have been able to catch up."

"You're probably right," Jace admits. He drops a quick kiss on my lips and then starts to pull me along. "Come on, Michael only gave me fifteen minutes."

I let him tug me back toward the car, surveying familiar pathways affectionately. I can see the outline of Kennedy Hall in the distance. Michael climbs out of the driver's side as we approach.

"Everything go okay?" he asks, smiling.

I roll my eyes. "Like I was going to turn him down."

Jace laughs, and Michael grins.

"Congratulations, you two."

"Thank you, Michael," Jace responds.

We drive back to the hotel to retrieve suitcases and the remainder of my security team before heading to the airport. I'm too keyed up to fall back asleep. The entire flight to Nebraska and drive to Fulton, I keep glancing down at my left hand.

Jace was wrong earlier; his proposal this morning was a surprise. He's right that our relationship has been largely defined by the fact I have to get married. And I know we will, now. But I didn't expect him to actually propose, to make it feel as though we're getting married because we want to, not because I have to.

I bounce in my seat as we drive up the infamous dirt road that leads to Dawson Farm. This is the one place I never thought I'd be able to return to.

Michael stops the car in front of the faded white farmhouse. "We'll head into town to get a hotel for the night."

"You'll have to go to the next town over," Jace tells him.

Michael sighs dramatically. "All right. If either of you need to leave this farm—call me."

The words are for both of us, but he's only looking at me.

"Okay, we will."

Jace and I climb out of the car. Thomas unloads our luggage from the trunk before the two cars of agents depart. I'm distracted by the mob that's suddenly descends on me. I'm passed and pulled between Dawsons. Jace grins broadly at the sight of his family surrounding me.

"Nice to see you all, too," he calls out to his family.

"Jace, we're sick of you by now," Mike replies.

"Of course we're happy to see...oh my goodness, look at that ring!" Mrs. Dawson catches sight of the diamond sparkling on my finger.

"Let me see! Let me see!" Claire chants, pushing her mother aside to inspect my hand.

I'm ushered inside the warm farmhouse to find it looks

exactly the same as the last time I was here. I glance fondly around the messy mud room and packed bookcases.

"Are you two hungry?" Ellen asks maternally.

"Actually, yes," I reply. "I'm starving."

"Me, too," Jace adds.

Mrs. Dawson bustles into the kitchen. The rest of us trail after her, watching her chop vegetables and toss chicken into a fry pan.

I sink down into one of the chairs at the kitchen table. Jace takes the seat next to me. I feel a yawn form, so I turn my face to muffle it against the soft fleece of his jacket.

"Tired?" he whispers.

"Some idiot kept me out of most of the night and then dragged me out of bed early this morning."

"You were the one trying to play poker when I carried you out the door."

I pull my face away so he can see me wrinkle my nose at him.

"I don't remember that."

"I'm sure you don't. You've got a selective memory in addition to selective hand-eye coordination."

"Well, you're already stuck with me."

"Yeah, I know." Jace grins.

I turn away from him to see Mrs. Dawson watching us with a wide smile on her face. I flush. She sets down a salad with chicken in front of us. I start devouring it immediately.

"This is incredible, Ellen," I compliment.

After eating lunch, Jace and I go out on a horseback ride.

"I was thinking we could get horses," I mention as we ride along past the barren dirt fields.

Jace looks over at me. "Seriously?"

"If you want. Or another sailboat. And I was also thinking—"

Jace cuts me off. "Viv. I don't need you to buy me anything."

"I want you to be happy in Marcedenia. I don't want you to... regret anything."

"I'm not going to, Viv. It'll be an adjustment, for sure. But I don't have any regrets, okay?" There's no hint of hesitation in his voice or face.

"Okay." I try to push away the doubts.

Following dinner, I help Ellen with the dishes while the Dawson boys and Claire watch sports in the living room.

"I can't tell you how thrilled I am things worked out between you and Jace, Vivienne," she tells me as we load plates into the dishwasher.

"That means a lot, Ellen," I reply. Hesitantly, I add, "I know this probably isn't what you envisioned—or necessarily wanted for Jace."

"It certainly wasn't what I expected," Jace's mother replies, laughing. "But all I want is for him to be happy. And I've never seen him happier than when he's with you."

I smile at her.

"So...you two are getting married."

"Yeah." What was once an impossibility, spoken as a statement. "We are."

"And it will be in your home country?"

"Yes, at the royal cathedral."

"That sounds fancy," Ellen remarks.

"The entire event is going to be pretty over the top," I respond. "I haven't been very—uh, involved in the details so far, so I could be walking down the aisle atop gold-coated rose petals at this point."

Mrs. Dawson lets out a disbelieving laugh, but I'm fairly certain I heard Joan mention that at least once. She keeps asking me questions about the wedding and Marcedenia as we continue cleaning up. Jace enters the kitchen as we're just finishing the dishes.

"Sam wants us to come over," he informs me.

"Okay…" I respond. There's something lurking in his expression I can't quite discern. "You want to go, right?"

Jace glances at his mother, and she's quick to excuse herself. "I'd better get Claire to bed."

"I think Gretchen will probably be there," Jace tells me.

"I already know she likes you, Jace," I reply. "It was fairly obvious the last time I was here."

Jace groans. "Do me a favor and don't mention that to Mike."

"Mike? How come?"

"Well, I came home after the first preseason game, you know when…"

"When I let the whole world know you getting knocked unconscious bothered me," I finish.

"Yup." Jace smirks. "Anyway, when I came home I ran into Gretchen. She suggested that we get drinks, and—"

"You got a drink with her?" I aim for nonchalance, but fall spectacularly short. It shouldn't bother me. I know he loves me. But Gretchen is someone who already fits in his world. Someone he wouldn't have had to give up anything for.

Jace's smirk morphs into a full grin at the blatant jealousy in my voice. "I had an idea she was interested in high school, but I didn't think…anyway, Mike suggested she still was, and I didn't listen to him."

"So, you got a drink with her?" I prompt.

"Yeah, I did. I literally had *a* drink, but she had several. And then she made it very clear she was still interested, and I turned her down."

"And you think she'll be at Sam's? That's why you don't want to go?"

"That, and she mentioned you."

I arch an eyebrow. "Really."

"She said I was turning her down because of you, which was partially true, and that I was only into you because you're hot, which is mostly true." He grins.

I scoff. "So you're worried she's going to say something if we show up together?"

Jace nods. "I've learned she's a little unpredictable if there's alcohol involved."

"Worried for me or her?"

Jace rolls his eyes. "Anne's assistant wouldn't even talk to me until you were out of sight. What do you think? I didn't want you to be caught off guard, though."

I head toward the stairs.

"Where are you going?" Jace calls after me.

"I'm getting ready to go. I know you want to see Sam."

Jace raises his eyebrows.

"I'll be nice if she says anything," I promise, giving him a cheeky grin. "Call Michael," I add as I start up the staircase.

"Nice of you to leave that task to me again," Jace hollers after me.

I shower quickly and get dressed in black jeans, black boots, and a cream-colored sweater. It's even colder here than it was in Michigan. Jace yells my name from downstairs as I'm brushing my hair.

"I'm ready!" I shout, grabbing my coat and rushing down the stairs.

Jace is leaning against the banister, wearing the same fleece jacket and jeans he's worn all day. The only thing he's added is a backwards baseball cap.

"Think you'll be warm enough?" he teases.

I scoff.

"Your entourage has arrived."

"Okay, let's go." We say good night to Jace's family and head outside to see the SUVs already waiting. I'm walking toward the rear one when Jace grabs my hand.

"Come on, we're taking the truck."

"Michael agreed to let us drive separately?"

"Yup." Jace grins at my obvious surprise. "Apparently, ten hours in Fulton is all it took to convince him you aren't in imminent danger here."

"And what did you have to agree to?" I question, having negotiated with Michael before.

"Taking a defensive driving course," Jace admits as we climb into the cab of the old truck. "I acted annoyed, but honestly, I'm looking forward to it."

"Devious."

"Thank you." He smiles at me before beginning the trek down the long driveway.

"So…is there anyone besides Gretchen I should be avoiding tonight?"

"What do you mean?" he asks, glancing away from the dark road at me.

"Girls, Jace. Are there any other girls I should avoid tonight?" The brief conversations I had with Sam and Gretchen during my last visit here made it pretty clear Jace's popularity among the opposite sex started long before he arrived at Lincoln.

"Sam didn't mention who all would be there…" Jace hedges.

"So, probably?" I infer.

"It's possible."

"Okay."

"Okay?" Jace glances at me again.

"What, were you expecting me to demand a list of every girl

you've ever slept with?" I ask, purposefully keeping my voice inscrutable.

"I really hope not," Jace replies, risking another glance away from the road at me. He visibly relaxes when he sees my expression.

"Thanks to Lincoln's gossip mill, I already know more than I ever wanted to," I inform him.

Jace winces. "I would love to discuss literally anything else."

I laugh. "We're good, Dawson."

I've always known Jace has a past; a past I fully expected to become a part of. Now? We're engaged before we've even ever been out on a date. Jace has spent his whole life being fawned over. Is settling down really what he wants?

I'm silent for the rest of the car ride, and I feel Jace's eyes on me a few times.

Jace turns into a paved driveway, which is a first for me in Fulton. It stretches for a while before I see lights up ahead that indicate we're approaching a building. Jace pulls off to the side of the driveway behind an assortment of trucks and cars already parked. I climb out and start striding toward the lights.

"Where are you going?" Jace asks, a hint of amusement in his voice as he climbs out as well.

"The gathering you brought me to?"

"Wrong way. It's behind the barn."

"Of course it is," I mutter before changing course toward the wooden structure barely visible in the light cast from the house.

"Whoa, you're not going anywhere until you tell me what's going on," Jace informs me, grabbing my arm and spinning me around. Headlights illuminate his stern face for a moment as the two cars of agents park behind Jace's truck. He follows my gaze. "They agreed to stay in the car."

I look up into the confused, stormy eyes that have always

served as some sort of truth serum to me, then glance away before I blurt out the niggling thoughts swirling beneath the joy. "I'm worried it's not going to be enough for you. That I'm not. You've been with all these other girls, and you're used to getting all this attention, and I—I'm worried you'll miss it once the novelty of us wears off. I know that you love me and the fact that you gave up football, and proposed, it meant—means—more to me than I could ever tell you. There's nothing that could mean more. But remember how surprised you were about the wedding we went to together? How young they were? That's us, Jace, and—"

Jace interrupts me. "Vivienne."

I look at him, bracing myself for anger that I'm doubting him, but his voice is soft.

"I get that you're scared. I do. But you're enough for me. You're everything. Give me a chance to prove it to you, okay? I don't want anyone else. This wasn't a rash decision on my part. I thought it through. All of it." He stares at me intently. Another flash of headlights illuminate their steely resolve.

"Dawson! Finally!" a guy's voice calls from the car that's just arrived. A tall figure bounds over to us.

"Hey, Jack!" Jace replies, slapping the newcomer on the back.

"I couldn't believe it when Sam said you were back in town! I mean…" the newcomer's voice trails off when he spots me. "Hello there." He grins. "I'm Jack."

"Vivienne." I smile back.

"I don't live under a rock, darling. I know who you are." Jack winks.

Several guys come over from the same car Jack arrived in, followed by a dozen more. Jace and I are quickly swept up in the raucous group that rounds the side of the wooden barn to the sight of a roaring bonfire surrounded by groups of people. One figure peels off from a group as soon as we appear.

"Dawson!" Sam greets enthusiastically, slapping Jace's hand and pounding him on the back. I tune out Jace's response as I glance around the grassy area we're standing in. Aside from a few large logs that surround the fire, there's just a folding table set up with an assortment of liquor spread atop it.

"Vivienne!" I'm distracted by the sound of my name, and glance back over to see Sam smiling broadly at me.

"Hey, Sam. Good to see you."

"I was expecting a crown this time," Sam jokes. "Or at least an armed escort."

"They're parked outside your house," I inform him.

Sam glances at Jace for confirmation. "Seriously?"

I laugh. "I'm going to grab a drink." I stroll toward the flimsy table. The roaring heat from the fire envelops me as I pass the periphery of the stone ring. Most of the alcohol spread across the table is beer, but I spot a bottle of bourbon in the back. I splash some into a red plastic cup, grab a bottle of beer, and turn around to see the one person I was hoping not to run into.

Gretchen looks shocked to see me.

"Vivienne. Hi," she finally says.

"Hi, Gretchen," I respond.

Her gaze drops. "I guess congratulations are in order."

I follow her gaze to the beer bottle I'm clutching in my left hand. The left hand displaying the diamond ring Jace gave me this morning.

"Thank you," I respond.

"You're lucky," Gretchen says softly.

"I know I am."

She smiles, then passes me to head toward the table I've just left. I feel eyes on me as I look around the assembled groups for Jace. He is standing next to the bonfire, talking to Sam. I approach them slowly. Sam spots me first and grins before saying something to Jace and heading toward a group of people. I reach Jace and hold out the plastic cup wordlessly.

He raises an eyebrow. "The beer is for you?"

"Uh-huh." I take a sip for emphasis and try not to make a face at the malty taste. I'm certain I don't succeed based on Jace's smirk.

He tugs me to his chest, and I go willingly, snuggling against the warm fleece. We stand in silence for a few minutes.

"I thought about it, you know," I tell the flickering flames I'm staring at.

"Thought about what?" Jace asks, playing with a piece of my hair.

"Abdicating." It's something I would never admit to anyone else, but Jace deserves to hear it.

I feel him inhale sharply.

"I think I would have. If my father wasn't sick. If there was time—"

"Viv, you don't have to justify anything to me, okay? I was able to give things up for us to be together. You couldn't."

"I don't want you to think that I wasn't willing to, that I don't know how unfair it was for you to have to make all the sacrifices—"

Jace cuts me off again. "Viv. You came here for Thanksgiving, even though you weren't supposed to. You told me who you really were, even though you weren't supposed to. You came to the hospital in South Carolina, even though you weren't supposed to. Those were all things that put yourself, or the monarchy, at risk. And you did them for me. I knew exactly what I was doing, and what you couldn't. Okay?"

"You could argue those were just reckless choices I made because I wanted to," I inform him.

"True. But you that's not why you made them."

"No, it's not," I confirm softly.

"So...are we really good on this now, or are you going to say we're good again and actually keep worrying about it?" Jace asks with an endearing smirk.

I laugh. "We're really good." I promise. "I think I've given you enough outs by now."

"You didn't need to give me any outs," Jace responds. "But I know why you tried to, and I love you for it. Just let me do this, okay? Let me choose you, Viv."

I study him for a moment. The gray eyes, the sharp cheekbones, the stubbled jaw, the dark hair just visible under the sides of his baseball cap.

"Okay," I whisper. "Choose me."

CHAPTER FORTY-ONE

JACE

I t's late when we arrive at the palace. I walk inside the imposing entryway with fresh eyes. I live here now.

It's a bizarre thought, to say the least.

For some reason, I expected the palace to be quiet and empty at this hour. Instead, there's plenty of staff bustling around. Two butlers descend upon us, picking up the luggage agents have already unloaded from the cars and carrying it upstairs. Most surprising? The queen and king are standing in the same spot as they were the first time I visited. The only difference from that arrival is that Vivienne is leaning against me, wearing my ring on her finger. Her feet drag as I walk us over to her parents.

"Hi Mother, Papa," she greets them, yawning widely. She raises her left hand to cover her mouth, and I watch as both of her parents spot the diamond she's now wearing.

Her mother is the first to react. "You're engaged?" she gasps.

Viv nods, glancing up at me and smiling. Her parents seem genuine in their excitement over our engagement, and I'm relieved. I left on good terms with them both, but I wasn't sure if that would transfer over now that Viv and I are a reality rather than an unlikely possibility.

After her parents finish congratulating us, we say good night. I surreptitiously pass Robert a piece of paper as we head toward the sweeping staircase. He seems to realize what it is, giving me a smile that has an additional tinge of respect. I'm glad he's not offended.

I have to haul Viv up the stairs, and I'm tempted to pick her up just to speed things along.

Halfway up the staircase, she asks, "What did you give my father?"

"Interesting how you were alert enough to notice that, but I'm supporting all your weight right now."

Viv smiles. "I like that I can lean on you," she replies simply.

I smile back.

"So?"

I sigh. "It was a check for five million dollars."

"*What?*"

"He sent it to me so I could buy out my contract. But I wanted to do it myself."

"He sent you money to buy out your contract?" Viv looks shocked by this revelation.

"I'm not sure if he wanted you to know…"

"I won't say anything," Viv promises.

"I had already made my decision. But it was nice to know he supported it," I share with her. She smiles before resting her head against my shoulder.

I huff out a laugh, then sweep her up into my arms. She snuggles against me as I cradle her against my chest, making me think this was actually her intention all along. Viv is no help with navigating, so I take several wrong turns before I spot the marble hallway that leads to the wing where Viv's room is located. We reach the door and I push it open, flicking on the light. It looks exactly the same as it did the last time I was in here. I carry Viv over to the massive bed and lift her on top of the comforter. She groans as her face smushes against the soft material.

I'm heading back toward the door when I hear her call my name. I glance back to see Viv's raised her head from the bed.

"Where are you going?" she asks sleepily.

"To figure out where my stuff got sent," I reply.

"Just come to bed," Viv mumbles.

I chuckle as she starts trying to pull her sweater off with her eyes still closed. She finally manages to as I reach the edge of the bed. Any amusement dies in my throat at the amount of skin suddenly on display.

Bleary blue eyes appraise me as she peels off her jeans and flings them on the floor. She climbs underneath the comforter, holding the blanket up. "Come on," she implores impatiently.

I shuck my shirt and pants, turn off the light, and slide under the sheets next to her. She immediately snuggles against me.

"Thank you," she murmurs.

I kiss her forehead.

I'm startled by how quickly I settle into life in Marcedenia. In many ways, it simply feels like a continuation of my last visit here. I'm given the same suite I stayed in before, but end up spending every night in Viv's room. Something I thought we were being stealthy about until my laundry started being delivered to her room.

Most mornings we go running together before Vivienne leaves

for her classes at Edgewood, while I remain at the palace for my daily lessons. They take place in one of the conference rooms by the room Viv and I had our ill-fated interview preparation in. This time my sessions are solo. I'm inundated with information about Marcedenia and the royal family in preparation of becoming a Marcedenian citizen.

I travel back to South Carolina three weeks after Viv and I returned to Marcedenia together to film the final advertisement Jeremy booked for me. This is the first time I'm leaving the palace without Vivienne, which means I have my own team of agents traveling with me. Now that we're engaged, I'm entitled to royal protection. It's completely bizarre.

When I arrive at the studio where the ad is being filmed, Jeremy is already there waiting. He eyes the agents behind me apprehensively.

"I know I gave you a hard time before, Dawson, but I hope this works out for you," he tells me.

"Thanks, Jeremy."

All I have to do for the ad is sit and drink the sports drink that it's for, and I almost feel guilty about the amount of money they're paying me for this. It's the only reason I agreed to do it. They ask me to take off my shirt for the final few shots, and I grin at the prospect of telling Viv. Maybe I'll simply surprise her. Give her a framed copy.

I'm leaving the studio when I get a call from Cooley.

"Hey, man," I answer.

"Hey! Are you back in South Carolina?" he asks.

"Yeah, how did you know?"

"It's all over the team fan accounts."

"Hopefully not rallying to run me out of town? I figured I'd be public enemy number one on those."

"Nope, you're still annoyingly popular. Left for love, and all that. Are you coming to the game tonight?"

"I wasn't planning on it," I admit.

"You should come, Dawson. I'll have a suite reserved. Give them my name if you decide to come."

"Okay, thanks," I respond. "Good luck later."

"Thanks," Cooley replies before hanging up.

My security team and I head to the hotel. Viv has a fundraiser she's attending tonight, so I don't bother calling her. I eat dinner and watch television for a while instead. It's long after my body is used to going to sleep, but I don't feel tired. I glance at the clock. The Sharks game starts in a half hour. I pick up my phone and call Marcus, the reserved middle-aged man who is the head of my security detail on this trip. He answers immediately, the same way Michael always does.

"Mr. Dawson?"

"I'd like to go out," I request. "To a football game."

There's silence on the other end of the line. Finally, "Very well, sir. We'll have the car pulled up outside."

When I arrive downstairs, the white SUV we've been using today is already waiting. I can see three agents sitting in the car, while the remaining two stand outside, holding up a phone they're listening to intently. One of them catches my eye and gestures I should get into the car. I comply.

"What are they doing?" I ask the agents in the car once I'm inside.

"They're speaking with Princess Vivienne's security team," one answers.

"What? Why?" I ask, panicked. "Did something happen?"

"No, nothing's wrong," another agent assures me. I think his name is Tom. "It's just they attended a game at this stadium over the summer. We…want to ensure we're navigating the building as efficiently as possible."

"Oh," I respond, feeling guilty for all the trouble this outing is causing. "You know, I'm fine not going if you guys think it's too dangerous. Or too complicated."

The first one who spoke scoffs. "Contrary to what *some* people think, we're plenty competent."

"Jim," Marcus barks from the driver's seat. There's a clear note of warning in his voice. The two other agents climb into the car.

"We got the all clear," one of them says.

"What took so long?" Jim asks.

"They had to get approval from Michael, too," is the response.

Out of the corner of my eye, I see Jim roll his eyes in the seat next to me.

"Okay… I feel like I'm missing something here," I state. The car is silent.

Marcus finally speaks. "Her Highness requested her own security team accompany you on this trip. Richard refused to allow it, since she has a public outing scheduled for this evening. So she insisted we run any unplanned outings past her team instead."

"I don't get it. You guys are great. Why would Vivienne want to send her team with me instead?"

"Agents are assigned in the Royal Guard based upon seniority, Mr. Dawson," Marcus responds.

I still don't get it, and Jim must see my confused expression. "The royal family gets the best agents," he states bluntly.

"Oh." I'm touched and annoyed. Touched Viv cares this much. And annoyed her way of showing so has resulted in the incredibly awkward moment I currently find myself in.

The trip from the hotel to the football stadium is a short one.

It's weird to enter through the side door that leads to the suites rather than pulling into the player's parking lot. I'm hustled past the security set-up and into an elevator. The attendant in the corner does a double take when he sees me, but doesn't say anything besides asking for the suite we're headed to.

The game is painful to watch. Not necessarily because I wish I was down on the field playing, although there are certainly flashes of that, but because the Sharks are trampled. The final score is 40-6.

I texted Cooley earlier, letting him know I was coming to the game after all, and he responds as we're driving back to the hotel from the stadium.

Bet you're glad you came, he replies.

There's always next season, I text back. He sends a series of beer emojis I take to mean he's more interested in a drink than a pep talk right now.

I fall asleep as soon as my head hits the hotel pillow and groan when my alarm goes off what feels like only seconds later. As much as I would love to go back to sleep, I'm even more eager to return to Marcedenia. I meet my security team in the lobby of the hotel, and we head straight to the private airport. I fall back asleep on the plane, and the five-hour flight passes quickly.

It's the middle of the afternoon in Marcedenia by the time we pull up at the front gate. We're waved through and stop in front of the main doors. My security team makes quick work of unloading themselves and the luggage. I've just stepped inside the door when a cloud of strawberry blonde hair blocks my view of the entryway. Years of football training are the main reason I manage to stay vertical as Viv leaps on me.

"Jace!" she exclaims.

"This is quite the welcome," I whisper into her hair.

"I missed you," she murmurs against my neck.

"Were you worried my second-rate security team might not get me back in one piece?" She pulls back, giving me my first view of her face, along with those of the dozens of people in the entryway staring at us. It's a mixture of agents, maids, a group of men in suits, and some women who I think are part of the team planning our wedding. They all glance away when they see me looking, but I'm already focused back on Viv.

She bites her lip. "You weren't supposed to know about that."

"It did make for an awkward conversation with my agents."

"Where did you go?" Viv asks.

"Huh?"

"I'm guessing you found out because they had to call my team. And they only would have done that if you went somewhere that wasn't on the itinerary."

"I went to the Sharks game," I admit.

Something in Viv's expression tells me she was expecting that answer. "I saw they lost."

"Yeah, they did."

"Too bad they didn't have you out there."

"I'm not sure how much use I would have been," I reply.

Viv raises her eyebrows. "Are you being modest about your football abilities?"

"No. But I would have spent the game thinking about how you were about to marry someone else."

Viv's face softens.

"I couldn't wait to come back," I whisper to her before I kiss her.

She hasn't brought it up again, but I'm sure she's still worried I'm going to regret my choice to move here one day. I'm not just saying the words to reassure her, though. I mean them.

Two months later, I drive my Porsche up the clamshell driveway of Glendale Cottage. I turn off the car. Mike and I climb out. Anderson, Owens, Kenny, and Sam are standing in front of the imposing building, just arrived from the airport.

"Dawson," Anderson breathes as we reach him. "This is the 'cottage' we're staying at? I thought you meant a glorified tent. Summer camp shit."

Mike laughs. "Dude, this is nothing. We went to brunch at the palace yesterday, and that place *does* make this look like a shack."

"I'm so glad I invited Vivienne to that party," Anderson says reverently.

"Yup, that's the only reason we're all here." I roll my eyes. "Come on." I lead my brother and best friends inside the admittedly impressive mansion to kick off my last night as a bachelor.

After we eat dinner, Owens comes up with the brilliant idea to go out to a bar, which Sam and Anderson eagerly support. Mike's just as enthusiastic, since the drinking age here is eighteen. It takes them twenty minutes to convince Marcus to tell us the name of the nearest bar.

My security team insists on accompanying us, which I expect, but my brother and friends are awed by their presence.

It's a quick trip to the seaside town closest to the cottage. We pull up outside a small, upscale bar. I receive plenty of double takes as we walk inside, even before my security appears behind us. We make our way over to the distressed metal bar top. I take a quick glance around the bar, and I'm distracted from the stares by a blond, combed head of hair.

I groan internally as I come face to face with the one person in Marcedenia I want to avoid. "Charles," I state. I'm not sure what else to say.

"Jace," he replies stiffly, glancing behind me at my friends

527

and brother. He looks to the bartender standing a few feet away, likely hoping he can order quickly and leave.

I don't know what else to say. I'm grateful when Marcus comes up to me, hoping he'll give me some sort of excuse.

"Mr. Dawson, it's the princess on the phone. She says it's urgent."

I hold out my hand, and he passes me the phone. Just when I thought the moment couldn't get more awkward, Marcus swoops in like an anti-hero, ratcheting the discomfort up several notches. I risk a glance at Charles. His face is stoic.

"Viv? Is everything okay?"

"Jace," Vivienne lets out a breathy giggle. "You weren't answering your phone."

"I forgot it at the cottage," I respond. "Owens wanted to see the local sights. Are you okay?"

"I'm fine," she assures me, her voice higher than usual. "Katie's here. We're hanging out. But I'm in the bathroom, and I really wish you were here."

"Why's that?" I ask carefully. I'm fairly certain she's drunk, or at least tipsy, which she confirms with her next words.

"Because then you could do that thing with your tongue when you—"

"Viv, I really can't talk here," I cut her off hurriedly. My body's already reacting to the way I know she was planning to finish that sentence, and I'm in a public place with her ex-fiancé about five feet away. "I'll call you back later, okay? Love you."

I hang up the phone and hand it back to Marcus, ignoring the shit-eating grin Anderson's giving me that suggests it might have been obvious why Viv was calling me.

"Enjoy the evening," I tell Charles, because I feel obligated to say something.

528

"You too," he responds before grabbing his drink and heading back to a group of guys who look as preppy as he does.

"Correct me if I'm wrong, but did your fiancé just booty call you in front of her ex-fiancé?" Sam asks.

Anderson laughs loudly. "I was getting the same impression."

I groan. "Let's get some drinks."

CHAPTER FORTY-TWO

VIVIENNE

For once, I don't slowly drift out of unconsciousness and begin gradually reacquainting myself with the world. I also don't try to fall back asleep. I bolt straight upright in bed the moment I start to stir.

I'm getting married today.

It still feels foreign, the excitement that accompanies the words, this event. The realization this is something I want to happen, rather than just a means to an end. I reach over to my bedside table and grab my phone. Ignoring the other messages, I tap on Jace's name.

We're getting married today, I send him.

Immediately, three dots appear that indicate he's responding. *That's today? If only anyone had reminded me...* He sends me a photo of the television set in the living room at Glendale Cottage. It's set to the main Marcedenian news channel, which is currently displaying the engagement portrait we took a few weeks ago. *ROYAL WEDDING THIS AFTERNOON* is the headline prominently displayed below it.

Wish people would pay us a little more attention, I respond.

We had a good run for a while there, Jace replies.

I'm distracted from my phone when Katie bursts into my room.

"It's your wedding day!" she shouts.

I can't help but laugh as I climb out of bed. "I didn't forget."

"Are you feeling okay?" Katie asks.

"I'm a little nervous, but…"

"You're not hungover?"

"Hungover?" I ask. "I didn't drink that much, did I?"

"You were definitely tipsy, and I'm not sure what you told Jace when you called him, but he called me right after and made sure I gave you nothing else but water." She grins. "It was really sweet."

I pick up my phone again. *Did I call you last night?* I send Jace.

He replies immediately. *Wasn't sure if we were pretending it didn't happen.*

Because… I reply.

It involved things you like about my tongue is how he responds.

I feel my cheeks heat as his words prompt a hazy recollection.

Happy to continue the conversation tonight he adds.

"Come on, let's head to the ballroom!" Katie exclaims.

For once, I'm just as excited as she is. I quickly pull on a robe and follow Katie out into the hallway. We giggle and squeal as we race through the winding corridors toward the cavernous room serving as my bridal headquarters. We burst inside to find everything's already been set up. All the furniture has been pushed against the walls to accommodate the buffet, salon, and changing areas that have been set up in the center.

My mother is already there, dressed in a navy pantsuit despite the early hour. She's speaking with Joan and beckons me over as soon as we enter the room.

"Good morning, Vivienne," she greets.

"Morning, Mother," I respond, grinning widely. Beyond just the burst of excitement I woke up with, I can feel exuberance bubbling within me. Rather than just Katie's infectious enthusiasm, I know this is all my own. A product of the place deep inside that thought I'd always have to wonder how the rest of Jace's life turned out, not have a front-row seat beside him.

Joan curtsies as I approach. "Your Highness."

"Good morning, Joan."

"We need you to select a second back-up entrée," my mother instructs.

"What? Why?" I ask. "Didn't the scallops and swordfish arrive?"

"Yes, they were both delivered a few hours ago," my mother responds. "But just in case they—"

"If this is what you're worrying about, I'm going to take it to mean we're in good shape for today?" I interrupt.

Joan nods vigorously.

"All right, then." I head over to the array of breakfast foods.

The morning flies by. Mrs. Dawson and Claire arrive just as we're finishing eating. I talk to them for a while before I'm pulled into the salon section. I lose track of time as I receive the full beauty treatment. My makeup is painstakingly applied. Each section of my hair is curled and brushed before being pulled back from my face in an elaborate braid. The rest of my hair is left loose. A diamond tiara is nestled in intricate twists, and then all that's left is my dress and veil.

I rise from the chair I've spent the last several hours getting ready in to find everyone else is already dressed. My mother has changed into a champagne-colored dress that shimmers as she moves. Jace's mother is wearing a blue silk dress, and Claire's is a similar style in pale pink. Katie's wearing a strapless navy number I helped her pick out a few days ago. And I'm still in my pajamas.

"Hurry up, get on your dress!" Katie urges. "Joan says we have to leave in five minutes."

"It's that late already?"

"Yes! Everyone else is already at the church. Hurry up!" Neither my mother nor Jace's say anything, but I can tell from their eager expressions they also want to see my dress before they leave. Claire is bouncing eagerly.

No one has seen my wedding dress. It's the one part of today I took complete control over. I selected the designer months ago and described what I wanted for my gown in excruciating detail. A sewing team took over a suite in the furthest wing of the palace and literally created the dress under lock and key.

I hurry into the changing room to find the black bag is already hanging. I unzip it slowly, careful not to snag the delicate fabric. It's exactly how I pictured it. I slide it off the hanger and let the white material pool on the carpet as I take off my robe and pajamas and step into the very center. I pull the dress up over my body slowly, luxuriating in the sensation of the flawless silk against my skin. I button the dress up as far as I can. There's a couple of inches I can't quite reach.

"Joan, can you come help me?" I call out. It's silly, but I want everyone else to get the full effect.

A moment later, I hear the curtain whisper as she enters. I look behind me to see Joan standing with her mouth agape. "Your Highness...wow."

I smile. "You like it?"

"I do," she confirms, coming over and helping with the rest of the dress. I pull the veil out of its bag and burrow the comb between two braids, allowing the silk tulle to float into place. I fling the top layer over my head and watch it drift down to my waist.

"Okay, I'm ready," I state. I pull back the curtain and walk out into the ballroom.

Katie, my mother, Jace's mother, and Claire all just stare.

"Is there something wrong? Something missing?" I glance down at the white satin and gauzy silk tulle frantically, worried there's some tear or stain I missed.

I look back up to see my mother dabbing at her eyes. "Vivienne..." she breathes. "You're stunning."

"Jace is going to pass out when he sees you," Katie tells me. "Like wow. Just wow. There aren't words."

Mrs. Dawson nods her agreement. "You're the most beautiful bride I've ever seen."

"You look like a princess," Claire chimes in with.

I smile, relieved. Everyone leaves in a flurry minutes later, leaving me alone in the massive room. It's the first time I've been alone since I woke up and texted Jace, and I wish I could talk to him now. I'm jittery, and I know the sound of his voice is the only thing that will calm my nerves. But I also know he was scheduled to arrive before my mother and his family. Meaning he's already at the church. I stand by one of the large windows and look out at the gardens.

"Your Highness, it's time." Joan reenters the room and interrupts my thoughts.

"Okay," I respond, turning away from the window slowly so that my long train has a chance to follow me. I follow Joan down the hallway. We don't pass a single person, which feels strange. Normally, the palace is bustling with activity at this hour. Either all the staff is busy with preparations or they purposefully had this section of the residence cleared.

I walk inside the entryway and finally see another figure. My father turns around. I watch his eyes well up as soon as he sees me.

"Oh no, none of that, Papa," I instruct him as I walk over and give him a hug. "We can't both show up at my wedding crying."

My father chuckles, pulling a handkerchief out of his pocket and patting his eyes. "You're a vision, Vivvi," he informs me. "A vision."

"Thank you, Papa," I reply, forcibly swallowing the emotion.

We emerge outside the main doors. The commotion that greets us is jarring after the quiet palace. A massive barricade has been set up beyond the columns that frame the main entrance to the residence, but I can hear the thousands of people who must be assembled outside the palace gates. Three cars are lined up in front of us: two SUVs and one sedan. Twelve agents stand waiting as my father and I approach. Two of them step forward, Richard and Michael. Both of them look awed as they take in my appearance.

"Have you two never seen a wedding dress before?" I tease as they reach us.

"Not one like this. You look beautiful, Princess," Michael compliments.

"Thank you," I respond. With each person I encounter, my excitement at seeing Jace's reaction to my dress grows. "Let's get this show on the road, huh?"

"As you wish, Your Highness," Richard responds, as formal as ever.

It's a logistical nightmare to load me, my veil, and my dress into the back of the sedan, but we finally manage it. My father climbs in next to me, Richard climbs in the driver's seat, Michael climbs in the passenger seat, and then we're off.

There's one SUV of agents in front of us and one behind us as we round the corner of the barricade and start down the tree-lined driveway to the main gate. It opens as soon as we approach, prompting cheers from the crowd assembled on either side of the street, straining against the metal barricades lining the edges of the road. I wave as soon as we come into sight, shocked to see the crowds continue along the entirety of the road. I look over at my father to find him already smiling at me.

It takes ten minutes to arrive at the stone cathedral where I'll be getting married. The crowds are even larger here than they were at the palace. All sound is muffled by the car's thick exterior, so it's a shock when my father's door is opened and the roar of noise inundates the car. My father circles the car, waving at the people packed behind the barricades.

My door is opened. I grasp my father's hand as I rearrange the white material I'm surrounded with and step out of the car. Somehow, a new decibel is reached as I straighten outside the sanctuary of the car, glancing behind me to ensure my train has followed.

Shouts fill the air and hundreds of shutters click as I smile and wave at the assembled audience. I shift my grip to my father's arm, and we begin the walk to the front doors of the church. Joan appears to hand me a bouquet of flowers for the second time in this spot. This time, I don't drop them.

We enter the church. The heavy wooden doors are shut behind us, muffling the sound of the crowds outside. The two of us pause in the lobby, alone again, waiting for our cue to enter.

"I'm really glad you're here, Papa," I tell my father. I mean more than just physically, and he knows it.

"Me too," my father replies. "I love you, Vivvi." A single tear rolls down his cheek.

I squeeze his arm twice. "I love you too, Papa," I reply, my throat tightening.

Despite the upheaval it's caused in my life, I'm suddenly

grateful for the marriage law. It's the only reason I'm allowed this moment. Without it, I wouldn't have met Jace. My father might never have been able to walk me down the aisle.

I study the patterns carved in the oak doors that lead to the inside of the cathedral as the music shifts, signaling our cue to enter. The old wood creaks as two attendants open them from the other side.

The hundreds of people seated inside the ancient church rise in unison as I step inside, clutching my father's arm with one hand and my bouquet with the other. The aisle is long, stretched to accommodate the dozens of pews that hold the dignitaries, ambassadors, politicians, and royalty attending this event, along with the more traditional family and friends.

This is the first time I've seen the inside of the abbey decorated. My mother offered to let me see it last night, but I wanted to wait and experience it for the first time now. I'm glad I did. It gives me something to focus on while everyone stares at me. I'm no stranger to being the center of attention, but this moment feels different. More intimate. I don't want to be the future monarch right now; I just want to be Vivienne.

I've always been awed by the interior of the cathedral. It's breathtaking. Ethereal. Ridged marble columns run the length of the walls, interspersed with windows boasting colorful mosaics accented with gold leaf. The marble floor has a golden runner spread down the length of the aisle. There are flowers and greenery everywhere. Lining the aisles, the pews, the walls. The heavenly scents of gardenia, freesia, roses, eucalyptus, and ranunculus mingle and swirl around us as we advance down the aisle. The rich notes of the organ reverberate and echo throughout the majestic building.

I struggle to shorten my steps to keep pace with the booming melody, eager to reach my destination. Progress is slow as I reach the halfway point of the aisle on my father's arm, watching a mixture of familiar and unfamiliar faces continue to pass by. I know we've almost reached the end when I begin to see nothing but familiar ones. I find Katie first. I see Anderson, Owens, Sam, and Kenny sitting together. Next, I spot my mother's tear-stained face, followed by the smiling faces of Jace's parents and siblings. Which means I'm at the end.

Finally, I allow myself to look at the one person I want to see the most.

I never want to forget the expression on Jace's face as we make eye contact. His smile is tender, wobbling as though it's on the brink of more sentimental emotion. His gray eyes are calm, like the surface of the ocean in the early morning. He's wearing a tuxedo, his face is clean-shaven, and I'm struck by the realization he's about to become mine. He looks similarly wonderstruck.

I ascend the two steps separating us and shift my gaze to my father. His final task is to raise my veil. I get my first unfiltered glimpse of Jace as the white tulle disappears. My father kisses me on the cheek and shakes Jace's hand before turning to take his place in the front pew beside my mother.

As soon as he departs, I allow my eyes to return to where they want to be. Jace and I stare at each other. I feel exposed. Vulnerable. This isn't a production or pageantry. It's real. I know my face is conveying exactly how I feel about the man standing in front of me, projected for millions of people around the world to see.

Jace holds out his hand. I grasp it. His warm, solid grip grounds me. I'm not doing this alone, the way I would have felt if I were marrying anyone else.

Simultaneously, we turn our backs to walk up to the altar. Jace squeezes my hand three times as we take the final few steps together.

Thirty minutes later, I hear seven words I've heard countless times before. At other weddings, in movies, on television shows. They have a different meaning to me now. A permanence I find comforting rather than constrictive.

I don't realize I've started crying until Jace wipes a tear from my face before he kisses me. I let myself have this one moment on the global stage and I throw my arms around his neck, molding our bodies together.

Long after the appropriate amount of time has passed, I pull away. Jace grins at me, his gaze heated.

"I love you," I tell him, finally voicing the words I've been wanting to say to him all day.

"I love you too, Viv."

We turn to face the cheering crowd. I'm beaming with happiness as I marvel over how unexpectedly, incredibly perfect this moment is. At the four months and three words that somehow got us here.

Together.

THE END

ACKNOWLEDGMENTS

Publishing a book is not an easy process. Beyond the time and the effort and the logistics, it's incredibly vulnerable—sharing words you wrote with the world. It's become less terrifying over time, as I've learned how to navigate the ups and downs better, but it's still scary. Every time.

This book—my debut—will always be extra special to me. Jace and Vivienne's story is the first one I put out in the world, and firsts are unique. Sometimes messy, sometimes awkward, but nearly always unforgettable.

When I published *Four Months, Three Words*, I honestly didn't think anyone would read it. I thought a silly story about a football player and a princess wouldn't be one anyone wanted to read. But I felt a sense of satisfaction about finishing it and it seemed sad to leave it forever as a massive document on my computer. I never, ever predicted it would become the first of many books I would write. Or that many novels later, readers would still tell me this is their favorite of mine.

Tiffany, thank you for all of your work on this one. Truly, I'm not sure what I would do without you.

Sam, thank you for this stunning cover. And for being such a kind and thoughtful person to work with.

Finally, a sappy reminder to believe in yourself. I published this book without telling anyone. Instead of being proud, I felt embarrassed. Instead of hoping people might read it, I figured they wouldn't. You don't need anyone else to assign your dreams value. You can make them meaningful and important all on your own.

ABOUT THE AUTHOR

C.W. Farnsworth is the author of numerous adult and young adult romance novels featuring sports, strong female leads, and happy endings.

Charlotte lives in Rhode Island and when she isn't writing spends her free time reading, at the beach, or snuggling with her Australian Shepard.

Find her on Facebook (@cwfarnsworth), Twitter (@cw_farnsworth), Instagram (@authorcwfarnsworth) and check out her website www.authorcwfarnsworth.com for news about upcoming releases!

Made in the USA
Columbia, SC
22 October 2023